Love, Sex, and
Understanding the Universe

By Harrie Farrow

Dedicated to all those
who dare to love,
especially to those
who have dared to love me.

Author's Note

The story I felt driven to tell, in my estimation, could only have evolved in the last years of the 1970's and the early 1980's. A story of the sort I intended, set during this time frame, would run into the brick wall of AIDS, would become a story about AIDS — just as so many people's lives became a story about AIDS in those years. Although this is a story of what AIDS dropped into the middle of - a story of how love, sexuality, and self-discovery were taking on new forms, forms which were aborted, or at best, drastically altered, in any case, drenched with death and suffering at the hands of HIV — the AIDS crisis was not the story I felt compelled to tell. For practical purposes then, in order to avoid having my story metamorphosing midway into a tragedy of AIDS, I decided that, though my novel extends well past the first half of the 1980's, in this fictional world I was creating, AIDS will not have become a reality yet. At the story's end, my characters have no clue that such a fate may await them, just as those who contracted HIV in the early years did not know what horrors their futures held.

Part One
New York

Chapter One

"What were you like as a caterpillar?" Mary Wallace gently urged a black and electric blue butterfly from its resting spot on her knee and onto her fingertips. "It's almost as beautiful as you, Jim." She held up the insect for me to see. We were in her tree house, at age eleven, in our suburban neighborhood fifty miles north of Manhattan.

This is the last memory I have before I headed down the emotionally searing path that lead me away from, and eventually back to, wholeness. My story begins when being me was easy — before there was any hint that I'd someday face seemingly insurmountable challenges in an often futile quest to be true to myself, before I had any clue that love and friendship would someday tear me apart.

I'm now a twenty-six-year-old physics Ph.D. candidate living in San Francisco; the year is 1987. Despite the often overwhelming complexities of my current love life, I'm finally once again, at peace with myself.

Though Mary was the first person ever I fell in love with, I didn't know it at the time, didn't realize that not all friendships were like that. She and I'd been inseparable ever since the day I looked out my kitchen window, when I was five, and saw a girl with wispy blond hair and a plaid dress dancing around the tree in my backyard. I ran out, the screen door slapping loudly behind me. It was early fall, and the air was filled with a dry warmth suggestive of crispy leaves. She was singing a song she'd made up about Popsicles. Later she taught me: "Yellow, green, and even blue too, sticky sweet, and how I love you. Purple, orange, oh isn't it good, yummy delicious, icy cool."

"That's a crabapple tree," I'd shouted. "You can't eat the apples, but they're fun to smash on the sidewalk."

She stopped and looked at me, surprised. "I like plums better anyway," she offered softly.

"What's your name?" I called in return.

"Mary Rachel Wallace." This time her voice was strong and proud.

"I'm James Jeffrey Landa. Come see my ant farm."

Mary was a tomboy; everyone said so. All I knew was that she was funny and clever and liked to do everything I liked to do. We spent endless hours creating villages in my sandbox, or flying on my swings straining to touch the sky with our toes. We splashed half the summer away in the plastic wading pool in her yard, our pirate ships engaged in fierce battle; ate strawberries dipped in sugar on my back porch; or drank lemonade on the front porch swing at her house. I still remember with chills, the day Mary fished an ice cube out of her glass, pushing a lemon slice out of the way to get at it. She'd pressed the frozen cube to my tanned dirt-covered thigh and, when I didn't cry out, ran it slowly towards my knee. Silently, we watched the dirt turn to muddy drops that ran off my leg, and fell like slow rain, onto the unfinished pine planks of the Wallace family porch.

Exploring every corner of the park, we knew where all the rabbit holes were and the best places to cross the creek. On bright cloudless days, we rolled down grassy slopes getting stains on our jeans — which our mothers would pretend to scold us for — and giggled helplessly in our dizziness at the bottom of the hill in a field of dandelion fluff.

No one else was allowed in Mary's tree house; it was our special place, perfect for make-believe. We'd go there too when either of us was mad at someone or sad about something, like when Mary's father was away on a business trip for far too long *again,* or when our neighbors yelled at my mom because I, overcome with desire, had stolen a juicy red tomato right off their vine.

There were more and more times when Mary was upset about her father being away, or about her parents arguing when he got back. I shouldn't have been surprised when one day — soon after she'd asked the butterfly what it had been like as a caterpillar — I found Mary crying on the tree house floor because her parents were getting a divorce, but this news shocked me.

Two days later, I climbed up the ladder to find her weeping again. I stood uncertain, listening to her sobs, watching the slight shudder of her shoulders. Finally, I sat next to her, putting my hand on her back. The floor of our hideaway was filthy I saw now — clumps of dried mud we'd trekked up over the years, debris from dead leaves, spilled juice. I spied a piece of popcorn wedged between plank and branch.

"Mary?" I inquired quietly, leaning in towards her ear.

"Go away!"

Huddling at the edge of the platform, hugging my knees, I listened for a long while to her whimpering. Mary had never rejected me before. Eventually, I gathered the nerve to ask, "Do you really want me to go away?"

"No!" She sat up, facing me with dirty, tear-streaked cheeks and a runny nose. Hair was matted to the side of her face that had pressed to the floor. She wiped her nose on the sleeve of her flannel shirt. "Do you want *me* to go away?"

"Of course not."

"Well, tough luck!"

I stared at her, frightened.

"Jimmy, they're going to make me leave!"

"What?" I whispered.

"My dad has a goddamn girlfriend in Georgia. He's moving there, and my mom's going to take me to Virginia where her sister lives. We're *moving!*"

"No." The word croaked out of me, a pathetic protest.

* *

Ronnie and Bill's Clip and Curl Salon, attached to the home of the proprietors and just down the road from us, was complete with a pair of fuzzy white poodles. Ronnie and Bill were always happy to see me, repeatedly told my mother how "outrageously beautiful" I was, and scolded me emphatically when I chased the dogs around the room. Decorated in pseudo-glamour, the place amazed me. Opposite a twenty-foot-long wall of mirrors, floor-length royal blue curtains graced an enormous picture window which looked out onto a storybook garden of azaleas and peonies.

The salon was like a concrete manifestation of the easy dream-like world I'd lived in, and nothing in that world had prepared me for the dissolution of Mary's family or the resulting consequences.

Mary and I had promised to write faithfully, but neither of us sent even a single postcard. I composed endless letters in my mind, sometimes even started to write them, but it felt so useless, so untrue to what we'd had. I figured she was experiencing the same sort of discomfort at the idea of our friendship being continued on paper. There had been so much that was physical about the way we related: chasing each other through the neighborhood, dancing in piles of yellow-orange leaves, building igloo forts, making goofy faces, and seeing who could hold out the longest in toe tickling contests. How do you do that via the postal system? How do you wrestle in snowdrifts, or... Or run an ice cube down a dirt-covered thigh?

4

I just couldn't seem to figure out how to be me without Mary, and I had no interest in making new friends. I spent hours in the park listlessly playing rounds of basketball against myself, or simply watching the clouds roll by. I got some joy out of taking my siblings, Elizabeth and Jesse, eight and nine years younger than me, to the playground, but watching them run and chase each other only made me prematurely nostalgic for my childhood, which seemed to have suddenly disappeared. I ended up spending more and more time in my room reading. I'd discovered the joy of books, and when I entered the sixth grade, I also discovered, much to my surprise, that I liked school. I liked learning. Previously, I had barely paid attention in class, had put only the absolute minimum effort into homework, and had always gotten Bs; I now sank myself into schoolwork and got the best grades in the class.

****

I studied the intricately muscled arm reaching up to make a shot. *Sports Illustrated* rested on my lap as I sat cross-legged on my bed. The basketball player was so strong, so powerful, so... What was I doing? I closed the magazine, looked out the window, past my faded cowboy and Indian curtains, and watched the soft December snow falling. Mary had been gone six months.

I opened the magazine again — the athlete's underarm thick with silky hair, his jaw so firm and... No, it was not as I had been telling myself all along. I did not stare at these pictures, running to the corner store excitedly in search of the latest issue, because I looked up to these men, wanted to be like them. No. That was not it at all. I could just taste the sweat, feel the slight roughness of his clean-shaven chin. I closed the magazine — this time because I knew, and I needed to think. I stared wide-eyed but no longer saw the snow. It was real what I was feeling,

5

undeniable, but how could this be? I reached under the bed and pulled out the copy of *Penthouse* that cousin Vince had left on his last visit. I opened it to a favorite photo. A redhead lay on her back, elbows propped up, long legs bent just enough to conceal most but not all of her pubic hair. Breasts fully exposed, head tilted back, her flawless face lost in an expression of physical joy even though no hands touched her — except perhaps my own. I placed the *Sports Illustrated* next to the *Penthouse* and looked alternately at them. I couldn't say that what I felt while looking at each was exactly the same. There were similarities, mainly desire. Looking at the woman was more arousing — perhaps because she was fully naked, poised for sexual pleasure. Yet, looking at the man was more alluring — perhaps because he was so forbidden. I closed both magazines and threw them under the mattress. I didn't understand. If guys turned me on, I must be homosexual. But how could I be homosexual and still get so turned on by a woman's body? One thing for sure, I was definitely turned on. I went into the bathroom and locked the door.

I studied the Penthouse carefully over the next days, to make sure. Yes, I was able to confirm over and over again, photos of naked women aroused me, and yes, in the one spread also involving a man, I looked at, and was turned on by, him too. So was I gay or straight?

****

The following month, Mr. Alma, my math teacher called a conference to inform my parents that I had quite the aptitude and should be put in a special program at another school. My mother threw a fit. A couple of days later my father recounted the story to Ronnie at the hair salon while Bill clipped away my sister's, bangs.

"Anna stood up and said to that Mr. Hazelton, "You are *not* going to make an anomaly out of my boy!"

6

"*Anomaly*, wow what a great word!" Ronnie interjected.

My father continued, hands on his hips, imitating my mother: "Of course he's smart! He's also athletic, should I send him to a training camp for Olympic freaks? He's adorable too, should I send him to charm school? He's a child for heaven's sake; leave him alone. He'll develop his talents at his own pace."

"Good for her!" declared Ronnie, his voice high pitched, his body moving in a sort of subliminal dance.

I was watching him carefully. When I realized that Bill noted this from the mirror, his eyes meeting mine, I quickly knelt down to scratch Golly-Girl under the chin.

My dad always encouraged me to watch the evening news, so I knew from clips of gay rights demonstrations in New York and San Francisco that not all gay men were like Ronnie and Bill — effeminate hairdressers with poodles. But even though I understood that if I were indeed gay, I would not grow up to be like the only two homosexuals I knew personally, they *were* the only ones I knew, and I was looking to them for clues about what being gay would mean. I suppose it was more, too. I watched with special interest the way they interacted with each other. The thought of two men making a life together especially thrilled me.

****

A couple of months later, Mr. McCuddy, stood at the chalkboard erasing the day's lesson. Margaret Jones finished folding the last of her secret notes and then headed for the cafeteria trailing behind the rest of the class. I stood among the vacant desks waiting, looking at the outline of muscles showing through the back of my science teacher's shirt. Finally, he turned around. A bit startled to see me, he pushed his glasses up with an index finger. I didn't much like Mr. McCuddy, he was dry and depressing, but to alleviate boredom in his class, I sometimes used his not so unattractive body as fantasy material. His face would look all right too with a pair of hipper glasses. But this had nothing to do with why I'd stayed after class. I had a question about electricity that was gnawing at me almost as much as the nature of my sexuality.

I asked the question, using the chalkboard to demonstrate the mathematical equation that was causing my confusion.

Mr. McCuddy stared at me. "Well," he said at last, "ah, yes, well, yes, I can see how you're entangled there, I... Ah, what I mean to say is... Yes, you have quite a question there Mr. Landa." He attempted to push up his glasses again, but they were already up as far as they could go.

We stood there, both of us painfully aware of his lame answer. His face flushed red. I turned around, embarrassed for him, and walked slowly towards the cafeteria. I wondered why the school had hired someone so inept. Then it came to me, a sudden realization. Mr. McCuddy was just your typical sixth grade science teacher. Sixth graders were not supposed to be asking those kinds of questions. It wasn't that he was unusually stupid; it was that I was unusually smart; my math teacher hadn't, in fact, been overreacting as my mother had seemed to want to believe.

By the time I made it to the lunchroom, most of my classmates had scarfed down their macaroni and cheese and hit the yard. I sat alone at a long table behind two older girls who were talking about a rock star.

"He plays his guitar like he's *making love* to it!" one girl crooned.

"I saw a photo of him with no shirt on and he's *so* hot," the other one countered.

I looked at my dessert, canned peaches, or canned apricots, I couldn't tell which. I was trying hard not to think about the level of my intelligence, and was not aware at first that I was overhearing the girls. I pushed a yellow-orange dome around in its sticky syrup.

"You know he's ac/dc, don't you?"

"Ac/dc?" the other girl asked, sounding almost frightened by her own ignorance.

Something in my too active brain told me that *this* was more interesting than canned fruit. I perked up my ears.

"You know," her friend teased, "someone who likes girls *and* guys — bisexual?"

I have no idea what the other girl said in response. That evening in my room, I tried to remember. I wanted to know. But I simply had not heard. The word bisexual had stood out so bright and clear in my head that all else had ceased to exist. *Bisexual.* I had a word. I understood; it was me. Hey, me and the rock star! I liked it — a nice clear label that said it all. I didn't have to choose. I didn't have to be *not* attracted to either guys or girls — a prospect I had found utterly absurd and likely impossible, but had thought was perhaps necessary. Now it wasn't necessary. Now it was okay to be me. I was not unheard of. Bisexual.

****

When you're twelve, and you discover something profound about yourself sexually, it's not something you think about discussing with your parents, even if they're like mine were — not only open minded, but also easy to talk to, and emotionally close to their children. So, of course, I didn't say anything to them about realizing I was bisexual. But, if I had known then how things would turn out, I would have told them right away. As far as I'm aware, they still don't know. I assume they continue to live in New York; my little brother and sister should now be just out of high school.

Chapter Two

I yawned. The TV was on, remote control in my hand, some bicentennial hubbub blaring over-bright colors at me. I'd just finished the ninth grade, and I would turn sixteen in September. My dad was at work, my mom out volunteering for the League of Women Voters, and Elizabeth and Jesse were at day camp. A Kool-Aid commercial came on and it dawned on me, in a moment of clarity, how much I despised television. So I was sitting there, with the damned thing still flickering at me, wondering what I *was* going to do all summer, when I heard knocking. I looked towards the entryway, but the knocking wasn't coming from there; it seemed to be coming from the kitchen. I got up slowly, perplexed, and headed towards the knock. Standing at the screen door — looking every bit the broken winged angel that she was — was Mary Rachel Wallace, sixteen and incredible.

"You're back!"

She stepped in and we hugged briefly, awkwardly.

"Just for the summer," she explained. "Mom sent me back to stay with Gran Wallace." Then she added proudly, "I'm incorrigible, unruly, and delinquent."

I smiled, raised my eyebrows. "How nice."

"God, look at you!" she said, stepping back.

I had, during the last year, gone from occupying a boy's body to occupying one more resembling a man's. Aunt Marie had remarked on several occasions that I had grown right into the cliché of, "tall, dark, and handsome."

I led Mary into the living room and promptly turned off the television. She sat very close to me on the couch and slipped her hand into mine. We watched the blank screen silently. Sexual energy was bouncing off the walls.

Eventually Mary asked, "Do you have a girlfriend?"

"No." After a pause I added, "Do you have a boyfriend?" This was meant to prompt her to ask me this question next, but as soon as I heard my words, I knew how she would take it.

"Yeah. His name's Phil."

I didn't want to hear about anybody named Phil. I wasn't even interested in knowing if she had a boyfriend. I understood that it didn't matter to her, so why should it matter to me? I hadn't seen Mary since she was eleven, but somehow I knew how her sixteen-year-old mind worked.

She squeezed my hand. "James Jeffrey Landa, are you still a virgin?"

I didn't like the question, and in searching for a response, came up with one of my own. "Why?"

"I'd hate to think of you missing out on all that fun."

Oh Mary! She was back. I turned and gave her a timid, uncertain, kiss on the lips, a kiss of childhood friendship, a kiss that rapidly developed into something much less innocent. In a short while, we were on my bed, partially, then half, then completely, naked.

The sight of Mary's breasts, the feel of them on my fingertips and tongue, the warm moist silkiness of her mouth and between her legs... all the rest as well: the soft curve of her hips, the look in her eyes when I entered her, these things rose up within me a wondrous passion. I understood resolutely that love and sex were good. A fact that I — as I lay afterward, my sweaty body curled in satisfaction around Mary's — gladly accepted as a clear and basic truth of life.

****

Mary was at my house whenever my parents and siblings were not. We spent endless uninhibited hours exploring ways to pleasure each other. When my family came home, we left to swim at the city pool, or picnic in the park. Evenings we spent at the arcade by the billiard tables. Mary was quite the shark. I'd never played before, but totally got into it. I liked the way I was able to apply basic principles of motion to get the best angle on a shot.

About a week after Mary re-entered my life, my father sat me down at the dining room table, with a very serious yet meaning-to-be-friendly look on his face. "Is there anything you want to ask me?"

"No." I shook my head.

"About birth control, maybe?"

"Mary's on the pill."

"Are you sure?"

"I've never known her to lie to me."

"Good. Is there anything you want to ask me?"

"No."

"Come talk to me any time you want."

"Thanks." I was grateful for having such cool parents. I knew that when I got involved with a boy, I be able to be just as obvious about it as I had been with my relationship with Mary. I just hoped the time would come soon. Making love with Mary felt so right, was such fun, and held such emotional joy, that it only peeked my desire to experience such things with someone of my own sex. Seeing how easily, how completely, my body responded to a woman, also — perhaps paradoxically — served to reinforce my understanding of how natural and right I would also feel with a boy.

I wanted to tell Mary I was bi, not so much because I felt I should, but because I wanted to hear her take on the matter. I figured I'd just fit it in casually in conversation. Maybe she'd point out a boy she thought was cute and I'd say, "Yeah, I dig him too." Or maybe we'd see something in the newspaper about gay rights, and I'd say, "Maybe I'll go down to Christopher Street and march with them," then as a footnote add, "I'm bisexual." But such an opportunity never presented itself, and suddenly the summer was almost over, and I thought it would seem odd if I were to bring it up abruptly, just before she was going to leave. So I never told her.

****

Sometimes, after playing pool, Mary and I'd have a couple of beers (I never knew where she got these) in the park, and watch the stars. I told her what I knew of astrophysics. She giggled delightedly and made up stories about red giants chasing white dwarfs across the sky. Invariably, the red giant went crashing into the oblivion of a black hole. On occasion, we fell asleep in the park, our backs on the grass, the moon washing us in pale white, two overgrown wood sprites depleted from the day's revelries.

Her grandmother began to give me evil looks every time she saw me. Mary had been sent back to New York to be kept out of trouble, not to spend all hours with a virile, teenage boy. I was all smiles and, "Hi, Gran Wallace!" She'd always had a warm cookie, a glass of milk, and a big hug for me when I was little.

Mary took it all in stride, laughing, wagging her butt, and, "I love you Gran," kiss, hug, and out the door, while the old woman was shouting, "Mary! You get back here this moment! Do you hear me? You're not going to spend another evening with that boy!" What resulted from all this was an understanding that Mary would not be returning to New York the following summer.

There was an afternoon when we sat on my back porch, solemnly staring at one another. At the time, I wasn't sure what was going on in either of our heads. We seemed angry, but for no apparent reason. Looking back, I think we were coming to terms with the fact that, that summer was all we were going to have together. She would leave in the fall, and we wouldn't write or call. It would be over. I'm not sure why we accepted this, didn't fight it. I loved Mary, and I let her go. Somehow, it seemed that this was how it was supposed to be. Maybe I understood that Mary wasn't someone anybody could ever hold on to. Maybe the experience of having already gone through the trauma of saying good-bye to her once made it that much easier to do it again.

I think I dealt with that summer as if it were a dream I had stepped into the moment I saw Mary at my screen door, and stepped back out of again when I saw her final wave, as the car that took her away rounded the corner and vanished. We'd not even made pretenses at intending to stay in contact. We'd hugged, kissed lustily, and then gave each other a long last look while Gran Wallace sat in the car beeping the horn impatiently.

In the weeks that followed, I felt mostly just very lonely. When school started, I sank into my studies again, but I also became consumed with trying to figure out how I was ever going to find a guy to be with. I began to understand that as long as I didn't look or act the way people expected homosexuals to look and act, no gay guy was ever going to suspect that I might be interested, and clearly the fact that I'd spent the summer traipsing around with a girl could only further cut me off from being considered a possibility for any guy looking for a guy. Making matters even less promising, was that the only boys I thought might possibly be so inclined were the few in school whom everyone thought of as gay simply based on their effeminate dispositions, and there was nothing there that interested me.

Chapter Three

The winter after Mary left, my grandfather suffered a heart attack. He was on his feet again within a few days, but my mother was never quite the same. She had run into a priest coming out of my grandfather's hospital room one afternoon, and said she nearly fainted at the sight of his white collar. As a teenager, she had rejected the church because she associated Catholicism with her family's efforts to control and dominate her.

One evening at the dinner table, she said, just as I was about to take in a mouthful of salad, "Where will my father go when he dies?"

My father, who came from a non-practicing Jewish family, gave her a sad smile and shrugged. Then she looked at me.

"Back to the universe," I answered, putting my fork down.

"Oh you and your universe!"

"It's not exactly *my* universe."

"Don't get glib with me," she snapped back.

I looked at my little sister, raising my eyebrows. Our mother was behaving totally out of character. My sister giggled.

"I love my father," my mother said as she and I washed the dishes a little later, while my dad got the kids ready for bed.

"I love Nonno too."

"But not like you love your own father."

"I guess."

"I disappointed him, broke his heart, by rejecting my faith." Her face was scrunched up with pain. She'd looked this way for days.

"You've lived your life in your own way; that's normal."

She paused, handing me a dish. "I wonder if God will forgive me."

"God?"

"Yes, God. Didn't your Einstein say he believed in God?" Her tone was suddenly high with irritation.

"He's not *my* Einstein, and I think for myself. He wasn't a cult leader."

"You'd never know it from the way you act."

"What does that mean?" Unaccustomed to my mother being critical of me, I was genuinely hurt and confused.

"Holed up in your room reading all the time."

I stared at her, disbelieving, but she just glared back.

"Fine," I said, throwing the dishtowel up in the air, "I'll start hanging out in front of the Seven Eleven talking about the latest crap on TV."

She looked at me now as though I was a stranger in her house.

I've often thought that things might have worked out better between my family and me if I'd only said the right things that evening, that this had been my one chance and I'd blown it. But even all these years later, I never could imagine *what* I might have said that would have made the difference.

****

It was true that it had broken my grandfather's heart when my mother renounced Catholicism, but I don't think it was the faithlessness itself that disturbed him, but rather that he took this as a defiance of him, the family patriarch. Maybe if I had pointed this out... In any case, it never seemed to disturb my grandfather that I didn't go to church. Back when I'd graduated Jr. High, he'd taken me to a huge bookstore in Manhattan. Through his thick mustache, he'd

16

rasped out with a heavy accent, "Tell me what books you want."

I told him the four I could think of off the top of my head.

"More," he'd said, "many more. I'll have an espresso on the corner; you browse. When you're done, I'll write a check."

I picked out twenty-two books in all: physics, astronomy, biographies of great physicists, two on electricity, and recalling information from an article I'd found in the library about homosexual writers, I threw in Allen Ginsberg's *Howl*, William Burroughs' *Naked Lunch,* and *Christopher and His Kind* by Isherwood.

I was prepared, if my grandfather inquired, to explain honestly the reason why I'd bought the few non-science related books. But instead, he asked, simply, "Did you get everything you wanted?"

Then he took me to an old-fashioned soda fountain. Seated at the long counter on spinning red stools, Nonno said, as we waited for service, "When I was your age, I wasn't nearly as studious as you. I dreamed of being an actor!" He laughed uproariously at this. "Like Charlie Chaplin!" Then, quieting down, he explained in a near whisper, poking an index finger into my ribcage near my heart, hard enough to hurt a little, "I didn't follow that dream because I thought it would make my life difficult. So I went against my nature and became a businessman, and that's how I discovered the true meaning of a difficult life!" Another big laugh. Relieving me of the jabbing finger, he put his thick hand on my shoulder and said, "How about a root beer float?"

****

I peeked out my bedroom window one morning, about four months after my grandfather's heart attack, and saw a woman in a plain dress with a huge wooden cross dangling from her neck. She held a large leather volume in one hand and a bundle of pamphlets in the other. I scurried downstairs.

"Who are those new people next door?" I asked my mom as she cored apples to bake. This was a family favorite — baked apples with cinnamon and whipped cream.

"The Elgies. Sam and Marissa," my mother said.

"What's their deal?"

She looked at me disapprovingly. "That's rude, Jim."

"Have you met them? Are they really weird?"

Again the same look. "I'm planning to take some apples over this evening."

"Apples? Really? Why?"

"They're our neighbors."

"They're religious fanatics."

"Jim!"

I looked at her curiously, started making myself some scrambled eggs, trying to stay out of her way. "What time are you going over there?"

"After dinner."

"If you're not back by ten, I'll call the police."

She stomped her foot. "Stop it, Jim."

She returned home before ten but she was back over there the next night. A few days later, I came home from school and found Marissa and my mom at the kitchen table with a bible, a *bible* spread out before them. I had burst in on them, swinging open the kitchen door, looking for a glass of milk, and actually gasped when I realized what I was seeing. I did a quick about-face and was out of there in a snap, as if I'd walked in on my parents having sex.

Soon after Marissa left, I met my mom in the foyer as I came down the steps. The kids were watching the Electric Company in the living room.

"What the hell are you doing?" I asked point blank.

"Don't talk like that in this house!"

I was flabbergasted. "Like *what*? *Hell*?"

"There are children in the house."

I looked at Elizabeth and Jesse, their eyes mesmerized by dancing kids on the screen. "They can't hear us, and so what anyway? What were you doing with her?"

"Talking, Jim, talking. Do I have to get permission from my son to talk to someone?"

"Why are you so angry at me, Mom?"

"Why are you so hostile to our neighbors? You didn't even say hello to Marissa. I was very embarrassed."

"Do you know how disturbing it is for me to see my mother consorting with a bible thumper?" Our voices had risen substantially, and Jesse and Elizabeth turned away from the television now to look at us.

"*Consorting*? You and your big words. You're not the only smart person around you know. Marissa has a lot of interesting things to say."

"No!"

"Yes! Why don't you come over with me tonight and hear for yourself?"

"You're going over there *again*? Christ, Mom!"

"*Don't* use the Lord's name in vain!"

I stood there with my mouth open.

"I have laundry to do," my mother announced and tromped off.

****

I knocked on the den door later that night. My dad was sitting in his black leather chair, a book open on his lap, a pipe in his mouth. He rarely smoked. As a small child, I'd loved the smell of pipe tobacco, and walking into the den that night brought back memories of a little boy running through the house, playing hide and seek with Mary, happy as a chimp in a jungle.

My dad looked up, over new bifocals.

"Mom's scaring me," I said, realizing my tone differed little from how I'd complained of monsters under the bed when I was four.

"Scaring you?"

"Yeah. It's those people next door. That woman. Mom's been over there a lot, and today... today they were reading the bible in our kitchen!"

I'd expected my dad to be horrified by this news, instead he took off his glasses, slowly laying them on his desk and said very calmly, in a drawn out sort of way, "Jim..."

It was then that I looked at the book on his lap. Big letters at the top of the page stood out, "GENESIS."

I slunk down into the chair across from my dad without making a conscious decision to do so.

"Your mother has always felt an emptiness within her where her faith use to be. She's struggled with this for years."

I buried my face in my hands.

My father continued, undaunted. "When I was a kid, I always wondered about the families who went to church or synagogue. It seemed to me that they had something that my family did not. A cohesiveness. *A faith.*" After a moment he continued, "Son, I think you could find a lot in this book that would help you understand better. I know you're always grappling with science to understand why we are here... but I don't think science is the answer."

I looked up, shocked at what my father thought about me, and told him with barely subdued anger, "I don't *grapple*! I'm not trying to understand why we exist. I only want to comprehend *how* we exist, and only because it's interesting and exciting. I don't give a damn why we're here. We're here. That's it. Accept it and stop reaching for false answers." I rose and pointed to the book on his lap. "That's craziness. Don't do that to yourself."

"I think you're forgetting who's the parent here, and who's the child."

"I think you're forgetting to use your rational mind."

"Rationality can only take you so far."

"Where the hell are you trying to go?"

"Not to hell."

I didn't know this man. He was not my father. As I was leaving the room, I turned around and said, "If you two get into that garbage, don't delude yourselves it to thinking I'll go there with you." Back upstairs, I pulled a book off the shelf, one my grandfather had paid for, and flipped it open to the sought after chapter, "EVOLUTION." If my dad's going to be down there reading Genesis, I thought, there needs to be an equilibrium established in this house.

****

I decided I had to take a proactive stance with my parents. They were intelligent people; I just needed to call their intellect into focus, get them to see how dangerous religion is.

Saturday night, at the dinner table, as we were finishing our pot roast, I calmly asked my mother if she wasn't concerned about all the harm that had been done in the name of Christianity.

"Whatever are you talking about?" She looked at me with her head cocked stiffly to one side, her brow in a furrow.

"What about rape victims who are told abortions are a sin?"

"Killing unborn babies *is* a sin!" Her head straightened now, her neck rising solidly above her shoulders.

"And bringing an unwanted child into a hostile environment isn't?"

"Are you implying that murder can be justified?"

Realizing I was going nowhere with this tack, I got more personal. "What about Ronnie and Bill?"

"Ronnie and Bill are very nice people..." Mom took a calculated sip of her water. Putting the glass down again, she added, "and talented hair stylists. But that doesn't mean they're not misguided, or that they're blessed in the eyes of the Lord." She patted her mouth with a paper napkin. "I plan to take some of Marissa's pamphlets with me when I have my next haircut."

"No! Mom, you can't do that!"

My mother's voice rose in return, "Do you want them to burn in the fires of hell eternally? If you'd *read* the bible, you'd know it says, as clear as day, right there in Leviticus, that..."

I felt my blood rise to a boil like an impatient volcano. I stared at my plate — half a dozen or so neglected peas on a yellow floral pattern. I put my thumb on the blue rim, grasped the underside, white showing up on my knuckles, and half rising, knocking over my chair in the process, I flung that piece of fine china as hard as I could across the room. The peas spun through the air like particles in an accelerator, and then there was the crash followed by the clamor of shattered pieces falling onto the hardwood floor. With my mother screaming holy terror, my sister crying in great gasps and my father and brother stone silent, I turned and bolted from the room.

****

The next morning, Sunday, I awoke groggy and thirsty. I wandered towards the kitchen, seeking orange juice, and at the bottom of the stairs encountered my family standing by the front door. Elizabeth was in a frilly pink dress, all got up like a birthday cake. Jesse wore something I'd expect to see on a used car salesman, and my parents looked the epitome of Mr. and Mrs. Conservative. I stared at them in gaping disbelief. They in turn gazed upon me as if I were The Creature from the Black Lagoon. I had on boxer shorts and a T-shirt that read, *Remember when the air was clean and sex was dirty?* Mary had brought this back for me after a visit to the city.

For a couple of moments none of us moved or spoke. Finally the spell was broken when I came-to and shouted, "No, not the kids!"

"Excuse me?" my father said.

I looked him in the eye pleadingly. "If you want to poison your own minds, that's your business, but don't do this to them. They're innocent children."

"We're teaching them the ways of Jesus," my mother said robotically. Then she ushered my little sister and brother away from me, out the door.

My father gave me a harsh disappointed look that frightened me more than any childhood monster.

"I'm your son, Goddamn it!"

His face softened. "Then come with us;" he held out his hand, my guide to salvation, "we'll wait while you get dressed."

"This is insane, Dad. Don't you know how much evil has been done in the name of religion?"

"That's the devil's talking through you!" He shut the door hard behind him. I stared at it, struck by an urge to run out and rescue Elizabeth and Jesse, forcibly if necessary. But by the time I swung the door open, our station wagon was already headed down the road. I stood barefoot on the lawn watching my family disappear from me.

****

Now that school was out for the summer, I spent enormous amounts of time at the library. I read anything that was written by or about anyone out or presumed gay, and everything I could find on the topic of homosexuality. There was no listing in the card catalogue for "Bisexual." I did find the word in the indexes of a few Psychology books though. These all led to one-liner definitions, which amounted to "latent homosexual" or "ambivalence."

Coming home from the library one day, unaware that my grandfather had died that morning, I walked in through the kitchen door. My mother turned abruptly and gave me a terrified look — as if I were a burglar. Her eyes were bloodshot pools, her face tear stained. Then my mother suddenly grabbed and hugged me. This was the first time she'd shown affection for me in months, and as it turned out, the last time ever.

"Nonno, Nonno" she moaned, weeping into my ear for her father. Realizing what had happened, I hugged her too, trying hard to express as much love and sympathy as possible without words — for what words could there be for this? My own tears came later, when I was alone in my room.

****

As we walked back to the cars from the gravesite, cousin Vinny said, "You should buy my Harley."

I just looked at him. What was he up to now?

"Ten thousand dollars."

"You're selling your bike for ten thousand dollars?"

"Ten thousand and a *hell* of a lot more later."

"What are you talking about?"

He put his arm around me. "The will."

I got ten thousand off the bat, and a fat sum labeled, "Higher Education" which was mine to manage as I saw fit when I enrolled in college. I bought Vinny's bike thinking:

wheels, freedom, a way to escape from the family. Vin stuck around long enough to teach me how to ride the bike, a few basic repair tips, and the joys of bowling. "Bowling was one of Nonno's great loves, you should learn in his honor." As with billiards, I found that the challenge of applying principals of motion made the game stimulating. My technique drove Vinny nuts. "Stop *thinking* about it!" he'd admonish.

"How's your sex life?" he asked one time to distract me.

"What sex life?"

"The one you're supposed to have! You're almost seventeen, Jim. Christ. You're not still pining over that blonde, are you?"

"Pining?"

"You need a good lay, that's what you need."

"I couldn't agree more."

****

I liked the Harley immediately, something I had to master and control or else have it ultimately, perhaps fatally, control me. I was totally taken in by its lion-like purr — there is something so patient about the sound of a Harley's engine, as if it is just waiting for something to happen — and the rugged luxury of the black leather seat. Within weeks, I was no longer able to imagine what life had been like without the bike. I'd ride over to the bowling alley and practice my game with men older than my grandfather had been. Or I'd drive out to the edge of town, to a funky corner bar where the aging bleach-blond barmaid was so drunk, and thought I was so cute, that it didn't occur to her that I shouldn't be in there sipping a draft and learning all I could from a boozed up eighty-year-old pool shark, Crazy-Man Al, whom I'd met bowling. He and I spent long afternoons under the blue cigarette-smoke halo of the overhead lamp, concentrating on our games as if they were events of great international significance. With watery pale gray eyes, Al watched intensely as I took my shots, scratching his head through a fine layer of white silken strands. Occasionally he'd grasp my elbow and move it back an eighth of an inch, or with an impatient jabbing, point out the ball I *should* be shooting for.

Chapter Four

In the fall of my junior year, I went to see the season's first basketball game at school. Watching sweaty athletic guys run around in tank tops and shorts seemed like a great way to unwind after class before I went home to hit the books.

I was no longer able to play pool with Al. A new bartender had taken over and with one square-shouldered vulture-eyed look, he'd let me know not to even entertain the notion of entering Happy Dreams Neighborhood Bar.

"Come on, come on," Al oblivious, tried to coax me in.

"No, not today Al."

"What's the matter with ya, Jimmy boy?"

Loneliness had become an issue, but even more pressing was a high level of frustration. Fantasizing about guys just wasn't enough anymore; I wanted to be with one.

A couple of the players on the court more or less appealed to me, and I indulged in a few daydreams, but I quickly found myself distracted by the futility of this exercise, and as the game itself was a particularly boring one, I started to look at the people sitting across from me on the bleachers. To amuse myself (barely) I did quick mathematical estimates: how many were actually watching the game; how many were talking to the people sitting next to them; how many were picking at their fingernails. One guy in particular caught my attention — Rick, the boyfriend of a popular and intelligent girl named Jenny. I was surprised to see him alone. Then slowly I became surprised by something else. Rick wasn't watching the game at all! Rick was doing what I had been doing most of the game; he was watching the *guys*! The ball would be at one end of the court, and his eyes would be all over the hunk coming in from the other end. I watched him for a while, becoming more and more certain of what it was I was looking at — a guy lusting after other guys.

Eventually, something in his peripheral vision must have made Rick realize that he was being watched, because suddenly he looked over at me. I almost panicked and looked away, but I managed to keep it together and smiled a knowing smile at him. Cautiously, Rick smiled back. Fueled by nerves and excitement, I was determined as all hell not to let this slide by me. I wanted to let him know that I knew what he was up to. I gestured with my chin towards the court, nodded slowly, and then smiled the knowing smile again.

Rick's eyes got big. Loud as my heart beat at the moment, the buzzer went off, marking the end of the game. Our eyes locked briefly, then Rick turned to get his books off the bench, and I, out of habit I guess, looked up at the scoreboard. When I looked back, Rick was gone; I couldn't make him out in the crowd. Frantic, I scrambled outside.

In the parking lot, people were everywhere. I stood off to the side of the gym door, my eyes searching, darting. Then, there he was, walking towards me. I swallowed hard. Rick was a sight. He stood about my height, a little shorter, but stockier — broad shouldered. He was clean-shaven, but a slight shadow made it clear that, given the chance, his beard would grow in full. His bronze skin, the gentle rolling outline of his nose, his pink lips, and strong jaw, made his face somehow both beautiful and super masculine. Longish curly hair, and golden brown eyes... I could find myself staring at Rick for purely aesthetic reasons.

He stopped in front of me, studying me, trying to read me. I looked back at him with alert unblinking eyes.

Rick pursed his lips. "Coffee?"

Coffee? It took a moment before I realized this was an invitation. I wasn't in the habit of drinking coffee, but the thought that zipped through my head was, *Yes, yes, whatever you want.* "Yeah," I responded with what I hoped was a really sexy whisper.

****

Leaving my bike at school, I rode with Rick in his Volkswagen bug across town. He snapped in a Pink Floyd tape, "Dark Side of the Moon."

I ran my thumb along the textured squares of the vinyl seat.

"I don't know your name," Rick said, as he shifted gears at a red light.

"Jim," I said, then I added, "I know yours."

"How come?" The light turned green and he shifted again.

"Oh, you know, Jenny's boyfriend — everybody knows your name."

"Oh, I guess."

In exchanging other basic information, we discovered that we lived about fifteen blocks from each other on the same street. Rick was also in his junior year. He asked questions about my bike, told me his car had been his dad's, bought new in the late '60s. It was easy conversation, easy to forget what the dynamics were.

Rick had neither asked where I'd like to go nor clued me in to where he was taking me. It turned out to be a place I'd never been to. We walked into a square room with rustic wooden booths along one wall, and lighting that was, if not truly dim, not bright either. Scattered mismatched tables and chairs filled the bulk of the room, but Rick headed to a booth, and we sat opposite one another on black upholstered benches. A waitress appeared instantly. Rick ordered two coffees for us, then turning to me, he said, "You did want coffee, right?"

I hadn't had coffee since my mother once spoon-fed me some of hers, at my insistence, when I was a little kid; I'd hated it.

"Ah, yeah, sure."

When the waitress was gone Rick said something forced and awkward to me, I don't remember what, about the restaurant's hamburgers, or fried chicken. But once our coffees were delivered, he seemed suddenly super relaxed again, very present. We smiled not shy smiles at each other, and it was the two of us there together, the rest of the world fading into a background mirage. At his lead, I poured cream into my cup. Taking a sip, I found my taste had changed considerably since I was seven. Rick cradled his mug in his hands, staring into it, concentrating, I could tell, on what he wanted to say. I had been thinking on the ride over that Rick and I could have a lot of fun together, but now, looking at him sitting there like that, it also occurred to me that I could fall in love with this boy, and then strangely, I thought that perhaps I already had.

Looking up at me, Rick asked with a soft smile, "Was I really that obvious at the game?"

"To me, yeah. But then," I added grinning, "I was there for pretty much the same reason."

He smiled at this, looked at me carefully. Rick took a sip of coffee then spoke quietly. "I said I didn't know your name, but I do recognize you. You ran around with a real cute blond girl a couple of summers ago."

"Mary Wallace." I smiled wistfully, remembering.

"I thought you were one lucky kid. Where did she disappear to?"

I told him, in more detail than I intended, through refills of our coffees, about my childhood friendship with Mary, her parent's divorce, and our summer together.

Rick listened carefully and when I was done he said, pensively, "So you dig girls too, not just guys."

"Right."

"Same here." Rick circled an index finger along the rim of his cup, looking down at it. His face fell sad, very sad. "Jenny doesn't know. That I'm into boys too." He looked at me quizzically then added, "I don't think she'd take it well." He chased this obviously distasteful fact with a long swig from his mug.

Reeling with all kinds of uncomfortable feelings, I said, "That's a drag."

"Yeah, it is." The sorrow in Rick's eyes, I saw now, was edged with anger, bitterness.

"Jennifer and I were in honors math together in the ninth grade; we competed for the best grade."

Rick shook his head, laughing in dismay. "Oh no, don't tell me, you're a brain too!"

The waitress came by then to offer more coffee. Rick looked at his watch and told me he needed to get home. "Big deal with my folks, that we all have dinner together."

On the drive back to my bike we, ironically, talked basketball. When he stopped the engine at the gym parking lot, Rick turned to me. "I'm doing something tomorrow with Jenny, but how about coffee on Thursday?"

Talking in low tones, I suppose in a futile attempt to cover up the excitement we both felt, we arranged a place to meet after classes. Then we sat staring at each other, our eyes saying things difficult to say with words, things that told both of us that something wonderful had happened to us that day.

****

Rick pulled up in his bug and I slipped into the passenger seat.

"Hi."

"Hi."

Yeah, we were both on a high all right, our faces beaming with joy. We drove in silence for a while, happy just to be beside one another, then Rick said, "I told Jenny I met you at the game. I asked if she remembered you from ninth grade math."

"What did she say?"

"She said that you didn't seem to get how intelligent you are, that you didn't take your smarts seriously, and that if you did, you would excel in whatever field you went into."

I laughed hard, then said, "She's probably right. I guess I make a pretty concerted effort not to be aware of my mind's capabilities. I like being smart, but I don't want it to become who I am."

Rick turned and looked at me and apparently had trouble looking away again, which nearly caused us to flip over as he sideswiped a curb. After that, we were silent again until we got to the restaurant. We sat in the same booth and the same waitress approached the table and said numbly, "Two coffees, right?" as if we had been coming in there every day for the past five years. I liked that; it made me feel like Rick and I were a couple that everyone was used to seeing together. Again, Rick seemed awkward and uncomfortable until the coffee came, but then he was all mine. I told him the story of my mother giving me a taste of her coffee when I was little, and how I didn't think I'd like it when I had a cup with him the other day.

Rick's eyes sparkled along with an amused little laugh. Then his laugh settled into a smile, and I found it was really too much to look at him when he was smiling at me like that. Then the smile too was gone, and Rick studied me intensely, as if trying to come to a decision. He leaned forward now, arms resting on the table. Looking right into my eyes, he said, "My folk's house has this basement apartment, with a separate entrance. Last year, I convinced them to let me stay down there. They had one stipulation

32

though," he looked down at his hand, and grinning to himself, said, "no girls." Rick looked up at me slowly now. "There's no rule however about guys."

Okay, I tried to steady myself, what I heard was that Rick knew what he wanted, knew what I wanted, and what would be the point of pretending otherwise. Jesus. I sat literally at the edge of my seat, waiting for an invitation.

Rick just looked at me, mischievously playing on the suspense. Finally, after taking a sip of coffee, he asked, "You have any plans for the rest of the afternoon?" Big grin.

"Yeah." I grinned back, my heart beat imitating the roar of my Harley. "I'm planning to spend the rest of the afternoon with you."

Chapter Five

Rick parked under a basketball net suspended from the garage at the top of a steep driveway, and led me down a short flight of concrete steps.

A couch and coffee table were positioned diagonally in the center of the spacious room. Several feet behind the couch, there was a twin bed against the wall. Above the bed a small rectangular window, at ground level with the driveway, let in the only outside light.

Rick selected a record from a large collection, which was next to a kitchenette alcove on the far wall, and placed it on the stereo. He was wearing green jeans and a yellow oxford shirt with rolled up sleeves. Very soon I'd be touching him, those big masculine arms. After a hiss and a pop, Credence Clearwater Revival's, "Good-Golly Miss Molly," came through clear and sweet. We stood a couple of feet apart, smiling at each other, nervously enjoying the anticipation. Then we moved towards one another, joined our mouths, and the nervousness was gone instantly. What I felt was passion. What I felt too was Rick's back through his shirt, solid and strong, against my hand. I was very aware that I was touching a man. I was also very aware that I was touching a particular man, a man who it seemed I was falling in love with, his tongue in my mouth thick and warm and excited. I felt Rick's hand, big and sure, moving down to my waistband, then continuing on to caress my ass through my jeans. I pulled the tails of his shirt out of his pants and slipped my hands up and onto the bare skin, silken as butterfly wings.

We parted, exchanged dreamy-eyed smiles. Then I unbuttoned his shirt, opening it to expose his chest. I took one look, then hastily pulled his shirt all the way off. Rick was breathing deeply, his chest slightly sweaty, alive with desire. I knelt down to undo his pants but ended up sticking my tongue into his belly button, and sucked and nibbled

34

hungrily. Rick moaned, his hands desperately kneading my shoulders. I moved back for a moment to gaze at the trail of curly hair that led from his navel down into his pants. I grabbed a hold of his belt and Rick let me unfasten it and unbutton his jeans, but before I had a chance to get to the zipper, he slipped his hands under my arms and pulled me up.

He removed my shirt, then while kissing me — our bare chests and stomachs pressing together — he slyly undid my belt and snap then unzipped me. I pulled down his zipper then too and we stopped kissing for a moment to remove our pants. We left our under shorts on though and, tonguing again, groped one another's asses and pressed into each other's erections. Yes, I was in love with Rick; there was more than just wildly intense lust going on here, and I didn't understand how these emotions could become so concrete so fast.

When the record ended, Rick went to turn it over, then led me to his bed as John Fogerty sang about being born on the bayou. I tried to remove his boxers, but he stopped me. "Let's make this last."

I nodded in agreement, and then lay stomach-down on the bed. Rick sat next to me and stared at my face, then at my ass. He broke out into a grin and proceeded to climb on top of me. Slipping his hands under my shoulders, he kissed my neck and back, then slowly mock-fucked me.

Feeling his hardness through my boxers on my ass, his soft moans near my ear, his hot breath and wet lips on my neck, the pressure of his fingers digging into my shoulders — which felt strong and powerful at his touch — feeling all this, and my cock rubbing against the bed with each of his slow grindings, I thought I might die right there and melt into ecstasy.

Mercifully, Rick stopped. Climbing off me, he removed my shorts, kissed my ass with soft pecks, then rolled me over and took off his own underwear. We studied

one another's erections with awe but did not touch —
because clearly that would be too much for either of us. So
we lay hugging, trying to cool down some, feeling the full
nakedness of each other's bodies — not, we quickly
realized, a great way to cool down.

Rick got up and headed across the room. I watched
his bare body — his firm ass cheeks — felt aroused beyond
belief, and was acutely aware of being amazingly happy.
He disappeared into the bathroom for a second, then
returned with a bottle of almond oil. Tilting the bottle
carefully, Rick poured a small pool of the gold liquid into
his palm, then gently rubbed the oil on my balls. My whole
body shuddered at his initial touch, then, after a deep moan,
I gave-in to the pleasure, but only for a moment, because I
became overwhelmed with a desire to do the same to him.
Motioning for Rick to lay on his back, I poured oil into my
hand and worked it into the smooth skin of his scrotum.
The hands-off-cocks policy we'd established was, by this
point, torturous. Staring longingly at his throbbing erection,
knowing it had to hurt as much as mine, I slid my oily hand
between his cheeks.

Rick's eyes were half closed. "Fuck me," he
whispered softly, like the dying request of a barely
conscious man.

I guided his legs back towards his chest and
carefully entered him. A moment of bliss was followed by
horror as I discovered that I would be unable to move
without ejaculating. I looked at Rick desperately. "Can I
scream?"

He held back a laugh, biting his lip before
responding, "Sure, my folks are at work."

I let out an agonizing cry, and then waited, holding
perfectly still. As soon as I felt brave and started a slow
thrusting, Rick grabbed his cock. The sight of this was way
too much; I came, screaming, feeling Rick's warm cum
splashing on my stomach, hearing his deep groans.

Three hours later, after fellatio in the shower, and fondling on the couch, Rick was inside of me. *Hurts so good* ran through my head like a mantra. I closed my eyes and lost myself.

****

We were quiet on the drive back to school where I'd pick up my Harley. Watching the manicured lawns as we drove by, this one with a swing set, that one lined with an immaculately trimmed hedge, I thought I probably should let Rick know. So I said, "That was my first time with a guy."

Rick looked at me in alarm, and quickly found a place to pull over. Turning off the engine he asked, "Are you okay?"

I laughed. "I'm *great*."

Smiling back, he said, "I'm feeling pretty wonderful myself."

****

Sunday morning, just after the family left for church, the phone rang. It was Rick: when could he see me again?

"After school tomorrow?" I suggested, and then a little more hopefully, "Now?"

"Now."

****

Rick saw Jennifer after school on Wednesdays, when his nosy neighbor got together with her bridge club, and he could sneak Jenny into the apartment for an hour before his folks got home. He also went out with Jenny on

37

Friday and Saturday nights, and spent most of Saturday day with her. Now Rick spent all the rest of his free time with me. Sometimes we shot hoops in his driveway, or went to a school game, or out for coffee, but for the most part, we were in his apartment. Rock music blaring, we fucked, loved, talked, away the hours.

Rick told his folks and Jenny about the conflicts I had with my family, and used that, plus something about me helping him with his chemistry, to explain why I was spending so much time in his apartment. Quickly, the family conflict alibi became more factual than not. Sure, I was with Rick because we wanted to be together, but I knew too that I came to need his apartment as a refuge. My parents and I could not be in the same room for more than ten minutes without a major confrontation erupting. Jesse would walk in singing, "Jesus loves me, this I know, for the bible tells me so..." and I'd explode. Or Mom would start telling me about a "lovely girl" at their church who could "help you discover the Lord's way." I was so tempted to respond, "Yeah, and after services we could get together with my boyfriend for brunch."

Frequently, I made myself sandwiches at Rick's instead of going home for dinner while Rick ate upstairs with his folks. On several occasions, his mom invited me to join them, but I felt that would be taxing the limits of their hospitality, and graciously declined.

For a while I made it a point to find dates for Saturday nights when Rick was with Jennifer. But conversations tended to center around trivialities and when I tried to steer towards a worthwhile topic, I found my dates didn't have hardly anything insightful to say.

A couple of girls made it a point to seduce me, which I admit was an easy thing to do, but compared to making love with Rick, it was like substituting filet mignon for mac 'n cheese. I couldn't shake the feeling that I'd rather be perusing Einstein's writings, and eventually that's what I chose.

I hung out at the library in the afternoons, but if I stayed too late, the librarian gave me bemused looks, and comments like, "A handsome young man like you should be out with a beautiful girl on a night like this." But by this point, my family and I had come to a temporary truce, where we avoided saying anything to each other more controversial than, "Please pass the salt." So, on weekend nights I ate a quick dinner then stayed in my room and read, waiting patiently for Sunday morning when I'd see Rick again.

Rick was a little put-off when I first stopped dating. He'd egg me on about how cute this or that girl was, and wouldn't Shelly or Tanya be great in the sack. This was in part, I figured, due to guilt about me being alone while he was out fooling around with Jenny, and in part due to him thinking my dating worked well to keep people from wondering about us. But even after I hadn't been out with a girl for months, no one seemed even the slightest bit suspicious, a fact that amazed me.

****

"Need help with that homework?" Rick asked one day, when he noticed I was doodling instead of doing my calculus.

I laughed.

"You gonna tell me what's on your mind?"

I put my pencil down. "Are you in love with Jenny?"

He looked at me quizzically.

"I'm not..." I said, "driving at anything, just would like to know."

Putting his homework on the coffee table, he repositioned himself to face me. "I don't know," he said

39

finally. "She's an interesting person to be around and..." Rick grinned now, "you'd be surprised how much fun she can be in bed. But," he thought a moment, "with Jen, I'm being a boyfriend, she's being a girlfriend. We're not just ourselves, so it's weird." He looked at me to see if I understood.

I picked up his homework and put an X next to an equation that I'd noticed he'd done incorrectly while I was doodling.

I felt a certain regret about being with Rick behind Jenny's back, but I was never jealous. I liked Jenny — admired her anyway — and was glad Rick had her in his life. Understanding the dynamics of my own bisexuality, I would never have dreamed of asking Rick to give up girls. But, I think the main reason I wasn't jealous of Jenny was because I felt so solid and confident about what Rick and I had together.

****

I was heading towards Rick's after school, the Harley scattering leaves, the sky dark and vaguely forbidding. I was taking the bike slow, enjoying the anticipation of being with my lover, when I saw my mom and Elizabeth walking towards home. Mother and daughter hand in hand, the wind whipping the little girl's hair across the back of a paisley print dress — a lovely image. Lovely but detached, part of someone else's family. Hearing the bike upon my approach, they turned around, and I waved. As I passed, my eyes back on the road now, I heard Elizabeth's joyous shout, "Jesus loves you, Jim!" the Jim trailing off in a distortion of sound waves.

I was glad to see the Volkswagen already in the driveway. My little sister's words had eaten away at me for the rest of the drive, and by the time I stepped into the apartment, I was literally shaking with rage. Rick sat me down on the couch and waited beside me. I wanted to destroy something. Finally he put his arm around me, and that calmed me down enough to be able to recount the incident.

"We use to have such fun," I said. "I'd love to be able to pick her up on the bike, just drive off, go to the playground, zip down the slide together, swing her up to the trees." I was imagining this in my head, like imagining some unattainable fantasy: flying a rocket ship to a far galaxy, swimming with a famous movie star on a Caribbean island — then reality takes hold, the rocket ship crashes, I'm attacked by a shark. "If I did that, tried to just go have a good time with her, it would be all, 'How come you don't love Jesus, Jim? Don't you want to go to heaven, Jim?' Can you imagine what she would think if I told her I had a boyfriend?" I paused to consider this. The rocket ship is attacked by some alien life-form. The movie star turns out to be Frankenstein in drag. "She'd probably break down crying, thinking for sure I'm going to hell; she'd probably pray for my soul every night." I thought about this too. The rocket ship was just a cardboard box in a garage; the movie star was my neighbor's dog in a wading pool. "She probably already does."

"Jesus loves you, Jim!" I imitated her, my eyes filling with tears.

Rick slipped his hand into mine. "If you told her about us, she'd miss the point altogether, not see how much love you were getting right here on earth."

Rick. Rick was real, not a movie star, not a far-off galaxy, not some lofty heaven in the sky. Fuck it. I got Rick.

"Oh yeah, it'd all be sin and condemnation," I said, feeling the full weight of what Rick had just told me, the part about how much love I was getting from him. This was some serious relationship I'd gotten myself into, no doubt about that. All the chaos in my mind was clearing now.

Sanity was taking over again, covering me like a soft blanket on a cool clear night. Where had those images come from? I'd never been one to have fantasies about rocket ships or movie stars.

Rick was telling me a tale now, about how his aunt kept trying to get his parents to let her take him and his brother to church. Finally, in a scene unprecedented in his home, his dad had told his sister to, once and for all, keep her "soul-grabbing little paws" off his kids.

"Now when Aunt Lil eats at our house she actually goes into the bathroom before dinner to say grace."

This perked me up considerably. "A closet prayer! I love it."

A short while later I was feeling lousy again. Rick had gone up to dinner leaving me with Janis Joplin, whom he'd put on repeat. I made a quick ham and American sandwich with yellow mustard. Why couldn't I be eating a real meal — Irish stew, or spaghetti with Italian sausages, maybe pork chops and mashed potatoes covered in gravy — with my mother and father, and brother and sister, my dad's cat coughing up hairballs in the kitchen, a glass of milk, and rice pudding for dessert?

I finished off the white-bread-gourmet-depression with the dregs from a plastic cup of tap water, then dove full force into my homework. I'd discovered I could lose myself pretty completely in books, in equations — block out the world, immerse my consciousness in the domain of the intellect. I'd been doing this for years, but I'd only recently realized that I'd been using this as a sort of a drug, a way to escape. It was, for me, a high. Yes, I, Jim Landa, do solemnly confess, that I get off on complex concepts. Trisexual if you will — boys, girls, and academics.

When I did this, got into the "think mode" as I began to call it, I found I got schoolwork done in an appallingly short period of time. So it was, I found myself done with my homework, while Rick was still upstairs playing nice-straight-boy whose buddy was waiting to play tidily-winks for a couple of hours, before he'd zoom off to sleep in his own bed. For lack of anything else to do, I began to think about my other big addiction — making love with Rick. By the time he got downstairs, I practically attacked him.

"You only want me for sex!" he complained.

I laughed. Then I laughed harder. It was an absurd statement. Then Rick was laughing. The more we laughed, the more we laughed, and pretty soon we were rolling around on the floor, in each other's arms, giggle-tears rolling down our faces. Then, suddenly, I pinned Rick's shoulders down, straddling him.

"You're my sex slave. I want you only for your big cock and," I considered, "your tight ass."

Rick continued to giggle, but he was also, I could feel, getting aroused. I moved off of him and, kneeling on the floor in the space between his legs, unzipped him.

"Come on, sex slave, I wanna suck you off." I undid his belt and yanked down his jeans and under-shorts, then gave him an outrageous blowjob. After Rick came, I lay down beside him pushing my hard-on against his leg.

"Fuck me," he groaned.

"No. You're *my* sex slave. You fuck me."

"But I just came," he protested.

"You'll just have to do it again."

We faced each other on our sides, talking, fondling, teasing, until, eventually, he was hard again. When he entered me — from behind, as I put my weight on the back of the couch — he put one hand on my cock, slowly sliding it up and down my shaft. Soon, as if a response to Janis' pleadings, Rick and I both came, quietly growling in unison.

After, we lay on the bed together for a while, catching our breaths, then Rick leaned up on an elbow gazing at me. "Spend the night."

"What?"

"Stay with me tonight. I'll tell my folks you can't handle going home. They'll understand."

"They'll figure us out."

"Would that be so terrible?"

I blinked. *What about Jenny?* went through my head quickly, but I didn't ask; that was Rick's business. Instead, I said what Rick already knew, "Yes, it would be terrible. If they don't want you screwing Jenny down here, there's no way..."

We lay there dismayed. Finally, Rick said, "But, stay over tonight. They won't think anything if it's just one time. The way they are, they'll be glad to help you out."

In fact, Rick's folks *were* fine with the idea once he relayed the "Jesus loves you" scene from that afternoon.

I called my house, and I simply told my dad, "I'm not coming home tonight; I'll be at a friend's."

"This guy, Rick?"

"Yeah."

He knew that's where I hid out from them after school. There was a long pause, then, "Okay." Clearly he did not like the idea, but what could he do?

Rick's mom gave him a pillow, sheet, and blanket, and we spread these out on the couch for appearance sake. Falling asleep in Rick's arms, I felt sad, sad that I would not be able to do this every night. In the morning we touched each other's faces and hair before getting up and getting ready for school.

This was Friday, so I wouldn't be seeing Rick again until Sunday morning. After school, I holed-up in the library, then sat down for dinner with my family. During grace I hummed to the tune of "Sodomy" from the Broadway musical, *Hair,* which my parents had taken me into the city to see when I was nine. For the rest of the meal, (at least it wasn't bologna) my family carried on as if I wasn't there. Skipping dessert, I shut myself up in my bedroom, poured through my books, recalled a lusty afternoon with Mary, masturbated, and fell asleep early.

Chapter Six

Saturday I drove my bike out to the river. Sitting on the bank, I dropped pebbles into the river, watching the ripples I was creating — the effects of a force radiating out well beyond the initial impact. I thought about how lonely I had been before I met Rick, found it amazing that my utter lack of companionship hadn't plunged me into the far depths of depression. I'd handled it "like a man," I supposed. This made me laugh, and got me to wondering why it was that I felt so much a man when I was with Rick doing things most people considered so... *anti*-man?

I put my hand in the river, watching the icy water flow under it, around it — following the path of least resistance. A path, I understood, I would never be able to choose.

****

I got out of the house early Sunday to be sure to miss the "family gets ready for church" scene. I had a greasy western omelet, and watery coffee, at a diner. When I drove up to Rick's, his mother was attending rose bushes along the driveway. As I brought the bike to a halt, she turned away from her roses and towards me. I took off my helmet and tried to read her face. She was smiling, but seemed to have something on her mind.

"Good morning, Jim."

"Good morning, Mrs. Bockley."

"How was your weekend?"

Still sitting on the bike, I said, "All right. How was yours?"

"Good." We looked at each other awkwardly, and I started getting nervous. Finally she said, "Jim... I know it has to be difficult, your family situation..." she trailed off.

46

"Yeah, it's pretty bad," I had to admit. Then I added quickly, "I've really appreciated you letting me hang out here and all." I was certain she was going to tell me enough is enough, and I was ready to put my helmet back on, burst into tears and zoom off.

But she said, "Rob and I have talked it over; we want to help as much as we can — while you're finishing high school." She gave me a sympathetic smile. "So please, feel free to come over anytime, and if you need to sleep here, that's fine too. Hopefully your parents won't make a fuss. I think they must realize they can't force their views on you and..."

I didn't quite catch her last words; I was still stuck on the bit about "if you need to sleep here." When she was done, I put a lot of energy into controlling my joy. Smiling an appropriate smile, I said, "Thank you, Mrs. Bockley. I'll probably take you up on that. It's very kind of you."

A cool breeze blew down from above the garage, and carried away any regret I might have felt for my deception, to a place well out of my reach. Mrs. Bockley pushed back a strand of hair that had been swept across her cheek and returned to her roses. I went to her son.

Rick was on his bed, the stereo silent for once. Dressed only in a pair of overly short cut-offs, a book was propped up on his bent, slightly spread, knees. He was being obvious about wanting to look sexy for me. I smiled at this, at him, and then, sitting at the foot of the bed, I took my gloves off and put my hands on his cold feet.

"You're like ice."

"Melt me."

I took off my jacket and slid myself up through the space between his knees, and lay on top of him. Putting my mouth next to his ear I whispered, "Your mom just *invited* me to spend the night as often as I like."

A moment of no response was followed by a whispered, "Are you serious?"

"Yes." I moved my mouth to his and proceeded to melt my ice boy into a mass of molten lava.

****

On Sundays we made it a point to get out of Rick's apartment for at least part of the day. It was one thing to hang out there after school three days a week, it was another thing to spend an entire day together in the Bockley basement; it wouldn't have looked right. Usually this meant lunch at "our" restaurant, sitting in "our" booth, being served by "our" waitress, whose bland indifference towards everything amused us greatly. Normally we managed fairly easily to put on a show of being buddies. This day however, I found the task difficult. I was too happy, too immersed in my feelings for Rick. I resented the fact that I couldn't touch his hand or even let our legs rest against each other's under the table. It didn't matter that we'd spent the morning with our bodies entangled, or that we would likely spend most of the afternoon, evening, and night touching each other in some way; I wanted to be able to put my hand on his forearm and run my fingers through the thick brown hair there. "How can it be," Rick asked, gesturing towards our waitress across the room, "that her new uniform makes her look both more feminine and more asexual?"

I stared at him blankly. Religion, I was thinking, is at the root of all homophobia.

"What's wrong?"

I leaned in towards him and said as quietly as possible — feeling ridiculous because the other customers were all well out of earshot — "If you were God, what reason would you have for hating what you and I have?"

He smiled, amused. Typical of Rick, he had an immediate answer, as if he'd just been waiting for me to ask

48

that question. "Fear." He ate a French fry. "Anything so beautiful has got to be scary to a god that wants to control."

I smiled, but only for a second. "I wonder what my parents think. I mean, in their understanding, God says homosexuality is evil. Do they ever question why? Do they ever think, now what exactly does God have against two men loving each other?"

"People tend not to make it a habit to question God. Your parents don't think about the psychological motives behind 'The All Mighty'. No one does," he chuckled, "just you, Jim. That's why I love you." He patted my hand.

Without thinking, I pulled my hand away, glancing around to see who might have been watching. "*Jesus*," I said afterwards, looking at Rick apologetically.

****

Rick and I were aimlessly making out on his couch when his phone rang. He answered, then handed it to me. "I think it's your dad." I now slept at Rick's four nights a week and didn't see much of my dad.

My father wanted to meet me after school the next day to talk. I thought, great, another effort to save my soul. But he must have guessed this, because he interjected, using my own slang, "I promise, no Jesus talk."

So with optimism as my motivator, I agreed to meet him. He chose the donut shop he use to take me to when I was a kid.

"Drinking coffee?" My father sat down on a chrome-trimmed stool next to me, just as my beverage arrived.

"Oh. Yeah." It felt odd that my father didn't know something so basic to the reality of my everyday life. But then he didn't know about Rick and me either, and that was pretty basic.

49

He ordered a jelly donut and a black coffee. After taking a bite, my dad said, "I don't like us being strangers."

"Neither do I."

"Well, I got the idea that I could teach you how to play handball and we could do a game once a week. What do you think?"

My father had picked up handball in his twenties and kept it up as a way to stay fit. He'd never talked to me about the game before, and as such, it held a bit of intrigue for me.

"Once a week?" I asked. "When?"

"Tuesdays after school?"

"Wednesdays."

"Okay, Wednesdays."

We sipped our coffee. "You sure you don't want a donut?" he asked.

"I'm sure."

"You always liked those chocolate cake ones. Remember the time you insisted on eating six?"

"Yeah."

"You threw up three times on the way home."

"Why did you let me do it?" I motioned to the counter boy for a refill.

"Sometimes," my father said with an excessive seriousness that he'd only acquired since he became a Christian, "it's important to let children learn about limitations first hand." He put his cup out for more coffee too. "My father did the same with me after he found out I'd been drinking beer when I was sixteen."

I smiled at my dad; he'd told me that story before, and now that he was recounting it, the Christian in him seemed to go out the window. I listened contently as he explained the details behind how my grandfather had challenged him to a drinking contest. My dad had gotten so sick he'd rarely touched alcohol since.

Finishing off his donut and wiping his mouth, my dad said, from behind the napkin, "Your mother would really like you to come to church with us on Christmas."

"You said no Jesus talk!" I shouted in disbelief. The counter boy looked at us with frightened eyes.

"Jim, it's *Christmas.*"

"Yeah, and I figure that's a good time to thank God I'm an atheist." I got up. "Forget it, Dad."

As I approached the door, he called after me, "Wait!"

Reluctantly, I turned around.

"What about the handball?"

"It'll just be another way to prey on my soul."

"*No.* No it won't."

"I can't trust you." I put one hand on the door. "You don't seem able to control yourself. We'll be talking about school, or your mother, or the moon, and the next thing I know in will come the religious crap."

"Okay, we won't talk, just play handball."

"We won't talk?"

"Just hello and good-bye."

I looked at him appraisingly. "If you say one word that's not connected to explaining the game, I'm outta there."

"Deal."

He kept his promise, and I loved the sport — the workout was tremendous. I looked forward to our games, and quickly the no talk rule seemed ridiculous. So I told my dad that if he thought he could keep a lid on the religion, I'd like to resume conversation. Under these new circumstances, we got along great, and one day he asked if I'd please start eating dinner at home again. This was after I'd boycotted Christmas — much to everyone's dismay, including Rick's — by eating Christmas dinner at a Chinese restaurant alone. I'd ordered the most exotic sounding thing on the menu, and that, in conjunction with the pretty waitress, kept me entertained. No way in hell was I going to partake in celebrating the birth that got perverted into intolerance. So now my dad was asking me to start eating dinner at home again, and I said, "I can't do that. I can't sit there and listen to you say grace."

He thought a moment. "You can stay in the living room and we'll call you in when were done."

"Mom won't go for it."

"I'll handle Mom."

"Okay."

He hugged me. Hugging him back felt very good.

****

The volume on the stereo was turned low — Cream's, *Tales of Brave Ulysses*. Rick was working on landscape layouts while I was engrossed in *The Tao of Physics*. We sat lengthwise on his couch, facing each other, our legs entwined. I'd just read something intriguing, and wanted to share it with Rick, but I knew he'd mumble something deep then change the subject. This always happened when I tried to talk to him about something that my readings had gotten me to thinking about. He'd invariably have something interesting or insightful to say, but, he'd made it clear, without actually saying so, that he did not want to get into it; he'd get agitated, his voice impatient, even while he was saying something truly profound.

It ticked me off to realize that I couldn't talk to him about things that were so important to me, so this time, instead of trying to engage him, I said, rather nastily, "You think I'm wasting my time with physics don't you?"

"No." He didn't look up from his work.

"Well, you think it's really boring then."

Now he looked up. "It scares the shit out of me."

I put my book down, sat up straight. "It *scares* you?"

He tapped his pencil on his pad. "I can't handle it, Jim. I start thinking too much and I feel like I'm going to go berserk."

I chewed on this for a while. Then Rick added, "I like that *you're* into it. I'll always cheer you on. Just don't ask me to think about that stuff."

Sometimes when Rick and I were making love, it felt so good I wanted to cry. Even though it upset me greatly to understand that I couldn't share the intellectual part of myself with him, hearing Rick say that he'd always cheer me on, brought on that same choked-up feeling.

****

Jennifer approached me at the stacks at the public library. "Have you decided where you're going to college yet?"

"Probably SUNY New Paltz." I did not look up from searching through titles. I was looking for Isherwood's, *A Single Man.*

"No!" Jennifer protested. "You could get into Harvard or Yale!"

"I don't want to get into Harvard or Yale." I pulled out the book, mentally daring her to notice the author, then realized she'd likely not know who he was anyway.

"They'd give you a full scholarship."

I looked at her carefully. She had bangs now, which somehow made her look smarter but not as cute.

"My grandfather left a trust fund for me."

"That's great! So why not go where you can have access to the best minds in your field?"

"Those places are riddled with cutthroat competition. I want to learn in peace," I said resolutely. Even with the haircut, it was easy to see what drew Rick to her. "I've heard enough horror stories about students contaminating one another's petri dishes." But, as Rick said, she wasn't herself. She didn't have a clue who she was, because she was so busy being who she thought she should be. "A guy who goes to Berkeley told me that when he showed up for an exam and realized he'd forgotten his pencils, the guy sitting next to him with *five* pencils refused to lend him one. I don't want any part of that scene."

Jennifer waved off my reasons with a delicate hand. "You're just an underachiever, and you know it." As she walked away she turned around and shook a slender finger at me. "The mind's a terrible thing to waste, Jimmy Landa." She left me standing there laughing to myself.

Another time she leaned over my shoulder.

"Physics, is it?"

"Yeah." I turned around to face her.

"I'm going to be a lawyer."

I almost said, Rick's told me, but I preferred to keep his name out of our conversations, so I just nodded.

"I like subjects that deal with people," she said.

"I like people too," I said, "but I prefer to enjoy them in nonacademic ways."

"You like people? You seem like such a recluse." She held a pile of books against her chest.

I shrugged. "I'm a recluse who likes people," *especially your boyfriend,* I was dying to add.

"You're strange." She turned and marched away, her impeccably trimmed honey brown hair swaying across her waistline.

Rick told me that Jennifer thought I'd gotten my heart broken by "that pretty blonde a couple of years ago," and that's why I didn't date much. He'd responded, "Could be," and changed the subject. Rick's mom's take was that I was depressed about my family life, and that's why I kept to myself so much (somehow she completely over looked the fact that I wasn't keeping to myself, I was keeping to her son). She asked him frequently how I was doing.

The truth was, with the dinner truces at home, and the handball games with my dad, the stress over my family had been greatly reduced. Things could have been better at home, but I was beginning to accept my lot. My lot, after all, included Rick. I was, in fact, as far as *I* could tell, actually rather happy. So it struck me as ironic that there was Jennifer concerned about my intellect and my heart, Rick's mom concerned about my emotional well-being, and my whole family concerned about my soul. I realized that I should feel fortunate to have so many people interested in my welfare (however misguided), and so I did — for a while.

Chapter Seven

The large pewter cross, that my mother had started wearing on a chain, dangled over her carrots or broccoli like a dark foreboding cloud. I knew she saw this oversized jewelry as a symbol of love — Jesus' love. But I saw it as a symbol of hatred, hatred for what I was, for the love that Rick and I had. I found myself, during dinners, fantasizing about ripping the died-for-our-sins charm right off my mother's neck. Meanwhile, Elizabeth and Jesse managed to slip religious innuendo into nearly all they said and did. Okay, they were just kids and did not really understand, but I found my stomach knotting up in response, and at dinner I could not eat. Eventually, it got to the point where I couldn't bring myself to go over there anymore, and I returned to eating sandwiches at Rick's.

It was shortly after this, that my father and I met on one of our Wednesdays, hugged, and discussed briefly my college plans. Dad wanted to know if I was certain about going to New Paltz; he tended to think the way Jenny did on this matter, but he didn't pressure me. I assured him that I was doing what was best for me, and he let it go. We got onto the court and worked into a good game. Our last game.

Breathless, between whacks at the ball, just as we'd worked up a respectable sweat, Dad said, "Elizabeth will be graduating," whack, "from the primary level," whack, "of her religious studies class," whack. "They have a little ceremony," whack. "She wanted me to ask you," whack, "if you would come."

I snatched the ball out of the air, gripped it so hard I thought it might pop. Giving my father a rage-filled stare, I slammed the ball down and started walking out.

"For your sister!" he shouted as I neared the exit.

"If she really knew me," I said, "I wouldn't be welcome."

As the door was closing behind me I heard, "What's that supposed to mean?"

I got on my bike and drove around, aimlessly, I thought, but I ended up at "our restaurant."

"Our waitress" was there. She seemed to be perpetually there. I sat in "our booth."

"Where's your friend?" She asked.

I looked at her hopefully. Could she know? Did *anyone* know? How could they not know?

She didn't know. He was my *friend*, my buddy. That I gave him blowjobs on a regular basis was as alien a possibility to her as the electromagnetic attraction between particles going on around her at all times.

"He's ahh..." What was he doing? *He's fucking his girlfriend.* "He's busy. I guess." Great answer, Jim. "Coffee," I requested with pleading eyes.

She shrugged. When all else fails, shrug. Shrug away everything confusing or not going according to normal conversational patterns. She shrugged and walked away, returned moments later with my coffee. I drank three cups, keeping my eye on the clock.

I couldn't keep going back to my parents, couldn't keep trying to work things out with them. I couldn't keep pretending to them that I was somebody I wasn't. If I was going to interact with them at all, I had to come out to them. But the more I considered this possibility, the more I found it unacceptable. I did not want to hear their ugliness, did not want to hear talk of Sodom and Gomorra, Satan and eternal hell. I was not willing to let them abuse me in that way, not willing to let them try to defile the love that Rick and I shared. Anyway, Rick and I needed to stay closeted to continue to be together in his apartment. I knew then, by the time "our waitress" poured my third cup, that I would break away from them. The handball games were over. The dinners were over. The nights when I wasn't at Rick's I'd eat fast food, be in the library as much as possible, or elsewhere, here, drinking coffee, then go home and hole-up in my room. When I left for college that would be it. They would be relegated to my past.

At five o'clock, I headed for a pay phone on a street corner.

"Hello?"

"It's me," I said.

"Hi. What's up?" He sounded bewildered. I never called him on the days when he'd been with Jenny.

"I want to see you."

"What's wrong? Are you okay?"

"Can I come over?"

"Sure. Yeah. Come over."

****

Rick was on the couch pretending to read his English Lit book. I sat down at the opposite end and he closed the book. Glancing around the room, I somehow expected it to look different. The bed was a mess. The bed was always a mess.

"Was Jennifer here?"

"Yeah," Rick said, almost as a whisper.

"Did you have sex?"

"Yeah," he answered again, this time with a disbelieving edge to his voice.

"Was it good?"

"Jim!"

"I'm sorry." I looked off into the corner.

"It was good."

I looked at back him. "I'm glad."

He smiled, letting me know that he knew I meant this sincerely, that I wasn't being facetious. Rick scooted next to me on the couch, took a hold of my hand. I told him about what happened on the handball court, and the decision I'd made about my family.

"Are you sure? About wanting to cut them off so completely?"

"It's like my family died, and I'm living with strangers who don't like me very much."

"They like you, Jim."

"But they don't like what I am."

"They don't know what you are."

"They don't want to know. I'm already this annoying unsaved soul wandering around the house haunting everybody. Meanwhile, for me, being around them without being honest about who I am is like a slow death. It's as if I'm constantly lying to their faces while simultaneously sticking a knife into my heart."

Rick looked at me knowingly. Then giving my hand a good squeeze, he said, "Why don't you start staying here Wednesday nights, you know, come by around six."

I studied his expression to see if he was just having pity on me.

Reading me, he said, "This is something *I* want. I don't like spending *any* night without you. I want your body next to mine when I'm sleeping."

The intensity of our love at moments like these, shocked me, even though moments like these were frequent. For instance, when we made love, the way I inhaled the smell of Rick's body, wanting to fill myself with him, and how this transformed me, took me to a place I can only call heaven — not my mother's sterile, asexual, pearly gates in the sky, but the blissful, lusty heaven of love experienced here on terra firma.

On Wednesdays I showed up after dinner. Fridays and Saturdays I was waiting for him when he got home from his dates with Jenny. It seemed to me that it should feel weird to be greeting him fresh out of the arms of his girlfriend, but all it ever felt was good to see him again.

****

Rick's brother Brian, a college junior just back for the summer, was taking shots on the basketball net, but stopped when I approached after parking my bike. Aside from the curly hair, he didn't look much like Rick. He was a rather gangly six-foot-four and wasn't nearly as good-looking.

Holding the ball in the crook of his arm, he spoke first. "So you're ah... Rick's ah... *roommate*." He gave me this peculiar smile.

"Brian, right?"

"Yeah."

"Jim." I put out my hand. He shook it hard, his eyes sparkling, his smile threatening to turn into a little laugh.

It was always like that with Brian. I always seemed to be running into him when no one else was around, and he always gave me, what I came to think of as the "I know your little secret," smile.

Eventually, when I felt fairly certain that I was reading him right, I said something to Rick about it. We were lying on his bed, staring at the ceiling, being worthless juvenile delinquents heavily under the influence of coffee, having had lunch at our favorite place.

"How would he know?" Rick asked.

"He sees what should be obvious to everyone. He's the only one not walking around with blinders on."

"You're just imagining things."

"Maybe he's gay."

"He's not gay."

"How would you know?"

"Because *I* don't walk around with blinders on."

"I think he knows."

"If he knows, why would he smile at you about it?"

"I think it amuses him."

"Maybe *you* amuse him; you're a strange person you know, Jim."

"And here I thought I was Mr. Normal."

"God forbid."

"Interesting choice of words."

"I thought you'd like that."

"Ever wish you were normal?" I asked.

"I'd rather be a slug."

"I'd rather be dead."

"I'd rather be a dead slug."

"I'd rather give you a bear hug."

We were laughing pretty intensely now, but we stopped suddenly.

Thud. Thud. It was Brian dribbling the ball directly outside our window.

"He knows," I said.

Rick got up and went to the stereo. In a moment The Kink's, "Lola," blared at high volume.

"Now he knows." Rick was standing next to the bed, looking down at me.

"Unless he's wearing blinders."

"Dance with me."

I got up and we whirled around the room in a frenzy of nervous caffeine joy.

****

One evening, in early June, I dragged Rick into the bowling alley. His game was terrible; he'd never played, but we had fun goofing around, and the night was made especially worthwhile because we ran into Crazy Man Al. He greeted me with a toothy, glossy-eyed, smile. "Oh Jimmy! Jimmy!" Big hug. He asked about my pool game, seeming genuinely hurt when I said I didn't play much anymore. Then, staring suspiciously at Rick, he asked if I might be interested in a summer job in his old buddy Clarence's motorcycle garage. Clarence, he explained, had retired from a promising life as a Hell's Angel when a biking accident landed him a prolonged stay in a hospital and the loss of all the toes on his right foot.

Clarence turned out to be a burly, bearded, guy with yellow cigarette stained fingers and a tattoo of a huge fish — blue and green — on the inside of his forearm. I took the job — running errands to parts stores and doing simple repairs — as soon as I realized my hours would overlap the shift Rick would be working at his dad's building supply business. Jenny was working at her aunt's law firm in Boston for the summer, so Rick and I would have lots of time for each other.

About two weeks after I started helping out at Clarence's, a biker with a handlebar mustache rode into the garage, the idling of his Harley's engine echoing off the walls announcing his arrival. He turned off the motor, removed his helmet, and wiped the sweat off his brow with the back of a hairy arm, all the while grumbling and swearing incoherently. Suddenly the words, "Goddamned faggots," came through loud and clear. I stood up from the crouching position I'd been in while fitting a chain on a Honda 250 at the other end of the garage.

"Goddamned homo faggots."

My black boots hit hard across the grease stained floor as I started towards him. But Clarence, who didn't seem to have noticed me, was now suddenly all over the guy, like a tornado in a trailer park, shouting in his face with threatening gestures.

"Get the *fuck* out of my shop! *Now!*"

The homophobe, surprised into fear, jumped on his starter, made a screeching U-turn, and high-tailed it, yelling back something about a "raving lunatic."

Soon as Clarence was good and sure that the creep was gone, he turned around to see me standing there staring at him with my mouth open.

"You got a problem with that?" he rumbled.
"No."

"Good." He ran thick grease covered hands over his balding head. I watched him the way one might a suddenly encountered poisonous snake. His nicotine scarred voice rose up again. "I had an uncle who was queer." He spat into a grimy garbage can. "But he was more of a man than most guys you see walking around. He's the only one who ever stood up to my Pa when the old man was beating the crap out of me."

Clarence hobbled off into the office, got a Coke out of the machine, and stood staring at the red and white dispenser while downing the cola. When he was done, he crushed the can and tossed it in the general direction of the trash bin. He came back into the garage then and resumed work without further word.

I told Rick that evening about the incident.

"What was it you were planning to do if Clarence hadn't reacted?"

"I don't know. *Something.*"

Rick's expression was full of alarm. "If Clarence hadn't had a gay uncle, the two of them might have killed you!"

I stared at him. He was so beautiful; I was so in love. Killed me, I thought. Killed me for loving you. Anger crashed through me like a tidal wave, and with a violence I'd never known before, my foot pounded into Rick's coffee table, as I shouted, "The world's all fucked up!"

A hollow silence ensued. The table lay on its side, one of the legs broken.

"Oh God, I'm sorry." I got down on my knees to look at the damage. "I'm sorry." I looked up at Rick, my eyes pooled with tears.

He joined me on the floor. "It's all right. It's all right, Jim. We'll fix it." But his eyes too were filled with anguish.

****

63

When the county fair came around, in the fall of our senior year, Jenny asked Rick, "Does Jim want to come with us?" Rick put the question to me, and I was surprised that I'd not found the notion utterly horrifying. "What do you think?" I'd asked, trying to read his face.

"Why not?"

I said, "Okay," as if there was no reason not to.

It turned out to be not nearly as awkward as might be imagined. I found it oddly fascinating to see Rick and Jenny holding hands, or even once, kissing. In place of jealously, what I felt was unrelenting frustration. If only Rick and I could do the same, openly, in public, in front of Jenny, and have her, like me, not mind.

Maybe it was the cotton candy and the roller coaster, but as I flew at high speed around a sharp curve, I got physically sick when, in an epiphany, I understood that the idea of Jenny being okay with Rick and I had little chance of ever ascending above mere fantasy.

Chapter Eight

"I'm really not liking the idea of not seeing you every day," Rick said. "New Paltz is beautiful, but I want to be in the city, be where there is a large out community. That's feeling very important. You could get a scholarship at Columbia."

We had just returned from a day trip up to New Paltz, and were sitting in our usual spots at opposite ends of the couch. For years, my family had gone on weekend trips to the funky little town surrounded by apple orchards and dairy farms. I had decided, as a little kid, that I wanted to go to SUNY New Paltz, and the fact that it was a state school, made it even more attractive. Sure, I could probably get a scholarship at a private school, but likely not enough to cover everything on through to a PhD. I didn't want to have to work while I was in school, and had no desire to be unnecessarily burdened by loans, so I needed to make my grandfather's money last. But I'd be about a hundred miles from Rick, whose heart was set on Columbia. We'd both gotten our acceptance letters, and final decisions had to be made soon.

Rick was saying he wanted me to be with him at Columbia, but he wasn't addressing the reality of the situation. He did not want to give up Jenny. Jenny would not accept us as lovers. Rick and I would not be able to bring ourselves to live closeted together once we left his parent's house. It didn't take a genius to figure out the math.

Rick gave me a sad smile. Then he looked away. He knew, but he wasn't going to say it; he also wasn't going to pretend we both didn't get it either.

I was angry that he couldn't talk about it, but I realized quickly that it wasn't Rick I was angry with, it was Jenny. I didn't want him to give her up; I wanted her to be okay with us. I looked at Rick; he was so beautiful.

Taking a couple of peaches out of a bag, I tossed one to Rick. He rolled it in his hands as if molding a ball of clay.

"Jenny's still saying she's only going to be able to come down from Boston one weekend a month, right?"

Rick nodded.

"So I'll come down the other three. It'll be fine," I said, trying to convince myself as well.

"One of us could always transfer next year," Rick added.

I didn't say anything to that. Just took a bite out of my peach, wiped the juice that spilled onto my chin with a finger, and licked it off. This would be a good time, I realized, to mention something I'd been thinking about. When I finished chewing, I said, knowing this might also help ease his sense of guilt, "I might like to dabble in a little heterosexuality again, myself."

Rick smiled. "It'd be good for you."

I was almost annoyed by how happy my statement seemed to have made him, but another feeling overrode any possible annoyance.

"I love you," I informed him matter-of-factly.

"I know. You tell me all the time."

Rick told me all the time too. For example, there was the morning we played a one-on-one game in the driveway before we went off to school. Sweaty and shirtless, Rick edged up beside me and whispered, "I love you." Taking full advantage of the situation, I stole the ball from him, making a quick shot. Totally incensed then, Rick played a relentless game, showing me an athletic side to himself that I'd had no clue about. We had wildly aggressive sex after school that day. Most of the time, though, he'd say he loved me when we were in bed together not having sex, his fingertips lightly touching my face.

****

I'd decided to live in a dorm at New Paltz —
splurging a little to get a private room — but Rick wanted
to find an apartment in the city, so we started going on
excursions down there to set him up. Apartment hunting in
Manhattan is a lot like elephant hunting in Manhattan, and
just when we were about to give up, Clarence told me his
aunt had a friend whose nephew... In any case, Rick ended
up with a small one-room deal that was, perfectly, just a
few blocks off of Christopher Street. In this part of the city,
we immediately fell into being very out about being a
couple, touching freely in public. We clearly understood
that at any time someone we knew might run into us, and
that was a possibility that, I think, we both actually hoped
for.

Chapter Nine

"Tell me you don't have a girlfriend. Or," she giggled wickedly, "tell me you do but you're not monogamous." I'd been sitting alone in the cafeteria, taking in a cup of coffee and feeling very serious — about college and physics, about my relationship with Rick, missing him terribly and wondering what had possessed us when we decided not to go to school together. It was the third day of classes. I hadn't seen her coming; I must have been looking at my fingernails, making a mental note to trim them before I went down to see Rick on the weekend. But there she was, pulling out a chair at my table. "You look cute," she had said first. She wasn't too bad-looking herself, quite pretty in a simple way — brown almond-shaped excitable eyes, dark lips, dimples that made her look like the child she more or less still was, and thin chestnut hair, shoulder length.

Amused by her come-on, I tried out: "I don't have a girlfriend, and I'm not monogamous."

She laughed uproariously and proclaimed, "We're going to get along great!"

"Actually," Amy told me over pizza at Chez Tony's that evening, "I do prefer monogamy; I was just trying to be clever. Are you really not monogamous?"

"I'm really not monogamous."

"Well, I don't know how I'll feel about that; we'll just have to see."

If there was ever a woman one could be monogamous with, Amy was it. I found out quickly that this girl understood pleasure. She was a pleasure *freak*. In bed, Amy was totally silly and wild; whipped cream, chocolate syrup, feathers, and tasty oils were par for the course. She actually dragged me into a discount store one afternoon so that she could buy a microwave, for the sole purpose of warming up honey, which she would dribble on my ass or beg me to suck off of her breasts. She had long delicate fingers, her hands beautiful and swan-like, and once, when we were buying fruit and cheese for a picnic, she put a tub of margarine in our cart.

"What's that for?"

"You'll see," and she waved her fingers dexterously in the air.

She enjoyed frightening me like that. Sure, I got scared, I knew I was in for some unbelievable form of debauchery or another. I was her perfect subject, always willing, always amazed by her sexual ingenuity, always able to match her playfulness once I picked up her particular angle of the moment. Frequently she got stoned before we had sex; occasionally I smoked with her. Either way, we were constantly giggling in bed. Sex with Amy was never serious or deep — just outrageous fun.

Okay, I admit, I was only trying to dramatize a point when I said it could be easy for someone to be monogamous with Amy. The truth is, pleasure gratification and playfulness are satisfying only to a point. If I hadn't had Rick to be serious with in bed — as well as silly and hedonistic — I would have grown restless with Amy quickly. Rick actually would be easier to be monogamous with, and until I met Amy, I had in fact been exclusive with him since the last one-night-stand I'd had early on in our relationship — which would make it almost two years.

But being bisexual and monogamous leads to certain obvious unsolvable problems, unless you're able and willing to close down completely one whole side of who you are. I don't feel I'm either able or willing — meaning, even if I was able I wouldn't be willing/even if I was willing I wouldn't be able. To say I did not think of women during those two years before I met Amy, to say I did not look at women, or fantasize about being with a woman, would be entirely false. Women were on my mind, but for a good while it was fine for them to be only on my mind, and then it wasn't fine anymore. I wanted to be with a woman. I wanted to touch a woman's breasts; I wanted to feel my mouth in the warmth between her legs, smell her, enter her silky wet body. I wanted to hear a woman's laughter, hear her sighs, feel long nails digging into my ass cheeks while watching her feminine face contort with pleasure as she has a woman's orgasm. I wanted to watch a woman walk across the room naked, her ass big and round and soft.

****

Kissing Rick right there in the middle of thousands of people's hustle and bustle at Grand Central, was utterly thrilling. We headed right to a hole-in-the-wall coffee joint — steam rising up from a manhole just outside the window. The tiny room was filled with people, and noise, and aromas of coffee and pollution. We sat in front of the window at a narrow counter on small wooden stools, drinking something very seriously coffee out of white paper cups, the coffee steam almost indistinguishable from the street's version.

"I've been unfaithful," I said.

Rick laughed, "Unfaithful?"

"I thought you'd like that."

"A woman?"

"Yes." I wondered briefly what he'd think if it had been a man; I found that hard to imagine, didn't want to.

"That was quick."

"She moves fast."

"Should I be worried?"

I turned to look at him. He looked worried.

"No," I assured him.

"Did you tell her about me?"

"We only just met; it might not last."

"Not telling her right away is only going to make it harder; take it from one who knows."

I watched the steam for a while. Ceaseless. "What should I have said? Hi, my name's Jim, I have a boyfriend, do you still want to go to bed with me?"

"It's not funny."

"I know it's not funny."

He took two big gulps of his milk-cooled coffee, as if it were a glass of scotch. "Tell me about her."

"Her name's Amy. Pretty, eighteen, smart but somehow not particularly bright. She's a sex maniac. Hedonist is a good word."

Rick grinned, despite himself. "I shouldn't be worried?"

"No, I like her; she's a lot of fun, but that's it."

"Tell her soon."

"Yeah, if we keep seeing each other."

We left then, to his apartment, to rejoin our aching bodies.

****

At a small corner grocery across from Chez Tony's, Amy and I bought a couple of Popsicles. We had been together now for nearly two months and I figured it was turning out to be something more than a few laughs, and though what was between us could hardly be considered a serious relationship, I thought it was high time I let her know who I really was. My plan was to come out to her that night. We sat at one end of the wide steps outside the store, quietly consuming our frozen treats, enjoying the Indian summer day. I started humming to the tune of Mary Rachel Wallace's Popsicle song. Then Amy began to get obscene with her Popsicle and I got in on the act too, letting her see just how skilled at fellatio I could be. We ended up laughing hysterically with Popsicle juice all over our mouths and chins.

A bearded man with long dark hair, and a woman with even longer blond hair, came and sat on the other end of the steps. Using old-fashioned wooden ice cream spoons, they started eating something out of a pint size container, and immediately began moaning in long ooohs and umms. This caught *our* attention.

Eventually they noticed us, smiled at our wondrous expressions. Amy, unable to contain herself any longer said, "Well, tell us what that *is!*"

"Carob Haagen-Dazs."

"What?" Were they speaking English?

They held up the carton for us to see. Haagen-Dazs was far from a household word back then, and their carob was one of only a few flavors they offered at the time. In a flash we were in the store purchasing our own container of the precious stuff.

Back at the dorm, Army immediately lit up a joint. I took a few drags, then pulled out the Haagen-Dazs. She spoon-fed me the first bite. It was glorious. I fed her a taste next; she feigned orgasm. Minutes later we were naked on the bed. There I was, nineteen, stoned, and licking this heavenly concoction off the tits of a pretty eighteen year-old who's giggling and squirming in pleasure, and the thought went through my head: I don't want this to end. I'd wondered a good bit about how Amy would react when I told her about Rick. She was so open minded, especially about sex, that I thought she'd probably think my bisexuality was cool. But then there was that monogamy conversation the day we met. She might not mind that I'd been with a man, but she might not be too happy to know that I was in an intense on-going relationship with someone else. Though if this *was* the case, I certainly had an obligation to tell her about Rick. But that particular evening was too fun, and I was way too stoned anyway. I'd tell her the next day.

The following evening, after we'd had sex, I was on her bed leaning back against the pillow. She sat on her rocking chair. I was psyching myself up to telling her, when Amy started talking about having a picnic the next day. The weather was *still* good. The question was where. I suggested a particular grassy spot near the Student Union.

"No, they're having some kind of gay demonstration there tomorrow."

I sat up slowly, tried to read her face. I couldn't pick up anything from it. "How do you know?"

"There are posters all over campus. How could you not notice?"

How *could* I not notice? "So you don't think we should have the picnic there then?"

"Well it's going to be crowded and noisy."

"You think so?"

"Sure."

"What do you think..." it would be handy to find out first if she's homophobic or not, "about the demonstration?"

"I think there will be a lot of commotion. I'm feeling like a peaceful quiet picnic — you, me, the birds and the ants."

"No, I mean..."

"What?"

Then appallingly, I found myself saying, "Well, were should we have it then?"

I didn't tell her that night. I was too frazzled. Too frazzled that there was a gay demonstration that I hadn't known about and wasn't going to go to. Too frazzled that I didn't even understand why I wasn't going. Too frazzled from thinking I was going to find out what Amy thought about homosexuality, and then not actually finding out anything. I knew I should have used that conversation as a way to bring up my bisexuality. After all, wasn't that what I'd been looking for that summer with Mary, a way to insert this revelation casually into conversation? Looking back, I could have invited Amy to go to the demonstration with me. Looking back, things always appear entirely different than they did at the time. Looking back, I can't help but think I was simply taking the easy way out.

I didn't tell her that night, and the next day at the picnic I decided resolutely that no matter what I'd tell her when we met that evening, but she announced as we were packing up our leftover brie, apples, and French bread, that she had an exam the following morning and needed to do a lot of studying. We had lunch together after her exam, but in the noisy cafeteria, and afterwards she arranged for quick sex in her room before we had to rush back to classes. We didn't meet that night. Then it was the weekend and I was back in the city with Rick, and Amy was at her parent's house in Kingston. And then, Rick was asking me how it went, coming out to Amy, and I said, "I didn't tell her." He gave me a weird look, and I gave him a weird look right back that said what I never said in words to him: "What about Jenny?" He knew what the look said, and he turned away and then changed the subject. Moments later we were in the kitchen chopping vegetables, a steak marinating in the refrigerator, and laughing about the futility of trying to cut a carrot with a dinner knife.

But I still planned to tell her. The following Tuesday evening she and I were in my dorm room studying separately together, when the phone rang. Amy was sitting right next to it so she picked it up.

"Hello?" After a short pause, she said, "Yeah, he's right here," and handed me the receiver.

"Amy I suppose?" Rick said.

"Yeah."

"Am I interrupting something?"

"No."

"Are you just saying that?"

"No. It's really okay." It felt strange having Amy in the room while I was talking to Rick. I kind of wanted her to leave so I could talk with him about whatever, the way we do when he calls, but I knew too, that if she did leave, I'd be alone again once we hung up, and I didn't much feel like being alone.

"I just wanted to say hi. I miss you." Rick's voice was so alluring. Why again were we so far apart?

I looked at Amy. She was leafing through my physics book. "I miss you too," I said distinctly into the receiver.

There was a pause. "Is she still there?"

"Yeah."

After another pause, he said, "Call me later. When you have a chance."

"I'll call."

When I hung up, Amy put the book down, and I knew I would tell her.

"Who was that?" she asked.

"Rick." Then I added, "Who I go to see in the city."

She picked up the physics book again.

"Amy..."

She turned a page.

"He... Rick and I..."

Pointing to a diagram towards the back of the book, she interrupted me, "This looks like two stick figures fucking."

I crinkled my forehead in distressed amused disbelief. I got up and went over to get a closer look at the diagram. Unable to see any resemblance to her interpretation, I looked to her for a clue.

"I bought olives," she said.

"Olives?"

"You know, like Martinis."

"Martinis?" I held up my hands in surrender. Surrender to whatever it was Amy had in mind for the night. Surrender to the understanding that I was giving up on coming out to her.

I gave up that fantasy, but did not give up the guilt. I tried to console myself with the concocted defense that Amy did not want to know. She'd heard me tell Rick that I missed him. Wasn't that a strange thing for one buddy to tell another? Especially when they spent three weekends a month together? Especially when they'd just been together two days ago? She'd heard me say, "I miss you *too*," so she would have realized that he'd also said he missed me. She heard all this, knew I went and stayed with him most weekends, and she heard me stammering, trying to tell her something important about Rick and me, and she'd changed the subject, come up with an utterly absurd remark about stick-figures. Some distant part of her mind must have understood about me and Rick, and must have decided that this understanding needed to be kept out of awareness.

This was the story I told myself. This was the story I told Rick that weekend, the morning after I arrived, as we ate bowls of savory Armenian soup he'd picked up at a restaurant around the corner. He'd laughed with me when I told him about the stick-figures, and the olives, and the old-fogies bar Amy had taken me to after dinner for Martinis, and what she'd had us do with the olives after we got back to her room. But when I told him my theory about how Amy didn't really want to know, he listened carefully, and then was silent for a long time. I think he liked the theory, liked it a lot, because he could use it to assuage his own guilt about Jenny.

Sopping up the last dregs in his bowl with a chunk of funky Armenian bread, Rick said, "So you're going to keep seeing her."

"I like her a lot; she's a riot." Then I told him another of the little self-defense stories I told myself. "I don't think she takes our relationship that seriously. You know, it's fun and games. It's not as if she's shopping for a husband." That last sentence I easily took for truth. The first part, I think somewhere in the back of my mind I knew wasn't quite on track. I meant a lot to Amy, at least as an important friend. But this was a knowledge that, at the time, I just could not allow to run around in my mind untethered. Later, over coffee, Rick said, "Jenny is definitely shopping. She's shopping for a career with a capital C. Having a hunky boyfriend is just part of her image of what it means to be a successful, modern, woman."

This wasn't news to either of us, and I knew Rick and his relationship with Jenny well enough to understand the emotions behind the look in his eyes as he told me this. He felt both rejected and relieved. Because of me, he could not have a truly serious relationship with her, and the fact that she wasn't seeking this is what had make it possible for them to stay together. Just as he would have ended things with her had she pushed for commitment, she never would have stuck with a boyfriend who at this time in her life pressed for marriage and children. Still, Rick did not like knowing that he ran second place to her career. Sure she ran second place in his life, but at least she came in behind another human. Being rejected for a deeper love was, for Rick, more palatable, though conceivably more painful, than being rejected for recognition, and wealth. He told me then, that even on the one weekend a month when she came to visit, she spent several hours doing research at the library.

"But," he mumbled into his coffee, as he brought the cup to his lips, "at least *I* know what I'm up against." At this, his face flushed with shame.

Chapter Ten

"The deadline for transfer students to apply for next fall is coming up in March," Rick said as we were washing the breakfast dishes. It was the beginning of the spring semester; he'd spent the previous weekend with Jenny.

I handed him a frying pan. "March?"

"Yeah."

For perhaps the tenth time during our years together, I did not ask, "What about Jenny?" But this time I knew the answer. If I decided to move to the city he'd tell her about us, and she could take it from there.

****

I stood in the bathroom doorway as Rick shaved, the following weekend. Watching his face in the mirror, I said, "My advisor said all my units will transfer. I just need to get an application."

Rick smiled at the mirror. "There's one on my desk."

There was no reason to believe that I would not get into Colombia, but Rick and I were waiting for that acceptance letter before we were going to let it sink-in that we'd be living together again. I envisioned all sorts of lewd and lascivious acts involving champagne that Rick and I could engage in once the letter did arrive. Amy's way of looking at the world was starting to rub off on me. Ah yes, Amy. When the letter came I would have to tell her, like it or not, and she would either like it, or not. Coming out to Jennifer and Amy would make the impending celebration especially meaningful — albeit tainted with regret. We would not only be celebrating living together again, but living *out* this time. Living openly together as a couple. What we both had really wanted all along.

****

I rode the train into the city a few weekends later, Rick slipping his hand into mine at the station, wordlessly offering me a yellow crocus and a kiss. I smiled at the flower, following him out to where even skyscrapers couldn't hide the brightness offered by the vast cloudless sky. We had dinner that night at a Thai restaurant, one dish of spicy green curry, another steaming with a pungent peanut sauce. Later, on a lark, as we passed a liquor store, we purchased a bottle of good California Cabernet.

We walked back to the apartment — the paper sack cradled in Rick's arm — quiet with satisfaction, happy to be together after another week of separation. Once inside, we carried wine glasses and the open bottle from the kitchen, placing them on the nightstand, and stood next to Rick's bed in dim light. Slowly, methodically, we touched, kissed, and undressed each other. I was reveling in tactile sensations, the softness of Rick's oxford shirt — like the one he'd worn the first time I'd loved him — the thick roughness of his blue jeans, the featheriness of his hair brushing the nape of his neck, the coarseness of the mustache he'd newly grown. One by one, pieces of our clothing fell together into a pile on the floor.

Now fully naked, we sat at the edge of the bed, sideways, facing each other, and tasted the wine. My senses already primed, I closed my eyes and took in subtle raspberry, and cherry, coming through a full body of sharp-sweet alcohol. Opening my eyes I noted the resplendent, equally sharp, and sweet, qualities of Rick. The moment was brilliantly clear, like the sky that morning. We lay back then, placing our less than half-empty glasses on the nightstand, and quickly got so caught up in our lovemaking that we forgot about the wine altogether.

I remember all this clearly, remember too, seeing, the next morning, our clothes together on the floor, the open bottle on the nightstand, the two glasses of wine next to it. I remember we made love again in the morning, then left without putting away the wine or picking up our clothes. I wondered later if Jenny had noticed the wine, recognized its quality. Did she stop and look at our underwear, stare at these for a while? She would have recognized Rick's, but mine, which partially covered his, what might she have made of them? And two sets of socks, mine gray, Rick's white. My T-shirt — if it was right-side out, I don't remember — she might have realized belonged to me, it was from the gym where Dad and I had played handball. Two sets of men's clothes, on the floor beside the bed, obviously taken off by minds distracted by other concerns, no thought given to tossing them towards the hamper, only feet away in the bathroom. Did she notice all this then notice the wine? The two glasses? What might she have thought?

Rick and I went out to brunch that morning. A magical place, orchids spilling from Greek-styled pots, the food artistically presented, full of fresh flavors, the waiter cute and funny, sunlight streamed through a glassed-in garden. We had champagne and chocolate cake for dessert. After, in the park, a group of conga players, in one of the band shells, mesmerized us for an hour and a half, such intensity, such power. Then we wandered about, looking at flower buds, roller skaters, laughed joyously at a group of toddlers chasing ducks.

Eventually we reentered the city, stopping for Italian ices, eating slices of wonderfully gooey pizza. We bought Baklava to have with coffee the next morning. Did Rick eat it alone? Did he throw it out? Did it sit untouched for weeks, turning hard?

As evening approached, we headed for Christopher Street, had a simple dinner of minestrone and crusty Italian bread. The rest of the evening we spent in a jazz club being blown away by Lionel Hampton. Finally, we headed back to Rick's place around eleven-thirty. As we got near, Rick began to whisper obscenities in my ear, telling me all the wild things we were going to do to each other in bed that night. Giggling, we touched and fondled one another as we headed up the steps to his floor. By the time Rick got his door unlocked, we were quite anxious to get into his apartment, and we sort of rushed in, all over each other, laughing.

Then there was a scream.

Jenny, horrified, on the couch, hands over her mouth, startled by the scream, her own scream. Rick and I were in an undeniable pose, one of his hands grasping my crotch, the other groping my ass, one of my hands up the back of Rick's shirt, the other squeezing one of his ass cheeks, pushing his groin into mine. Stupidly, we stood there, frozen, unable to comprehend. Then we began to understand, and slowly released one another, separated. We looked at each other, not willing yet to acknowledge Jenny.

Seconds only, the time between unlocking the door to our parting, yet it all went by in sickeningly slow motion.

Jenny jumped up from the couch, her own shock wearing off. "How long's this been going on?"

We were speechless.

"How long?" she shouted.

"Jen..." Rick turned towards her now, took a step in her direction.

"Get away from me!" She jumped back as if she were being attacked, nearly stumbling over the couch.

Rick stopped. "Jenny, I..." He shook his head. "I'm sorry..."

"You're *gay*?" Her expression was utter disbelief.

And while Rick stood there facing her off, I was crumbling. I wanted to disappear, evaporate into thin air. I slunk off to the corner, crouched on the floor, and buried my head in my arms. I felt sick, a nausea so strong it threatened to devour me.

"I'm bisexual, Jenny. We're both bi." I heard Rick's voice quiet, breathing a sigh of relief with these words.

"You both need *help*. This is *wrong*." Her voice hysterical.

I tried to make myself smaller in the corner, drew my legs up closer to my body.

I heard Rick's outrage now, his words coming through to me despite the utter chaos in my head. "It's not *wrong*! What Jim and I have is *beautiful. Beautiful*!"

Then, "Jim..." Rick calling out to me.

I could not respond.

"Jim, tell her. Jim!" His voice like hot thunder now.

I kept thinking, I don't exist; I don't exist; I'm not here.

One more time, "*Jim!*"

There was a horrible long silence, a space where hell reigned.

Then Rick again, "Get out! Both of you. *Out!*"

Get out? I looked up. Jenny was collecting her things franticly. Then she was gone, didn't even bother to slam the door.

"Get out, Jim!" This was a command.

I stood slowly, took tentative steps towards him. We looked into each other's eyes, and I saw it then, knew it was the end, unbelievable, but there it was. He wanted me gone, for good.

"Please, get out now." His voice quiet this time, terribly sad.

****

I rode the train back up to New Paltz in a trance. In the dorm, I lay in bed staring at the dark, not feeling, not here at all. When the sun came up, I fixated on the ceiling, trying to will it to come crashing down upon me. At some point I got up to use the bathroom, after which, I sat on the window ledge in a numb stupor watching the world go on as usual. Students, professors, walked along calmly, couples — heterosexual couples — held hands. Finally the tears came. I went back to bed clutched my pillow and sobbed. When the tears stopped, I stared at the wall, while my mind slowly began to function again.

Thoughts reeled. Rick had needed me and I hadn't been there for him. Our relationship had needed me and I had copped out. *Why?* What I had felt was extremely ashamed. Was my homosexuality so abhorrent to me? That was certainly how it appeared. But I couldn't buy this theory. It just didn't sit true with me. I could not convince myself that I thought there was anything bad or wrong, sick or evil, about two men having sex with each other. To the contrary, everything within me said that it was good and normal, beautiful and right. I *knew* this, felt it to my core. Then why did I react like that? Why did I react the way society/religion would have me react: filled with shame and disgrace? Why would I take on horrendously wrong attitudes that I had never been capable of even *understanding*?

I tried to put myself back into those nightmare moments at Rick's only last night. *What* had I really been feeling? I remembered Jenny's face, the horror that then melted into disgust. Rick and I in shock. It was as if a bubble, a protective shield around us had suddenly been popped. *What* bubble? It dawned on me then, it wasn't that I had been ashamed of my behavior, ashamed of being in a homosexual relationship. I was ashamed of Jenny's thoughts, ashamed of the ugliness through which she looked at our relationship. Of course. I had always known that this was precisely why I didn't want to come out to my family — I did not want their evil, sinful, bad, thoughts, and words, to adulterate our love. I did not want to expose myself, Rick, to their sick distorted perceptions of our relationship. Last night I was ashamed that someone who didn't understand had penetrated the sanctity of our love. In curling up into a ball, I was trying to protect myself from Jenny's ugly, ugly, thoughts. I wasn't running away from facing my homosexuality; I was in that corner *dying*, bombarded by ignorance and wrongful judgment.

Rick's words to Jenny, so loud and forceful: "What Jim and I have is *beautiful!*" And it had been. *So* beautiful. I fell into a choking sob. Why couldn't I have stood beside Rick, and told Jennifer that no matter what she thought or felt she could never take away what Rick and I were to each other? Instead, I let her take it away, let her steel it like a cunning thief. Rick would never forgive me, even if I explained, apologized, and I didn't think that he should. I would never forgive me. My actions were unforgivable.

I don't know where the day went, but at some point I realized that the sun was going down again. I snapped on the radio, found some crackers on my bookshelf, and nibbled on them half-heartedly while I tried to lose myself in the music. I found out then approximately what percentage of rock songs were about lost love, and shut the damn thing off.

I awoke in the morning, still in my chair, half-eaten cracker in hand. It was Monday; according to my clock, I had fifteen minutes before my first class. I debated whether I should go. This came as a bit of a shock since I hadn't even entertained the notion of skipping school since the fifth grade, since the days before it dawned on me that I like learning. I resolved that yes, of course, I'd get up and go to class, and then I sat there and watched the time tick away. Apparently I fell back asleep because the next thing I knew I had missed most of my second class as well. In a half hour, I realized, Amy would be looking for me in the cafeteria. Amy... I did not want to see her.

I got up and opened my books to see what I'd likely missed in class. But I found the words dancing on the page, swimming through tears.

"*Rick!*" issued from within me in the form of a primal scream. My body racked with terrible pain, I tumbled to the floor. Yanking a blanket off my bed, I hid myself in it, rocking, crying, and torturing myself by remembering loving times with Rick.

An hour, maybe two, later, I sat facing the wall wondering how I was ever going to get over this. How?

At four-thirty the phone rang. I knew it was Amy. I let it ring. Rick would not be calling me; this I was certain of. It rang. But what if I was wrong? What were the chances it would be Rick? I thought of that look in his eye, no it would not be him, chance: one in about five hundred thousand. So, what if this is that one chance. I knew it was Amy but I picked it up, just in case.

"Hello?"

"When did you get back? I was worried when you didn't show up for lunch."

I wasn't even disappointed; I knew it would be Amy.

"I don't feel too great; I'll call you later, okay?"

"What's wrong?"

"Please, Amy; I'll call."

"Is it your stomach, or what?"

"I just feel lousy."

"Let me come over and take care of you. Why didn't you call? Have you eaten?"

"I just need to be alone." I hung up.

How do I not think about Rick? How do I think about him and still go on? I started cleaning my room, which I rarely did. At least this meant that there was plenty to do. I cleaned and daydreamed about graduate school where I would finally sink my teeth into some real interesting work in physics. Maybe I'd be living with some wonderful guy not much unlike Rick, or maybe a smart sassy woman with a great sexual appetite.

When everything was clean, neat, and put away, I sat feeling very much disoriented by my unfamiliar surroundings. I wondered what Rick was doing just then. Eating our baklava? Maybe finishing off the wine with it. Maybe crying on the bed. Maybe cleaning his apartment. I laughed, remembering the few times he and I'd gotten totally disgusted with the shape of our basement hideaway, and had gone out to our favorite booth, drank lots of coffee, then came back and buzzed around tiding up in a most neurotic fashion. He'd told me once that Jenny liked the mess, had said her folk's house was always so clean it made her feel inhuman.

Maybe, it occurred to me, Rick will go out to a bar tonight to pick someone up. I felt jealous. Not jealous about Rick being with someone else, that I actually found arousing, but jealous of him having that option. Maybe that's what I'd do tonight if I was in the city. It'd certainly be a great distraction, better than the hell of this dorm room. If there was a gay bar in New Paltz, I didn't have a clue about it.

The phone rang again.

"I'm really worried about you. Can't I come over?"

"No!"

"Something's wrong; you're acting so strange."

"You mean queer."

"What?"

"Oh never mind, Amy. Forget it."

"Jim..."

"I'll call you. I'll call. Just... Just, please Amy. I'll call." I hung up.

Chapter Eleven

Amy didn't put a cherry in her belly button, or run down to the cafeteria to get a frozen chocolate banana she'd managed to convince someone to let her stow there. She did not write "fuck me" across her breasts with red frosting squirted out of a pastry bag. She did not play Jimi Hendrix's red vinyl bootleg, "High Live and Dirty Rated X." She did not put on the Beatles, "Why Don't We Do It in the Road?" — something she actually had us do at three a.m. a few weeks earlier (I'd been terrified and intensely horny; she'd been her typical stoned giggly self). She did not fill squirt guns with Drambuie.

Amy wanted to, for once, just simply make love with me. The worst thing she could have done at this particular space in time. It was Tuesday, and I had finally given in to her phone requests to see me, feeling that any distraction might save me from insanity or possibly suicide — my acceptance letter from Columbia had arrived that morning. I went to her room, and to avoid conversation, responded to her sexual overtures, not realizing that she was going to play it so straight laced. I wasn't sure what her point was. Perhaps she was making a desperate response to my recent odd behavior. Perhaps it was just an exploration of what — for her — was simply another novelty. But regardless of her motive, I didn't like it. *Rick* I made love with. With Amy I had silly, carefree, highly erotic encounters. That is what I was looking for that afternoon, an escape, something that might actually release me, if only for a moment, from the oppressive gloom that I'd been drowning in. But no, she wanted to make love.

There was nothing I could do, no way to snap her out of this. I could not insist she be silly and bubbly. So I went along with it, and as I lay on top of her, inside her, kissing her neck, I began to cry. It was useless trying to fight it; my emotions were bigger than me. As I sobbed into her neck, she moved her hands, which had been clutching my biceps, around to my back and hugged me, whispering softly, "What's wrong? What's wrong?" I found her gentleness, her concern, unbearable. Pulling my now flaccid self out of her, I rolled onto my side, facing the wall, and bawled helplessly.

Amy covered me and got up from the bed.

Eventually, I was able to get myself together again, and I turned around, reluctantly, knowing I was going to have to face her sooner or later. She was in her rocking chair, a few feet away. I sat up, my mind blank.

"Jim," she said quietly, "tell me. *Tell* me."

"I can't," I said, realizing that this summed it up entirely. I can't. I can't tell her. I can't love her. I can't be her lover or her playmate. I can't do any of it. I got up and pulled on my jeans. She watched me, stupefied.

"Amy, I can't. I can't do this anymore."

"Tell me. I'll help you."

"I can't; I'm sorry." As I closed the door behind me, I was overwhelmed by, what had now become such a familiar companion, regret.

****

I realized that I could spend a lot of time being depressed and angry with myself and the world, or I could get my act together and go about the business of having a worthwhile life. In choosing the latter, the one thing that seemed eminently clear was that being out was the most important thing I could do for myself. Otherwise, nothing in my life would ever be right.

There was nothing keeping me in New York. A change would help — get a new start. San Francisco seemed to be the answer, a place where I would surely be accepted for who I am. There were only a few more weeks left in the semester. I would concentrate on my exams, then ride out west. The idea of leaving behind my family, Amy, and yes — if we weren't going to be together — even Rick, felt good. New York would be my past, San Francisco my future.

I knew that I might never return to New York, or if I did, it wouldn't be for many years. I wanted to see Rick one last time, say good-bye. We'd been too close to have the last words between us be: "Please get out now." I also needed him to know how I'd really felt about us.

The day before my first exam, I sat on my window ledge, phone in lap. Rick's number rang three times. There was heavy cloud cover outside, and I thought about lightening so as not to think about Rick. The thing about lightening is that no one knows exactly what triggers it, just like love.

"Hello?"

For a second I just took in the sound of his voice. Finally I said, "This is Jim."

Nothing.

"Will you talk to me?" I asked timidly.

"I don't know. But it looks like I'm not going to hang up."

"I'm moving across the county. I'll be in the city next week; I'd like to say good-bye."

There was no response.

"I just want to say good-bye."

A horribly long time went by with no answer.

Finally, I added, "Please, Rick."

A sigh was followed by a reluctant, "All right."

****

We met in a cafe just off of Christopher. Rick had picked the spot; some place that we never went to together, I figured, was his criteria. It was dark, slightly smoky, one of these put-together-out-of-a-box decors — fake Tiffany lamps, dark wood, dusty ferns — the type of place we never would have gone to.

I had just walked in, was looking around to see if he was already there, when I heard, "Jim," and turned around.

Rick looked good, a little tired though, and very uncertain. He did not smile. I wanted very much to hug him, feel him close to me. Damn, I wanted to make love to him. I could sense his body urging towards mine too. But instead, we stood too many feet apart and each said a feeble, "Hi," choking back tears.

Mercifully, a young waiter with a swish and a jovial demeanor came to our service. With the utmost proficiency, he escorted us to a table, took our coffee orders, and then left us alone again. At which point, Rick said, unable to look me in the eye, "I'm already sorry I agreed to this. It's too hard."

I had to wait until I could speak without the words getting stuck in my throat, but finally, I said, "I want to apologize. Though I know it won't fix what happened, I want to explain something to you."

"I'm listening."

Undaunted by his sternness, the words I wanted to say came without hesitation.

"I have never been ashamed of our love. I want you to know that." *Now* Rick looked me in the eye. "I was always proud of our relationship, and you were right — what you said to Jennifer. What we had, was beautiful, really beautiful." I stopped for a minute to wipe a wet spot off my cheek with the sleeve of my shirt. I sat back as the waiter placed our coffees on the table. He looked alternately at each of us, smiled sympathetically, and scooted off.

Leaning forward again, with my arms on either side of my cup, I continued, "I reacted the way I did because I couldn't take the ugliness that Jenny was projecting onto our relationship. It's like someone was throwing rocks at an elegant bird, and I couldn't bear to look, couldn't bear to face it." I pushed aside an ashtray near my elbow. "I know a brave man would have tried to stop the hurling rocks, would have tried to protect that bird. I acted as a pathetic coward; I wasn't there to protect our love." Cupping my mug in my hands, I pulled it towards me, its warmth a futile attempt at comfort. "I'll live with that for the rest of my life," I said. Then I added, "But I wanted you to know that an inability to face what I am, or who we were to each other, was not what my reaction was about."

For a long while Rick was silent, a pained expression on his face. I took sips from my cup, dismayed by this drug's utter impotence under the current circumstance.

Then Rick said, his voice very formal, stiff, not at all the way we use to talk to each other, "I'm not sorry anymore that I agreed to meet you. I'm glad you told me that." He nodded, affirming his own statement. "That makes a lot more sense to me. I'd been thinking that I didn't know you at all, didn't know your perspective on our relationship, and that was very upsetting. This feels better. But you're right too; it doesn't fix what happened."

"I know."

We drank our coffee, an awkwardness settling between.

The waiter approached with a steaming pot. "Refills?"

We both hesitated. Then in a panic, fearing that this is how we'd part, I held out my cup, and Rick followed in kind.

"Are you really moving?" he asked when the waiter left.

"Yeah, San Francisco. I want to be out."

He smiled. "And Amy?"

"It's over. I didn't tell her. After... Well, when I got back from the city last time, I just... couldn't. I ended it. It wasn't right."

"I came out."

I felt a rush of excitement. "You came out?" I repeated his statement, just to be sure I heard him right; he'd said it so offhandedly.

Rick had a great big smile, sparkling eyes. "Yeah."

"Your parents?"

His smile faded now; he looked worried. "I thought about calling you — to let you know — but I don't think..."

Then I understood; of course.

"They asked about you; I had to tell them. They're not going to broadcast it. But, sooner or later, I mean if I go home with a boyfriend, people who knew us will realize... I don't know if Jenny's said anything; I haven't seen her. I'm sorry. I don't know, maybe it wasn't fair; maybe I should have lied about you..."

"No!" I interrupted. "No, you shouldn't have lied about me. Tell everyone. I mean it. My folks... You know I haven't talked to them in months. I won't come out to them, but I don't give a damn if they find out. I'm happy for you, really glad." Then I asked, "How were they, your mom and dad, about it?"

"Angry," Rick said. "I mean, about you, the deception, breach of trust and all that."

I thought of San Francisco, and how I would soon cease to live a life of regrets. "Tell them I'm sorry," I said. "I really did appreciate their help."

He nodded. "I tried to get them to see how it was for us, told them how in love we were. They sort of understood."

"And about you being bi?"

"Oh they're grappling with it." Rick ran fingers through his curls. A gesture I could have done without. I knew exactly what his fingers were experiencing; my own had been there many times. Rick caught my eye, realized, and then quickly removed his hand. Covering up he said immediately, "It's like they're trying to reach the top of a mountain; they're determined to get there, but not always sure they have the right shoes for the job. But," he grimaced, "they're not dealing with me being *bi*. It's crazy; all my life I'm seen as straight; I tell people no, I'm bi, and all of a sudden I'm *gay*. They don't understand bi at all. I'm gay and confused about it; that's what my dad says. That part's a drag, but at least I don't have to hide anything anymore."

"Your brother?"

"You were right; Brian had us pegged."

"How was he about it?"

"Interesting. He said he'd thought about it for himself — doing it with a guy — but decided it would make his life too complicated; it'd be easier just to stick to chicks. I told him I didn't think that was a choice I could make. He shrugged and said, 'Everyone's different.'"

Some fifteen minutes later, taxis honking impatiently, a siren wailing from a nearby street, we stood outside the cafe with our hands stubbornly in our pockets, a Milky Way wrapper swirling in the dust and wind at our feet. Afraid to hug, unable to accept the notion of a handshake, we said highly unsatisfying, choked-up, good-byes, stealing quick glances at one another's faces. And then, from Rick, there was a hesitation, like he was about to do or say something meaningful, but instead he turned abruptly, and ran up the street.

Part Two
San Francisco

Chapter Twelve

Driving out west, I kept thinking I should enjoy the trip, take my time and see the sights, but I just wanted to get to San Francisco and start my life. I was looking forward with great enthusiasm to beginning all over again, this time totally out. Being bisexual seemed like a blessing, a blessing that could only be abused if not fully appreciated.

So I stuck to the highways. At rest stops I ordered apple pie from lovely all-American girls who smiled shyly, and sometimes not-so-shyly, at me. In their invariably pink uniforms, they were so tempting. I wondered about their Saturday night dates, the lucky boys who got to slip their hands between their legs.

Along the way, small towns cropped up amongst muted hills appearing suddenly on the horizon — the church steeple always the foreboding precursor. These towns appeared so innocent and vulnerable and yet scared the hell out of me. Born of isolation is fear. Different becomes equated with evil, conformity transforms, without notice, into intolerance. They were, for me, these towns, like the monsters of my early childhood fears. Had one of them risen up on its hind legs and roared at me, I would not have been surprised. As each one slipped behind me on my road out west, I shuddered with relief.

By the time I got to San Francisco, I was ready for the different-ness I knew I'd find there. I'd looked forward to exploring the city and gay nightlife, but I felt a strong need to settle in before starting to have fun. So I got right to taking care of details, and within a couple of days I'd found a large efficiency apartment, with shared garage space, on the edge of the Sunset district. It was a quick ride to San Francisco State. Castro Street was just over the hill and Haight-Ashbury and Golden Gate Park were within walking distance. I bought yardsale furniture, registered at State, and shopped for much needed new threads. I found myself purchasing black jeans, black shirts, black boots, and a black leather jacket. I told myself, jokingly, or perhaps not so jokingly, that I was in mourning over the loss of Rick.

On some level, I must have been nervous about doing the bar scene, because I seemed to be putting it off, but several days after I arrived, I realized that all the books I'd mailed to myself at general delivery were in place in newly purchased used book shelves, and there was milk for my coffee in the fridge, and even a set of salt and pepper shakers on the funky wooden table I'd bought at a Pilipino family's basement sale that morning. I'd paid the teenage son to deliver it in the family's truck.

"You got a girlfriend?" he'd asked, after we got the table in place.

"No." Remembering that first conversation with the resurrected Mary I almost added, "Do you have a boyfriend?" but I stopped myself.

"Do it drive you crazy?"

"Sometimes," I said.

"Man! It drive *me* crazy. I *need* a girl." He was kind of half dancing, half doubling over in mock pain. But now he stopped, focused on my blank reaction. "Oh, or maybe you gay?"

I smiled. "Sort of."

He looked at me sideways, then laughing good-naturedly said, "Maybe I go now," and he made his way hastily out the door, waving my ten dollar bill, for the delivery, over his head. "Thank you!"

It was that night, salt and pepper shakers, which I found somehow amusing at the moment, in their place, that I decided to finally go out to a bar.

****

Once, when Rick and I were in a jazz club on Christopher, I overheard a gay couple near us talking about the Power Tool in San Francisco. So it was there I headed, not to Castro, but to SOMA, the old warehouse district south of Market. There were lots of other bikes parked in front of the bar. Inside, it was all men, a large percentage of them in leather. The speakers were pounding out a rhythm that commanded bodies to dance.

I got a longneck beer at the bar, then found a space to settle into, leaning one shoulder against a wall, watching. I couldn't quite put my finger on the theme behind the decor, "minimalist-masculinity" maybe. Everything — what little there was of it — was in unfinished wood, and was, in some less than obvious way, aesthetically pleasing.

I was taking the scene in, enjoying the variety of male bodies, faces, when a sweet-looking blond, wearing an immaculate blue work shirt neatly tucked into tight new blue jeans, sauntered over to me, smiling. "I don't think I've seen *you* here before."

He had an incredibly slow drawl that got a big smile out of me. "Just got into town a few days ago," I said, looking him over.

"Welcome to San Francisco." His eyes flirted unabashedly. "Where from?"

"New York — upstate."

"Running away from home?"

Smiling again, I said, "More or less."

"Me too. Got here two years ago from Kansas."

"Farm boy?"

"That's right. They ran me out of town."

"How's that?"

"Me and my boyfriend? After school, we'd go back into the wheat fields together? Behind an old barn? Had us a hell of a time. Some classmates followed us out one day? Gave us the surprise of our *lives*. Caught us with our pants down, literally! I left town the day after graduation, didn't stop till I got to San Francisco." He took a swig of his beer, staring at me seductively while he mouthed the tip of the bottle.

"And the boyfriend?"

Farm Boy took another big swig. Removing the bottle from his mouth he swallowed dramatically then answered, "He stayed. Said what we did was wrong. Said he had to make up for the shame he'd caused his family. He was gonna get married, 'go back to girls' as he put it. None of that for me. No sir!"

I liked this guy, his look, his attitude, so when he put his empty bottle down, started rocking his hips and said, "Come on, dance with me," I moved real close to him and allowed the music to do what it wanted with my body.

As we danced, I leaned towards his ear and said, "Sounds pretty exciting, screwing in the wheat fields."

"Sure was."

We grinned at each other. Totally turned on, I put my hands on his ass and brought our bodies together. "Tell me about it."

He gave a beautifully descriptive account of hot sun, sweat, lust, and wheat-dust that got in his lover's nose and made him sneeze.

****

Farm Boy lived in a small one room in an old apartment building high above the smelly streets of the tenderloin. A beautiful yellow and green quilt on the twin bed dominated the otherwise undecorated room.

"My grandma made it for me," he said in response to my staring at it. "The only thing I took with me, besides clothes and a couple a pictures of the boy who forsaked me."

I studied the two framed bedside photos of a brown-haired blue-eyed darling whom anyone could see was gay.

"How will he survive?" I asked.

"He'll do what he thinks he has to." He flicked back a blond strand that had crossed into his eye. "People do it all the time."

Fucking him from behind, Grandma's quilt carefully folded and placed on the windowsill, I thought of the farm towns I'd passed in Kansas, and I thought of my parents and the illness that had come over them, rendering them helpless to the charms and seductions of "Our Lord Jesus Christ." These thoughts immersed me in desire for this sweet young man whom I did not know, made me mad with desire to somehow fill him up with the understanding and open-minded nurturing that he should have received from his family and neighbors. It seemed, or so I imagined, that he understood what I was doing, and took it in hungrily. *You are good, you are beautiful*, I said to him with my body.

I spent the night with Farm Boy, thoroughly enjoying touching him, his broad shoulders, the details of which had lain concealed under his work shirt at the Power Tool. His masculinity was undeniable and I felt drawn to it the way I had been to those photos in Sport's Illustrated all those years ago. Oddly, there was almost nothing about this experience that reminded me of Rick. Rick was about love drenched with passion. Farm Boy was about lust and desperation. Experiencing this kind of sex, especially in its anonymity, seemed almost like losing my virginity all over again, now for the third time.

I headed back towards my apartment in the early morning light, the city glowing golden with promises. I knew I'd never be with Farm Boy again and that felt right; it was beautiful for what it was. I was on a high; San Francisco was living up to my expectations. I was finally going to live my life open and free and me.

****

A blast of dance music greeted me as I pulled open the heavy wooden door of HUNKS, a bar at the opposite end of the block from the Power Tool. I thought I wasn't going to get in at first; there was a large burly guy up front carding. But he looked up from the driver's license he was studying and waved me in with a weary smile.

The interior of HUNKS was huge, dark, and totally to my liking. White candles, in votives, burned at close intervals on a two-sided antique bar which ran through the center of the room. A massive mirror backed the bartenders on both sides. At the far end of the room, where the bar ended, was a large dance floor. Lining the walls were long wooden shelves, just wide enough to rest a drink or an elbow. Tables, chairs, bar stools, were nonexistent.

It was just after eleven. I'd known the bars would still be dead, but I'd been restless, lonely, and horny. There were maybe a couple of dozen people scattered about. Immediately I noticed that, unlike the Power Tool, there were also a few women here. The rest of the crowd was gay, or possibly bi, men, far fewer of whom were in leather than at the Power Tool. The bartender, who had a ponytail down to his ass, and Mic Jagger lips, was enthusiastically batting his eyelashes at his customer, a small muscular guy with jet black hair, majestic blue eyes and — I found out a good bit later that night — a pair of nipple rings. Soon as I approached, Ponytail abandoned the object of his affections and eased over to me. "Ooo, *la, la!* What's *your* name big boy?"

"Jim."

"I'm Danny," smile, wink. "Whacha drinking?"

I couldn't help but crack a smile back. "Beer."

Pointing at me now, he informed me, "Heineken."

"Okay."

After dancing for over an hour, and watching Majestic Eyes dance (which convinced me to go after him — anyone who moved like that had to know how to enjoy himself in bed), I went back for another beer. By now the place was packed. I squeezed in next to the guy Danny was taking an order from. He too had a ponytail, almost as long as Danny's, only gray. Gray beard, sparkling impish gray eyes, and a silver peace sign dangling from a silver chain. He ordered a Cruzan rum and soda with lime.

"Cruzan!" shouted Danny over the boom, boom, boom, of a disco beat. "You're always crusin' with Cruzan, Bill. I love ya! Marry me, Bill! Will you marry me, Bill?"

Bill turned to me. "Marry? Marry?" like he was stunned, "Marry?"

Danny gave him his drink and patted my hand. "He'll get over it." Then with raised eyebrows, he asked, "Heiny?"

It took me a second to realize he was inquiring about my drink order, not my ass. "Right," I responded, trying not to look flustered.

Bill took a sip of his drink. "Ah... good stuff! Virgin Islands rum." Turning to me he said, "Try it sometime." When my Heineken arrived he added, pointing at it, "That's not bad, but try this sometime. Try it." And with this, Bill turned away, the crowd near us parting temporarily to allow him in, and then closing around him, swallowing him whole, Virgin rum and all.

****

When I entered A Kiss of Heaven Bakery and Coffee House on Haight Street a few days later, a wired

Bill approached my table, tray in hand, smiled broadly — clearly recognizing me — and asked, "Something strong and hot?" A Kiss of Heaven became a regular hangout. The front room had about ten small tables, most of which were crammed into two triangular window alcoves, which allowed sightseeing of Haight's endlessly entertaining pedestrians. A small back room was cozier and darker. The coffee was perfect, and the service, from Bill — who like our waitress in New York, seemed to be perpetually there — was always great and often amusing.

Another place I began to frequent was Lucky Paul's Bar and Grill farther down on Haight, where I played pool with contemporaries of Al's and Clarence's, guys whose wild and woolly youths had rendered them scary-looking — old-before-their-time — gruff men with bad coughs, greasy balding hair, and interesting — even amazing — personalities that were almost without exception riddled with hostility. I looked around Lucky Paul's one particularly crowded afternoon and wondered if any of these former-tuffs was perhaps gay, a latent homosexual, as it were, who'd in reaction to something undesirable perceived within, gone hyper-masculine, become everything that a fag wasn't supposed to be. I looked at the gray-speckled beard of the guy I was playing pool with, his beer gut, the filterless cigarette pinched between yellowed fingers. He scowled at me. I laughed to myself and, focusing back on the game, pocketed my third shot in a row. I missed the next one, but only by a hair. He guffawed loudly, slapped me on the back hard, grunted past the butt now clenched between his lips, "You're not bad, kid."

I got the feeling that as long as I played a good game of pool and had a beer in my hand, these guys didn't care who else it is I might happen to be. I thought of Clarence and his defense of homosexuality, and felt what I knew was a totally delusional sense of safety.

Love, Sex, and Understanding the Universe

****

I was taking my black-garbed self to the bars almost nightly. I'd considered then dismissed the baths as too distasteful: not just anonymous sex, but it seemed, dehumanizing sex. By day I explored the city's book stores. City Lights was my favorite, the cramped creaky shop overflowing with knowledge and information, explorations, sensuality and outright sexuality — so much to challenge the status quo. Or I picked up handball games in Golden Gate Park, playing hard against intolerable yuppies. I slept in the afternoons, or drank coffee, then played pool buzzing, shooting down a beer or two to take off the edge. Then the world of night again: another beer or two, dancing, flirting, then hot sex with some sexy hunk or another.

****

The cheap curtains I'd gotten together didn't quite close all the way, and this morning, splinters from the sun streaked in and pierced through my throbbing head. Grumbling, I covered my eyes with my pillow, a lumpy thing I should never have bought. Another thing I should never have done: gone home with that guy last night. At the bar on Castro I'd thought his gruffness sort of charming. I'd been horny and had not bothered to think twice before I jumped into his Mustang. When we got to his place, I discovered quickly he was quite the screwed-up case of a homophobic fag. He hated himself, hated me, hated both of us because we were men who liked men. He smoked too much too. I'd gotten a headache from all the smoke, still had the headache. He'd turned his face away when I tried to kiss him, fucked me angrily, then had gotten dressed in a rapid-fire hurry, as if the very reality of his naked body was more than he could take, and immediately upon completion of tying his shoes (in double knots!), he told me to, "Get the fuck out." Nice.

I'd showered when I'd gotten home, but my hair still stank, that lovely stale of tarry smoke. I'd had, up until that night, a lot of fun with the men I'd met. But I didn't have any actual friends, and as I lay there, lumpy pillow insulating in the tobacco stench, I began to think of all the things I did not have, or more specifically, all the things I'd lost: Rick, Amy, Mom, Dad, sister, brother, Mary (oh God, Mary), Grandpa, even Jenny and Gran Wallace, even Rick's parents, and Vinny (Christ, good old Cousin Vin), and Al and Clarence. Lost them all. I was alone in the world. Me, my lumpy pillow, cheap curtains, and wretched stinky hair. School would start soon. School would be my saving grace, light at the end of the tunnel. I rose and went to my calendar, literally counted the days. Then I headed to A Kiss of Heaven where an upbeat Bill asked, "Java fix?" Small talk with Bill and a coffee buzz served to just barely lift me out of my gloom; it was enough anyway to get me through the day.

Chapter Thirteen

I stood in the doorway of my first class on the first day of school. There was an array of faces — Arabic, Chinese, Vietnamese, Japanese — mostly men, one black woman, and a couple of nerdy white boys. Then there, in the front row, middle seat, sat a guy who, as soon as he spotted me, cracked a grin that had to pretty much match the expression he saw on my face. What we found so amusing was how much alike we appeared: dark hair — his perfectly straight — just past the collar, dark eyes, black jeans, black boots, tall, fit, good-looking. Our facial features different of course, his nose sharp and his lips thin. Immediately I processed cues from the way he sat, held himself, very masculine, very controlled, and very hetero.

I sat in the empty seat next to him — front row had long been my normal classroom space — putting my stack of books on the desktop. He took a good look at the books, his head bent sideways to read the titles. Then he turned, opened his backpack, and placed his books on his desk, titles facing me. We each had six books; all were identical. He was a sophomore physics major too, and we had the same advisor whom had recommended the same classes, all of which were scheduled for the same days and times. His name was Derek, and he had been born and raised in San Francisco.

The next day, as I was locking my helmet to my bike in the school parking lot, I heard another Harley approach. I watched as it drove up and was parked next to mine. Pulling off his helmet was a laughing Derek. We walked to class talking about our bikes. Over the next couple of days, mostly over coffee in the cafeteria, I discovered that Derek was at least as smart as I was, maybe smarter, had opted out of Berkeley for much the same reasons why I had, and was as passionate about physics as I was.

The third day of classes, Derek came over to my place in the evening to study. We started by going over class material, but quickly veered off into a long philosophical/theoretical discussion concerning current physics research. After four hours of intense intellectual focus and the better part of a large, delivered, sausage and onion pizza, Derek asked, after licking tomato sauce off his thumb, "You play pool?"

I laughed. "Yeah, I do."

On the way to Lucky Paul's we stopped at Two Times Over — a large cafe with high ceilings and huge picture windows looking out onto Haight — for coffees to go. As we passed A Kiss of Heaven a couple of blocks later, Bill who was standing in the doorway gave me a wave, then pointing at our logoed cups, shook his head disapprovingly. I held mine up in a toast to him, and he laughed.

"Maybe we should stop there for another coffee after our game," I said to Derek, expecting him to say something about not wanting to drink coffee so late at night, but I should have figured better by now. He responded, "Sounds good."

Lucky Paul's was quiet, a couple of has-been tough guys drowning at the bar. The pool table sat at peace in its dank backroom. We downed our coffees and ordered a couple of longneck Buds, the bartender looking over Derek as if deciding whether he should be allowed into this exclusive club. Apparently he passed muster because we were handed two beers with a friendly nod.

Derek played a damned good game, but I beat him three in a row.

"So," he said, scratching his chin as we put our cues back on the rack, "do you bowl?"

A Kiss of Heaven was closed by the time we passed by, but we decided to meet there the next evening at six, and then I'd follow Derek to the bowling alley in Daily City.

****

Derek and I arrived at the cafe simultaneously at five forty-five. Bill greeted us with an expression of exaggerated relief. "That's much better, boys."

Though Bill's looks didn't fit any gay stereotype, many of his mannerisms would certainly have made him suspect to anyone who was concerned one way or another. If Derek noticed or cared, he didn't let on.

In front of the bowling alley later that night — after Derek's bowling skills continually out did mine — a couple of young women were about to get in a car next to us, when two men — blue collar types in their thirties — approached them.

"Hi, girls! What are you up to tonight?"

The women were obviously not interested, and tried to be kind in their refusal of an offer to have drinks bought for them, but the men persisted. Finally, the taller woman said bluntly, "We're lesbians." The other woman shot her an amazed look. But the men backed away, laughing good-naturedly, jabbing elbows into each other.

Derek shook his head, which I interpreted as sympathy for the guys who got turned down.

"Want to go to the 9er's game tomorrow?" Derek asked, as I was thinking this might be an easy time to slip in that I was bi.

"Umm..."

"They're gonna have a great season."

"Yeah, sure." I put on my helmet, feeling relived that he hadn't asked me to a basketball game instead.

****

Derek and I sat together in every class, had morning and afternoon coffee in the cafeteria, grabbed lunch together. Four or more nights a week we studied at my place, took in a game of pool, or hung out at the bowling alley; we shared pizza, or Chinese food. We had amazingly intense theoretical conversations about physics that went on for hours. After these talks, I always felt exhilarated — for the first time in my life, I had someone with whom I could discuss physics on deeply intelligent levels. Every morning I woke up looking forward to my next encounter with the mind of Derek.

****

San Francisco State is, more often than not, shrouded in a blanket of chilling fog, but this day — about two weeks after Derek and I met — was one of those unusually clear days when everyone spills out onto the lawns and gets a good dose of sunshine. While walking across campus to the Student Union, maneuvering around a group of pseudo-hippies playing a reckless game of Frisbee, Derek and I nearly collided with a couple of guys sitting under a tree kissing. Public display of gay love was not actually all that typical of a sight on campus, but there they were, and since we'd been busy trying not to get decapitated by a red, white, and blue, tie-dyed flying disk, we hadn't notice these men until we were practically on top of them. I saw them first and swerved so as not to step on their toes. Derek however jumped away drastically, his face horrorstricken as if these two lovebirds were actually a swarm of fang-exposing cobras.

As I continued to head towards the cafeteria, brushing off Derek's reaction as merely odd, I heard from behind, muttered disgustedly into my ear, "Fucking faggots."

107

Derek had said these words, then quickly, as he stepped alongside me, recomposed himself, back to the controlled macho guy that stones could only bounce off of.

An overwhelming urge rushed into me full force — I would grab Derek, shove him to the ground, and mercilessly pound his face with my fists. Sort of the antithesis of gay-bashing, I guess.

Derek had said, "Fucking faggots," and had recomposed himself and kept walking. He hadn't expected me to respond, nor did he even look to see my reaction. He was a few feet in front of me now, as the power of my emotions had brought me to a near stop. Watching him, the caveman in me swiftly gave way to a crushing disappointment. I imagined myself grabbing his arm, whirling him around, and saying right into his face, "I've been thinking of you as a great friend, but I like kissing men just as much as those guys do, and if you can't handle that then fuck off." But I didn't do that either. No, I would approach this in a calm, collected, manner. Once we were sitting down in the Student Union with our coffee, I would very matter-of-factly tell Derek that I was bi. I'd tell him that I hadn't appreciated the way he'd reacted out on the lawn. I'd explain that I wasn't interested in him sexually — he wasn't my type, too macho — but I did want him as a friend. However, if he's got issues with homosexuality then he needs to get over them real quick.

As we entered the building, I played this scenario out in my head and realized quickly that it was obvious, from his behavior moments ago, that Derek was not going to stick around for five seconds after I came out to him. Here we had become such great friends so quickly, and with one statement I was going to push him so irrevocably far away from me. But there wasn't any alternative.

We took a table in front of a triangular picture window that looked out onto the art buildings beyond. I stirred cream into my cup. Derek drank his black —

predictable, I thought now. Maybe he'll throw his steaming drink into my face. Maybe I'll throw mine into his face. He was squinting out the window, with a very stern, angry, expression. He was thinking about those "Fucking faggots." Screw him.

I opened my mouth. "Derek."

He looked at me expectantly, the sternness, the anger, gone now.

I took in his face; I remember that, looking at his face, not just looking at him, but really *studying* his face, and something gripped me. I tried to speak; my outrage at his words was boiling over, but...

I hesitated, then I heard myself saying, "I don't feel too good, I'm gonna head home." And I stood up and dashed out of the building.

My Harley sped up 19th Avenue, then barely slowed enough to successfully make the turn onto Sloat Boulevard, the roaring of the engine like the angry declarations of a caged lion. The bike flew along the long length of Sloat, my head in a frenzied rage, but I slowed down as I approached the zoo. The roaring now a steady purr, I craned my neck, looking through the entrance gate. Maybe I could get myself locked up here. People could point; I could roar back, or sulk in a corner. I pulled up at the beach and sat on the cool sand, staring at the Pacific. Now the ocean roared at me, a methodical, indifferent roar. I lost myself in the physics of waves, light refractions on water, tides, planets revolving through space. Tell Derek I'm bi, I like fucking men, and what? Sit on opposite sides of our classrooms hating each other? I took off my boots and socks, watched the sand particles disperse as I slipped my toes in, felt the transfer of cold from sand to foot. Thermodynamics. Derek had some interesting thoughts on thermodynamics. The man was smart. Smart and apparently stupid. No, really more like smart and ignorant. He'd been born into an ignorant world. Was that his fault?

But why couldn't he, why hadn't he, especially since he was raised in San Francisco, moved beyond that? Maybe he'd never had to face this issue personally. Maybe he'd never met anyone who could pull him through the stereotypes. But why would any thinking person, which Derek certainly was, embrace stereotypes? Maybe if I just gave us time. If he got to know me really well. He wouldn't be able to hate me, won't be able to hate anyone gay anymore. Maybe. But it didn't matter. Because that wasn't going to happen. Because I was going to tell him now — well tomorrow anyway. What was I going to do? Lock myself into a foul suffocating closet after living in "Gay Mecca" for less than two months? Not a chance. That's not what I came to San Francisco for. I owed it to Rick to be out. I owed it to my own damn self. I couldn't believe I was even wrestling with this at all. I could just ignore Derek. Yeah, that was it. Just avoid him and eat pizza by myself and play pool with ridiculous old-men thugs, and talk to a spot on my ceiling about anti-mater, create an invisible friend who could spin equations around his little finger like the magician Derek.

****

I got back on my bike and drove home in a solemn mood. All that evening in my apartment I kept telling myself, *I'm not going to hide in a closet; I'm not going to silence myself; I am going to tell him.* Midnight, I went down to a bar on Castro and found someone to go home with. As I kissed his chest, sucked on his cock, grasped his ass and fucked him hard as per his pleadings, I was intensely aware of how much I enjoyed being with a man, how much I liked this part of who I am. I would no sooner give up my homosexuality then give up my intelligence.

Later, when this man I had "made-love" to, but had not loved, slept next to me — telling me before he fell asleep that it was all right to spend the night — I decided resolutely that I would tell Derek immediately after our morning class the next day. As I thought this thought, as these words went through my head, I knew something, something terrible, and I fell asleep devastated. I was not going to tell Derek the next day. I was, despite everything that I understood to be true and important, going to wait until Derek's friendship with me was like reinforced concrete, then let him swing a homophobic fist at that!

During the drive to school the next morning I wondered how I was going to pull off a smile, wondered if I could pull this whole thing off at all. Something inside me, some invisible *force*, something physicists haven't yet identified, had made the decision not to come out to Derek, but the rest of me resisted, hated this decision. I walked towards class thinking: maybe when I see Derek I'll just find myself blurting out, "I'm bisexual and damn proud of it," right there in class in front of everyone. I hoped beyond all hopes that this would happen.

As it turned out, the second I saw Derek's face grinning at me, happy to see that I hadn't died overnight, I fell very easily into a very familiar closet. It was, after all, something I knew how to do.

Chapter Fourteen

About a month after I stepped back into the closet, I was on a bus, going to pick up my bike at a shop where the engine was being overhauled. I'd taken a crowded streetcar down Judah, squeezed myself in amongst punk rockers, old ladies, black drag queens, a Vietnamese family, and Mexican dykes in full leather, and had now transferred to an electric bus rambling through the Fillmore district quite empty. In the back was a group of Japanese-American teenagers, who were arguing loudly, in broken English, about whether Madonna or Michael Jackson is the coolest. So I sat all the way up front, where the seats face the seats on the opposite side of the bus, rather than facing forward.

At the next stop, I watched a businesswoman come up the steps — coral-pink short-skirted business suit, expensive leather briefcase, long beautiful legs. She sat down across from me, an incredible face, smiling at me. I realized that she was very young, maybe twenty-three, way too young to be in such a serious get-up. The door hissed shut, and with a slight lurch, the bus continued on. Her eyes — intelligent long-lashed hazel eyes — looked me over. I returned the interest, noting lightly tanned skin, high cheekbones, brunette shoulder-length hair, sensuous lips — did I mention smiling at me? There was a silk blouse under the open tailored jacket, very inviting. I smiled back.

The bus rode on through some of the scarier parts of town in a semi-darkness created by thick fog lolling above. Occasionally, new passengers got on, but I barely noticed, the businesswoman and I too busy unabashedly studying one another. Eventually the bus came out into the bright sunlight of the Civic Center, where City Hall, the public library, opera house, and other momentous white buildings, converge in a sort of oasis of civilization. My bus companion had looked beautiful in the fog and poverty riddled Fillmore district, and she looked beautiful too in the sunlit and culture riddled downtown. When the bus pulled to a stop, she rose to get off. I thought once, twice, then jumped up and got off too.

Hearing my boots on the sidewalk behind her, she turned around, smiled.

"Do you have time for a cup of coffee?" I asked.

"Do you work around here?"

"No, I'm a student — at San Francisco State."

"Oh, so why are you out this way?" Her voice was soft and teasing.

"I have to pick up my motorcycle..." I paused awkwardly, "out near the highway." I gestured in the direction of the East Bay.

She looked confused.

"I got off the bus because you did."

She liked that, told me so with her eyes.

Over coffee, she informed me that her name was Carol and that she was indeed twenty-three. She worked as a personnel officer for a large conglomerate, and traveled often to aid in interviews of prime candidates for upper level positions. She liked her job, and would I give her a ride on my motorcycle sometime, say this afternoon when she got off work, she has a pair of jeans in her office she could change into.

That afternoon, at five I sat on my bike, helmet removed, waiting for her at the agreed upon spot. I watched her approach from a distance, now in jeans and white tennis shoes. Her hips were broad. She was a large-boned woman, tall and self-assured. Nothing could knock this one over. On the bike she pushed up close against me and wrapped her arms around my waist, her hands gently gripping my rib cages. I drove up Powell through Chinatown, came out at Washington Square in North Beach, then took Columbus' diagonal towards Fisherman's Wharf. We sat on benches by the Maritime Museum, overlooking Aquatic Park. We watched pigeons and tourists, talked about pigeons and tourists, laughed about pigeons and tourists. Back on the bike, Carol held on tight as I drove along Marina Green and through the forested Presidio. I rode through Golden Gate Park, turned on Judah, taking a slight detour to point out my apartment. Then I headed down Haight to take Carol home just off Alamo Square. She lived in the penthouse apartment of a four story, lacy Victorian. In front of her turquoise-colored door we exchanged phone numbers and light playful French kisses.

As I walked to Haight Street later that night to meet Derek for coffee and spaghetti at Del Grande's, I made a game plan. I would take Carol out to dinner some place where there were bound to be gay couples, see how she reacts, and either come out to her and take it from there, or drop her like a hot potato. No matter what, I was not going to get into another closeted relationship. This had to be handled properly this time.

The next day, I made the phone call short and concise. Would she like to have dinner with me Friday?

"Yes." She was enthusiastic.

"Eight o'clock, then? I'll pick you up."

****

I knocked on Carol's door, hoping she wouldn't ask me in. *Don't get too close, too intimate, until you know.*

But no worry, Carol, ready and eager to get out and about, shut the door behind her, giving me a killer smile. She wore a white tight-knit cotton dress, cut low on the shoulders. It showed off her hips, accented her cleavage, and allowed a clear calculation of just how long her legs were. Oh how badly I wanted this night to go well.

There was a second-story restaurant on Upper Haight that I'd gone to once during the summer, with a guy whom I'd picked up at a bar the weekend before. He and I had spent the night together, and there seemed to be some possibility for more between us, so I'd asked him out to dinner. Everything had gone fine until he started talking about cocaine like it was some sort of a God (he'd done a few lines the previous weekend but I hadn't thought much of it), and then went on to relay get-rich-quick schemes that would bring him in a more steady supply of this glorious white powder. Anyway, it was to this restaurant that I planned to take Carol, the food had been great, the atmosphere romantic, and most importantly, the clientele had consisted of a good mix of gay, lesbian, and straight couples. The restaurant featured an eclectic menu, a series of small dining rooms glowing with candlelight, and a staff with a relaxed, you're-at-home, attitude.

Carol and I were led through a full dining room, and then we were seated in an adjacent room next to a gay couple. One more gay couple sat in the opposite corner.

Carol's first reaction wasn't encouraging. She looked around uncomfortably. "Have you been here before?" she asked.

"Yeah, it's a great place. Don't you like it?"

She looked around again. "Well, it's... It is *pretty* in here, "she said with a disconcerting, frown.

But within minutes, I began to feel that I must have misread her initial discomfort. She relaxed quickly, and we had an enjoyable conversation, even as a lesbian, then another gay couple, then two straight couples were seated in our room. Carol had a great sense of humor, was quite bright, oozed sexuality, and appeared to be explicitly interested in me. She asked a lot of questions about physics that seemed to come from a genuine curiosity. She told me funny anecdotes about her family in Iowa: her Aunt Sally who baked pies incessantly to keep from facing the realities of her life, and her Uncle Bud who drank like a fish but was well-loved by the kids because he had a hundred and one ways to make them laugh. Carol, it seemed, might just have a hundred and one ways to make *me* laugh. Her stories were told with enthusiasm, hand gestures, and a good deal of intentionally obvious embellishment. But for all her family's amusing traits, she said, she'd just had to get away from them, go somewhere where she could be, "my own damned self."

"They would have had me married, raising little monsters, keeping house, and working as a sales clerk at K-Mart. But they couldn't keep *me* down. The summer after high school graduation, I packed my bags, said, sayonara, and hopped a bus out here."

She'd gotten a filing job at the company she still works for, then had taken classes at City College, and quickly moved her way up.

I had been really looking forward to watching Carol eat the chocolate cake she ordered for dessert (certain aspects of Amy's hedonism had latched on to me), but just before it arrived, the gay couple next to us left. Apparently, this was the moment Carol had been waiting for. She leaned towards me and whispered, "I just wish they didn't have to flaunt it so much."

Carol might as well have hit me over the head with my Grolsch bottle. Words reverberated in my head: *they, it, flaunt*. Flaunt! There were just some couples *eating dinner* together. I was not conscious of what my external expression was in reaction. Likely horror. But Carol wasn't looking at me; she was looking with disdain at the lesbian couple across the room.

Okay, it was over. She wasn't for me. No point in making a scene about it. We'd finish our desserts; I would not even notice how she ate her chocolate cake. I'd drive her home; we'd go about our separate lives. I was not going to try to educate her. I was not interested in putting *any* energy into her; she did not exist.

In defiance, I spent the rest of the time at the restaurant thinking about the last man I'd gone home with. He'd been well hung, and mildly aggressive — I'd liked that; he wasn't ugly about it, just very lusty: "Take off your pants! Get on your knees!" Firm commands I'd gladly obeyed. To hell with Carol. As we ate our desserts, I was cold and absent. She became nervous. Tough shit. I drove her home without a word. After she got off the bike, I forced a solid, firm, "Good-bye."

She smiled, looked confused. "I'll call you."

I drove off without responding.

****

Carol did call, four days later. I told her schoolwork was keeping me busier than I'd expected, I needed to concentrate on my studies, and didn't have time to date. I hung up with another firm, "Good-bye," before she had a chance to get a word in edgewise.

Two days after that, in the early evening, I was sitting alone in my apartment, twiddling my thumbs, lonely and melancholy. There were the bars of course, but not much would be going on with that scene for several hours yet. I was hungry, didn't have much in the fridge, didn't feel like eating alone somewhere. Derek. Derek would be nice right about now. Well, yes, he and I had spent the last five nights setting our intellects on fire, and I had thought a break would be all right, but what was the point of that? We could have pizza on Haight, play a game of darts, or go bowling; Derek was always in for bowling. I rose to call him. The doorbell rang. Derek! Sure, he'd had the same idea. I went to the door, pulled it open eagerly, smiling.

Carol came bustling in, chipper as a nymph on a moonlit night, bearing parcels of wonderful-smelling food. No, "Hi," or "Can I come in?" she just danced right past me, waving the bags in the air. "Thai food! Tom Kha Gai, Pad Thai, Evil Jungle Prince."

117

****

Carol put the bags on the counter, pulled out little aromatic boxes, placing them one by one on my table, while I continued to stand by the still open door, shocked by her audacity. My mouth opened to speak... but what do I say? *Get the fuck out, you homophobic...* what? You homophobic *cunt*? *Bitch*? I don't like using those words, not in that way. *Please leave, Carol*? Or like Rick, *Please get out, now.* That hurt, like a stab in the heart. That was a no-no. I don't think about Rick, don't think about him because that is what I have to do in order to survive, not think about Rick.

Carol was in the kitchen now, finding plates, talking about the Thai restaurant, talking about how she almost picked up French food instead, but thought Thai might be more my style, lighter, funnier, spicy and full of exotic flavors, not so overbearing and heavy like French food.

I shut the door. But I did not move from my place next to it. I could open it again at a moment's notice. I watched her move. This tall, solidly built woman sailing somehow with such lightness around my apartment. She did not ask where anything was, found glasses at first guess, found a bottle opener, poured Thai beer.

Now she was saying she'd bought tickets to see Jaco Pastorius at a club in North Beach. We'd once, almost, Rick and I... No, don't think about Rick.

"I remember," Carol was saying, "you told me you use to go listen to jazz a lot in New York."

Did I tell her this? Go ahead, I thought, *you* remember, I won't. *You* do it for me.

Carol set the table, confident, self-assured, full of vivacious energy, her slinky blouse showing off firm, braless, breasts.

118

I sat on the couch, helpless, suddenly *wanting* to be helpless, intrigued, and wanting her, wanting her full round ass, wanting her body badly.

She picked up a glass of beer, held it out to me. I got up off the couch, got out of my funk. Carol was trying to make me happy, and she could do this, could accomplish this task, at least to a point. I was already in the closet... already in the closet... What the hell, why not take it all the way? I was, after all, an "all the way" kind of guy.

The Thai food was great. The jazz was great. Sex with Carol was great.

In the morning she was still there. I had eggs and cheese in the refrigerator; I could make us omelets. I had eggs and cheese in the refrigerator... Why hadn't I realized this last night? Why hadn't I realized this, and gotten up and made myself an omelet, and then when she showed up I could have said, "Sorry, I just ate; good-bye." But no, I was glad that this was not the way it turned out. I made us omelets while Carol talked. She talked about how ugly her cat is, and I should come over and meet the cat, but, she wondered, could I stand the mess at her place? She glanced around my apartment. "I guess you could." She was certain the cat would like me, and, "By the way, you have a beautiful cock, and do you think you could explain Einstein's Theory of Relativity to me?"

"How about Saturday night?"

"Perfect!"

****

I had a dream: Carol wanted me to explain Einstein's Theory of Relativity while I was fucking her. A new twist on kinkiness — sex with physics! Why hadn't I thought of this? I told her I couldn't. She said I could. I told her maybe I could if she got her ugly cat to stop staring at us. She put the cat in the kitchen and closed the door.

119

Something about a kitchen with a door that closes... What for? You could close the door and have sex in there and no one else in the house could watch you... humm. I told her to put the cat in the living room, and we'd have sex in the kitchen. I explained the Theory of Relativity to her while she sat on the counter, legs spread, her hands on my hips, guiding me firmly in and out. I found talking about physics got me off all the more. Carol went wild, groaning in all the right places.

This was the dream I had that night — the night before I went to Carol's to explain relativity. In reality, I told Carol about Einstein's theory as we ate by candlelight at her dinner table — delicious red snapper with a West Indian sauce that a classmate from City College had taught her how to make. She followed my explanation, concentrating to get it fully. Carol's mind was sharp. We had sex on her bed, the cat watching us. In the morning, I fell in love with the cat, who *was* truly, truly, ugly.

****

Carol, I came to discern over the following weeks, did not want marriage or children. She did not even want an intense love affair. What Carol wanted, it turned out, was pretty much what I was able to offer her: a nice face, a nice body, good sex, and an enjoyable enough personality that made almost no demands of her. Carol wanted a man in her life, but she clearly did not want that man to *be* her life. She wanted her job to be her life. All this sounded all too familiar.

While I was what Carol was looking for, she was, obviously, not what I was looking for. I wanted someone to love fully — someone who would love me, the complete me. This could never be Carol. But she offered me plenty none-the-less. She was a nice place to channel my sexual desires for a woman; she was good company — always upbeat, full of life; she also, depressingly enough, proved very useful in presenting the image of heterosexuality to Derek. And, in all honestly, we got along extremely well. Conversations with Carol continued to be both interesting and amusing. In addition to our shared enjoyments for jazz and ethnic food, we were both found of lazy times in bed interspersed with hot sex. The initial feeling I experienced the day I met Carol on the bus, that attracted me to her, was intrigue, and that intrigue, perhaps more than anything, was what continued to draw me to her. I had no doubt that her personality was fixed, it just somehow eluded me, went completely over my head, and oddly I liked that, found that it even turned me on, never knowing what she might do or say, continually being surprised, and yet never feeling as though her actions were at all out of character.

If I was going to be involved with a woman whom I couldn't be out to, then Carol was probably the perfect choice. A relationship with her still allowed me much time and space within which to pursue other interests, so to speak. And this brings me to the one thing that Carol wanted in a relationship that I couldn't offer, but could at least offer the illusion of: sexual fidelity. Carol never came right out and demanded this, but it was clear from comments she made that she would be faithful to me (she never inquired about my opinion on this matter), and that she expected the same in return. For some reason this was important to her. I'm not sure why. I guess it's important to most people. Perhaps if I were monosexual it would be important to me too. I don't know; I never really explored the issue, as it isn't an option. So as I continued to see Carol, so too, I continued to enjoy the bars, or more precisely, the men in them. I insisted on using a condom with Carol — STDs ran rampant in the gay community — making up a story about an aunt who got pregnant despite her IUD.

Chapter Fifteen

One particularly cold night, I went home from HUNKS with a handsome man nearly a generation older than me. What had attracted me to this guy, besides his looks, was that he wasn't drunk and didn't seem intent on playing games. He'd approached me confidently, watching for my reaction to him, which was cautiously enthusiastic. Sliding in next to me, resting his elbows on the same ledge mine were on, he'd asked right out, "What are you looking for?"

I answered, "Nothing too specific, a nice time, hot sex."

"That," he said with great promise, "I can do."

He mixed us Kir Royales in a modern dimly lit kitchen in his flat near Coit Tower. Walking with stemmed blue glasses down the hall towards his bedroom, we passed a room filled with toys.

"My son. He stays with me every-other weekend."

"Were you married?"

"Yes. His mom and I still get along quite well."

When we got into the master bedroom he sat down on the edge of the king-sized bed. He had silver-gray accents in his hair, and I kept expecting to find a way that he reminded me of my father, but he didn't. The bed was covered with a plush chocolate brown bedspread, and perched upon it he looked rather regal, but in a totally unassuming way. He took a sip of his drink, and I thought him to be tremendously sexy, his calm demeanor quite alluring.

I stood very close in front of him, feeling bold and comfortable. I took a sip from my glass then hazarded, "Are you bi?"

He looked at me now as if I was a lunatic. "I'm *gay*."

I knew that I should leave it at that, but I couldn't. "You didn't enjoy sex with your wife?"

"Of course I enjoyed it," he said, impatiently, "it just wasn't anything like what I experience with a man." He reached out and took the drink from my hand. Placing both our glasses on the nightstand, he pulled me towards him. His mouth tasted of lemon and lust. It was a long sensuous night.

In a way, I was just as much closeted about my heterosexuality as I was about my homosexuality. But while none of the men I'd had sex with knew I liked sleeping with women too, it was also true that few of them ever knew that I was a physics major, that I was a coffee junkie, or that I was a damned good bowler. The difference, however, was that I would have felt comfortable revealing those later attributes, and on occasions did, while it became increasingly clear that my attraction to women wouldn't be something I could comfortably talk about with any of the men I had slept with in San Francisco. For example, there was the stud with the handlebar mustache. We'd walked from a bar on Castro, down to his place in Noe Valley, for some good wholesome sixty-nine fun. Along the way we'd passed a hetero couple pressed up against a wall, faces locked in desperate exploration.

"Yuck," said my man for the night.

"What?" I inquired, wanting to be clear.

"The most disgusting thing I can think of: kissing a woman."

I hadn't responded, just processed this information. I found it interesting even if alarming. But why hadn't I been anywhere near as outraged by his comment as I had been by Derek's response to the guys kissing under the tree? Why hadn't I told Mr. 100% homo that kissing a woman was among the most beautiful things I could think of? Because tolerance, I had begun to realize, is a selective concept that has, within the gay community, very clear limits.

Ironically, being closeted about my straight side was somehow comforting, as if this were confirmation that not being out had nothing to do with internalized homophobia — after all, that would imply I was heterophobic as well. The way I preferred to look at it, I wasn't out simply because nobody wanted me to be who I am. This was, paradoxically, both an easy cop-out and a realistic assessment of the world I lived in.

****

Getting up from a table at A Kiss of Heaven, I pulled on my leather jacket, hitched my backpack over my shoulder, and waved good-bye across the room to Bill, who had, for no reason at all, brought a peanut butter cookie with my cup of coffee and said, "It's on the house." The cookie had reminded me of the ones Gran Wallace use to have waiting for us, on winter days, when Mary and I were kids running into her aroma-filled kitchen after school.

As I stepped outside, I noticed the fog had rolled in, dropping the temperature considerably. Stopping to snap close the sleeve of my jacket, I admired an old Indian bike parked at the curb. Then turning as I snapped my other sleeve, I realized, from the corner of my eye, that I was being observed. I glanced over to see a guy sitting length-wise on a ledge that was at about my chest level. He was leaning back against the adjacent wall with long legs bent at the knees, on which rested a sketchpad. In his left hand was a stick of charcoal. His crew cut, dyed pale orange, and his dark eyebrows, highlighted a striking face. He focused back on his sketchpad when he realized I'd noticed him looking at me, but when I kept my eyes on him, he returned my gaze.

We exchanged smiles. "Hi," he said.

"Hi."

"Getting pretty cold, isn't it?"

"Yeah." I zipped up my jacket. He was wearing torn blue jeans and an old army jacket. "What are you drawing?"

He held up the picture for me to see. It was a male nude with an unmistakable sensual quality to the man's pose. He put the drawing back on his lap.

I went and stood next to him to get a better look. "Nice. Really nice. Are you an art student?"

"Yeah, Oakland School of Art."

We talked briefly about his school, then he asked my name.

"Jim."

"Pleased to meet you." He stuck out his hand to shake. "I'm Flash."

Letting go of my hand with unaffected reluctance, Flash added, "I'd offer to buy you a cup of coffee, but I guess you already had one." He nodded towards A Kiss of Heaven.

"How about I buy you a beer instead," I suggested.

"Great." He jumped down off the wall and stood taller than me, at about six-foot-three. As we moved down Haight together, towards a club called the Night Cat, I was impressed by how comfortable this trim, but not thin man seemed with his height, how completely he possessed his body.

As we walked he asked if I was in school. When I told him I was majoring in physics, he said, "Wow!" then asked, "What does one do with a degree in physics?"

"You get a masters, then a PhD."

"Then what?"

"Teach or research, most likely. I'd prefer research."

"Doesn't that usually lead to developing wretched weapons, things like that?"

"I think I'll find a way not to do that. Anyway, teaching isn't an entirely repulsive notion."

"But wouldn't you just be teaching people who will go on to make," and here his voice took on an especially ominous quality, "*implements of destruction?*"

I smiled at his dramatics. "My choice would be to teach high school. Most of those kids don't end up with careers as Physicists. I'd just be getting them off on trying to understand the Universe."

"Trying to understand the Universe!" Flash laughed. "That's cool."

At Night Cat, we talked in a corner of the dark, nearly empty, room. To the question where are you from, he responded, "New Orleans."

I raised my eyebrows. It sounded so exciting, so far away. I wondered why he left, so I said, "It must be alright there. Gay-wise, I mean."

"Yeah, it is."

"So why'd you come here?"

"Change of pace. See something different. Where are you from?"

"New York, just upstate from Manhattan." I took a sip of my Bass Ale.

"How's that gay-wise?"

I laughed. "It's suburbia."

"Why didn't you just move down into the city?" He put his beer bottle against his cheek as if to cool himself.

"Got my heart broken there," I explained.

"Male or female?"

I studied him for a moment, disoriented. "Male."

After taking a swig of his beer, Flash asked, "How long ago was that?"

"Few months."

"Feel any better?"

"Long as I don't think about it... or talk about it."

He winked. "Gotcha. You live around here?"

"Few blocks up the hill. And you?"

"Just the other side of Haight — Page and Cole."

"Sounds like a nice location."

"How about I show you in person?" He winked again.

I nodded yes, taking a good long look at his body, imagining.

Grinning at the attention, Flash held up his beer. "Here's to sex on the first date."

****

Sitting at the kitchen table, in Flash's apartment, was a woman with purple and black hair, and a green-eyed man with bleached blond spikes sticking out of his head. The guy had a large safety pin for an earring, and a leather jacket with chains and padlocks all over it. The sleeves of the jacket had been torn off and a thin frayed long-john top with holes at the elbows was worn underneath. A beautiful Japanese tea set sat on the table next to them; pale green liquid shimmered in porcelain cups. These two punkers sat facing each other, the woman's foot resting in the guy's crotch. She pressed against him as she leaned forward to pass him a joint. He took the jay from her, his free hand running along the inside of her thigh, which was covered with torn fishnet stockings.

In a vague disinterested way, they glanced up and waved as we walked by. However, when we were halfway down the hall, the guy's voice called out, deep and gruff. "Flash, your mother called!"

Without stopping, Flash responded, "Yeah, yeah."

"She said she..."

Flash closed his bedroom door behind us, but the voice from the kitchen rose louder now. "She said she just got out of jail!"

Flash smiled, opened the door a crack and shouted, "Good one Zeek!" then closed the door again.

Intricately patterned Indian blankets were everywhere in the small room — one as a bedspread, one as a curtain darkening the lone window, another draped over a table. Two more billowed from nails on the ceiling, and one acted as a door to a closet.

He sat on the bed and motioned for me to sit next to him. "Never mind Zeek," he said, "he's my boyfriend and," Flash brushed cat hair off the bedspread, "he always finds a way to harass me when I bring someone home."

"Boyfriend."

"Yeah." He got up and started lighting candles. There must have been near a dozen in all, scattered around the room. Blowing out the last match he said, "We don't even have a telephone."

Flash and I lay down now, facing each other sideways on the bed. We fondled one another in silence, enjoying each other's bodies, faces, and expressions of pleasure. I pulled off his pants a little later — the man was big — and lying back down beside him, ran a finger down his long, sinewy arm. "What's your preference?"

"I'm a strictly versatile kind of guy," he said, breaking out in goose bumps.

I smiled. "Me too."

"In that case, I think I'd like you to fuck me. That is, if you don't mind."

I liked Flash's use of politeness as a subtle form of ironic humor. "I don't mind," I said.

He responded by pulling my body tight against his and sticking his tongue deep in my mouth.

Later he walked me out into the afternoon air. The fog had burned off and it was considerably warmer. "I'm sure I'll see you around Haight again," he said. "In any case, you know where I live."

As I walked home, the words, "I'm sure I'll see you around Haight," struck me. Derek and I were on Haight together a lot. Had I been crazy, picking up a guy on Haight, in the middle of the day no less? Suppose Derek, or Carol, had seen me looking this guy over in front of the cafe? I felt my mind twisting about. No, *that* had not been crazy. What was crazy was me being a closet-case. I had enjoyed Flash, and it was all backwards for me to feel that by picking him up I had done something I shouldn't have. It was strange and nice how well Flash and I hit it off. Not someone I could develop a serious relationship with, but... I realized now, no, as much as Flash would make an interesting friend/lover he could never be... we just didn't have... well, it just wasn't anywhere near as profound and deep as the way in which Derek and I connected.

I kicked a can near my apartment, then, approaching my door, pulled keys out of my jacket pocket. The scenario was too symbolic: unlock the door, step inside, close the door, lock it behind me. Back safely in the closet.

Chapter Sixteen

Knowing that it was ridiculous, that it couldn't go on for long, I went out of my way to avoid going near Haight unless I was alone. That was fairly easy when it came to Carol; she didn't like that part of town all that particularly much. Derek was a little trickier, but I managed for three weeks. During this time I was often on Haight by myself, and hoped to run into Flash, but he didn't seem to be around.

Eventually there was no way to keep Derek off Haight without seeming really weird about it. One afternoon he just got it into his head that he wanted a slice of Run to Roma's pesto pizza, and after that, coffee and lemon cake at A Kiss of Heaven.

The pizza was great as always. Derek and I laughed uproariously, getting into a juvenile conversation about naming discovered outer space objects food-oriented terms: Comet Kumquat, The Great Gelato Galaxy. Later, when we walked into the cafe, Bill greeted us with a black-power fist in the air, "Hey bros!" I smiled dimly at him as I glance furtively around the room. There was no sign of Flash. Then Derek suggested we go into the back room. I led the way. And there he was, coffee cup and sketchpad on the table in front of him. Flash looked up at me.

I shook my head no, almost imperceptibly, and mouthed the word, "Please."

He frowned and went back to his sketching, obviously pissed. I managed to convince Derek to sit in the front. "There's more light," I explained lamely, and escorted him to a corner table well away from the line of traffic.

****

The next day, I went to Flash's to apologize. We sat in the kitchen where Zeek and the purple-haired one had sat a few weeks back.

"I'm sorry."

"You should be." It was clear he hadn't appreciated what had happened at A Kiss of Heaven, but clear too he was glad I'd showed up to apologize.

"He's my best friend and he thinks I'm straight," I explained, gaining a sense of what it's like to be a Catholic at confession.

"What kind of friend is *that*?"

"I don't know."

"Do you want to do him?"

"No!"

He gave me a strange look.

"He's too stiff, too uptight," I elaborated.

Giving me a wicked smile, Flash said, "*Stiff,* and *tight,* are words I usually associate with..."

"There isn't anything sexual about him," I interrupted.

"Oh, I don't know..." Flash was grinning.

"Look, can we not talk about this?"

"Sure. But I think you should tell him."

"So do I. But that doesn't seem to count for much. How's school?"

"Great. I have a couple of really cool teachers this semester."

"I'd love to see more of your work."

We sat on his bed looking at the sketchpad. There were several pages with the same male nude he'd shown me last time, in various alluring poses. In all of the drawings he wore only a black leather cap.

"Is this someone you know?"

"He's a model at the school. They have him sit on this pedestal and I'm supposed to draw him like that, but that's not how I see him."

The next picture was of a guy shooting up. It was drawn with great detail: the veins in the arm, scars from previous punctures, the hand that had just pushed the syringe limp and seeming to tremble just the slightest, a thin trickle of blood, the rubber-hose-pinched-skin, the ecstasy on the face. The face was undeniably familiar.

"Zeek," I said.

"Yeah." Flash didn't look too happy. He flipped the page over. Zeek again, on the telephone, naked from the waist up, having what appeared to be a lively conversation. Faint track marks could just be made out in the crook of his arm.

"Zeek's pissed," Flash said, "that we don't have a phone. He makes a lot of pretend calls: to the Easter Bunny, President Ford, the Dukes of Hazard..."

"Dukes of Hazard?"

"Television?"

"Oh."

"Sometimes he pretends to call members of his family. That usually gets pretty weird." Flash turned to the next page; a woman stood naked with her hips turned slightly sideways and her torso facing forward. Her fingertips lightly touched her breasts. I studied the picture awhile, the seductive look on her face, the realistic details and imperfections of her not overly opulent breasts, the way she touched them, the inviting manner even in how her legs were posed. Plenty of gay men enjoy a woman's beauty and sensuality, in a purely aesthetic sense I guess, but there was no way this picture could have been drawn by someone who didn't thoroughly appreciate a woman's sexuality. "You're bisexual," I said looking up at Flash.

"So are you."

I stared at him, appreciative. "How did you know?"

He shrugged. "It takes one to know one." Then running his fingers through my hair he cupped his hand at the back of my head, brought me towards him. Coming up for a breath, moments later, he said, "Do you have any idea just how square you are, Jim?"

I laughed, hard. He put a quick end to that by pressing his mouth into mine again.

When he fucked me, he looked into my eyes. I saw total joy on his face, as if the process that led up to coming inside me was the only thing that existed in the universe. Just as he so completely managed to encompass his tall body, just as he managed to put himself so completely into his art, Flash now was completely immersed in the act of sodomizing me. It was clear that he knew exactly who he was with at that moment, and that it mattered. He fucked intensely, groaning loudly with each thrust. I found myself moaning deeply in response, more turned on by his pleasure than my own. There were other people in the house now. I heard footsteps, quiet short laughter, and a name being shouted at full volume, "Louanna!" a proclamation of sorts, Zeek's hoarse voice.

****

A couple of weeks later, I saw Flash across the street as I was coming out of the produce store on Haight. He was walking slowly, and — I was shocked to see — a bit hunched over.

"Flash!"

He smiled and waited for me, but the smile disappeared quickly as we headed down the street together. Eventually Flash said, "I'm moving to Berkeley." I waited for him to say more. As we passed a vintage clothing store he told me, "When Zeek first started using I didn't want to say anything. Didn't want to tell him how to run his life. *That* was a *big* fucking mistake." He stopped and leaned against a light post. "Zeek's an addict."

Flash looked far down the street. "Life with a junkie is fucked." Then turning back to me, he added, "The worst part is..." he searched my eyes for understanding, "The worst part is, every time I see Zeek's bliss after he shoots up, I'm envious. I want to be there too. I want to be there with Zeek."

I nodded.

"I've got to get away. Now. I have a couple of friends I can crash with for a while." Then he said, "I love Zeek. A lot. I've been in love with him for four years."

I felt awful, couldn't help but think of Rick and I. "Maybe Zeek will clean up eventually," I offered, wanting to grasp onto some hope.

"Maybe." He sounded doubtful. "Do you want to come over for a while?"

He didn't seem to really want this, so I told him the truth, that I was on my way to class. "I'll stop by tonight," I suggested, somehow understanding that once he left San Francisco I wouldn't ever see him again.

"I'll be saying good-bye to Zeek tonight."

So Flash and I said our good-byes at the corner of Haight and Cole. Seeing the sadness in his eyes, I felt a great urge to kiss him. But I thought, I can't do that, Derek... Carol... Then I thought, what the hell's wrong with me? I moved to him, kissed him long and lovingly.

"Good luck," I said, as a final farewell, when we parted.

"Thanks," Flashed winked. "*You too.*" Then he turned and headed down the street.

****

When I got back to school after saying good-bye to Flash, Derek was all upbeat. "Hey, Jim!"

"Hi."

"What's the matter?"

I stared at him hard and long. "Nothing." I sat down, scowling at the top of my desk.

"Are you pissed about something?"

"No." Then, "Yes." Then, "No." Finally, as the professor came in, I said, "I just need to work through something."

After class, I told Derek I was going to skip our between-classes coffee and take a bike ride, clear my head.

I rode up the Great Highway, along the Pacific, until I came to the remnants of the Sutro Bath House. I found a good spot at the edge of the cliff and sat looking at the ruins and the ocean. Eventually I convinced myself I should be happy. Happy that Flash had enough sense to not fuck up his life. I found a smile somewhere, my pocket, under a rock, somewhere, and talked my face into not rejecting it.

If I ever see Flash again, I'll ask for one of his sketches. Anyone would do. It could be of a turtle. But one of a woman would be ideal.

****

As the weeks rolled on, I found I thought less and less about my hypocrisy, less and less about my duplicity. I concentrated on Derek, school, Carol. But there was still always an underlying current of self-loathing at being a closet-case, and a subterranean hatred towards Derek and Carol for being homophobes. Additionally, I began to notice another feeling gathering momentum. As the friendship between Derek and I solidified, began to take a strong hold on both of us, I couldn't help but feel I was betraying that friendship by hiding so much of who I was from him. There were so many times that I directly and indirectly lied to him, yet I wouldn't think twice about asking Derek to hold on to a million dollars for me. I knew he'd trust me with his life if it came down to it. So when I told him I was tired because the neighbors had gotten into 3am fight again, when in actuality I was exhausted from cruising the bars and having sex with men several nights a week, I felt as if I were despoiling something sacred. In companion with this guilt, of course, grew my anger towards Derek. If I was being a lousy friend by withholding the fact of my queerness from him, what kind of friend was he (as Flash had asked), whom had made it clear that knowledge of my gay-side would cause him to reject me with the utmost efficiency and disgust? But in time these feelings too became concealed under blankets of denial, only coming through like the annoying hum of an appliance. Come out to him? Sure someday. Usually, I was able to dismiss such thoughts rapidly, as if this concern actually belonged to someone else, and I needn't let it interfere with my happy existence.

****

After having taken all our spring classes together, Derek and I signed up for a couple of summer courses at City College. On a Friday morning, about a week before summer school was scheduled to start, I met him for coffee in the Mission district. Derek always seemed especially comfortable at this coffeehouse where the walls were lined with rows and rows of books. Across the street was a historic movie house where he and I'd once seen Herzog's, *Aguirre The Wrath of God*. Next to the theater was a great health food co-op squeezed into the space of an alleyway. Carol sometimes bought obscure items there for something exotic she was planning to cook, like seaweed for sushi, or bulgur for tabouli. On the corner of the block was a small bar with a pool table in the back where Derek and I'd gone for beer and a game on several occasions.

Derek sat back now with one black boot resting on the crossbar of the chair opposite him, taking macho sips of his still way-too-hot coffee. In a moment one of us would get up to start examining books, and the other would follow.

I almost ordered a cappuccino just to unnerve Derek, but I really just wanted a good old cup of something warm and substantial, and Derek was in such an up mood that I thought it would be a shame to go and spoil it by doing something totally frou-frou. Anyway, I had an image to protect.

"Wanna do bowling tonight?" My coffee sat untouched in front of me; burning my tongue was a bit too far to go to prove my masculinity.

He answered with a grin. "Not tonight."

He wasn't going to say more, but it was clear from his expression that there was more to say. It was this kind of inability to open up that really bugged me about Derek. I wanted to say, "*What?* Just tell me; don't be such a controlled son of a..." But, *I* too was playing the he-man game, so I just sat there looking disinterested, and then told him about the chopped Harley I'd seen on Haight that morning. I'd liked the airbrushed painting on the gas tank — a sexy woman in a desert setting — and described this for him. Nice safe topic between buddies.

Later that night, I got picked up at a bar on Castro by a well-dressed good-looking man in his early thirties, who told me he was an investment banker. In a powder-blue BMW convertible, he drove us to his place atop Russian Hill. After he'd had his way with me — as I leaned over the railing in a dark corner of his porch, which had a magnificent view of the city — he asked if I'd spend the weekend with him. I was fine with the idea, seeing as how I didn't have much else to do — Carol was out of town, Derek, for mysterious reasons, was unavailable. And, yeah, I always hoped that one day a pick-up would turn into something a bit more substantial. But while the investment banker and I got along well enough for a sex-filled weekend together, there didn't seem to be a basis for us to connect on a deeper level. That was just as well, because I was uncomfortable with the fact that he was a "top" only. I ran into this plenty in the bars — guys who have roll-playing fetishes. Normally this didn't bug me much because with a one-night-stand, if a guy only wants to be fucked, or only wants to be the one doing the fucking, it's no big deal. But I couldn't sustain a long-term relationship with someone who, sexually speaking, wasn't more interested in simply enjoying one another, and going with wherever that led, rather than following some dominant-submissive script. Hell, I didn't even play that kind of a game when I was having heterosexual sex. The idea of a totally submissive woman sounded about as exciting as macaroni and cheese. Meanwhile, I spent the weekend lost in this guy's world, gladly, repeatedly, allowing him to enter me, wondering more each time if being a top only, might not have a lot to do with homophobia.

When he told me his coming out story, recounting, over Veuve Clicquot and raspberry tarts, how he tried to convince himself for a long time that he was bisexual and thus not wholly deviant, I listened mutely. When he said he finally accepted that he was gay, I wanted to tell him that I had not had any problems accepting my homosexuality, but the fact that I'd pretty much always been a closet-case made this seem like a ridiculous thing to say. I knew too, if I told him I was bi, he'd laugh knowingly, thinking himself superior for having gone beyond this "juvenile phase" of coming out to one's self.

Chapter Seventeen

I found out what was going on with Derek about two weeks later. We'd gone over to his apartment after our morning class at City College. We were taking Logic — a required course for all students at State — from a former actor who paced the width of the classroom bellowing out his lectures as if they were Shakespearean. Despite his antics, he was a good teacher, and the subject matter totally turned us on. We were now sitting at Derek's 50s vintage kitchen table, happily pouring over our battered used textbooks, when the phone rang. It was clear from the quiet shyness with which Derek talked to the caller, that there was a woman on the other end. I'd never seen Derek like this before, and it made me uncomfortable even though I couldn't hear what he was saying since he'd gone into the bedroom. In any case, he cut the call short. When he came and sat back down, I raised my eyebrows questioningly.

"Alice," he said.

"Alice," I responded.

"She works for an accountant, downtown."

Realizing that this was supposed to explain everything, I said, "Oh." Derek then went back to the extremely complex if/then sequence we'd been in the middle of when the phone had rung. I'd been looking it over while he was speaking to Alice, and it blew me away how he was able to step right back into it without any apparent thought.

****

I drew a diagram of a particle under stress. The sketch came quickly, out of nowhere. This was a few hours after the Alice phone call. When we'd finished our homework and the inevitable accompanying intellectual banter, I'd left Derek's, telling him I had to get to the bank before it closed. The truth was, I badly needed sleep. But I ended up popping into A Kiss of Heaven for a cup on the way home. The cafe was quiet — me, Bill, some anonymous soul in the back making homey kitchen sounds, and a young woman heavily engrossed in a volume of sheet music.

Coffee is sometimes merely a drink, sometimes it's mostly warmth, often it's clearly a drug, and then there are days such as this one, when coffee is just a simple pleasure. I'd been happily nursing a ceramic mug in the back room, when the crisp white pages I'd bought that morning to type a report on, called out to me and I began sketching the particle diagram. When I was finished, I stared at it, picked up my pencil and scribbled, "ME" on the trembling particle about to break apart and loose itself to otherness. I hastily tore up the drawing and dashed out of the cafe.

Once home, I collapsed and the bed, and slept until midnight. I awoke with an intense desire to commit the act of fellatio, and headed for Castro.

****

A month later, I finally met Alice. Derek had asked me to stop by his place to help move in a new desk, and Alice was there with him when I arrived. She was friendly towards me, but the friendliness seemed to be of the sort that comes from force-of-habit, friendly because friendly is what one is supposed to do, not what one necessarily feels like doing. She was pretty in a very ordinary way, simple inoffensive face, long straight dark hair, much like Derek's. She would really be *quite* pretty if it weren't for the resigned vague animosity that came across in her expressions despite the attempt at friendliness. It dawned on me through the course of the desk moving and placement, that the resigned look was a permanent feature, while the vague animosity was a reaction to me in particular.

Later, when Derek and I were having coffee at Cafe Trastevere in North Beach, I said, jokingly, awkwardly, "What horrible things did you tell her about me?"

"Who?"

"Alice."

Derek smiled. "She doesn't like you."

"She just met me."

Derek took a bite out of a slice of lemon cake. Talking with his mouthful he said, "She thinks I spend too much time with you."

Inexplicably embarrassed by this, I got up to get a refill on my coffee. We talked football when I got back to the table.

****

Alice and I rarely crossed paths, and Derek talked about her only incidentally: "I'll be at Alice's tonight," in response to, "I'll give you a call later," or, in the hallway before class, "Alice's boss said there's a good act at Cafe Some Place Else this weekend." Derek and I had recently discovered stand-up comedy, which became a brief obsession for us. Brief because of all the gay oriented jokes. I always worried I'd laugh in the wrong way at the wrong joke. Derek, I noticed, usually found some way to not even hear these jokes. He'd get up to order us another round of drafts, or whisper to me about a cute chick at the next table. One day after class when Derek was waiting for me to finish stuffing my books into my backpack, I asked if he knew who was going to be at Some Place Else that Friday.

"Some fag."

I looked up at him angrily.

"What?" he asked.

"Nothing," I responded with a great deal of acrimony.

He looked back at me, frowning, grasping to comprehend, and I became fretful that I'd blown it, blown my cover, and this fear rapidly grew to where it was larger than my anger, and I two-stepped it quickly, corrected the look on my face. "Oh, I thought I'd left my chemistry notebook somewhere, but it's right here." I pulled out the black spiral book to show him. "Coffee?"

****

Carol took me to eat at Le Bigamist, a Vietnamese restaurant on Haight that one of her City College friends had told her about. The restaurant's name came from a fantastic story involving a cow, a duck, and a goat, or an ox, a cat, and a pig — some unlikely barnyard triad. I glanced at the menu briefly, then looked around the large semi-darkened room. Bill, I discovered, sat across the way, his hand entwined with that of a very pretty, sever-looking, woman in her early fifties. She was draped in a multitude of fabrics and colors, her wrists and neck ornamented with assorted beads and tiny silver bells. Bill and I noted one another, briefly studied each other's girlfriends, then exchanged smiles. When they got up to leave a bit later, Bill and I waved friendly good-byes. I explained to Carol's questioning look that he worked at the coffeehouse down the road.

I saw Bill with the same woman only once more, months later, strolling hand in hand through Golden Gate Park near the arboretum. I ran into him at HUNKS that same night, and approached him as he stood in a corner sipping on his Cruzan and soda.

"Saw you in the park today," I said, cold Heineken in hand.

"Nice day for a walk."

"Yeah it was." I had actually been on my way to a handball game.

Bill and I watched the dancers silently for a long time. Much later I noticed him walk out with a tall hefty bald guy in biker's leather garb, whom I'd seen him with at HUNKS on several other occasions.

****

"Uggh!" I awoke with a start one morning after Derek and I had studied late into the night.

Slowly I replayed the nightmare I'd woken from: I was in the S.F. State campus bookstore; Derek had just driven off, to be with Alice. I approached the section that contained the Human Sexual Studies books. I took down *The Philosophy of Sex*, and started leafing through it. As unannounced as the Cheshire cat, someone was standing next to me. "I'll be your professor for that class."

Alarmed, I looked up at a handsome guy who seemed too young to be a professor. "Oh I'm not taking the class, just thought the book looked interesting."

"Why not take the class?"

He was gay; it dawned on me. "Ah... it's complicated," I stuttered.

"The class? Or the reason why you don't want to take it?" He smiled a beautiful smile.

I smiled back. "The reason why I don't want to take it."

"Maybe it's just as well." He stuck out his hand. "My name's Tim. I saw you once at the Dancing Flamingo on Polk Street; I stayed clear because I'd also noticed you on campus and I figured, what if you wanted to take a class from me some time? But now that we've gotten that out of the way..." beautiful smile again. "Join me for coffee in the cafeteria?"

I was so filled with desire to have coffee with this man, and so filled with terror at the idea of having coffee with him in the school cafeteria — the same cafeteria where Derek and I had coffee daily — even though I knew Derek was nowhere near campus.

He laughed, apparently at the expression on my face. "*What?*"

"I can't." I was startled to hear myself say these words, because when I'd opened my mouth I'd fully intended to say, "I'd love to." Enough was enough, I'd thought, to hell with Derek and all this closet shit.

"You *can't?*"

Horrified, I said, "Sorry." Then I put the book down and ran out of the bookstore without looking back.

I rubbed my forehead with my fingertips now. Only a dream... Only a dream... No. Not only a dream. This was, in fact, my life! I went into the bathroom, looked at myself in the mirror. "What the fuck is wrong with you?" My reflection stared pathetically back at me.

****

I was lying on Carol's queen size bed in her spacious airy apartment. She had a lot of peach and pale blue colors, which gave the room a certain sort of refreshing quality. The sort of refreshing that's great for a temporary change of pace, but which I sensed I'd find suffocating after an extended stay (which never happened, so I can't be quite sure). It was early evening, and we'd just had a wild romp on the bed. She'd called from the airport, having returned from a business trip. "Jim, meet me at my place," in her sexiest voice. When I'd arrived, I found her removing diamond stud earrings, silk stockings, and an outrageous pink-grapefruit linen business suit. We'd been frantic with each other. Now all was quiet, she lay peacefully, silently, next to me. I stroked the cat, which slept on my bare chest, and admired its ugliness. Then Carol got up and started walking around, and I admired her naked beauty instead; she really did have a killer body.

She went into the kitchen and I heard her put coffee on for us, then she came back into the bedroom and brushed her hair. After that, she started looking through drawers. She worked her way through the dresser, then went to the closet. Finally she came back to the bed with a small box and opened it.

"I made this in high school, but it never fit. It's too big for me. Maybe it'll fit you." She held up a wide brass ring. Etched into a flat surface was a series of connecting V's. With the power of an archetypal image, the ring stirred something within me. Carol took it out of the box, tried it on my right ring finger. Too small. She tried it on my pinkie. Perfect.

A pinkie ring! How apropos.

"It's perfect," I told her.

Derek noticed the ring right away the next day, and admired it enthusiastically. Everyone admired it: the produce store clerk, the bank teller, Bill at A Kiss of Heaven, Danny at HUNKS. I should have realized then that the ring was not going to play an innocuous role in my life, but if there was something ominous about the way people noticed it, this escaped me at the time, and I proceeded to wear it night and day, every day.

Chapter Eighteen

Somewhere during our second semester together, Derek and I became known in the physics department as the "Jim and Derek Team" — a result of the facts that we: took all our classes together, nearly always got the highest grades on tests, always sat front-and-middle, and had a tendency to challenge our professors with insightful questions. Thus it was, that we were in our physics III class on the first day of our junior year, and the professor, a Mr. Kline, whom we knew of, but had never met, walked up to me, stuck out his hand and said, "Derek, right?"

"Not quite." I shook his hand.

"Jim then. Privileged to meet you." He turned to Derek said, "Derek," nodded his head in a little bow, and shook my buddy's hand. Then, standing in front of the chalkboard, he announced to everyone, "It promises to be an interesting class; we've got the Jim and Derek Team with us."

The guy who'd sat down on the other side of me laughed softly in disbelief at the spectacle. I'd noticed him as he'd walked into the room and passed in front of Derek, and then me, to take his seat. He had short dark hair, was maybe five-foot-eight or so, and though he wasn't particularly attractive, he wasn't unattractive either, and though he had all the trappings of a straight man, I was aware that on some vague unidentifiable level he appealed to me. I'd been aware of this, and then dismissed it as pointless. When he made that breathy laugh in response to the teacher's announcement, I turned to face him.

He raised his eyebrows and whispered, with a slight chuckle, "Jim and Derek Team?"

I smiled, then looked back to focus on what Mr. Kline was revealing on the chalkboard. When the bell rang, the guy next to me left quickly, but the next time the class met, he arrived early and approached Derek and I where we were standing in the hall. We looked at him quizzically.

He got an amused look on his face and said, "I already know your names. I'm Jeff."

During a brief exchange of information, in which Derek and I awkwardly attempted to explain the "Jim and Derek Team," we found out Jeff was an electrical engineering student who'd just relocated from Cambridge, Massachusetts.

****

A few days later, Derek and I were indulging our caffeine habit at the Student Union and going off on a bizarre tangent relating to electrical reactions on the subatomic level, when we saw Jeff walking across the other side of the room, and decided to snag him in hopes of picking his brain. An electrical engineering major might know a thing or two that we didn't.

Jeff was well versed in his field but, in the end, he picked our brains more than we did his; Jeff, it turned out, was fascinated by physics. When it was time for Derek and me to get to our next class, Jeff accepted an invitation from Derek to join us for studying that night at my place. This became a regular habit. Sometimes Jeff showed up even when we were going over notes from a class unrelated to his studies. He could usually keep up with us for a while, but eventually we'd lose him. He'd stay on a bit, seeming to enjoy just sitting and listening to us banter, though, as late night dipped into early morning, he'd get up and say something along the lines of, "I think I'll go touch base with what the rest of the world sees as reality."

One night when Jeff left, Derek, taking advantage of the break in our studies, went to the john, and I got up and crossed to my window to watch Jeff drive off in his funny little green hatchback. Something about him made me recall how I felt when I first arrived in San Francisco. It struck me that he'd probably left Cambridge running away from reminders of a girlfriend he'd recently split up with.

****

Carol's time was mostly spent on work and work related matters. What little time was left over was more or less divided evenly between City College classes (technically this should go under work related matters), the friends she made at City College, me, and a combined category called "cat and time to myself." So, it had been a while since I'd seen her, when an evening with Derek, Jeff, and books, at my place was interrupted by a phone call from Carol.

"I have a pot of black bean soup."

"Hi Carol."

"Are you hungry?"

I looked at Derek and Jeff. "Black bean soup?"

Derek nodded enthusiastically; he was always in for Carol's food. Jeff, clearly not sure what was going on, signaled his approval.

"Everybody's hungry," I told Carol.

"Everybody?"

"Me, Derek, and one more — guy named Jeff."

"Oh good; there's lots!"

"Is she Cuban?" I inquired.

"Brazilian actually."

Carol befriended an apparently endless stream of women she met at City College, new transplants from an array of different countries. She collected them like postage stamps — the more exotic the better — and always, or nearly, these women were great cooks. Carol would take them shopping for ingredients — Chinatown, Japantown, Mission district, wherever they needed to go. Then back to her apartment and brew up some amazing concoction. Often I was the beneficiary.

"My girlfriend," I'd explained to Jeff after I'd hung up. He'd smiled, rather lamely, and nodded. He looked preoccupied and was quiet until the food arrived.

Carol came bustling in, much in the same manner as she had that first night we'd slept together. She held a shopping bag containing sour cream, cheddar cheese, chopped onion, and Brazilian hot sauce. She handed me her keys, and I went down to her car to get the huge pot of soup. When I got back upstairs, Jeff and Carol were chatting and laughing together as if they'd been buddies for ten years and running. I looked at Derek; he shrugged. They talked about Cambridge — Carol had never been there, but she had this girlfriend at City College who... It turned out, also, that Jeff had once had a summer job in a personnel office screening applicants. Somehow they got around to politics, something that both of them found fascinating (I hadn't known this about Carol) and on and on. Jeff even recognized Carol's scarf as the work of a particular Italian designer. "I had a friend who was in the fashion business," he explained.

Derek and I sat through the whole meal talking only when an occasional question or comment was thrown in our direction. Mostly we watched them, as if watching TV. It was rather entertaining.

****

Derek and I were served pizza by a gay waiter at Your Every Desire, on Haight. Derek always shifted uncomfortably in his seat after a gay server approached our table, but other than an occasional mocking of excessively nelly behavior, done in a subtle, almost subconscious manner, he rarely responded with much else anymore. I think he'd finally gotten the message that I wasn't into queer bashing.

After we ate, we played a couple of games of pool at Lucky Paul's with, what Derek liked to call, "Real Bikers" — guys who had tattoos, scraggly beards, and big guts. Our game blew them away. Another time, months earlier, when this had happened, one of the Real Bikers had said, as we were on our way out, entirely jokingly, I'm sure, "You're not bad for a couple of fairies." The whole gang of them laughed uproariously. I'd shrugged it off — our superior pool playing had insulted their masculinity, so they had to insult ours. But Derek's whole body tensed. I got the impression, from the look on his face, that if these guys hadn't been the types to certainly have knives up their sleeves, or in their boots — somewhere — he would have turned around and punched one of them in the nose, and taken from the others a broken rib or two and a black eye in the bargain. Derek had been icy towards me the following couple of days, made it a point to be occupied with Alice after school, rode off campus during lunch, and went to the library instead of having coffee with me. I'd found all this amazing, and disturbing, but hadn't expected for a moment it would last, and it hadn't.

On this night, after the pizza, this particular group of Real Bikers treated us like Real Men, telling us horrendously misogynous jokes, which Derek actually laughed at, although he turned and made disgusted faces in my direction. They talked bike talk with us, and billiard talk, and then one guy, who'd told us his name was Zip, got all excited, practically started jumping up and down when we told him we were physics majors. He was a good six-foot-four, and instead of having an exceedingly large girth like most of his peers, he was grotesquely thin. His nose was big and bulbous, and his skin was over-run with speed-freak pockmarks. A beautiful tattoo of a cheetah ran the length of one forearm. With great enthusiasm, Zip got into an intensely philosophical conversation with us about the parallels between advanced physics and theological theory. His ramblings included an amazing amount of scientific knowledge interspersed with LSD induced understandings about it "IT ALL," as he kept saying, and Zen Buddhist teachings mixed with a quasi-schizophrenic view of what the New and Old Testaments are "*really*" all about.

When we left, our heads reeled as much from the secondhand smoke as from the surprisingly insightful ideas this guy had thrown at us — what we were able to decipher out of all the chaos coming out of his mouth.

"Fitting," Derek said, "chaos."

"He took it far considering the total absence of math."

The night seemed unusually dark. We walked several blocks towards the park end of Haight, deftly dodging groups of loitering freaks of one kind or another — potheads, skin heads, nuvo yuppies... The two of us in black, our boots thudded softly on the gum and spit littered sidewalk. We got occasional glances from both women and men, some out of curious desire, some — from certain elements of the freaks — clearly hostile. We ignored it all, our thoughts out in the Universe. When we approached the Night Cat, our minds were still not quiet in the here and now. But entering the club quickly forced us back.

A new wave band was jumping around spasmodically on the stage, blasting out emotionally ripping guitar lashes, and banging out the equivalent of primal screams on an abused-looking set of drums. The bassist was lost in an orgasmic trance, as he appeared to fuck the hell out of his obviously loved instrument. We eked out a space at the bar and stood observing. Conversation was entirely out of the question. There were two men dancing together not too far from us, looking as weirded-out as all the hetero couples. Following Derek's lead, I systematically avoided looking in their direction.

I spotted a guy, dancing by the far wall, with blond spikes for hair. I thought it might be Zeek, but it was too hard to tell from across the dark, smoky, room. Eventually, I used the excuse of having to get to the men's room as a way of getting a better look. It wasn't him, the face was all wrong. The guy stuck his tongue out at me, like a bratty little kid, when he realized I was looking at him. He had a nice tongue; I was tempted to tell him so.

Soon as I entered the restroom, another guy, who'd tried to catch my eye just outside the door, popped in, hovered vaguely to my left for a moment, and then slowly washed his hands. I made a point of pretending he wasn't there. I wondered if Derek ever caught on to these subtle overtures or if, more likely, his extreme body language warned these guys off. I thought then that perhaps it was *because* these kinds of possibilities exist in the city that Derek had adopted such excessive posturing.

I'd had a draft with the pizza, two long neck Buds at Lucky Paul's, a Bass Ale at Night Cat, and later, I was three quarters the way through a Heineken at HUNKS, when a young male-female couple walked in and stood next to me at the bar. The five beers had been over several hours, but still it was more than I was used to, and I had a bit of a buzz going. The man had a dreamy, dark, mustache and a long, curly, ponytail. The woman, a pretty blonde, wore a tight sweater that showed off enticing, small breasts. They stood very close together at the bar and seemed to be filled with a spooky sort of joy for existence. Projection, I thought, I'm drunk.

Danny approached them, and winked. He held up three fingers, and with the index finger of his other hand, pointed first to the man, then the woman, then himself, raised his eyebrows, and nodded enthusiastically. The couple laughed happily at the proposition, but seemed to know Danny well enough not to take it seriously.

"Hey," he shouted above the din, "you two've been holding out on me!"

They smiled angelically back.

I found this scenario excessively funny and after a good loud laugh (which scored a wink from Danny), I walked away from the bar shaking my head and went to look at the men dancing.

Standing in a corner, I was approached by several guys, one after the other, as though I were in a receiving line. The first was totally inebriated and actually fell on top of me. I, not so gently, pushed him off and away. The second had psycho written all over his face — glazed hungry eyes, and a crooked luring smile that scared the hell out of me. I glared at him and said slowly, "I'm not your type." He stared at me a moment, and then, apparently unable to think-up a good comeback, slinked away. The third guy poured out lines like, "This is my first time; be gentle with me and I'll do anything to please you." I ignored him, but he persisted. Finally I said, point blank, "I'm straight."

"The *hell* you are!"

I liked that; it cheered me considerably. I patted him on the shoulder and said, "You're right, and you're a good boy. But I can't be your daddy. You're probably older than me anyway." He pulled his shoulder away defiantly and marched off.

I went home alone, thankful that none of these guys had gotten ugly when I failed to respond positively to their advances. I wasn't disappointed to be going home by myself. Sometimes, it seemed, I went to the bars more to give expression to my gay self than to necessarily get laid. I was tired anyway; it'd been a long day.

****

On a Tuesday night, about seven weeks into the semester, Carol was on an extended business trip to Milwaukee, and Derek was helping Professor Kline with a lab class. I was home alone, trying to take advantage of the chance to get my apartment into some semblance of order. But the fact that I hadn't bothered to go get pumped up on Java juice before attempting this task, struck me as a terrible mistake. But that thought itself was a terrible mistake. A memory of Rick and I cleaning our basement hide-away while buzzed out on caffeine — Rick tossing musty towels at me and laughing at my exaggerated disgust — tried to sneak in, but I shoved it back hard and fast.

Falling into a somber mood, I sat cross-legged on the floor sorting through a pile of gay newspapers that I kept buried in a dark place in the back of my closet, as if they were pornographic. I gathered up the papers periodically and took them, along with my copies of the San Francisco Chronicle (these were in open view), to the recycling center down on Lincoln. The act of pulling paraphernalia from my gay world out of the closet sunk me further into the glooms. I was looking at a front-page photograph of Sister Mish, of the Sisters of Perpetual Indulgence, flaunting her pride, when the phone rang.

"Hello?" I answered, suspiciously.

"Jim, it's Jeff. I'm not getting this differentials stuff; can I come over?"

I glanced at my black trash bag of inversion newspapers. He doesn't get differentials? It seemed to me that he understood the concept perfectly well when we'd all gone over it last night. "O... kay," I answered Jeff, rather doubtful. Really it wasn't okay. I wanted to be left alone to wallow in self-pity and the chaos of my material world.

After I hung up, I slowly stuffed the stack of Bay Area Reporters back into the bag, and stashed them safely where they could do me no harm. Hell, I thought, it's a good thing Jeff was coming over, otherwise who knew what depths this night would have sunk me into. I folded a pile of laundry, re-shelved a few books. Yeah, Jeff was good company. I liked Jeff. So, by the time he arrived, I was actually quite happy to see him.

But Jeff did not greet me back with the same enthusiastic smile. Well, okay, Jeff wasn't exactly the most chipper person on the planet. But no, this wasn't the usual serious, quiet, Jeff. He seemed edgy, uncharacteristically uncomfortable, said only a monotone, "Hi," with shifty eyes — odd in response to my happy, "Hey Buddy!"

He immediately sat down on the couch, his posture tense. While I re-bolted the door, it occurred to me that Jeff and I had never been alone before. I sat on the couch next to him and opened the textbook in front of us on the coffee table. "How's it going?" I ventured.

"Okay." He did not look at me.

"Do you want a beer? Or some water?"

"No."

Jeff's obvious discomfort was making me nervous. I figured let's just get to the books. I pointed to a graph I was sure he'd comprehended last night, and started to go over it. But he wasn't listing to me, wasn't paying the slightest bit of attention to the graph. I stopped, mid-sentence, looked at him. He looked back at me, directly into my eyes. Hazel staring into brown.

"What's up?" I said finally, getting a bit peeved.

"I like your ring." He pointed at my pinkie.

I looked at the ring, realizing the copper needed polishing. He likes my ring? I frowned at him.

"It caught my attention the first time I saw it," then he added, very deliberately, "three months ago."

Now I knew something was wrong, very wrong. My heart was beating too fast. "Classes only started two months ago," I offered hopefully.

"Yeah, that's about right." Then, again looking right in my eyes, he added, "That was the *second* time I saw your ring."

We stared at one another for far too long. I searched his face for a clue. Why were we talking about my ring? *What* was going on here?

"The first time," he said calmly, "was at HUNKS." Then to spell it out perfectly for me, he added, "Some guy was hanging all over you."

HUNKS. When two worlds, kept apart for so long, suddenly come colliding... I could not reconcile that *Jeff* was in my apartment speaking *this* word to me. All I could register was that my closet doors had suddenly been blown wide open. Anything else that Jeff's comments implied escaped me for the moment. I was overwhelmed by a quick surge of horror, and then panic — adrenaline rush, urge to flee, the whole bit. I'm searching for some place to hide, and the feeling is too reminiscent, too reminiscent.

"Are you gay, Jim?" Jeff's voice came across so sane and smooth in contrast to the crisis going on in my head.

Then it dawned on me. What was Jeff doing at HUNKS? I stood up. "What about you?"

"I'm gay." There was no hesitation.

I walked to the window, stared blankly at the street below. I was trembling. He knows Derek and Carol, is *friends* with them.

I turned around and said, "I didn't know."

"Now you do."

"I'm bi." A heat, a kind of gentle fire, came over me as these words, unspoken for far too long, finally met their freedom.

Jeff watched me, must have seen the relief, the joy even, that came into my eyes. But then he said, "Derek and Carol don't know, do they?"

Hearing Jeff utter these two names at this moment... My jaws locked, my fists clenched, my stare pierced through him.

Jeff's eyes widened. Clearly taken aback, he responded quickly, "Whoa... Hey, I don't appreciate you being closeted, but I'm not in the habit of outing people."

I stood my ground for a moment trying to determine if I could trust him. Then I realized, of course I could. I let out all the air I hadn't realized I was holding in, and swallowed hard. My heartbeat began slowing back towards normal.

I found though, that I now could not look at Jeff. I turned around and faced the window again, slunk my hands into my pockets. A moment ago I had felt large and powerful, ready to tear Jeff into pieces if necessary. Now I felt small, deflated. A new feeling had rushed in to take over where the protective fear had been — shame, utter unrelenting shame. It had been a good while now that I'd been leading a double life. The sense of things not being right, the sense of self-disgust and frustration, these feelings were contained in a small box in the back of my mind. I was continually aware of this box's existence, aware of its contents, but though every day its existence ate at my psyche, I rarely felt the full intensity of the impact it had on me. I'm a closet-case; I lead a double life; I find my behavior despicable; yes, yes, but life goes on. Now here I was, confronted with the truth about myself in a way that forced me to deal with it head on. There was a man, a gay man, a friend of mine, sitting in my living room, and he knows what a two faced, lying, hypocrite I am. And there's no way he could possibly realize that I do, in fact, embrace my homosexuality. Yes, I felt small, and unbearably embarrassed.

I heard Jeff's voice behind me, from the couch, very quiet, "Do you want me to leave?"

I turned to face him.

I did not see the disgust and pity in his eyes that I had expected. There was something else there entirely. Something surprising. Yet... now that I thought about it, not all that surprising. It brought back a feeling I'd done a good job of repressing — my initial reaction to Jeff when I saw him that first day of class.

Very carefully, because I was still reeling from all that had just transpired, I asked, knowing that I already knew the answer, "Was your purpose in coming over here tonight to confront me with my duplicity?"

He responded with a soft, "No." Then Jeff got up and walked slowly towards me until he was about two feet away. "Now do you want me to leave?"

Jeff was standing so close. His face, not a beautiful face, his nose a touch too big, his eyes and mouth too plain, too ordinary, but yet the way they all came together, or perhaps how he presented himself to the world.

I answered him with a kiss.

Chapter Nineteen

Derek, Jeff, and I were winding down from what had ostensibly started off as a study session, but had rapidly disintegrated into a bullshit session. Our background music was the muffled sound of a steady torrent of rain. We'd been waiting for the weather to clear so we could go get something to eat, but it hadn't let up. A discussion, about whether to have pizza or Chinese food delivered, was interrupted by the phone.

Carol's voice on its natural high — she'd been making curried chicken all evening with a woman from Guyana — "So I'll bring some over?"

Just one problem. If Carol came over, she'd expect to spend the night, but Jeff was expecting me to show up at his place after Derek went home. I had to think fast. If I told Carol I'd already eaten and then didn't suggest she come over anyway, that would be the end of that, but how could I lie about having already eaten when Derek was sitting right there?

Trying to buy time, I said quietly into the phone, almost as a whisper, totally disbelieving, "Curried chicken?"

"You like curry."

"Yes," I paused, then threw out, hopefully, "Derek and Jeff are here."

"Great! There's plenty of sauce; I'll defrost more chicken."

"Oh, you don't need to go through all that!"

"All what? Opening the freezer, popping it in the microwave? Don't be silly. I'll come over in twenty minutes."

Feeling inane and helpless, I looked at Derek and Jeff. "Curried chicken?" I tried to make it sound as unappealing as possible.

Derek's eyes lit up enthusiastically, like those of a puppy being offered a bone. Jeff stared at me, open-mouthed. He knew what this would mean.

"With potatoes," Carol was saying on the other end.

Anger. I felt anger. Anger directed at Carol for not knowing, for being homophobic, for being so damned alluring. Anger at Jeff for doing something that might give us away — what if Derek had seen the look on his face. Anger at Derek for not knowing, for being homophobic, for liking Carol's cooking so much. Then I realized, in an instant, that all that anger was displaced, that I was really angry with myself — really hated myself at that moment.

For the next twenty minutes, I kept trying to mentally will Derek to get up and go to the bathroom so that I could have at least a moment to speak with Jeff alone. I even went so far as to get us all a round of water. But Derek didn't touch his, and fifteen minutes later, I was the one who had to pee. I carefully avoided the mirror in the bathroom, didn't want to look at that despicable creature.

But before then, about ten minutes after Carol's call, Jeff started to rise. "I'm gonna head on home."

"You don't want any curry?" Derek couldn't contain his shock.

"No," Jeff said.

"But you were just saying how hungry you are, and you loved the curry you had with Jim and me at that Indian place on Van Ness a couple weeks ago."

Good old unobtrusive Derek. The man of few words just couldn't control himself when it came to someone passing up a good meal.

Jeff looked at me, jaw clenched. I became frightened that he was going to do or say something that Derek just couldn't miss. I quickly gave Jeff pleading eyes, then looked away, deciding suddenly to water my sole houseplant, a coleus with red and pink leaves.

Jeff stayed, spent the time until Carol arrived leafing through an astronomy book I'd purchased all those years ago with my grandfather's money. Once Carol got to my place, she managed rather easily to bring Jeff out of his funk. They got into a discussion about the art teacher she had in high school, and the story behind her making my pinkie ring. I heard very little of the story because, out of nervousness, I'd enthusiastically engaged Derek in a conversation about motorcycles made in Eastern Bloc countries, rattling off statistics I'd read in a gay biker magazine. Some twenty minutes after we ate, Jeff got up, and said he was leaving. Then he asked Derek if he wanted a ride because of the rain; maybe they could stop in North Beach at Shades for a beer.

The prospect of them going drinking together made me uncomfortable. I'd never been around Jeff when he'd had more than a beer or two. What if he and Derek decided to have a few? Would he start to lose control of what he was saying? In order to cover up any possible signs of my anxiety, I ended up saying to Derek, "Yeah, and you can ride the bus over here in the morning to pick up your bike." His Harley was parked safely next to mine in the garage.

Derek nodded in agreement, and rose to join Jeff. It felt oddly disconcerting to watch them walk out the door together, something more than just a fear of disclosure... I sat there momentarily, staring at the door, trying to comprehend... But then I turned my attention towards Carol who had started to clean up. We did the dishes together, then fell into bed.

Sex between Carol and me that evening was as hot as her curry, a fact that annoyed me as I lay awake beside her most of the night.

****

As Carol toweled off from her shower the next morning, I told her to give me more warning when she was going to be bringing over food.

"It's just that I want to be sure it comes out right first," she responded.

"Doesn't it always?"

"Not *always*."

"Well, if it doesn't turn out good we'll go to a restaurant or make spaghetti, whatever. I really don't like last minute calls."

"I didn't realize." She used the towel now to scrub her hair dry. The rest of her stood naked for all the world... no, for only me, to see.

"I'm not mad or anything, just call the day before or something."

"All right, Jim." She kissed my cheek.

Shortly after she left, Derek showed up to get his bike. There was nothing amiss in his behavior; apparently Jeff hadn't done anything to alert him to the deviant nature of our relationship. I was glad it was a Wednesday since Jeff only took Tuesday/Thursday classes, and I wouldn't have to face him publicly before I had a chance to talk to him privately. After classes, and coffee with Derek, I rode over to Jeff's place off of Mission Dolores Park. His apartment consisted of two rooms in a large Victorian house that had been divided into several units.

After discovering that Jeff wasn't home, I crossed over to the park and sat on the small hill opposite his windows. Stroking the closely cropped grass, feeling its coolness, its scratchy stubbiness, all I could think about was how good Jeff was for me and how bad I was for him. His heart had been broken back home — by a guy named Bob. While Jeff had brought a sense of serenity and comfort into my disjointed world, I didn't see how I could ultimately bring him anything but more heartache. I lay back with my hands behind my head. Across a sharp blue

162

sky, wispy white puffs skirted by at a rapid clip. Looking at these clouds was like watching your life spill away from you.

After a while, I started hearing a cup of coffee calling me. But I resisted and, with the sun and a light breeze on my face, let sleep overtake me.

I awoke twenty or so minutes later, sat up slowly, rubbed my eyes, then glanced over at Jeff's place. There he was, standing at his window, looking out at me. I scrambled to my feet and did a half jog over to the apartment.

Sitting at his kitchen table, warming my hands on a cup of coffee he'd had waiting for me, I said, without fanfare, "I'm sorry."

"Don't be." He was very stern.

"Well, I am," I said just as stubbornly.

"I knew what I was getting myself into when I got involved with you."

I didn't have anything to say to that. I sipped my coffee, which felt undeservingly warm and soothing. We sat awhile, Jeff staring out the window, me staring into the blond brown of my drink.

Jeff said, not moving his eyes from the view at first, "You looked beautiful laying out in the park like that." Now he moved his gaze to me.

"How long were you watching me?"

"Maybe fifteen minutes."

I felt a not unpleasant mixture of embarrassment, flattery, and lust. But lurking just beneath these emotions was a subtle yet pervasive sadness. A long silence ensued.

Later, over dinner at a Mexican restaurant, I let Jeff know that I'd told Carol to give me at least a day's warning. He seemed happy about that. Less, I think, about knowing that in the future there wouldn't be those kinds of surprises, than about knowing I'd put some effort into sparing him these situations. He was relieved to see that I cared enough to have made this demand on Carol. Jeff didn't trust my devotion, and my clear understanding that Jeff's doubt was totally justified, served to further depress me.

"Let's go to HUNKS tonight," Jeff suggested as we were finishing up our chili rellenos.

"I thought you didn't like the bars." Jeff had told me that he only went barhopping a few times when he first got to San Francisco to help keep his mind off Bob. Back in Cambridge, he said, he'd only gone to gay bars on rare occasions with groups of friends. I myself hadn't been out in that scene since a couple of nights before Jeff and I first slept together.

"I don't," he confirmed, "but I figure that's one public place where you'll let me touch you."

I'd been pushing grains of rice around my plate with a knife, but now the knife dropped with a clatter; I'd flashed back to the day in "our" Restaurant when I'd asked Rick what God had against homosexuals, a day when I'd felt great anger at not being able to touch my lover in public.

I dashed into the bathroom. Turning the cold water on full blast, I desperately splashed much unwelcome tears out of my eyes.

When I returned, Jeff studied me cautiously. "What happened?"

I shook my head.

He looked hurt.

"Rick," I said, "my first... It was just... a memory." I looked in Jeff's eyes. "Please, I'll tell you about it another time; not now."

"Okay." Jeff understood; he'd been there.

I smiled appreciatively. "Let's have some flan for dessert, then go to HUNKS." Raising my eyebrows hopefully I added, "Will you dance with me?"

****

164

Danny was happy to see me. He winked at Jeff, who I had my arm around, and told him, "Lucky guy."

Jeff did dance with me. We had, actually, a wonderful time. Afterwards, we stopped at the Power Tool, where we stood in a corner and, giggling, pointed out guys, or parts of guys, that turned us on. It was the first time Jeff and I were truly relaxed with each other. Which was sad and telling because we'd been sleeping together regularly for over a month now.

I was at his place again the following evening, and as we lay in bed together, I told him about my family, and Rick. I then explained, as best I could — fumbling all along the way with words that struck me as grossly inadequate — why I wasn't out to Derek and Carol. I realized when I was done that the reasons I'd given for being closeted hadn't made much sense. But Jeff said he understood my pain, so he at least got that out of it. "However, I don't," he added, with a very disapproving tone, "understand your choices. It is *your* life though; I'm not going to pass judgment. But being in a closeted relationship is really rough on me." His eyes got narrow. "Like being trapped in a bizarre nightmare."

"That's a good way to describe it," I said.

Chapter Twenty

I got up and walked with Derek to the door as he was leaving. Derek had gotten used to, by now, the fact that Jeff occasionally fell asleep on my couch with one of my books.

"See ya in class tomorrow," I said, as Derek hoisted his backpack over his shoulders.

"Yeah, all right. Have a good one." He stepped out into the night.

"You too. Watch out for that fog." The street was a thick white.

I watched his black jacket slowly descend, then disappear, down the steps. I locked up, turned around, and smiled at Jeff who'd come back to life. It was a weird feeling: alone at last! There was joy at this, but sorrow and even anger, subdued it. The moment when the door closed behind Derek, and Jeff and I could be ourselves with each other, was such a potent reminder of just how closeted our relationship was. I also resented the implication that Derek was an unwelcome intruder.

I sat down next to Jeff and put my arm across his back. He put his hand on my thigh.

"Someday you're going to have to tell him."

"I know."

"What exactly are you waiting for?"

"That, I don't know." I looked down at a worn spot on the knee of my jeans. "I keep thinking that one morning I'm going to wake up, and I'll just know *that's* the day." I worked my hand under Jeff's collar, caressed his shoulder. "How do you think he'll react?" I'd thought twice before asking this; it was a scary question.

He sighed. "You know him a lot better than I do, but I can't imagine him throwing away your friendship..." Jeff stopped as if he were rethinking what he intended to say, and then eventually in an odd voice added, "You're too important to each other."

Brushing away an alarm of confusion that went off in my head triggered by Jeff's tone, and focusing instead on what Jeff actually said, I responded, "Yeah, I use to think that — you know, when we first met — I thought once Derek and I'd been friends for a long time it would be easier; he'd know me; we'd have been through some things together, and he'd try to understand. But now I feel like the closeness between us would only make..." I felt uncomfortable talking about this. "I mean, would he want to spend hours alone with me in my apartment... if he knew? Sure, he might try to deal with the truth about me, but I don't think our friendship would be the same."

"Well, you've managed to keep your hands off him all this time; why would he think that would change?"

I cringed at these words; there was something so abrupt about the way he said that. But Jeff didn't seem to notice my reaction, and he went right on. "Things would probably be a lot *better* between you and Derek if you came out. There'd be an honesty that's seriously lacking now, and you wouldn't be consumed by guilt every time you look at him. Anyway, you'd feel way better about *yourself.*"

"I don't know," I said, "how good can it feel to know that your best friend thinks you're disgusting?"

Retracting his hand from my thigh, Jeff said harshly, "By knowing that that's *his* problem; not yours."

"You don't think I already know that, Jeff? Nothing Derek could ever do or say could make me feel bad about loving men, but that doesn't change the fact that I couldn't handle it if Derek despised me."

"He already despises what you are."

"Do you hate him for that?" I asked softly.

"I hate that part of him."

"But you don't hate him."

"I like Derek plenty, but I really have to question how anyone of Derek's intelligence doesn't see that ignorance for what it is."

"It's so unlike him too," I said. "He doesn't harbor other prejudices. He dated a Vietnamese girl in high school. The only thing he's prejudice against is what *we* are."

We sat for a moment considering this, then, mercifully, Jeff put his hand back on my thigh and turned to give me a passion-filled kiss.

****

"What do you do for Christmas?" Jeff inquired, as he and I climbed Coit Tower.

Studying the New Deal murals, touching them lightly with my fingertips — as if some wisdom from that era could rub off on me — I ascended the wide spiral staircase slowly, Jeff at my side. Reading between the lines in his question, I responded, "I figured you'd be going back to Cambridge to be with your family."

"No," he said bluntly. "So, you do something with Carol."

"No," I said back, mimicking his terse tone, "she goes to visit her family in Iowa; it's the only time she sees them."

"Derek, then."

"He spends a couple of days with his folks."

"So, what do you do?"

"Nothing."

"Nothing? Come on, you do *something*."

"Okay, I go to a restaurant in Chinatown. A place that doesn't even have a menu in English."

"How do you order?"

"They have a wall of tanks overflowing with wild looking sea creatures. I point, and smile a lot."

Christmas night, a waiter brought by a tray of assorted appetizers, and I picked out some bright green seaweed in a spicy garlic sauce. Halfway through eating this, Jeff started to laugh rather boisterously.

"What?"

"It feels so naughty, eating here on Christmas."

Now I laughed. Jeff seemed to be such an innocent. This prompted me to ask, "How are your parents, about you being gay?"

"Oh, really okay." Jeff wiped his mouth with a cloth napkin nearly the same color as the seaweed. "My mom's uncle is an old queen who was out pre-Stonewall."

"Wow."

We were distracted for a moment, watching a waiter with a net chase down a large fish in one of the tanks. When this task was accomplished, I asked, "So when did you tell your folks about yourself?"

"Right after I split up with my girlfriend."

"Girlfriend?" I made no attempt to hide my shock.

"Well, I wanted to be sure; you know, give heterosexuality a try at least."

"And?"

Jeff folded his hands in front of him on the table. "There was this girl who I always thought was real nice. It was our junior year in high school, and she had a reputation for being very priggish about sex. That felt safe. So I started dating her. And here I was with a girl who wanted to save her virginity until her wedding night, and I felt like *she* was rushing *me* to go further than I wanted to go. I knew then, you know. I mean, she puts my hand on her breast and I feel nothing."

"Nothing?"

"I just felt like... it's just so ridiculous. I'm not interested; so it's this big charade."

"No sexual response at all?"

"No."

"I find that amazing."

"Really?"

"I find it difficult to grasp strict homo- or hetero-sexuality; it eludes me. How does one not feel attracted to either men or women? Do you find my bisexuality odd?"

"No. To me it's like some people are straight haired, some curly, and some an in-between wavy.

I pushed the last remnants of seaweed and garlic together and, picking up the blue and white bowl, guided them onto my tongue with my chopsticks. I chewed carefully, savoring, trying to commit to memory the exotic taste and texture. When it was gone, I said to Jeff, "You think it's genetic then?"

"Or possibly hormonal."

A big plate of erotic looking abalone arrived at our table. Jeff looked at the plate, then at me, and started to laugh again. Still smirking to himself, he dished out platefuls, serving me first, and then himself. He sat smiling at his food for a moment then asked, "You ever been here with Derek?" He looked around the room as if trying to imagine Derek in this setting. We were the only non-Orientals there.

"No."

"Carol?"

"No."

Finally, Jeff braved a taste of his food. Taking a tentative bite, his face first registered unintentional alarm, and then his expression settled on interest and pleasure.

"I met a guy at the Mirage once," I said now, speaking between mouthfuls of abalone. "He was probably around thirty. We found a corner where it wasn't too loud and got into an interesting conversation. He was an attractive man, and at first I was real flirtatious with him, but he didn't respond to this, though he clearly enjoyed talking with me. So we had this great asexual conversation. Eventually we walked down to Francine's Fries and talked more, over cheeseburgers and coffee. At about two o'clock we got up to leave." I tasted a helping of spicy eggplant that had just been delivered to our table. "Did you order this?" I asked Jeff.

"No."

I shrugged. It was divine.

"Anyway, I'd assumed we'd go home together. Sure, he hadn't wanted to flirt, so maybe he preferred to save that sort of thing for the bedroom, right? I mean, I found this guy intriguing, and I definitely had the hots for him, so I'm all geared up for a fun time in bed. And what does he do? Once we're out on the sidewalk, he says to me, 'Can I buy you dinner tomorrow night?' Flustered and intensely frustrated, I found myself suggesting this place." I gestured around the restaurant with my chopsticks.

Jeff, still eating with relish, looked at me expectantly.

"Maybe I suggested coming here out of spite. But he liked it, seemed to be right at home. He was well traveled: India, Thailand, South America, even Syria. I loved talking to him. I loved looking at him. I thought I could really love loving him." I paused, thinking back. I had very much liked this guy.

"So just as the meal's ending, I'm sucking on a lychee nut, being very obviously sensual about it, but he completely ignores my attempts at seduction. Finally he puts his hand - nice and big, and tan, as I recall - on mine and says, "Jim, I have herpes, genital warts, and hepatitis B. Three months ago I was treated for a rare parasitic infection. I'm off sex. I'm really into yoga now. In India, a man's considered truly virile, and powerful, if he can suppress/overcome his base sexual desires, channel his energies towards more spiritual matters.' Then placing his hands back in his lap, he says, 'Can you handle a nonsexual relationship?' Nearly choking on my lychee nut, I said, trying to sound nonchalant, 'Sure, we can be friends.' 'No,' he responded, 'I'm looking for a *boyfriend*. I've got lots of friends.'"

I stopped eating. Put my chopsticks down on my plate. "I was so disturbed by this — I can't tell you."

Jeff started laughing and laughing. "Poor Jim!"

"I mean, for *days* it left me out of sorts."

Jeff laughed even harder. Then I started laughing too.

****

Ella Fitzgerald sang sweet notes as Derek and I studied in one of the music cubicles at the San Francisco State Library. Whenever we needed to do research, we gathered up the books we needed, then found some old recordings in the library's stacks, and sat in one of the soundproof booths with a turntable.

Ella's voice, a powerful, mood-altering substance, put us into a quiet, dreamy, space. And when we headed back to our bikes, Derek looked up into the cloudless sky, in which hung a full crystal-ball-like moon, and said, "I'm going take a ride out to Fort Funston, check out the reflection on the ocean."

This sort of statement from Derek was always an invitation, so I responded, "Sounds good," which he knew meant I would join him.

We parked our bikes, and walked to the hang glider launch site at the edge of the cliff. The ocean was big that night. Large unruly waves tossed and turned the moon's path of light on the Pacific's dark surface. We stood there silently, only a few inches apart — two dark-haired figures dressed in black, the moon illuminating our faces, our motorcycles parked back behind us. We stood there, not speaking, for close to an hour. I wanted to speak. There was something I wanted to say. It gnawed at me, seemed to be screaming to be let loose, and I had no idea what it was. I could just barely taste it on my tongue, feel the words forming in my throat, but then, just when I'd think I had it, it would melt away, disappear. Then I would start to feel it again, the pressure, the unrelenting urge to say it, whatever it was, and I'd start to know, start to understand, and then whoosh, it'd be gone again. I wanted to come out to him; that was the logical assumption. I had to tell him, and now would be the moment. But as obvious as this seemed, I knew that wasn't it. That was not what was torturing me inside. Not this time. Something about how beautiful the night was, the moon, the ocean, the cliffs, and the little flowers blooming just beyond the tips of our boots, dangling down towards the water, just barely hanging on to the western edge of North America. I wanted to speak of this beauty to Derek, but words like beautiful, and lovely, were not words I could use with Derek unless we were speaking about a woman, and even then they would be awkward. So it was something about beauty then that I wanted to say, but not *quite* this. There was something else, something more, something about beauty, but more, and I couldn't get at it; I couldn't lay my hands on it and present it to him. It was out there, beyond me, and yet inside me; it was circling around, pushing on me, yet just outside my grasp.

My feet began to ache. I wanted to sit down, but I didn't. Derek didn't. We just stood there, silently surrounded by beauty. Eventually, a lone cloud moved in, veiling the crystal ball, and we walked back to our bikes. Derek headed home, or possibly to Alice's. I went to Jeff.

Jeff's lights were off, so I crept upstairs quietly, let myself in with my key, stripped, and crawled into bed next to him. I lay awake for hours, listening to his breathing, unable to sleep. He smelled good. Smelled like Jeff.

Chapter Twenty-one

I sat by the window in a coffee house on Castro Street one morning, looking out as a car with Arkansas license plates drove by slowly. The gawking family within pointed out a couple of drag queens, who looked like they might just now be winding down from last night's revelries.

Jeff brought two lattes and chocolate biscotti to the table. We had been together for nearly a year now. This morning followed an especially loving night at his place. I put my hand on his, which was resting on the table near the sugar shaker. Jeff broke out in a big smile. He'd been fighting a patient battle to get me to show affection towards him in public places other than just the bars — at least in gay parts of the city. The lattes were good. I felt especially at peace.

Four hours later, Derek and I were, between summer school classes, eating lunch in the City College cafeteria. He took a large bite out of a roast beef sandwich, and appeared to suddenly remember something.

When he finished chewing, he let out a short brief laugh, then said, "Alice had some kind of appointment down near the Western Addition this morning, and had to change buses on Castro." He wiped mayo from the corner of his mouth with a flimsy cafeteria napkin. "She looked in the window of a cafe and saw two queers holding hands. Said one of them looked just like you."

****

I'd just stepped out of the shower when Jeff let himself into my apartment. Instead of reaching for my robe, as I normally would have under the circumstances, I found myself putting on jeans and a T-shirt. Meanwhile, Jeff took off his heavy suede jacket and put it, and his backpack, on the couch.

"Hi." He was cheery, glad to be with me.

"Hi." I walked over to my bookcase, not to him.

He took a good look at me. "What's wrong?"

I looked blankly at my books. "Alice."

"Alice? Who's Alice?"

"Derek's girlfriend."

"Oh, yeah."

Turning around now, I said, "She was on Castro this morning changing buses."

Jeff watched me with unblinking eyes.

Unable to meet his gaze, I looked away. "At lunch Derek tells me that Alice saw a guy who looked just like me — could have been my twin — holding hands with another guy. He thought it was funny."

"What did you say to him?" Jeff's tone was accusing.

I didn't answer.

"What did you say?"

"Nothing."

"Nothing?"

"Nothing."

"You had to have said something. You said *something*, why else can't you look at me? What did you *say?*"

I turned my head briefly in his direction and said angrily, "I laughed!"

"You *laughed*?" Jeff was livid.

"What else could I do? Derek was laughing; I laughed with him." I was acutely aware of how pathetic my voice sounded.

"What else could you *do*? You could have told him that it *was* you, that it was *me* you were with. That I'm gay and you're bi. That we're lovers. That..." he almost stopped himself, but then said it anyway, "That we're in love with each other."

I was in love with Jeff, knew he was in love with me, but we had never told each other so, not in words.

"I can't tell Derek that," I said sadly.

"Why? Because it isn't true?"

"Because it *is* true."

Jeff's voice rose even louder, "I'm not a closet-case, Jim Landa! I'm *not* a closet-case!" He snatched up his jacket and backpack and headed for the door.

When he put his hand on the knob, I said softly, "Please don't go."

He stopped, turned around; his expression was riddled with conflict.

"I'm sorry," I said.

"Fuck sorry; I'll never forgive you for this, Jim. *Never!*"

"I'll probably never forgive myself either."

Jeff grabbed my thickest physics textbook, which was on a table next to the door, and whirled it across the room, his voice thundering, "*Goddamn you!*"

The book flew into the opposite wall with a loud smack, and landed like a broken winged bird, wounded, on the floor. We stared at it.

I walked over to Jeff and put my arms around him. He began to cry. Then my tears came too.

****

More than once, I wanted to ask Jeff why he got involved with me when he knew it would be a closeted relationship. But it seemed like a cruel question, and really, I knew the answer: he had followed his heart.

It had been only a couple of weeks before the Alice incident that it had finally dawned on me that I was in love with him. My feelings for Jeff were so different from how I had felt for Rick, that it took a while for me to recognize that it was love. What I'd had with Rick was intense and profound, while my love for Jeff was a quiet peacefulness inside me. I felt happy and comfortable when I was with him.

I considered Jeff a blessing in my life. A *temporary* blessing. I knew, *knew*, that it was not going to last. What did I really have to offer him? A partnership in duplicity? I can't see you Friday night — my girlfriend's expecting me for dinner. You need to leave my bed before five tomorrow morning, because my buddy's meeting me for a before classes bike ride, and I don't want him to see you here. No, my relationship with Jeff would not last.

As if falling right in step to fulfill this prophecy, arguments between Jeff and I became frequent. I'd now become adamant about playing it strictly as friends except when behind locked doors and closed curtains. If Alice had ever met Jeff, that day on Castro would have meant an instant outing for me. I was not willing to risk this. Jeff couldn't, wouldn't, understand. I couldn't blame him.

****

Two months before Jeff would graduate at the end of the fall semester, as we sat on my couch, eating delivered Chinese food, Jeff said, "Bob's been calling."

So the end was near. I put down my chopsticks and gave him my rapt attention. Bob, Jeff's ex, was of course the reason why he'd left Cambridge. Bob and Jeff had been together nearly three years when, as Jeff told it to me, the relationship got stagnant; Bob decided he wanted out. Now I hear Jeff telling me Bob wants him back, and almond pressed duck is getting stuck in the lump in my throat. Jeff tells me Bob wants him back, and then he is silent, and I hear in Jeff's silence, *Tell me something earth-shattering;*

tell me something that will make me stay; tell me you'll come out.

I say nothing of the sort. I say nothing at all. Instead, I reach out for Jeff's hand, but he pulls it away.

That's when I got up and went into the bathroom and said to the man in the mirror, "I hate you." He said back, "I don't hate you." I said, "Go to hell!" and went back to Jeff who was poking around angrily at his chop suey.

"I'm going crazy," I told him as I sat back down. "There's nothing I'm capable of doing or saying that will make you stay. You're better off with Bob."

He sat motionless, chopsticks still in hand.

"I love you," I added, finally saying these words to him.

He looked at me, stunned.

I kissed him, pulled his body to mine. Jeff allowed himself to respond, and soon we were on the bed expressing our love.

****

It was another month before Jeff brought up the subject again. He told me he'd gotten a great job offer in Cambridge. He said this in a happy, excited sort of way, which told me that he had come to accept that he was leaving me, and was looking forward to being with Bob again. But I had not come to accept any of this, not at all.

I said in a monotone, "Congratulations. When do you leave? Why does everything have to be so fucked up?"

He said, without sympathy, "You'll have to answer that last question for yourself. I'll leave right after exams. It didn't have to be this way."

"Unfortunately, it did," I said.

"Why?" Jeff took my face between his hands, forcing me to look at him. "Why, Jim?"

178

I looked right into his eyes and told him the horrid truth. "I don't know."

Jeff dropped his hands in disgust, turned away. "Jim, you're a mess." He stated this, without anger, as a simple fact.

And my messed-up self said in response, "Will you keep seeing me until you leave?"

"Yes."

After that, of course, we got along wonderfully. There wasn't anything to argue about; it had all been resolved. We both knew that I was a shit. Jeff was leaving, going back to Bob, to an out relationship. I would be left to stew in my closet. With this knowledge all neatly tucked in, we had a hell of a great time.

Jeff left early on a Sunday morning. I did not see him off; instead I stayed in bed the whole day, wondering what the fuck was wrong with me. How could I have let him go? I tried to will the tears to come, but they did not; my heart had turned to stone.

I was listless, vacant, over the next weeks. This new self-loathing quickly began to grate on me. When it gets to the point where you get up in the middle of a conversation to look at yourself in the mirror and say, "I hate you," it's clear that something has to change. I knew I could not continue in the closet much longer. But I had felt this for years, and here I was nearing twenty-three and... and... and even when it meant loosing Jeff, I would not open the doors to what had become one hell of a dank, stinking, den of mental chaos. I half expected to find cobwebs in my hair.

The closet in my apartment was small, with a slatted door. A few mornings after Jeff left, I squeezed into that tiny space and shut the door, wanted to see what the allure was. It felt, actually, at that moment, there in that closed darkness, really rather nice. There wasn't the discomfort and claustrophobia that I had expected. I felt safe, warm, surrounded. I knew it was a false sense of security — at any moment someone could open the door, leaving me fully exposed — but still it felt good. Stepping back out of the closet again, everything felt vast and frightening. I felt very alone.

Chapter Twenty-two

Although I made efforts towards trying to seem happy enough around Derek, this was a futile exercise. He easily picked up on the fact that I was not in high spirits. Though, of course he did not connect this to Jeff's leaving. In Derek's usual macho-guy ways, he tried to cheer me up. Never once did he ask what was wrong, or offer an opportunity to talk, but he got us tickets to a Forty-niner game, something I'd normally enjoy.

So here we were in Candlestick Park, surrounded by thousands of raving fans. The Forty-niners were playing another great game, and through all the roaring, I stared blankly at the field, mentally reliving the first time Jeff and I slept together, the night he came out to me.

Derek jabbed me every once in a while with his elbow. "Wow, Montana's killer tonight." I'd snap out of it momentarily, try to focus on the game, then feel myself slowly slipping back into self-pity land.

After the 'Niner game, I decided to avoid Derek until the spring semester would start in a couple of weeks. I was afraid that he would either eventually ask me what was wrong — then what might I tell him? another lie? the TRUTH? — or that he would *not* ask what was wrong, and this would piss me off and depress me all the more.

I did not go to the bars. Though I'd stopped cruising when Jeff and I'd gotten together, that had been from lack of interest, but now, though the sexual desire was there, I found the idea emotionally repulsive. I'd been able to pull myself sufficiently together when I'd first arrived in San Francisco, to approach the bars with an optimistic up-beat attitude, but now I knew, I'd be in that scene as one of the pathetically sad and lonely. Not a fate I was eager to step into.

Meanwhile, I saw as much of Carol as possible, even went so far as to give her a key to my place. Being with Carol was about the only thing that appealed to me. While with her, I was able to forget Jeff. The more the time I spent with her was spent in bed, the better. I wondered at this. Was it because I had no other sexual outlet? Or was I preparing myself for coming out, making a last ditch effort to cling on to something, someone, I knew I'd soon lose? The notion that the time was nearing grew steadily stronger. Coming out *would* mean saying good-bye to Carol; I had no doubt. What it would mean for Derek and I, I found I could not even venture to contemplate.

Carol responded to my newfound enthusiasm for her with, I don't know what else to call it but, glee. That was Carol for you. I hadn't been with another woman for more than two years, a fact that only now struck me. But it made sense; Carol had an amazing body, and was always a joy in or out of bed. She never ceased to charm and intrigue me. I guess, I loved her in the way you love anyone who you've spent that much time with, shared that much fun with, but I wasn't in-love with her. There just wasn't that deep emotional, spiritual, connection. I began to wonder now whether I would ever love a woman in that way — whether I could. I supposed that what there had been between Mary and I had been that kind of love, but we had just been kids, and it was hard to compare that to what I'd had with Rick or Jeff.

By the time classes were well under way again, despondency over Jeff's leaving and over knowledge of my, as I'd come to think of it, fundamentally screwed up nature, had become partially dissipated and partially absorbed into my personality. Derek and I were spending lots of time together again. And by the time Derek and I skipped our graduation ceremony to study golf ball trajectories at the Olympic Club, I realized, much to my dismay, that the feeling of my coming out being imminent had faded. It was business as usual, except I had no homosexual interactions — which had really started to grate on me. My body ached to be with a man, and my psyche felt equally disoriented. I did not like living the life of the "happy heterosexual," complete with his girl and his buddy. In fact, I found this lifestyle felt excruciatingly weird. But still I could not bring myself to go to the bars.

****

The week after Derek and I first met, I'd asked, "Play any handball?" and, it had been almost a relief when he'd answered with that grin of his, "Never been near it." He said he got his exercise by messing around with a set of weights. So we'd kept it that way. It was good to have *something* that I didn't share with him besides my love life. I picked up games at the courts in Golden Gate Park — for fun, and to stay fit for cruising. In late April, a new gym with a handball court had moved into a space not far from my apartment. I joined, and as if I didn't already have enough pent-up lust in me for men, I ended up with a handball partner who made every cell in my body scream with desire. Mike was a paradigm of masculine beauty — a tall, sandy-blond, with a tan sculpted face, and the body of a Greek God. Subtle, yet overt body language, and an over attention to self-appearance, rendered Mike's gayness unmistakable.

We got out on to the court the first time without much more than a simple introduction. I soon found myself in the midst of the hottest handball game I'd ever played. I'm not referring to the presence of sexual energy; I'm talking about the game itself. Our skill levels were near equally matched, and our individual strengths and weaknesses seemed to create the perfect challenge for both of us. More importantly though, Mike approached the game with the same attitude that I did. We were both very competitive, but being The Winner wasn't the point. It was about playing the game, being out there, sweating, and concentrating, pushing our physical limits, feeling that powerful energy.

After that first match, when we sat at the juice bar still high from the game, I tried to strike up a conversation. I knew Mike assumed I was straight, and I knew I could set his thinking otherwise with one lusty look at his body, or even his gorgeous face. But I'd not done this yet, wanting first to establish some sort of rapport with him.

Mike had a strawberry and banana protein shake in front of him. His breathing was still deep from the game. I felt my own pumped-up athletic power slowly, sweetly, draining from me, my heartbeat returning to almost normal (a bit faster than normal due to the present company).

"You live in the neighborhood?" I asked.

"Naw, across town." He waved his hand ineffectually in the air, not looking at me.

"I'm a few blocks from here."

"Nice for *you*."

Touchy subject, I figured. I tried another tack. "I like your game."

He smiled.

"How long you been playing?"

"Few years." He took a sip of his shake.

"Juice bar's nice." I glanced around as I said this. Some effort had been put into the place; it seemed not so health-freak oriented, more designed for aesthetics and relaxation. There was a lot of dark blues, instead of sterile white. He didn't say anything so I asked, "Don't you think so?"

Mike made a face equivalent to that of a six-year-old presented with a plate of steamed spinach. "Well, if you like coffee houses," he sneered. "It doesn't come off much as a place to get something that's good for you. Makes me not trust their shakes, you know, like maybe they added a little sugar on the sly just to make it taste good." He jabbed his straw into his drink. "Court's nice though, but I was hoping they'd have more than one. Shit. I hate having to sign up way in advance and all that *crap*."

"Uh..." I said, trying to hide my devastation.

"Speaking of which, are Tuesdays good for you generally? I could sign us up for the next few weeks... unless you're too, too, busy to make that kind of a long-term commitment." Mike was standing now, waiting for a response.

"Tuesdays are good." I didn't care how much of a jerk he was; I wasn't going to pass up that kind of a game.

So, we became regular weekly partners. I confirmed quickly that *any* attempt to exchange words with Mike resulted in a disastrous excursion into the wastelands of the unpleasant. Since Mike was not inclined to strike up conversation on his own, and I now avoided it like the plague, every week we'd have an amazing game, the entire transaction taking place with few, if any, words exchanged. And, every week I'd become overcome with physical lust for Mike, stealing furtive glances that filled me with unbearable frustration. I kept thinking: what if sex between us would be like our games? However, this fantasy was always tempered by the thought: what if sex between us would be more like our conversations?

****

Regardless of what I thought sex with Mike might be like, the fact was, lusting after him was driving my homosexual longings to new levels of insanity. So, despite my newfound aversion for the bars, I was on the verge of going back to the old haunts — but, that never happened. About five weeks after we first started playing together, a lover of Mike's, a burly Latino, showed up to give him a lift. Mike introduced him quickly by mumbling his name, "Tony."

The following week, when Mike and I had just started playing, the room loud with our breathing, the squeak of our shoes, the smack of the ball, Mike says to me, out of the blue, "You're gay, Jim?" and he keeps playing, not missing a beat.

Mike and I rarely talked, but on the court, without exception, we'd *never* uttered a *word*. Now this. First I tried to recover from just hearing his voice during a game — that in itself was a sacrilege.

Finally, while concentrating on a hard slam, I answered, "I'm bi."

Grabbing the ball midair, Mike put a dead stop to the game, glared at me. "*Bi*, what's *that?*"

"Play ball, Mike."

He stood grounded, eyes pinned on me, demanding a response.

Enraged, I snatched the ball out of his hand, hit it hard as I could. We continued the game — with unrelenting intensity — in silence.

Later, when we were at the juice bar, mutely hydrating as usual, my anger dissipated now by the energy I'd put into the game, my curiosity got the better of me and I asked, despite my better judgment, "How did you know?"

"How did I know what?"

"About me."

"About *you*. Well, let's see..." Mike looked up at the ceiling, as if expecting an explanation written there. "Oh yes, Tony. You know, that big strong Mexican *fag* I introduced you to last week? Seems he use to see you at the *Power Tool*, oh... lots of times. He'd thought of hitting on you. You do have a nice ass." Mike glanced briefly in my direction. "But it seems you were a little too *straight-*looking for his tastes." He paused a moment and dramatically played at scratching the absent stubble on his high cheekbone.

Then he went on, "I had told him that my handball partner was a het-er-o-sexual, but on that fact, he set me straight — oh dear me, a pun! I said, 'Tony, you *must* be mistaken.' But he assured me he'd recognize that ass anywhere, and besides," Mike pointed to my pinkie, "he knew it was you for certain because of the ring." He looked at me now deadpan.

I studied Mike's face. Those incredible eyes — deep-sea blue — the long pale lashes, that classic nose, full pink lips. How could such an ugly mind be lurking behind such a work of wondrous beauty? He turned and took hold of his straw, putting it in his mouth, taking a long drink from the mango shake. I watched his puckered lips embrace the straw, watched his smooth, tan cheeks curve in with the effort of sucking.

He looked up now, and as a footnote to his earlier rantings said, "So you're *bi*." He practically spit out the word. "What? So, does that mean you're, like, too *homophobic* to admit you're *queer*?"

He'd gone too far! Hit a raw nerve. I wanted to shut him up — fast! And, I wanted to show him just how comfortable I was with my gay side; oh how I wanted to show him!

I stood up. "My apartment's a ten-minute walk, you interested?"

Mike's face first registered utter surprise, but then his eyes lit up and, licking his lips, he nodded an enthusiastic approval. The nod, instead of a "Yes," I took as a sign — much to my relief — that we were back in our more congenial nonverbal mode. Being sexual with Mike was either going to be utterly wonderful or utterly awful. If he was going into this without speech, it seemed wonderful had a much better chance.

****

Forget awful, forget even wonderful, the word, as it turned out, was more along the lines of unbelievable. Having sex with Mike *was* like playing handball with him. *Some* part of our brains connected perfectly. Whereas sex with someone I love is a glorious emotional, spiritual, and physical rocket-ship ride to the stars, sex with Mike was a purely physical experience. But, oh what a physical experience! We understood completely how to arouse one another, how to take each other to the brink, hold him there for a tortuously long time. There was nothing playful or loving about what Mike and I did in bed; it was all very intense — like our games on the court. Though we of course never discussed it, it was clear to me that this was not the usual sexual experience for Mike either. Somehow, on these two very specific levels, we seemed to have been made for each other.

****

Tuesday after Tuesday, Mike and I met in the early afternoon, played an extraordinary handball game, in silence, and then walked to my place, in silence, to have extraordinary sex, in silence (with the exception of speech-eluding expressions of ecstatic pleasure). We rarely said more than two words to each other all afternoon.

We admired and appreciated each other for our sexual and athletic talents, and for our compatibility in these areas, but that was all Mike and I had. Really, I didn't know what to make of our relationship. Was it a relationship? It was weird; that was clear. I truly wished that I had someone to talk to about it. There were plenty of times like that over the years, where I felt, profoundly, the absence of someone to bounce things off of. "Hey, Derek, I'm in this really bizarre relationship, give me a little perspective, would ya?" Ha! And what are friends for?? I resented more and more that Derek didn't truly know me.

Every Tuesday morning, just a few hours before Mike and I would be taking each other to sexual nirvana, I'd be sitting in the cafeteria drinking coffee with Derek. "Hey, Derek, would you like to know how I'm spending the afternoon?" "Hey, Derek, you ever have sex with someone you really couldn't stand?" "Derek... Derek... WAKE UP!" How could he not know? Goddamn me for being so good at playing Mr. Hetero.

This kind of thinking got me worried that I'd cop out and, instead of telling him, I'd somehow let it slip, that I'd just stop trying so hard to hide things from him. What if I just sort of left a copy of the Bay Area Reporter laying on my coffee table, and there's the headline staring up at Derek: "Bisexuals Demand More Recognition from Gay Groups." I knew, too, exactly what would happen. Derek, if he noticed the paper at all, would assume it was a mainstream newspaper reporting on a gay issue. Maybe if he saw a new B.A.R. there every week for a month, he'd say, "What's the deal?" But I could say anything, make up any far-fetched story, and he'd believe me. I could say, "I have a gay neighbor and they keep delivering the papers to the wrong address," and he'd be satisfied. I could even tell him the truth, point blank, and he still wouldn't know. I could say, "I read the gay papers because I'm bisexual and these issues concern me," and he'd laugh, think it an off-color joke, and leave it at that. I was invincible, and I knew it. Invincible, like invisible — Derek could look right at me and not see me — and yet I continued to make every effort to keep my "Big Secret" hidden from him.

Except once. This was seven and a half months after Mike and I became sexual partners. In a moment of emotional chaos, I decided to let fate determine if Derek would find out — Carol being fate's vehicle.

In magazine comics depicting a husband or wife walking-in-on their spouse cheating on them, the adulterers are always sitting up in bed, their mouths opened in surprise, clutching sheets they'd hurriedly pulled up to their chins. This was not what Carol was presented with when she walked in on me and Mike. In fact, so lost were he and I in the thralls of physical ecstasy that we didn't even know she was there until we heard a loud gasp that wasn't coming from either of us.

What Carol saw was much more than she needed to see in order to get the picture. There was her gasp, and startled, Mike and I snapped out of our revelry. The sheets were in a pile on the floor somewhere; I didn't have a clue. That was my first thought, where are the sheets? My second thought was, it finally happened. My third thought was an awareness that the emotion accompanying my second thought was immense relief. All this, of course, flashed through my head inside of a couple of seconds, after which Mike suddenly seemed to understand what was going on. He scrambled for his clothes and ducked into the bathroom. At the sight of Mike's naked body flashing across the room, Carol let out a blood-curling scream, face contorted, fists clenched at her sides, and my fourth thought was: Carol doesn't deserve this. But the emotions behind that thought was an odd mix of tremendous regret and tremendous hatred for an intolerant world — which to me at the moment Carol represented.

I found my pants, pulled them on while Mike, now dressed, dashed out the front door. Carol looked at me, disgust, shock, horror — you name it — written all over her face. I don't know what she saw on my face, probably anger. Anger at what she was thinking.

And then she said it. "You're a *homo*!"

She could have been saying, "You're a Cyclops!" or, "You're an ogre!" You're a *homo* — like that was the worst kind of terrible monster. Then she added — for precision I guess — yelling in rage, "You're a goddamned sodomite!" Clearly worse than a bloodsucking vampire.

Carol stared at me: a werewolf growing fangs and pointy ears right before her very eyes.

"I'm bisexual," I told her in an amazingly matter-of-fact tone. There, I had said it, told Carol, *I'm bisexual*; it was that easy. I'm bisexual; that's who I am.

"You're a faggot!" This was said clearly as a way to hurt me, like, "You're a stupid-head;" "You're an ugly jerk."

"Okay, I'm a faggot," I told her. "I'm half faggot, half he-man. However you want to see it, Carol."

Half bad, half good; half freak, half normal; half right, half wrong; half perverted, half sexually well-adjusted.

"I'm sorry; I should have told you when we first met." I looked at her sympathetically. I was sorry, deeply, profoundly, had always known I would be.

"Sorry? Sorry? You're *sick*."

I'm not sorry; I'm sick. Half sick, half healthy.

She looked around frantically. "Where are my files?" She grabbed a folder, which I hadn't noticed she'd left last night, off the kitchen counter, and stormed out, slamming the door as hard as she could.

I stared at the door, my mind blank for a moment. Then a terror surged through me. DEREK! She would tell him. Would she? She would. I saw myself lunge for the door. I would plead with her, reason with her, beg her, whatever. I saw myself open the door, tear down the hall after her. But I wasn't. I wasn't doing any of those things. I was standing perfectly still, staring at the door. Then I just let go. Let go of all the control I'd had over keeping myself a secret from Derek. I let go of that control and placed it directly into Carol's hands.

It occurred to me that I could go over to Derek's and tell him myself before Carol had a chance to. That's probably what I should do, I thought. But I went and sat on the couch instead. Sitting there, I felt three things: the tremendous relief of Carol having found out, amazement at how deep and how wonderful that relief was, and utter terror at the possibility of losing Derek.

Chapter Twenty-three

I headed for class the next morning, scared to death that Derek... wouldn't be there... would sit in the back of the class and pretend that we'd never met... would jump out of the bushes and beat the crap out of me.

He was sitting front row center, empty seat beside him, looking over the previous day's notes. I walked towards my seat cautiously, studying him.

"Hey," he said, half absorbed in his notes, glancing at me briefly. Then he did a double take. "What's the matter?"

I sat down slowly, taking my place beside him. She hadn't told him?

"You okay?" He seemed concerned.

She hadn't told him.

"Jim?"

"Carol..." I said. "We ahh... split up."

"Oh." Then he asked — as a reluctant courtesy — "What happened?"

What happened? What? "We... She... She found someone else." What a stupid thing to say. Why didn't I just tell him? Yeah, sure, right there, two minutes before class.

"That's a drag."

That's a drag. Good, Derek. I go out with a woman for three years and she leaves me for someone else, and, "That's a drag"? I shook my head. Get a grip. What am I thinking? She left me for someone else? Here I am getting pissed at Derek's inability to be there for me, and I've told him yet *another* lie.

Derek was squinting at me. "How 'bout we take a ride out to Mono Lake this weekend? Weather's good."

"Sure."

I was despondent. Derek could see that. But it wasn't about Carol; it was because she hadn't told him. She hadn't relieved me of that burden.

We went to Mono Lake. Got absorbed, and lost in the place, the way Derek and I tend to do. I forgot to look heartbroken. Derek didn't notice. Maybe he thought I was just being a man about it. Life went on. But now no Carol, no Mike. There was only Derek. I didn't go to the bars; I didn't ask any women out. I was, actually, celibate. What a concept. It felt unnatural, dehumanizing, but it was what I wanted at the time — by way of default.

Derek and I were spending amazing amounts of time together. Now well into our first year of the graduate program, school had become especially interesting. Hours were spent discussing the implications of current astrophysics research. Our ideas went from words, to equations on paper, back to words, then off into the realm of the beyond, where numbers become so meaningful that they become almost meaningless. It was easy to lose track of reality when we were discussing a reality where everything is relative. At the end of these nights we felt exhilarated/exhausted.

Exhilarated/exhausted, gay/straight. What was stopping me now from coming out to Derek?

I had fantasies: end of a long night, sitting on the couch together, and mater-of-factly, "You know what, Derek? I'm bisexual."

You know what, Derek? I'm bisexual, and he's out the door, and I never see him again.

****

Derek didn't ask why I'd switched my handball games to Thursdays. I played whoever was available. One time it was a good-looking, eighteen-year-old, Italian-American. After the game, when two gay guys in short shorts walked by, he said to me, "Seems like queers are taking over this gym. Kinda gives you the creeps, doesn't it?"

I looked at him stone-faced, and said, in my most masculine voice, "It seems to me you don't know a queer even when you're looking right at him."

Seems to me there are an awful lot of homophobes running around San Francisco. I never saw the Italian Stallion again. Poor little boy almost wet his pants. I had no sympathy, no mercy. I hated them all... except Derek. Not really, part of me hated Derek with a passion — but it wasn't enough. The hatred that festered in me for Derek, no matter how intense, never could get a good foothold, it just sort of tagged along on a very tenuous string.

****

I began to miss Carol some, but I never missed her as much as I was glad to be rid of her. I missed the sex, and I missed her laughs, her *being*, but how could I miss the lies, the duplicity, our damn fucking closet, her filthy, disgusting, homophobia?

So wouldn't I also be glad to be rid of Derek in the same way? Wouldn't it be just as well if I came out to him, and he told me to go to hell? Wouldn't life simply be better? To live every day with the overwhelming frustration of my inability to be true to myself: this was eating me up, tearing my insides to shreds, had been for years. Like all forms of self-loathing, it wasn't pretty. I was a hideous coward. I knew very clearly that being closeted with Derek was making me feel this way about myself, and still I could not tell him.

Our friendship went on as always: we talked through the nights, went for rides, ate pizza and Chinese food, drank coffee, played pool, went bowling. Derek saw Alice sometimes too. Alice in Bernal Heights, like Alice in Wonderland. She existed to me almost as a fiction. They were together a night, an afternoon. What they did, what they said to each other, how Derek felt about it, how she felt about it, I had no clue. Derek didn't talk about her. Every couple, three weeks, or so I might hear, "I'm going to Alice's tonight."

He wasn't with her on his birthday. He was with me. We hiked up to the top of the Golden Gate Recreation Area, watched the fog devour the bridge and the city, then had Guinness Stouts and played darts at a pub up in Napa. He was with Alice the following weekend. Did she bake him a cake? Did she know that Derek has an affinity for lemon cake? It's the only sweet thing I've ever seen him eat. He turned twenty-three. In a few months, I'd be twenty-four.

Twenty-four, a closet-case, celibate, and living in San Francisco — one hell of a pathetic joke. I was not looking forward to my birthday, and before that, I would have to endure the extreme effort I put into ignoring Gay Pride Day every summer. I carefully avoided Market Street, the Civic Center, and the greater-Castro-Street-area, on Pride Day. I didn't read the papers that week either. I was certain that if I were to see or hear anything connected to the activities of the day, I would drop dead instantly from shame and self-disgust. The Bi-Center would no doubt have their contingency in the parade. I could join in, waving a sign, "I'M BI, AND I'M ALL FUCKED UP." I had thought, at times, of going to the Bi-Center, but I always imagined myself in an AA type of meeting where I'd stand up and say, "I'm bisexual, and I have a closet fetish."

****

About two weeks before Gay Pride Day, I walked into a corner bar in the Mission district, a little after five on a Friday evening. There was a pool table in the back; Derek and I came here to play sometimes. On this night we'd made plans for bowling at seven-thirty, but I'd gone down

196

to the Mission to hang out before meeting him. I'd had coffee at the cafe full of books — one of Derek's favorite places — and bought some dried peaches at the co-op to share with him later.

Coming from the bright outdoors into the dark interior of the bar, I could initially only make out two vague shapes at the billiards table. I got a glass of draft, then headed to the back in hopes of picking up a game.

A beautiful redheaded woman incorrectly held a cue, lining it up for a poor choice of a shot. She concentrated on the table, smiling, it seemed, at her own incompetence. From my peripheral vision, I was aware there was a man with her, standing in the shadows, but I didn't even give him a glance, so mesmerized was I by this sight. Her face was so perfectly pretty that it might have been boring if it weren't a bit of asymmetry in her smile that clued me in to the interesting person inside. Light from the imitation Tiffany lamp seemed to set her auburn curls afire, and a sage colored blouse exposed, as she leaned over the table, plenty of braless cleavage. I was intrigued by how this very feminine figure managed to hold herself in such a firm solid stance. I rested my elbow at the edge of the bar and watched her eyes as she made her shot. They registered uncertainty and self-amusement. The ball ricocheted off the side and missed the pocket by a couple of inches. She looked up then. Goose bumps sent me into chills as her beautiful eyes looked straight at me. An impish smile was her reaction to me, or the fouled shot, or both.

Damn, I thought, too bad she's not alone. At which point I finally looked to see who the lucky guy was, walking out of the dark to take his turn. I laughed, because my immediate thought was: too bad *he's* not alone. Tall and fit, with over-the-collar, curly, brown hair, he stepped up to the table. He exuded masculinity, yet there was a vague softness about him — just enough to smooth out the edge on that harsh angularity that makes some men seem so inhospitable.

He also missed on his try. As he moved out of the way so that she could take her turn, he noticed me finally, and smiled at my facial reaction to her planned shot. She looked at him to see what he thought, and when she realized he was looking at me, she asked, addressing me, "You know how to play this game?"

I walked up to the table and showed her what to shoot for and how. As I continued to coach them, there was an incredible sort of... *electric* feeling. Every movement, every glance, felt charged. I knew that they felt it too; that we were all aware that we were all feeling it. We kept smiling at each other, laughing for no apparent reason. Although they wore matching wedding bands, I noticed that when I had to get real close to the guy, to show him the best angle on a shot, he did not edge away from me the way any straight man automatically would. In fact, he seemed to be enjoying, as much as I was, our bodies being so close that if either of us so much as sneezed, we would be touching. I wasn't sure what to make of this. I mean, they were married, but then I thought, this *is* San Francisco.

When the game ended, I offered to buy them a beers, but the guy said, much to my horror, as he actually began to walk towards the door, "Thanks, but got to run; our car's in the shop. Have to pick it up before they close."

The woman added, with a wave, as they neared the front, "Thanks for the pool tips!"

Then they were gone.

I couldn't believe it! I stood there unable to accept that they had left, that I'd likely never see them again. Then, like a miracle, she came rushing back in. Her hot breath whispered huskily in my ear, "We're at 2119 Fulton; dinner's at seven-thirty, if you can make it," and she zipped out again before I could respond.

Elated and breathless, I couldn't remember when I'd ever felt so excited, but my hand reached into my jacket pocket and found the dried peaches — Derek... bowling... I headed to the pay phone just outside the restrooms, dialed Derek's number. I'd tell him something came up — not a lie. He wouldn't ask what. But my call went unanswered. I hung up. I'd never done anything like this to Derek before, but I wasn't going to not show up for this dinner invitation, not with the way we all felt together just playing pool.

Chapter Twenty-four

I rang the doorbell at Fulton, and in a moment heard footsteps. The hunk from the bar opened the door a bit, smiled broadly, and then opened it wider. I stepped in. A narrow landing led to a flight of steps going up. We stood just inside the doorway, this man, whose name I did not know yet and I — stood there taking each other in. I felt, paradoxically, both extremely nervous, and amazingly calm. That we were attracted to each other in a physical bar-pick-up kind of way was apparent beyond a doubt, but there was something else, something powerful and profound. I felt that I'd been waiting for this my whole life — even though I hadn't realized that fact until now — that we'd always known each other, always been a part of one-another's lives, even though we'd just met. I felt too, with unshakable certainty, that he was experiencing these same sensations.

"I'm Hank," he said, awe slowing his voice almost to a drawl.

"Jim," I responded in an equally dreamy tone.

He looked up the staircase. "Rebecca's in the kitchen."

I followed him up, and he led me down a long hallway with a hardwood floor, to the spacious room at the end. Rebecca was standing at a cutting board, and turned around as she heard us approach. In her hand was a very large knife, covered in blood.

I looked at the knife first; I couldn't help it. She realized then, and laughed. Putting the sullied utensil back on the chopping block, she explained, "Quartering a chicken."

So lovely, these words, *quartering a chicken*. Our eyes met and held. There was that electricity again.

Hank, who had gone directly to the stove to stir something, said, "His name's Jim."

"What?" Rebecca seemed bewildered.

We both looked at Hank.

He smiled at our expressions. "His name's Jim."

"Oh." She looked back at me to register the name with the being.

All I could think was, *electricity*, and I had the totally incongruous feeling of wanting to sit down with Derek, throw some books on a table, and study this thing — whatever it was — going on between me and this couple, get it into our skin, get lost in it. I started to feel dizzy.

"Beer?" Hank asked.

"Sure," I answered through the swirling in my head.

I watched him cross to the refrigerator. It was really way too much to be there with them: one quartering chicken (the words as she'd said them could easily have been "passion flower," or "sweet scents") yes, one quartering a chicken, the other getting me a beer — his ass peeking from behind the refrigerator door as he searched for the beverage. Hank wore coffee-colored drawstring pants. I stood staring at his obviously firm cheeks, knowing that his wife might notice me doing this, and thinking that if she did, she would like it. He brought out a beer finally, handed it to me, standing so close that I could feel his body heat. I took the beer, and after an extended eye to eye glance, he returned to the stove, stirring. I looked at the label: *Pete's Wicked Ale*.

"Can I help with dinner somehow?" I'd had to concentrate very had to get the words out.

"Peel garlic?" Rebecca said, turning around with that knife again.

Responding to my nod, she got out a small cutting board and placed it next to hers, putting a few cloves on top. Handing me a paring knife, she looked as if she wanted to say something, but she held back.

I took the knife. "What?"

She smiled, hesitated.

I raised my eyebrows as encouragement.

Rebecca held up her knife. "Mine's bigger than yours."

I broke out in a hardy laugh. After that it was a bit easier to function. I was still moving in some sort of a dreamscape, but I was no longer in a state of near shock.

A little while later, while I was helping Hank set the table, I asked if they'd gotten the car fixed all right.

"Oh yeah. Brakes. Looks like they did a good job." He placed a pair of candle holders with tapered lavender candles on the table, then bamboo placemats. "Do you have a car?"

I folded the three Indonesian-print cloth napkins Hank had handed me. "I drive a Harley."

He smiled without looking up from lighting the candles. "Did you find a place to park all right?"

"It was a little tricky."

"You can park in the garage..." wooden salt and pepper shakers beside the candleholders, "next time."

Rebecca chimed in from behind a pile of red pepper slices now gracing her cutting board, "It's a big garage; there's plenty of room next to our car."

Next time. It was already clear to all of us there would be a next time. And a next, and a next, and on and on...

Over potato leek soup, we talked quietly. I learned Hank was an editor for a publishing company, and Rebecca was a paramedic. They'd met at UC Santa Cruz, and were both now thirty. Rebecca moved out west with her family when she was fifteen. Her mother and father were minor IBM executives. Hank had been happily shipped away for college by conservative parents, who were from old money in Connecticut, his father in the newspaper business, his mother, a socialite. When I told Hank and Rebecca that I was going for a Ph.D. in physics, they were intrigued, and a bit — but not too — surprised.

The table was set against a window; darkness was settling in. The candles' flames flickered double in the glass, our reflections like a mirage set behind them. The soup was rich and satisfying, and the conversation flowed as smooth as picnic honey on Amy's sun warmed thigh. The more we talked, the more we understood how insanely well we were getting along; it all seemed beyond earthly pleasures. Just talking!

No sooner had we started the entree when — in the middle of a discussion filled with vague sexual innuendo about the merits of various hot sauce brands — Rebecca slid fingertips into a hole at the knee of my jeans, a hole I hadn't even known was there, a hole that had, it seemed, materialized specifically for this purpose. I stopped talking midsentence, closing my eyes, while a rush of fire flashed through my body and settled succinctly in my groin. When my eyes opened again, Hank, who apparently realized what happened, was grinning vicariously at my reaction. Rebecca's face was alit like an angel. I couldn't imagine for the life of me how we were going to make it through dinner. We did though, somehow, although the peach custard pie had to wait until well after midnight.

****

An array of candles filled their bedroom with a soft glow. The three of us were crouched on our shins, naked in a circle on their bed. Rebecca's nipple was pointy in the cradle between my thumb and index finger. Hank's hand caressed her other breast, as he watched me studying her — Rebecca's eyes half shut, her lips barely parted. Then I studied him — Hank's lips were soft with desire, his eyes filled with untranslatable feelings. My hand trembled slightly as I explored the curves of his ass. Rebecca had one delicate hand on my shoulder, tracing muscles, while her other grasped her husband's biceps. Hank's fingers stroked the smooth hairless space of my inner thigh. Rebecca's red curls fell softly, softly, on her pale cyan-peppered shoulders. A few hours earlier, I had walked into a bar, and had somehow ended up here in heaven. I was — like with Rick — much too quickly falling in love: falling in love with a man; falling in love with a woman; falling in love with a man and a woman who were also in love with each other, who were also both falling in love with me.

When we moved our bodies together, the three of us, when we brought our mouths together, and kissed, a three-way kiss, a phenomenon I'd never even considered, I knew my life was flowing into a whole new realm of possibilities, a whole new way of understanding what it means to live and love on this planet.

At four a.m. I got dressed. We were all exhausted, physically, emotionally. I needed rest, and time for reflection. Home sounded real good. We made plans to meet for a late brunch that afternoon, and I kissed them each, individually, good-bye.

****

Waking up leisurely around eleven, I sat up, a bit groggy, and waited for the fuzziness of sleep to settle into consciousness. As the events of the night before came into focus, I closed my eyes to enjoy a wave of pleasure that washed over me. Hank and Rebecca — like stumbling upon hidden treasure.

Picking my jeans up off the floor, I inspected the hole in the knee, smiled and stood to pull them on. I headed for the kitchen — no ordinary night, not at all — put a pot on for coffee. No ordinary night, and, I realized, it would have no ordinary effect on my life. I found butter and rye bread in the refrigerator, put them on the counter, brought out milk for the coffee.

The phone rang.

I stumbled over a pile of books on the floor next to the couch, "Damn!" but made it to the phone in one piece, and plopped down on the couch.

"Hello."

"Jim!"

"Derek." A surge of nausea overtook me. "I..." my voice halted. *Say something about last night, about why I didn't show up at the bowling alley.*

"Jim? You there?"

"Yeah."

Silence, then, "Are you okay? Were you sick last night or something?"

"No, not sick. I..." Where had my voice gone? I swallowed. "I'm sorry," I croaked out, "I tried to call. I guess you'd already left. Umm, something... something came up."

"Okay, that's cool."

No it's not! Derek, it's not cool. Not cool that I'm telling you another lie.

"Just don't let it happen again."

Don't let it happen again? Okay, I won't, won't let it happen again.

"How 'bout I stop over later?" he suggested.

"Later? I... no. I don't think later... No. Later's no good." He had to have heard the panic in my voice.

"Oh, I get it, you met a chick and..."

I felt, there was, this incredible, a great deal of... energy, I had to put into not blanking out. Gathering up what little strength I could, I blurted into the phone, "I'll call you... tomorrow, or Monday. *Monday.* I'll call you Monday." I hung up.

I hung up, and hung my head down, closed my eyes. A moment later I stood and crossed to the window.

Staring at the rain-drenched street, hands in my pockets, I was overcome with a panicky sort of fear and a kind of elation. The kind of elation one experiences when standing on the precipice of freedom. And then I knew. It had finally happened. Today was the day. Today was the day when I woke up — so to speak — knowing that I was going to tell Derek. I was going to tell Derek.

Chapter Twenty-five

As I drove my bike to Hank and Rebecca's for brunch that afternoon, I relished in the cool mist of a light rain. I could remember having driven in weather like this before. Then, the rain had felt like a swarm of attacking needles. I had ducked in a futile attempt to protect my face from the mini torture session and still somehow watch the road. Today, same weather, it was as if the tiny droplets of water were rays of joyful light, which, upon contact, bathed me in euphoria. I couldn't get over how sure I was — about everything. I was sure of my love for both Hank and Rebecca, so quickly and firmly established, sure about their love, each of them, for me. I'd seen enough game playing in the bars, been with enough men who approached one-night-stands with a forced sense of emotional connectedness, to know that what I had with Hank and Rebecca was real. And I was so sure about telling Derek, so sure that whatever the outcome of this long overdue revelation, it would be the right thing for me.

I pulled my bike up in front of the garage, removed my helmet and smoothed back my hair. As I walked over to ring the bell, anticipation, and the euphoria from the mist, filled me to overflowing.

Hank greeted me, his smile as big as mine — like a beauty pageant winner. We enjoyed each other's expressions until our smiles turned to sweet soft laughter. Then I said, "My bike's in front of the garage."

"Oh." He came to. "Okay."

"Looks like fun," Hank said, stroking the gas tank after I'd settled the bike next to their Toyota. We stood about a foot apart.

"Yeah, it has been. I've had it since I was sixteen. My cousin said, 'Wanna buy my bike?' I thought, now what's Vin up to? But soon as I got on it..." My words trailed off. Our eyes turned away from the bike and to each other, then we were kissing. When we parted — ever so reluctantly — Hank took my hand. "Come on," he said, and headed us up the steps.

Rebecca was in the kitchen again, juicing oranges. When our eyes met, I realized, with a pulsating intensity, like a ball of fire dancing around inside me, that I had never desired a woman in this way before, that, in fact, there were only two other people I'd ever desired in this way — Rick, and her husband.

We diced potatoes, separated broccoli flowerets, and grated cheese, to a background of light jazz coming in over NPR. Our conversation about good restaurants to go to for brunch, led into a discussion about good ethnic restaurants, which led me into telling them about Carol and her hobby. They were thrilled with the stories of the various new immigrant girls and their great recipes.

"Carol sounds interesting. How long were you with her?" Rebecca asked as she scrambled eggs, adding a dash of pepper, a dash of salt.

"Little over three years."

"What happened?"

"Well..." I hesitated. Tell them about Mike? About Derek? About my clos... not a pretty past. I wanted to tell them everything. I wanted to open up my heart and soul and mind, hand them the keys and tell them to feel free to rummage. But not now, not until I was out to Derek. So I said, "It was never so much serious as convenient, more fun than deep. She's a workaholic; on average we didn't see each other more than a few days a month."

Nervously anticipating a question about Carol's attitude towards my bisexuality, I said, after taking a sip of coffee, "What kind of beans are these? Guatemalan?"

Hank answered — onion scented steam rising up behind him from a pan of sautéing potatoes — "Yeah, French roast." He watched me take another sip, then smiled broadly.

"What?" I mouthed the word across the room.

"You like coffee."

No one had ever said this to me before. "How'd you know?"

He laughed. "You should see your face when you've got the stuff in your mouth. When you swallow."

"I like coffee," I confessed, holding his gaze over the top of my cup as I took another sip. Hank watched me unabashedly. I thought of saying, "And you like me," but that was already well established. I realized then that Rebecca had turned around from the cutting board. She was resting her back against the counter, smiling with satisfaction at the way Hank and I were flirting. The three of us looked alternately at one another. This nice neat triangle, all points firmly connected.

****

As we ate our spinach, mushroom, and cheddar omelets with home-fries and fresh orange juice, it dawned on me, during a moment of sudden comfortable silence, that the reason I had decided to come out to Derek was that I could never tell these two that I had to hide what was between us. No, not just that, not just that I couldn't tell them this, but that I couldn't *do* it. I couldn't lie about something this beautiful. I had done that once before, with Rick, and I could not do it again.

I felt amazingly calm there at the table with this man and this woman whom I had made love to the night before. There was no anxiety, nor panic, about telling Derek. That, I knew, would come later, as I contemplated how and where and when. There would be plenty of time for anxiety later. I did not even feel the joyous excitement that I'd experienced earlier, simply relaxed... at home.

Chewing on buttered cracked-wheat toast (everything tasted unnaturally good; I had never been aware before of enjoying toast!) a bit of irony occurred to me. Had I been able to lie to Derek about Hank and Rebecca, but not been able to confess this horror to them, not been able to sit there, look them in the eye and say, "Yes, this is glorious, *but* I have this friend see, and he doesn't know about me, that I love men." Had I tried to keep *Derek* a secret from them... Yes, that would have amounted to being closeted about being closeted. Just the type of mess I was likely to get myself into. But not this time.

As we cleared the table after brunch, I found myself unable to resist the pull of Rebecca's body, and Hank seemed unable to resist mine. I was sandwiched between them as we groped and kissed and somehow made our way to the bed and nirvana.

****

After we finally got around to cleaning up the kitchen, we went for a walk in the park. The sky had cleared; the sun was out, rapidly drying everything it touched. I remember hoping that Derek wouldn't happen upon us, and I was thrilled that this was not due to a fear of being outed, but rather because I didn't want to miss the opportunity to tell Derek myself. All the fear — it would soon be over.

We walked a long way through the park, to Mallard Lake, where old men sit on benches and young families with kids feed the ducks. Pigeons were everywhere vying for a piece of the action. Hank, Rebecca, and I, totally high on life, stood quietly, taking it all in.

I spent the evening with them, in front of the fireplace, listening to Miles Davis, and this time I spent the night. The next day, Sunday, Rebecca had to work, so I would spend the day alone with Hank.

****

Early Sunday morning, I awoke to the view of Hank's well-manicured hand resting on Rebecca's ribcage, her breast hidden beneath streamers of amber curls. I sat up slowly, dazed by happiness, and slipped out to use the bathroom.

When I returned, to Rebecca sitting naked at the edge of the bed brushing her hair, and Hank bare-chested, hands folded behind his head, watching her, I had an overwhelming desire to drop to my knees, and give thanks to the Lord. But instead, I slid in behind Rebecca and next to Hank. He put his arm around me, and together we watched Rebecca dress for work.

Then she was gone.

"Just the two of us," I mused, turning to face Hank.

"Yeah, you and me."

"So..."

"So..." He ran his hand up my thigh, towards my groin, while simultaneously pressing his parted lips on mine. I got an instant erection.

I'd received an education during the last two days in the dynamics of threesomes, something I'd been totally ignorant of. Erotically speaking there's an ever-mounting level of stimuli. Not only do you experience the direct interactions between you and your lovers, but the interactions of your lovers with one another, each of their reactions to what you're doing with the other person, your reactions to their reactions etc. etc. etc. In conjunction with this virtual cornucopia of sexual stimuli, for Hank, Rebecca and I, there was also a powerful overabundance of love-saturated emotions. Because this love was so equally shared among us, it didn't always matter whose hand you were caressing; in fact, sometimes, in the acrobatic passion of the moment, it wasn't easy to know; in fact, you could be caressing your own hand without realizing it at first. It was as if we threw ourselves into a gigantic pool of love, melted there together, swam unencumbered in its pleasures, and then came up bathed in joy, gasping for breath, for release, from what was an almost unbearable ecstasy.

Though I was still reeling from the wonders of being in a threesome, Sunday morning I discovered that being alone with Hank was far from anticlimactic. It was another kind of heaven, floating on another kind of high. I understood immediately that it would have been a terrible deprivation if we'd not allowed ourselves to experience one another individually. There are ways in which we connect with other people that are unique to the individual. Certain aspects of our personalities are understood, appreciated, or even elicited, by few others — sometimes no one else, sometimes just one other. There were parts of me, parts of Hank, which we discovered and relished in only when it was just the two of us. Quickly on our first day together we understood the profundity of the relationship that was just ours — independent from what the three of us had. Our lovemaking that morning was insanely intense, as though we were both trying to devour the other with our bodies.

I was still coming down off my orgasm when Hank said, "So tell me about physics." He paused to catch his breath. Then added, "When did you first get interested?"

I was laying on my back, the cool room bringing down my body-temperature, drying the sweat. No break between sex and physics, humm, okay; I'll let Hank take me there.

"Pretty young," I said, the sound of his breathing intoxicating me, loosening my tongue. "I was fascinated with the structure of things, but not on a mechanical level, on a molecular level, and then on a grand scale — these microscopic particles making up this vast, poorly comprehended, universe. It was such a huge challenge, you know, to get any kind of a grasp on it."

Hank kissed my hand. "You're smarter than most people I come across."

I turned to look at him. It was funny, the way he said it. "Well, I guess that's it; I needed to channel my tendencies to process and analyze, into something that would keep me on my toes. So tell me about publishing."

He sat cross-legged next to me, looking at my arm as he ran fingertips slowly along its length. "That was an obvious choice for me," he said. "I love communication — the transmitting of ideas and feelings. When people actually get across what they mean, connections become so much more pure." He bent over to lick a droplet of cum off the tip of my cock, then continued, "Communication is fundamental to the growth of humanity. Umm." He savored the taste in his mouth a moment, then added, "Individuals have all these ideas, which, when expressed and brought together, can move things forward. And the *written* word is this great re-viewable, editable, form of communication."

"That's pretty deep, Hank."

He gave me this look that said all kinds of deep things without using any words at all.

While Hank showered, I thought of Derek and all the words we'd shared, ideas we'd melded, and all the books — other people's ideas — we'd poured-over together.

****

That afternoon, Hank and I were in bed chatting and eating delivered Chinese food. I sat against the wall, wearing boxer shorts. Hank was at a right angle to me, his knees pulled up, a blanket draped over his naked body.

"The parade's in a couple of weeks." Hank stretched a toe out to be warmed under my knee.

I looked up from my cardboard container; I'd been searching for another cashew. "Parade?"

He looked at me oddly. "Gay Pride Day?"

"Oh! Yeah." Funny I should forget.

"Rebecca's scheduled to work. I made plans to go with friends. You'll join us?"

Finding a cashew, I held it in front of me between chopsticks and thought, Gay Pride Day... I stuck the nut in my mouth. Next year. Next year I'll go to the parade with Hank. This year I have something much more important to do on that day — something highly appropriate. School was out, and the German 101 summer class we'd signed up for wouldn't start until right after Pride Day, so I could avoid Derek for the next couple of weeks. It would take some doing, but I'd find some excuses, use them all up; I wouldn't be needing them soon. Waiting would be good too, I realized, because I not only needed to come out to Derek, but also to tell him about Hank and Rebecca, and that would seem less ridiculous if I'd been involved with them for more than just a couple of days. Anyway, I needed time to consider exactly how to tell him.

****

I called Derek on Monday as promised.

He picked up, apparently expecting me. "Hey."

I was really glad to hear his voice. "How's it going?"

"Not bad, how 'bout you?" He sounded happy too.

"I'm great actually. But, listen, I want to talk to you about something important." To hell with the excuses, I had decided. "Can you meet me at A Kiss of Heaven, a week from this Sunday? Around one?"

"Sure. What's all this about?"

"I'm gonna have to tell you in person."

"Okay, but you sound kinda..." and then, totally out of character, he asked, "Is it something bad?"

I hesitated. "I guess that's a matter of opinion."

He laughed. "Okay, so... Well... How about a game of eight ball tonight?"

"It's..." I was trying to finish the sentence but my throat was not cooperating.

"It's what?"

"It's better if I don't see you until then. Until we can talk."

There was a long silence. Finally Derek said, "What's going on?"

"Derek... Just trust me on this." Then I blurted out without intending to, "I don't want to be making up any excuses."

"Excu..." Now Derek seemed to be at loss for words. Eventually, incredulously, Derek said, "Why would you be making up excuses?"

The tone of his voice in particular got to me. I involuntarily sighed loudly into the receiver. "I'll see you in a couple of weeks," I said, and hung up.

My old friend regret, in the form of grief, moved in, a thick gray cloud of gloom. There were no thoughts, only feelings. I went and lay down on my bed, my face buried in the crook of my arm. After a while, I realized I was sobbing.

****

My experiences with Hank and Rebecca thus far were like having shackles released. Tuesday, I got to find out what it was like to be alone with Rebecca. Teenaged Mary aside, a holding back that's always there when your lover is not someone you love was gone for the first time with a woman. The closet I'd so laboriously dragged along with me every time I'd ever bedded someone of the opposite sex, also gone for the first time — Rebecca not only knew I had a thing for men, she'd actually witnessed me fucking and being fucked by her husband — how out

215

can you be? Making love with Rebecca was a welcoming of freedom, characterized by utter abandon and passion.

As with Hank, parts of who I am, parts of who Rebecca is, were released and celebrated now that it was just the two of us. With both of them, the elements of my personality that came to the forefront were traits that I embraced like lost friends, aspects of who I am which had suffered for lack of expression. I could have met either Hank or Rebecca, had they been single, and immediately started up a serious relationship as a twosome. But I was glad that this was not how it had happened, not only because I wanted both of them in my life, but because I wanted to be able to be with both of them simultaneously — to experience with them this amazing thing called a threesome — and because I wanted them to have each other.

****

I thought a lot about coming out to Derek. I couldn't imagine him walking away from me, just turning his back and walking away. But I knew too, Derek couldn't imagine me lying to him, couldn't imagine me having a secret life, couldn't imagine me making love with a man.

The possibility having a future without Derek, was terrifying, but it was a terror I'd always lived with — at any time I could have been accidentally outed. The difference was now I was finally ready for this. Ready to lose him, or else finally really gain him — in a true *honest* friendship. There was no longer room for other options. If he disappeared out of my life, I could accept this as an alternative to continuing the way we had been. When I was alone, a mixture of anxiety over coming out to Derek, and joy over my new love life, consumed me. When I was with Hank and/or Rebecca, I found it easy to just focus on what we had, and not think about Gay Pride Day. I had decided to wait to tell them about Derek until after I came out to him — more palatable to say I *was* closeted than to say I *am* closeted.

When I said good-bye to Hank the following Sunday, I told him that I had something rather urgent to take care of the day of the parade.

"More important than Pride Day?" He obviously found this hard to believe.

We'd spent the afternoon making love, and lingering sensations still dominated parts of my body. "More important," I said. "I'll explain next week."

He studied me carefully. "Why do I get the impression you're up to something mischievous?"

"Because of the way I'm looking at you, but that's only because I still can't believe how beautiful you are; it has nothing to do with what I'll be doing on Sunday."

Chapter Twenty-six

There was what appeared to be a vacuum of feeling as I headed down Haight Street on Gay Pride Day. I wasn't sure if there were so many conflicting feelings that I was unable to identify any of them, or if on some level I knew not to feel or think anything, just allow myself the space within which to experience and process whatever was going to soon come my way.

I sat in an alcove, against a window, and was immediately shrouded in the fog of other people's cigarette smoke. I felt very serious and, for the moment anyway, calm. The day, the event, had been so frequently in my thoughts over the years, that the reality of it took on a surreal quality.

Bill approached my table. "Cup-o'caffeine?"

"Yeah," I responded, looking him in the eye. Had I ever looked Bill in the eye before? I had chosen A Kiss of Heaven as the location for my "coming out party" because I didn't think a private setting would be comfortable for either Derek or me, and also, I liked the idea of Bill being around — it was possible Derek would become violent.

Bill smiled, then turned away to get me the usual dark-roast. It occurred to me then that he could easily have not been here today because of the parade.

I glanced at the clock behind the counter; I was fifteen minutes early, but of course Derek could possibly arrive early too — we both had tendencies in this direction — he might, in fact, arrive at any moment. Nervousness, like a venom, crept through me.

Bill placed my coffee on the table. I was too distracted now, said only a half-present thanks; this could be the last time I ever see Derek. As Bill walked away, I realized that I was gripping the handle of the coffee mug — as if it were Derek, as if I could somehow physically hold on to our friendship, keep it from slipping away into empty blankness.

Sunlight, which was reflected as a laser point of brightness in my coffee, was suddenly eclipsed by a figure moving across the front of the window. It was Derek — black jeans, black boots, black jean jacket — just as he'd been dressed the day I met him. And now he had come through the door, and was standing at my table. I looked up at him, frightened, not at all self-assured like I'd hoped I'd be.

Derek looked concerned and a bit annoyed. He held my gaze as he sat down. Almost nostalgically, I took in the straight line of his nose, the dark dark brown of his eyes, those thin lips, not grinning at the moment.

Then Bill was there. "What'll it be, Bud?"

I turned my attention to this crazy hippie, and, noticing now that he was wearing a long strand of electric blue love beads, I involuntarily laughed.

Bill raised his eyebrows.

"I like your beads."

Derek squinted at me oddly, and I realized at once, I never would have said something like that in front of him before.

Bill touched the beads, and said, "Why, thank you."

"I'll have a cup of dark-roast," Derek interjected.

The familiar huskiness of his voice struck me; I wanted to fill myself up with it, hold it inside me forever. I forgot about Bill. He was gone now anyway — but he returned almost immediately with Derek's coffee, then left us alone again.

It was obvious from Derek's expression that he had not been happy about the two-weeks distance I had imposed, about the mysteriousness of this meeting. He was uncomfortable. Little did he know just how uncomfortable he'd soon become.

I took a sip of my coffee, hoping for a sense of sanctuary there, but the warmth, the rich flavor, were no match against that which I now faced. I leaned forward, my hands clasped before me on the table. Looking directly at Derek, I took the first step in what promised to be a long journey.

"I want to start by saying I'm sorry. But those words seem so inadequate, in the context of what it is I have actually done."

Derek's eyes expressed uneasiness and...and doubt. We stared at each other silently, gravely. I saw a thought forming on his lips and waited for it. Finally, firmly, with anger, he said, "You don't need to apologize to me." Like how dare I think he would ever expect an apology for anything I had done.

I sat up, swallowed hard. "I've lied to you. Lied all these years, systematically, repeatedly, consistently."

Derek laughed. A nervous disbelieving laugh. "About what?"

"About who I am."

"Your name's not Jim." His sarcasm was born of frustration, of confusion.

"My name's Jim." Picking up a pink packet of artificial sugar, I felt the powdery granules between my fingers. Studying this in my hand, I said, "Carol didn't leave me for another guy. She left me because," and now I looked at Derek again. "She left me because she walked in on me in bed with someone else."

"Why would you lie to me about that?" Total incredulity coated his voice.

I took in his face again carefully; he hadn't shaved that morning. Then I looked right into his eyes, made sure I had his full attention, opened my mouth, hesitated, just a second, and then the words, I felt them taking shape in my mouth, savored them like expensive chocolate, "It was a man."

Derek looked at me blankly, and then, "What was a man?"

I'd expected this, expected that even when I told him right to his face, he still wouldn't know, and so, with unbelievable ease, I spelled it out for him now. "It was a man I was in bed with."

Derek's eyes widened, froze momentarily, then he pulled his gaze away and stared, without blinking, at an unidentified spot on the wall.

"Look at me Derek."

He did. Fierce eyes, clenched jaw.

"I'm bisexual." Again, the words like a delicacy in my mouth.

He sat perfectly still, except to look away again. Despite the lack of movement, I sensed complete restlessness — a beast who'd suddenly found himself imprisoned by a clever trap, a trap more clever than he. He wanted to escape but didn't have a clue how, dared not even try. And I, as if the captor of this volatile angry creature, watched him carefully, fearing escape, ready to jump to action if the attempt were made. A long space went by like this. Then finally, looking as if he'd just been told that his lunch was monkey intestines, he said to the wall, as a half question, half statement, swallowing on each of his words as if he might throw it up instead, "You're telling me you're gay?"

"Bisexual."

He looked back at me, gestured helplessly, as if I were speaking Arabic.

"I enjoy women, I'm sure as much as you do, but I also enjoy men. *A lot.* Sexually, romantically."

Derek shook his head, as if attempting to knock right back out the information he'd just taken in.

But I had to tell him all of it; if he ran off now, and I never had a chance to confess...

"There's more," I said. "More I have to tell you."

221

"More? *What?"* He squirmed in his chair, the tiger beginning to search for an out.

"Jeff and I were lovers."

There was a second, only a second, then Derek jumped up, pushing back his chair violently. But he just stood there staring at me. He seemed to be surprised, and thrown off center, by his own reaction, as if he wasn't sure where he was or what he was doing. He seemed to be assessing *what* to do. Then he saw me look at Bill, who appeared behind him, and he turned to face this long-gray-haired sage.

Bill stared calmly but sternly at Derek.

"What do you want?" Derek demanded.

"I've seen you two come in here together for years."

"What of it!" Derek seemed as if he might take Bill's head off in one clean bite.

"I think you should hear him out," Bill said with a shrug.

Derek looked at me. And I smiled. I smiled a smile that was so typically me that Derek couldn't help but *see* that it was me. And he did see that it was me, a fact that registered on his face as total confusion. Giving Bill a curt nod, he sat back down, reluctantly, as if at a loss as to what else to do.

I gave Bill an appreciative glance. He winked then returned to his job. Derek was calm, though far from relaxed, more a calmness resulting from exhaustion. He gestured in the general direction of where Bill had been, and asked, "What's with him?"

When I failed to answer immediately, Derek crossed his arms and looked out the window. I pick up my cup, attempted to bring it to my lips, but my hand was shaking, and I put it back down again. I'd come way too close to losing Derek. Finally, when I could, I answered, "I'm fairly certain he's bi too." My voice was as shaky as my hand, and this scored a quick glance from Derek, but he clearly found the outside world a lot safer and turned back to it.

"I see him at the bars sometimes," I explained, "but I've also seen him out with a girlfriend."

"The bars," Derek repeated to the window. Then he added without apparent anger, "I have no fucking idea who you are."

"Yes you do!"

He looked at me as if I were completely insane.

"Okay, maybe you don't." I thought for a minute. "You do, and you don't."

Derek nodded his head slowly. "I do and I don't." His tone was totally sarcastic.

I searched desperately for the right thing to say.

But then Derek queried the widow, "Jeff, huh?"

"Yeah," I sighed. "I didn't know he was gay either, at first. He wasn't closeted, but because of me... Well, anyway that's why he left me."

"Left you. *I* thought he went back east because of a job offer."

"Job offer, ex-lover..."

Derek looked at me. "Ex-lover?" as if I'd said ex-Martian. He was quiet a moment, then he said, matter-of-factly, "I'm sorry, Jim, but I just can't listen to this." He pushed his chair out, much more quietly this time, stood, turned, and took a step.

"Derek..."

He stopped.

"Please, don't go."

He turned back to face me. Derek stared at me for a long while. Anger and uncertainty, gave his face a particularly scary look. Then his expression changed; he looked sad. He didn't want to go. He sat back down.

The third time I'd slept with Rick, the nervousness of being with someone new was completely gone, any sense of being unsure if what we had was real, gone too.

We had copulated lustily after school, and then we lay in each other's arms, exhausted, in love, at peace. I remember feeling an overwhelming sense of safety. I was with Rick, in his bed; nothing could harm me. Though that feeling came over me many times when with Rick, I hadn't felt it again, since we'd parted, until there, that moment, when Derek sat back down across from me at A Kiss of Heaven. I found this odd, and tried to make sense of it. Derek was still visibly disturbed, still full of uneasiness and rage, yet I felt extraordinarily safe. I knew I wasn't home-free yet. At any time he still might walk, walk out and be gone — for forever. That moment felt, actually, extremely odd. Here was a Derek who knew I was bi. Here was a Jim who wasn't closeted. It was a completely new world. I understood then — the sense of safety came from knowing, for the first time, that there was hope with Derek, that being out and still having Derek in my life *was* a possibility. I had to find a way to bring him through this.

"Why did you want to leave?" I asked softly. "Because I'm bi, or because I betrayed our friendship?"

"Both."

"I understand completely why you're angry about the betrayal. But I don't get homophobia. I've tried to understand it, but I can't; it eludes me. Why does the reality of me loving men make you angry?"

"Loving?" He still had that sad look on his face. Sad, and I now realized, also frightened.

"Yes, loving."

He studied me, squinting with knit eyebrows as if he were in a great deal of pain. Finally he said, "It doesn't make me angry." He paused then added, "I guess it does make me angry. But it's more than that. It makes me..." Derek looked as if he might choke or cry, and then the word came out, as if on its own, "*uncomfortable.*"

"But why?"

"Why? Because..." He stopped. He stopped because he knew the answer.

"Yes?" I knew the answer too.

"Because... Because we were friends." He said this harshly, leaving me to read between the words.

I stared at him, right in the eyes, for a long while. He glared — the terrified tiger — back at me.

"And what?" I finally said. "Do you think I've been lusting after you all these years?"

His whole body tensed; the clear message being: you so much as touch me and I'll tear you to pieces.

Undaunted, I matched his anger. "Do you really think you're so hot? I'm not in the slightest bit interested in you in that way. I find the idea as repulsive as you do. You're not my type, *Derek*." I said his name with a particularly nasty tone that I immediately realized I'd borrowed from Mike.

"Not your type?" Now Derek was being snide. "What's your *type*, Jim? A prissy little *fag* with a dainty swish?" He had said it; he *had* to say it.

"Fuck you, Derek!" This was something *I* had to say. But I realized what an insanely poor choice of words I'd made under the circumstances. Covering up quickly, I scowled at him and added, "You wear your masculinity like a protective shell; it's so..." I wanted to use the word "impenetrable," but stopped myself, and for lack of a good quick substitute said, "unappealing. It's like you're not really human. Who'd want to have sex with *that*? How does anyone make love to someone who's on-guard all the time. It's..." hard enough? no... "difficult enough to be friends with someone like that. So don't worry, I have no desire whatsoever to be lovers with a macho-homophobe who wears a thick defensive armor as a goddamned permanent *overcoat*."

He gave me a particularly unattractive forced smile. "I can't tell you what a relief it is to know that I don't turn on queers."

"*Relief?*" Why should he care?

"Half the guys you see, you wonder what's going on inside their heads when they look at you. It's scary walking around this city."

"Scary?"

"Yeah, scary."

It was amazing to realize how heteros think.

I sat there feeling simultaneously happy that I'd told Derek things that I'd felt about him all along, and regretting tremendously that I'd criticized him so harshly. Not that I thought it upset him. Sure, he'd take it as confirmation of his masculinity. Well, good for him. What a jerk.

He was fuming; I could practically see the steam rising out of him, the air around him melting. But he wasn't a jerk, just... Just... *What* was it about him? How many times had I cursed the day I met him? How many times had I wondered what mysterious force of nature had brought us into each other's lives? How many hours had we spent together? How many truly great moments? Many, many, many — like grains of sand on a beach, stars in the sky, atoms on the head of a pin. Some nights, when we'd been talking, we'd looked at the clock clueless — it could have been seconds or centuries — and found it was four or even five AM. Yet, I realized now, Derek had never slept on my couch; I'd never offered; he'd never suggested. This wasn't within the realm of possibilities...

"You lied to me for five goddamned years!" This quiet shout, squeezed out between Derek's teeth, pulled me jarringly back. God, he was angry. Well, I guess I would be too. But he hadn't given me a choice, had he?

So I told him, "If I had been honest with you from the start, there wouldn't have been five years. There wouldn't have been five minutes."

"What gave you the right to take that option away?"

"The fact that it would have been based on ignorance and prejudice."

"So you were just trying to protect me from what you considered my ignorance?"

"I was just trying to protect our friendship, which you can't tell me hasn't meant a lot to you over the years."

"*Friendship*! What friendship? Friendship isn't built on a foundation of lies."

"Fine, okay, I should have told you right away. At least then I wouldn't be sitting here now, looking at the disgust in your eyes, watching all the respect you ever had for me circle up with the cigarette smoke, and get sucked out the vents. At least..." I had to stop to catch my breath, "at least I wouldn't have spent five years living a totally fucked-up, closeted life, hiding who I am, which happens to be someone I like a lot, hiding and lying, and losing Jeff." Anger alone kept back my tears now. "Goddamn it! I came to San Francisco to be *out*! To hell with it! To hell with you, Derek! To hell with the last five years! It was all a mistake, a terrible fucked-up mistake."

I clenched my jaws to keep my teeth from chattering. Shit! The cafe wasn't even cold! I put my arms around my waist to hold in my rage.

Derek was watching me wide-eyed. Then he was staring at the tabletop. He was thinking, processing; I knew the pose well. But I just wanted him to go away. Leave, Derek. Fine. Be gone for forever. Go ahead, do it already. Go!

But he looked up now, and said, "The last five years weren't a mistake. The lies were a mistake. But not the last five years. Don't say that."

It was something, I realized, what he was saying. It was the most emotionally deep thing he'd ever said to me, and he was saying it to an *out* me. Of course I didn't want him to leave. No. But what he'd said was illogical, and

Derek had a mind that picked up on errors in logic almost by instinct.

"You can't have one without the other," I told him. "The lies, the five years, they go hand in hand. It's a package deal. That's the point, Derek. That's the whole point."

He was processing again, but I interrupted. "Damn it, why *are* you so screwed up about homosexuality?"

"Screwed up?"

"Yes. It's a perfectly normal, natural..."

"I'm sure you don't want to think there's anything wrong with it, but *of course* there is."

I looked at him bug-eyed. *Of course?* I couldn't even respond to that.

"Propagation of the species?" he reminded me, as if perhaps I'd forgotten this basic evolutionary principle. "That's what sex if for. Fags..." he stopped himself, "Gay people" — forced political correctness — "don't propagate."

"Neither do you, Derek. According to that argument, every heterosexual act involving birth control is *just* as unnatural, just as *wrong,* as gay sex."

"No, because even though I'm not trying to produce offspring, I'm engaging in an act that consists of what nature intended."

"Get off it, Derek. When *you* have sex, you're engaging in an act of physical pleasure, intimacy, sometimes maybe even love. That's exactly what I'm doing weather I'm with a woman *or* a man. Procreation is for *rabbits*! For us it's just *one* of the possibilities. Humans are different, remember? We have speech, the ability to split atoms..."

"All right!"

"Anyway, study a little zoology, you'd be amazed how much homosexual stuff goes on even with the 'lesser' creatures."

"I said, all right."

All right? "All right what?"

"All right, maybe homosexuality isn't so unnatural. *Maybe*; I'll have to think on that."

"All right I'm bi?"

Derek's face flushed red. "I don't think I can understand that. I don't think I can understand who it is you're telling me you are. *Maybe,* it's not unnatural for two men to..." he seemed to be searching.

"Fuck."

"*Fuck.* But look, it's difficult for me to even *say* that. It's not something that I get. I don't know this person who you say you are, and I don't know that I *can* know you, or that I want..." he stopped himself there; he wasn't able to finish that sentence. In a moment he picked up again with, "You're not who I thought you were. You're not my friend Jim. You're some *other* Jim."

"I'm not your friend Jim. All of a sudden I've turned into someone else."

"Right. All of a sudden you've turned into someone else."

"This is who I've been all along, Derek. But you want me to be someone I'm not."

"I want you to be who I thought you were, who you presented yourself to be." He scowled. "You're getting pissed off because I'm not saying I understand, understand your secrets, your lies," his voice rose rapidly now, "your Goddamn impersonation of a perfectly normal heterosexual!"

Something inside me unraveled. As much as I wanted to keep Derek in my life — and I was all too aware of that desire at that moment — I wasn't going to put up with *any* of his garbage. Our friendship had to continue on my terms or not at all. So I found myself nearly shouting back, "*Normal*? *Normal*! Heterosexual is normal. So I'm some kind of freak? An anomaly. Is that it? Do you want to know what I think about people — gay or straight — who are attracted to only one sex? Do you really want to know? Because I keep my mouth shut about *that*; *I'm* the freak; *I'm* the pervert, right? So yeah, I keep my mouth shut about all those close-minded, repressed, *normal* people walking around, just ready to point a self-righteous finger at the likes of me." I stopped for a second. Did I really think gay and straight people were repressed? But I was on a roll, so I continued, "Just what *is* your problem, Derek? You want me to explain why I'm bi? I'm much more interested in hearing why you're *not*."

Derek shot out of his seat, almost knocking over the table. Cold coffee splashed out of our cups.

"Watch yourself!" He glowered at me.

"Fear!"

"You *mother*..." he stopped himself suddenly, and in a mutual abrupt disorientation, we stared at each other. What the hell was going on here?

Deflated, the rage gone from both of us, Derek sat back down. I was thinking, trying to make sense of the things we'd just said. Why was I challenging Derek's sexuality? What was I trying to say with the word, fear? But Derek allowed his mind to wander elsewhere, and now something else occurred to him, and he interrupted my thoughts with, "That time Alice was changing buses on Castro and saw two men..."

"That day would have turned out very differently, wouldn't it, if Alice had ever met Jeff."

"That was you and Maguire?"

"Yeah," I responded faintly, remembering the horrors of that day.

Derek frowned in an especially disturbed sort of way. "You laughed about that with me! And what? Were you laughing *at* me? All this going on for all these years and I didn't have a clue. You must take me for such a fool!"

230

"Derek," I said harshly, leaning in towards him, "do you have any idea how it felt for me to laugh with you about that? I was betraying Jeff, and myself, and every damn gay and bi person on the planet! *And* I was lying to the best friend I've ever had. *No*, I was *not* laughing *at* you."

Derek stared at me for several seconds with a perplexed look I'd never seen on his face before, then resting his forehead in his hand, he squeezed his eyes shut and was quiet for a long time.

I had a tremendous headache. I focused on that and the jumble of protesting chaos in my stomach.

With his head still in his hands, eyes still closed, Derek mumbled, "Some best friend I am."

I waited a moment, and then whispered, "What?"

"Some best friend." He looked up now. "You're right; I would have avoided the hell out of you had you told me when we first met. The first thing I thought today when you told me, was: if we hadn't been such good friends for so long I'd be outta here in a flash. That's what I really felt like doing — just get the hell away from you." Derek looked out the window but continued to speak. "Yeah, and here I've been thinking, some friend, he's lied to me for years." He paused for a moment, eyes widening. I looked to see what it was outside that alarmed him so, but there was only an idling Corolla at the curb. "But maybe," he went on, "maybe I'm the one who's not been a good friend — that you couldn't tell me, that you knew my prejudices would be greater than our friendship."

I was too scared to say anything, afraid I'd break the spell, make him rethink this.

"Why did you finally tell me?" he asked, turning back to me.

Just the thing to break the spell, just the thing to change his mind. I looked into my cup at the cold lifeless slosh. Where was Bill?

231

"I'm in love," I said finally. "Big time." I couldn't help but smile now; I'm in love.

"With... a man," Derek stated with what appeared to be reluctant distaste.

"A man and a woman."

Confusion registered in Derek's eyes.

"A couple; not a hermaphrodite." I knew this was the wrong joke to make with Derek, but I couldn't resist.

Derek wasn't laughing. Spell broken. Confusion and disgust were written all over his face.

"Degenerate," I said. "Okay, I'm a degenerate."

He shot me a hate-filled glance — could have been a bullet.

"I fell in love with a man and a woman — at the same time, yes, in the same bed — who happened to already be in love with each other. There you have it. Want to make me feel bad about it? Good luck. I feel great about it. Degenerate or not."

"Look, Jim, give me a frigging break! I came here today thinking that you're going tell me you decided not to go for a PhD..."

"You thought *that*?"

"Well, you sounded so serious and scared on the phone, that was the only thing I could come up with. I've always been aware that something was wrong, that something was bugging you; I just didn't know what. So I thought maybe school, maybe physics..."

"No way. How could you think that?"

"What?"

"I wouldn't do that to you, flake out on the PhD; I love school. I love physics. I..."

It seemed there was more to this thought, but Derek cut in. "You wouldn't do *that* to me, but you've lied to me, led a secret life?"

"I'm glad I did."

Yes, we were both glad, weren't we, that we'd had each other these years, even if it had to come the way it did. But, it was clear too that this way of relating to each other had run its course, had necessarily come to an end.

After a long silence, Derek spoke in a monotone to his hands on the tabletop. "A couple." He picked at a fingernail. "That's pretty weird." He reached now for a coffee spoon and fidgeted with it nervously.

"So it sounds weird to you, to other people. I don't give a damn." I thought of Hank, Rebecca, and I, together. "It's intense," I said. "There's a lot of emotion bouncing around in a threesome. You know, if you think about it, it's like an exponential equation."

"A *threesome*." The disgust and sarcasm, in his voice was undisguised.

Without premeditation, I lunged, and grasped Derek's wrists. The spoon dropped from his fingers, clattered onto the table. I put my face right up to his. "Listen to me," I said in a hissing whisper. "Hear what I'm telling you. I feel more whole now than I have *ever* felt. All my life I've been splintered, alien in my own world. All that's gone. I can be with Hank or Rebecca or both and just be myself, no secrets, no other life. I can't be running around anymore behaving as if I'm ashamed of who I am — because I'm not; I never have been. And, I've come to the understanding that if that means giving up our friendship — despite how unbelievably important you are to me — then so be it. And as you said, anyway, what friendship? Who are we really to each other if there are these prejudices, these lies? I'm in love. I'm happy. And I want to, for once, be whole. Give me that."

Derek yanked his hands away from me. Claiming them for himself again, he folded his arms across his chest. In a moment, when the steam settled, Derek said, "I need time." He sat up, smoothed out his hair with an unsteady palm. "It's a lot, Jim. It's a lot."

I nodded. "Okay."

He stood up. Looking down at me with those frightened, sad, eyes, he said, "I guess I'll see you in German class, Monday."

"Yeah, all right. Monday." Then I watched Derek leave. Watched him pass by the window in front of me. I wanted to jump out, crash through the glass after him.

I got a big wordless bear hug from Bill when I was leaving — he'd waved away my five-dollar bill.

Chapter Twenty-seven

Tuesday, Rebecca and I went for a walk at Land's End, where the Pacific greets the San Francisco Bay. We allowed ourselves to get caught up in the surreal landscape, but it wasn't long before — giggling at the hopelessness of avoiding coupled men behind bushes — we opted instead to dose ourselves with art at the nearby Palace of the Legion of Honor. Rodin's The Thinker greeted us on the lawn out front, comically reminding me of Derek — the great thinker in my life.

Inside, Rebecca and I said little, allowing the paintings a chance to speak to us instead. In light of the conversation we'd have when Hank got home, I was glad for the quiet prelude.

But evening came soon enough, and Hank and I sat at the kitchen table with coffee mugs in hand. The kitchen was warm and steamy; a zucchini-nut-bread, made by Rebecca and me, had just been taken out of the oven. Coffee aromas and sweet baked smells filled the room.

"I missed you at the parade."

"You have no idea how much I would have liked to have been there."

"You really couldn't put off your plans?" Hank leaned over his coffee and blew. A waft of steam rose up and disappeared into the cooler air.

"No. That's what I wanted to talk to you about."

Rebecca joined us, baring plates of the bread and her own cup of coffee. After we'd all taken bites — the bread delicately sweet and richly laced with allspice and cinnamon — I said, somewhat abruptly, "I have a friend — Derek." The word friend seemed inadequate. "He's..." I wanted to say, *more than a friend*, but that didn't sound right either. "We're actually pretty close," I offered.

Hank and Rebecca were listening intently, sipping coffee, so I continued. "I met him my first day at State, and we've gone through the physics program together. I really mean *together*. We take all our classes together, study together — several times a week — go bowling, play pool..." my voice trailed off as I thought once more of just how much time we'd spent with each other. "He's got a Harley," I said. "We meet for coffee." I raised my cup, as if to illustrate. What if Derek doesn't get over this? I considering this horror, then realizing — Hank and Rebecca looking at me a little oddly — I lowered my cup and went on. "He's straight." Now the bombshell: "Until Gay Pride Day, he thought I was straight." My embarrassment hit me like a rock in the chest. I looked in Hank's eyes; there was disappointment, disturbance. From my peripheral vision I'd picked up a sudden movement from Rebecca, a sort of full-body twitch.

Still looking at Hank I said, "I don't know how to make this make sense to you. Being closeted with Derek and," I added, glancing at Rebecca now for a second, "also with Carol, was totally against my principles. I've never thought there was anything wrong with being queer. I am ashamed of having been a closet-case, and I never claimed to understand why I was doing it. It even cost me a man I love." I looked at the refrigerator. "Anyway, all that's over now. Maybe my friendship with Derek is over too; I don't know."

"I don't understand," Hank said. "Is this guy homophobic?"

"Yes."

"Then he's a jerk."

"He's not a jerk; that's the problem."

"You're in love with him."

"No!" I shifted uncomfortably in my chair. "I love him like a friend, yeah. But not otherwise; not in the other way."

"The gay way."

"*Any* way. Just as a friend."

"What's the difference? I mean the fact that you stayed closeted all these years..."

"Look," I cut Hank off, "he's like a totally asexual person to me. He's very macho — but not in a sultry way — in an uptight, closed-off way."

"He sounds like a jerk." Hank's tone matter-of-fact, not ugly or accusing.

"I know; but he's not." I looked at Rebecca.

She sighed loudly. "Maybe we don't know you well enough. To understand."

So, over more coffee and zucchini bread, I told them, with heavy emotion, about Rick and my family, about coming to San Francisco alone, about all the commonalties Derek and I had, how we could talk about physics in ways that were beyond anything I'd ever experienced, how quickly and intensely we became a part of each other's lives. I explained how I had assumed Derek wouldn't be homophobic, how open-minded he is about everything else. Then, over more coffee, I told them how Derek *had*, in the end, heard out my confession, had wanted to flee but *didn't*. It was important to me that they not hate him.

Hank and Rebecca sat through it all, silently, sympathetically, listening.

"I want you guys to understand," I said finally, "but ultimately, I can't make you understand, because *I* don't understand," and with that, I had nothing left to say; I was emotionally exhausted.

Hank got up and stood behind me, kneaded my shoulders. "It's okay; I understand enough. I understand that you feel deeply." He bent down and kissed my cheek. "And I understand that Derek's not a jerk, just somehow screwed up." He kissed my mouth. Oh God. I was totally vulnerable to that man at that moment. It was a perfect feeling.

Hank went to put on another pot of coffee, and I looked to Rebecca. She smiled serenely at me, like a Buddha.

"What?" I asked gently, when she said nothing.

"I like loving you."

I exhaled a little laugh. "I like loving you too."

We never did get around to drinking that second pot of coffee. Our lovemaking that evening was of a rolling-hills, voluptuous, sort. Afterwards we went for a tromp through magical Chinatown — made all the more magical from the high we were on. All this we chased down with a late night dinner of spaghetti, Chianti, and spumoni on Polk Street. Still, later that night, when I chose to return to my apartment, I worried about Derek.

****

I got home from classes Wednesday afternoon and searched around for my neglected address book. I found it between the *Toa of Physics* and an old Chemistry text, then sat on the couch next to the phone and dialed.

There was a pick-up at the other end. "Hello." The greeting was so nostalgically sweet.

"Hello," I said back. Jeff had always recognized my voice immediately in the days when I use to call him frequently at his place on Dolores Park.

There was a short silence, then an uncertain, "Jim?"

"Yeah."

"Are you okay?" He sounded very concerned.

"I'm great."

"Great?"

Well, that was to be expected; I was never great back then.

"Totally," I answered. Then, after pausing for effect, I said, "I came out to Derek."

"*You did? Really?*"

"Yeah, on Pride Day." It was so nice to be able to say this to him.

"Wow! So it went all right?"

"I think so. He didn't exactly give me his blessing, but he didn't give me a black eye either. It was difficult to weed out his reaction to my homosexuality from his reaction to finding out I'd been deceiving him. The combination hit him pretty hard. He said he needed time to think."

"No doubt." There was a bitterness, a sarcasm in his tone. I ignored it.

"He came to our German class the past few days acting as if nothing has changed, but I haven't seen him outside of class. I don't know how things will be between us ultimately. But in a way it doesn't matter."

"Of course it matters! Why would you say that?"

"I took five years of it his way; if he can't..." I felt myself starting to choke up, and couldn't finish. *Of course it matters.* "It just doesn't seem possible that things could be the same between us."

"No, it probably won't be the same."

"But I had to do it."

"It's always been something you had to do." There was that bitterness again. "What about Carol?"

"She walked in on me screwing my handball partner some months ago. Not a nice scene. But I was so glad it was over with her. I know you liked her, but that was as really fucked up situation."

"Yeah; it was. So what prompted you to finally tell Derek?"

"I've fallen in love."

Jeff didn't respond. Oh God, I felt like kicking myself. Trying to cover my tracts, I hastily added, "For the first time, I'm in a situation where I feel like I can make my life work."

"Meaning what?" A stiffness distorted his voice.

"I'm involved with a couple." Perhaps he could see the difference here. "Rebecca and Hank."

More silence.

"Jeff?"

"Yeah. I'm just trying to process... A couple? It sounds scary, Jim. I feel like I should be afraid for you."

"*No*. Be *happy* for me. It's wonderful. They're incredible people, and what we have... I've never experienced anything like it. It's like discovering some new law of physics..."

Jeff laughed. "You had to bring physics into this."

"Well, sure."

"I hear how happy you are. It's nice for a change. I just hope you know what you're doing."

"I know what I'm doing."

"Anyway, if it brought you out, it can't be all bad."

Hanging up a little later, after asking how things were with him and Bob — very good as he told it, and I believed him, he sounded good — I felt a sense of peace that I had not experienced since the days before Mary's parent's divorce, a level of calm even more fundamental than the safeness I'd felt at that one point with Derek at A Kiss of Heaven, and I fell into a deep sleep there on the couch.

When I awoke, it was early evening, the faint glow outside oddly more like dawn than dusk. I went to the window in the kitchen and watched the slice of sunset I could see between buildings across the street. Somehow, it made me recall the night Derek and I watched the moon on the water at Fort Funston, and I got a strong urge to call him. I decided not to fight it.

He answered almost immediately.

"Game of pool?" I said, bypassing the hello.

"And pizza," he added, taking the next words right out of my mouth.

"Twenty minutes?"

"Fifteen, I'll grab a cup with you."

"All right." I hung up. Could Derek tell from my voice that I'd just woken up and planned to get coffee first? Did I always get a to-go cup from Two Times Over before we played pool? No. Occasionally, but not usually. Maybe he just made a lucky guess. Maybe, but I knew better. We hadn't even talked about where to meet, we both just knew.

****

At the end of the night, as we were about to climb back on our bikes, the night having gone like any other, with just a faint edge of awkwardness at first, I said, without planning to, "You don't have to forgive me. Ever. For the lies." These I knew were unforgivable, and I wanted to let him off the hook.

But immediately, serenely, he shot back, "I already have."

We stood there a moment looking into each other's eyes. I wanted to hug him — a feeling I could not remember ever having had before. Instead, I quietly mounted my bike and roared away. It wasn't until I was several blocks away that I heard Derek's Harley start up.

Chapter Twenty-eight

"I should tell you about Ted," Hank said over lattes at Two Times Over. Our legs were entangled under the small table. "We've been lovers on and off since college."

"Ah, I've been wondering about the other men in your life."

Hank smiled. "He's married now, but we get together occasionally."

"Open relationship, like you and Rebecca?"

"No."

"Oh."

"He's distressingly charismatic and unnaturally good-looking."

I smiled at Hank, studying him for a clue. "Is that supposed to make me understand, or are you trying to make me jealous?"

"Are you?"

"I could probably work myself up to that."

Hank moved his leg against mine affectionately. "No need. I was totally infatuated with Ted in college, but that's mellowed to fondness. Though it's steamy between us when we do get together, it's nothing close to what I feel for you."

"Maybe I should be jealous of *you*." I suggested. "He sounds hot."

"You wouldn't like him."

"Why not?"

"Ted's always been a mess, especially so back then. He insisted he was straight — had all these girlfriends — but then liked screwing around with me and a few other guys too. He treated the whole lot of us like crap. But I couldn't help myself when it came to him. No matter how many times he was late to meet me, I'd always be there when he asked. That's how I met Rebecca — we kept crossing paths when I was waiting for Ted in the dorm they both lived in. She and I would talk; in the beginning it was mostly me complaining about Ted, but soon we got into all kinds of conversations. One day she said, 'You're looking at me kinda funny for a gay guy,' and I responded, 'Who said I'm gay?'"

"If you're not gay, you might want to tell your boyfriend to take his knee out of your crotch," said a girl walking by our table at that moment.

We laughed, and gave her a thumbs up.

"Anyway," Hank continued, as I inched my knee a bit farther in, "Ted thought it was really funny, when he found out that I'd spent that night with Rebecca instead of waiting around for him. Everyone had assumed I was a confirmed homosexual." Hank grimaced, "You're giving me a hard-on, Jim."

"Sorry." I moved my knee back a tad.

"Forgiven."

"So, no one had ever seen you with a girl?"

"No, I'd never gotten around to exploring my straight side much — except for some girls I'd messed around with on summer vacations at the beach, in my teens; there's just something about a bikini..."

Hank's eyes suddenly sparkled. "See, being gay was a great asset in the rebellion against my ultra-conservative parents. I came out to them when I was fifteen."

"Fifteen?"

"Yeah, I was involved with this nineteen-year-old college freshman, and one night he drove me home hours after my curfew. We got out of his sports car and were arranging our next tryst, when I noticed my parents looking down at me from their bedroom window. I grabbed Steve and gave him a totally randy kiss."

This elicited an involuntarily, "Wow," from me.

"You should have known me back then."

Now, I was jealous. I had been such a coward most of my life — a fact that struck me hard. "Didn't you have any fear?"

"I more or less expected to get kicked out of the house, but I was too naive or too stupid to realize how bad that might be. I didn't get thrown out though, instead, my dad treated me with utter contempt from then on, which, honestly, was a lot more interesting than being ignored — as had been the case up to that point."

"What about your mom?"

"She became all skittish, like I might bite her."

"Did they ever say anything?"

"No, even though every chance I got, I made sure they knew their son was queer. You can imagine how happy my dad was to ship me off to college and be rid of me once and for all."

"You've never been back?"

"No, but they did come to the wedding. My father came up to me at the reception and mumbled over a glass of champagne: 'What a farce.' Later, Ted told me that towards the end of the evening, my father, seriously drunk by now — and of course, having no clue who Ted was — leaned into him and sang, "Hi-ho the dairy-o, the fairy takes a wife," then settled himself into an arm chair, and passed out."

Hank laughed, then smiling wickedly added, "We *could* go back east; I'd love to take you home to meet the family sometime."

The idea terrified me, and I couldn't even muster a faint smile. I folded my arms at my chest, sat up straight, and crossed my legs ankle over knee.

"Oh Jim, I'd never ask you to do something you didn't want to." Hank's tone suggested amused annoyance at how uptight I am, mixed with genuine sorrow at having upset me. I stared at him, frowning. He was infuriating me, he knew it, and he was doing it because he knew that it turned me on. Hank leaned forward, reached out a hand, and ran fingers through my hair, looking at me with an expression that read, "Do please forgive me."

I licked my lips. "Let's go home."

****

A couple of weeks later, I unlocked my door to find Derek sitting at my desk talking with Hank who was on the couch. Rebecca had been assigned a late shift, and Hank had come over to my place for a change. I'd run out to get cream for our coffee and had only been gone a few minutes.

They both turned and smiled at me. I blinked a couple of times to clear my head of this possible hallucination, then remembered that Derek had mentioned something earlier about wanting to borrow a book. Okay, so here he was.

Derek started to get up. "I'll just grab that book and..."

"Stay a bit and have a cup of coffee with us," I said, reminded with a bitter taste in my mouth, of all the times he'd left Jeff and I alone, having no idea what would take place when he was gone.

While I was making the coffee, I listened as Derek and Hank continued a conversation about the parallels between modern physics and Eastern Mysticism.

My return with the coffee prompted silence. I watched the dark liquid flow as I poured coffee into Derek's cup, then Hank's and mine. I sat down near Hank on the couch, and finally said to Derek, "They were out of Nicaraguan, so I thought I'd try something different."

Derek chuckled.

My involuntary chuckle followed. What were we laughing at? I looked to Derek for a clue; he seemed equally confused. Derek and I took sips of our coffee, looking at each other, embarrassed. Something about the idea of trying something different... I rose and got Derek a glass of water, which he drank ravenously in big gulps.

"One of the teachings of Taoism," he said now to Hank as he put down the empty glass, "is that ultimate understanding cannot be expressed in words."

"But we physicists come along," I continued, "and try to explain it with math."

"And?" asked Hank.

"And," said Derek, "we seem to be approaching it."

"But," I went on, "how do we convey our findings to the general public?"

"What you need," said Hank humorously, "is an ace linguist who can translate math into English."

"Or German," Derek said.

"Yes," I said, "something very structured."

When our cups were empty, Derek fished out the volume he'd come for, shook hands with Hank, said he'd see me in class tomorrow, and left.

Sitting with Hank and Derek in my apartment over coffee and conversation had been symbolic proof that everything was right about my life, *finally*.

Over a second cup of coffee, Hank recounted what had happened when I left for the store. Just after I'd gone, there'd been a knock. When he opened the door, there stood a man whom, surprised and embarrassed, said, "Oh!" then, "Ah... is Jim in?"

"He went to get milk. For coffee," Hank told him.

The guy at the door had nodded knowingly at this. Hank realized who it probably was, and introduced himself. After a pause he asked, "Derek?"

"Yeah. Oh, ah... nice to meet you. Look, I'll... I'll give Jim a call later."

"He'll be right back. Come on in."

"Oh. That's okay. I just ah... I just wanted to borrow... I'll give him a call."

Hank opened the door wide. "Really, I don't bite."

Apparently Derek appreciated Hank's sense of humor because suddenly his uneasiness melted, and he stepped in. Hank told him he was reading *Tao of Physics* at my suggestion in response to him wanting to know more about physics.

"He's seems like an all right guy." Hank said now. "Interesting, smart, intense. A lot like you. I see what draws you two to each other. Actually," Hank said, "it's kinda fascinating to be in the same room with you guys."

"How do you mean?"

He thought a moment, then leaning forward, explained, "It's like half of what you're saying to each other isn't expressed verbally. Even when you're talking about coffee."

"That happens with you and me too, Hank. Actually, it's different with us," I corrected. "It's not as if we communicate without speaking, it's more that you know what I'm thinking. You're very in-tuned to the way my mind works."

Hank smiled. "And with you and Rebecca?" he asked.

Ah, the thought of Rebecca, picturing her in my mind, thinking of us together... "She and I communicate really well with words, and with body language — I don't mean just sex. Do you know what I'm saying?"

Hank nodded. He looked kind of sad but in a beautiful way. "I love watching you and Rebecca together," he said, "it's like watching a perfect snow shower."

Then Hank added, "You know, except for those first couple of minutes at the door there with Derek, I found it difficult to believe that I was talking to someone who's homophobic."

"I guess..." I said softly, "he's changed." There *was* something different about Derek, something... "Hey," I said, "let's eat in tonight. How about pork chops with mash potatoes and gravy?" I was suddenly ravenously hungry.

Chapter Twenty-nine

Rebecca stood in the bedroom doorway wearing a white camisole trimmed with lace, and a pair of pink silk and lace bikini underpants. I'd just come running up the stairs. It was a cold day, and I was fully dressed in leather — jacket, pants, gloves, and boots. I'd had a nice ride along the park, thinking of Rebecca as I watched the trees whizzing by. Standing there in the hallway, I had a flashback to the day Rick's mother invited me to spend the night whenever I wanted, and how Rick had greeted me on his bed wearing only cut off shorts. When I told him his toes were as cold as ice, he'd responded, "Melt me." I smiled at the memory, then at Rebecca. As I approached her, it dawned on me that this was the first time since Rick and I split up that I was able to think of him without sorrow or regret, the first time I could look back and feel happy about what we'd had. I stopped a couple of feet in front of her.

Rebecca grinned. "Damn, you look *hot*."

I took off my gloves and put my hands on her shoulders, which were cold. Unzipping my jacket, I pulled her towards me and wrapped the jacket flaps across her back. She moved her small hands around to my back and held me tight. I smelled Hank in her hair, felt her hard nipples and soft breasts pressing against my thin shirt. "Let's go into the bedroom," I whispered.

I took off my boots and we sat on the mattress cross-legged facing one another, smiling foggy-eyed, like a couple of blissed-out yogis. After a bit, I knelt to peel off my jacket, then slipped fingers behind the waistband of Rebecca's underwear, pulling it out to take a peek at that pretty red triangle of hair. As I sat down again, I let my fingertips brush lightly against the silk covering her clitoris. She moaned softly. We sat for a long while devouring each other with our eyes.

More often than not, Rebecca greeted me on our Tuesdays dressed in old jeans and some oversized T-shirt or another. Usually that was all she was wearing — shoes, socks, underclothing, all absent. And then there were times, such as this day, when sexy underwear was the only thing she was wearing. Though Rebecca's physical features were undeniably feminine, her personality was totally androgynous. I was always in awe of the way she moved in and out of femininity and masculinity — in clothing and behavior — with such ease, such grace, thoroughly enjoying the contrasts, without signs of awkwardness. Witnessing how much she enjoyed herself in a slinky red dress and heels gave me a better understanding of male transvestites. A woman can get away with a lot more versatility in her behavior. Rebecca was able to have fun with this license without it coming across as distorted. As far as my response to Rebecca, and I know Hank's as well, no matter what she was wearing, it always had a sexual allure. She was a highly sensual person, utterly comfortable with her sexuality, and that always came through.

We made love that afternoon, a lovemaking that started out slow and teasing and left us eventually sweaty and short of breath. In bed afterwards — naked, sticky, the smell of sex still heavy in the air — we lay side by side on our backs, one of Rebecca's knees resting on my abdomen. I stroked it as one might a cat's belly.

"You and Hank," I said, "that's quite a relationship you got going."

"I like it."

"So do I." I thought about how much I liked it, then asked, "Did you ever consider forsaking all others?"

"No." She put a hand between my legs and started toying absentmindedly with my limp cock. "We were very certain to have that not included in our vows. For one thing, there's always been Ted. And 1974, college, California, you know, free love was the standard assumption. I guess most people blew the concept off eventually, but monogamy isn't something that either Hank or I have ever had any interest in."

"Nineteen-seventy-four, I lost my virginity that year; I was fifteen."

"You lost your virginity the year Hank and I met," Rebecca mused, "I like that. Boy or girl?"

"Girl. Mary Rachel Wallace. God," I laughed, "I wonder what she's up to these days." I was enjoying Rebecca's fondling without actually getting aroused; that didn't seem to be her goal anyway. "It's never been difficult?" I asked, returning to the original topic, "being involved with other people?"

"It isn't, is it? I mean with the three of us." This was a statement; not a question — the answer had been obvious from the moment I stepped up to the pool table the night we met.

"Jealousy," Rebecca said now, "is all about insecurity. It can be tricky when one of us has a sexual partner that the other one doesn't know. It helps if there's a lot of clarity in the air."

I was starting to get hard. Realizing this, Rebecca stopped playing with me. I was glad; we had all afternoon. She turned on her stomach, and I ran my hand along the back of her thigh, up to her ass. Rebecca's ass, smooth as a nun's belly. Smooth as a nun's belly, a phrase my father had used a lot — in reference to bread dough, about infant Jesse's bald head, about a salesman's pitch — before my father had "found religion," before religion had gobbled up my father and made him disappear.

"Like with Ted," Rebecca was continuing, "we both knew him before we knew each other. I know Ted's not about to try and *steel* Hank from me, run off with him. And Ted and I *like* each other, in a sort of very distant way. Why should I object to him and Hank sleeping together? I have no qualms about it." She paused, and sat up. "Except maybe now that Ted's married." She bit her lip. "I don't like that Ted's wife doesn't know. But — and I've given this some thought — Hank was involved with him first, for years, it's hard to say it's wrong. I think the moral issue's Ted's, not Hank's. That may be a cop-out, but it's hard for me to be sympathetic towards people who demand sexual fidelity. I don't relate." She looked down at me beside her. "What do you think?"

I sat up too and studied the paisley pattern on the Iranian bedspread that covered us. Eventually, I said, "Love is so rare and precious; it doesn't seem right to ask people not to act on it."

The words hung in the air, suspended in the steaminess still lingering from our lovemaking. I felt such a nervousness within me surrounding this idea, and I wasn't sure if it was because this philosophy needed more thinking through, or if there was something else.

"There was a time," Rebecca began, filling-in the silence that I was beginning to find displeasing, "when I felt uncomfortable about a woman Hank was going out with. I hadn't met her, and that's fine with a one-night-stand, but he started seeing her a couple of times a week while I was at work. Back then I often worked late-nights. Anyway, I didn't know where this woman's head was at, how she perceived the situation. It made me nervous."

I turned to get a good look at Rebecca. "But you didn't ask Hank to stop seeing her." I knew she never would. Rebecca's hair needed washing, I noticed now. It was a little oily on top, stringy at the ends. This made her somehow *more* beautiful. The many versions of Rebecca, each more alluring than the rest.

"No," Rebecca conceded, with a faraway look in her eyes.

"What did happen?"

"I ended up going to bed with her." Rebecca laughed. "Her name was Sheila." She said the name as if it were some type of exotic flower; obviously Rebecca liked the taste of this woman's name in her mouth. "She was very sexy. She'd seen a picture of me one day and said, 'Wow! Hank, why aren't you sharing her with me?' When Hank told me this, I rolled my eyes. But eventually, reluctantly, I agreed to Hank setting us up on a weird twist on the concept of a blind date. I thought it was important that I meet this woman anyway."

Taking all this information in, I picked up a strand of Rebecca's hair and played with it, twisting it around my finger, then watching it unravel; tugging it lightly to make it straight, then releasing it again to watch the curls bounce back into form.

"Sheila was a trip. She was total high-energy and, oh what's the word... *vivacious*! She was just like this flighty butterfly dancing around from flower to flower tasting them all and saying, 'Yum... what's next?' She had ideas... acupuncture, aloe vera juice as *the* cure-all, astrology, you know, all *Oh, Rebecca, you have to let me read your chart sometime*! She was, anyway, interesting, and she had a good heart. But Hank and I were just another faze, another concept to explore. *Oh, a* threesome, *humm, a married couple, wow...* She twirled through our lives and then spun her way right back out again. We missed her when she left."

I had stopped playing with her curls. When Rebecca combed back a lock with her fingertips, I caught a glimpse of the feathery red hair under her arm, which sent a feathery red fire through me.

"She sent us a post card about a year later from a pot-growing commune in Hawaii. Said she was setting sail for Jamaica with a Rastafarian she'd met in New York. They were going to live off the land up in the mountains. But first she had to make airfare to get to Florida, so she was giving "tantric massages" to tourists through one of the hotels. She could be on Jupiter now for all we know."

I leaned back, placing my hands behind my head. "I feel amazingly stupid," I told her.

"Why?"

"I didn't know you were bi."

Rebecca smiled, "Well isn't everybody?"

She had said this flippantly, but I stared at her with raised eyebrows, and asked quite seriously, "Are they?"

"Oh, who knows?" She waved a hand in the air. "Personally, I find that I'm more attracted to men, but if someone, a situation, like Sheila, comes my way... Well, let's just say I'm not about to kick Kim Basinger out of my bed. I just wouldn't."

"Kim Basinger?"

"Yeah, she's sexy."

I tried to imagine for a moment then said, "I suppose I wouldn't kick her out of my bed either."

Pulling back the blanket, I knelt in the space in front of Rebecca's bent knees. She parted her legs, and I moved my head down, my nostrils filling up with her scent, and then my tongue playing eagerly at the moist silkiness there. Between my own legs, I felt my cock growing quickly with each of Rebecca's moans.

****

Hank asked me to go to a pre-season basketball game with him. My immediate thought was: how do I get out of this? Then I realized I didn't want to get out of it. "I haven't been to a game in six years," I told him.

Hank waited, so I added, "I use to be a fan."

"Rick," he said.

It frightened me more and more, the way Hank knew where my mind was at, as if my face were nothing more than a plate of glass he could look right through to effortlessly read information off my brain. It frightened me in the way that love is frightening — frightening in that it's so terribly comforting.

"Rick," I confirmed.

I'd been with Hank and Rebecca for nearly five months now. The two of us were in the laundry room, running a wash. Hank sat on the dryer. I stood next to him in this small window-filled room. Condensation obscured the view and created a cozy warmth.

"We met at a basketball game," I explained, going on to relay the details. It felt good to have Hank laugh with me sympathetically over the innocence and charm of this early momentous occasion in my life. "Basketball games," I added, "were also one of the only places Rick and I went to together in public." I pulled myself up onto the washer. "When I got to San Francisco, I let Derek turn me on to football."

"The only part of football I like is when they pat each other on the ass."

"My favorite part too!"

With his left foot, Hank caressed my right foot. "You'll go to the game with me," he said.

"Yes."

He took my hand. "I'll dry your tears."

****

My first basketball game since Rick, did turn out to be a cathartic experience. Not the least of which was due to the fact that Hank was there with me. Yes, I had loved Jeff, but not like Rick, and not like Hank. And, as with Rick, I found myself continually shocked by the depth of my feelings for both Hank and Rebecca. It was as if I didn't really believe these kinds of feelings were possible, but at frequent revealing moments was forced to face the truth — I was deeply in love.

255

I hadn't cried about Rick in I don't know how long... years. But there at the game with Hank, my throat started to choke-up, and I didn't fight it. Hank put his arms around me, held me close to him while seemingly ceaseless drops of sorrow spilled from my eyes. Nothing in particular had touched this off; I had not started remembering a particular moment with Rick; I had just been watching the game and then suddenly I was flooded with emotion. Perhaps I had forgotten for a moment where I was, whom I was with; perhaps for a moment I was back in high school, sitting next to my first boyfriend.

When the game was over, Hank drove a ways and then parked in a quiet spot under some trees. After a bit, he said, "You know, Jim, I don't want to ever be without you."

I put my hand on his thigh. He put his hand on top of mine and we laced our fingers together tightly.

"You won't ever have to be."

For a good long while we sat there — as much together as when one of us was inside the other. My thoughts eventually went to the basketball stadium, and how Hank had, in front of all those people, held me while I cried. Then something occurred to me, and I asked, "Who won the game?"

He turned on the engine, and as he started to back out, he said, "Hank, Rebecca, and Jim won the game."

Chapter Thirty

I suppose I should have seen it coming. These sort of things don't just pop out of a void. Looking back, there were red flags all over the place, but the extent to which I chose to notice them at all, I found them disturbing and unprecedented and thus completely dismissed them. In other words, I was walking around with blinders on. That changed as I received the shock of my life, a week after the basketball game.

Hank and Rebecca left on a Saturday morning to stay with Rebecca's sister, Sharon, for a few days up in Napa. A good friend of the family was getting married, and a mini family reunion would follow. Rebecca, had seen to it that I got invited too — Sharon considered herself open minded, and thus was "accepting" the "choices" Hank and Rebecca had made concerning their marriage. I would be "welcome with open arms" — Sharon's words — "tolerated with forced smiles" — Rebecca's translation. Still Rebecca wanted me there. But I wasn't up to missing out on classes. I'd meet her family another time, when they could come into the city and be on our territory.

Saturday evening, Derek came over early. We worked hard for a few hours — Derek's mood edgy, sharp, and oddly chipper-happy. He was pushing me, pushing me to keep up with him. I loved it, egged him on. At eight we walked down to a Chinese restaurant, got silly with our chopsticks and lo-mien. Back at my place, we got lost in a spiraling tangent that proved more relevant than our original focus. It was late when we found a place to call it quits.

"Never fails, Chinese food always makes me thirsty," I said, closing my notebook, then went into the kitchen and poured water into a glass.

"Jim..." Derek had apparently followed me.

"Yeah? You thirsty too?" I hadn't turned around.

He didn't answer. I took a sip. Finally, I turned to see what he wanted. Derek stood there staring at me, not saying anything. His expression was all wrong. I was grappling, trying to figure out what exactly... He stepped towards me. Before I could comprehend, Derek brought his face to mine. I felt his tongue in my mouth, felt my mouth responding.

"*No!*" I pulled away, slammed my back up against the counter, getting as far from him as I could. I stared at him in horror, my breathing as heavy as if I'd played a rough game of handball.

Derek looked back at me, calm, patient, intensely alert.

"What the hell! Did you just kiss me?"

"Yeah, I did." He had a dreadful smile.

"What the fuck?" I wiped my mouth harshly with my sleeve. "Like kissing my mother," I gasped.

"*What?*" He was smiling, amused.

"I mean..." I searched for words. Finally I found something that might work, "*Taboo!*"

"Taboo?"

"Jesus Christ, Derek!"

"How about we go sit down?" He gestured towards the couch. "I promise I won't touch you."

Derek was promising not to touch me!

He sat where he'd been before on the couch. I pulled out the chair at my desk, on the far side of the room, near the door, and sat uncomfortably gripping the armrest. "What's wrong with you?" I spat out.

"This'll be easier if you calm down."

"*Calm down*? You just kissed me!"

"I know."

"You know?"

"I knew exactly what I was doing."

"Well *what*? What were you doing kissing me?"

"I was doing precisely what I've been dying to do for the past couple of weeks." He had this terrible terrible smile that wouldn't go away.

"What's that? Freak me out?"

Derek grinned now, the old familiar Derek grin, shook his head back and forth slowly. "No," he said softly.

I tried to process this. No, he did not wish to freak me out. He wanted to kiss me. Derek wanted to kiss me, had been wanting to, dying to, for a couple of weeks. He wanted to, and *did*. "Shit!" I said.

Derek laughed.

"What are you laughing at?"

"I don't know, your reaction, I guess."

"Well, how did you expect me to react?

"I wasn't sure, but I figured I'd never find out if I didn't do something. And," he added matter-of-factly, "it got to the point where not doing something wasn't an option anymore."

"What the fuck are you talking about?" I was almost certain I did not want to hear the answer.

"I've been doing a lot of thinking since you told me you were bi," he said. "I'd harbored a prejudice all my life that I'd never questioned, never held up for scrutiny, which seemed really strange to me. You know how I analyze everything. And it just really bugged me too, that I couldn't understand who you are. Not understanding totally pisses me off, right? And because it was you at issue..."

Picking up again, he said, "So I set my mind to it. First of all, I knew you were right, about nothing being wrong with homosexuality. I mean the minute I gave the issue *one* objective thought, that much was clear. But when I tried to comprehend your attraction to men, tried to imagine you enjoying sex with a guy, it seemed beyond my abilities. But the more this task seemed impossible, the more I felt driven to conquer whatever was holding me back." Derek took long measured glances around the room, as if he were in unfamiliar surroundings.

"I didn't suspect that understanding you would change me. I thought I would figure out this homosexual thing and then go on with my life." Derek raised his eyebrows in my direction. "But that's not what happened." He blinked a few times at the Bay Area Reporter that lay in front of him on my coffee table. "When I first tried to imagine you and Jeff in bed together, I felt sick." Derek laughed. "Literally sick. I couldn't do it. It was terrible. Nausea, and I broke out in a full sweat. I was *shaking*. So I backed it up. You're not in bed together; you're just alone in your apartment, fully dressed." Derek now realized what he'd been looking at. He picked up the paper, read a few headlines, then placed it carefully back on the table.

"Not difficult to do," he said finally. "Imagining you and Jeff talking football."

I did not interject that Jeff was not a sport's fan. I could not interject anything; my mind was on hold. I was a vegetable with ears that were hearing unbelievable things.

"I could even imagine," Derek went on, "you guys sitting close to each other here on the couch." He patted the spot next to him. "After that, I tried to picture the same scenario, but no football, just like maybe you're talking about something more personal — how your day went maybe. And okay, I could do this. But to think of Jeff's arm around you... I had to *force* myself to not block this image out. But once I was able to stomach that, I found that I had a sense of you two enjoying this — that you felt comfortable, happy together. I could see you two hugging to say good-bye or touching each other's hands while you studied. All this made me very uneasy, but I could do it. But you and Jeff in a sexual scenario... No!" Derek's voice was suddenly loud. "No way! I absolutely could not do that. And then I thought: I don't want to do this. Why am I trying to force myself to do something I find repulsive? So

260

what if I can't do this? Who the hell wants to subject themselves to something that disgusting? Was I crazy, spending so much mental energy on thinking about fags fucking? I was beginning to unravel, really questioning my sanity, because I felt driven, despite what I thought was my better judgment, to conquer this fear — because at some point I did come to recognize it as fear."

With a slow careful hand, Derek brushed bangs off his forehead. "But I knew too that I'd never feel comfortable around you again until I understood you. And I couldn't be satisfied with that; I wanted to be your goddamn friend, even if it drove me to the brink of insanity. So I tried another tact, returned to how you and Jeff must have felt about each other. And this worked. Focusing on the emotional aspect of your relationship, somehow freed me to understand how Jeff might not only feel good enough about you, that he'd like to hug you, but that he might also experience some arousal in doing this, feeling your body against his."

He took a good long look at me, smiled — I guess at my catatonic state — and then after staring off into nothingness momentarily, said, "One of the things that most attracted me to you as a friend is that you were very much a man. You know, masculinity in its true form. I thought of myself in the same way, but I had doubts, parts of me that were insecure — was I man enough? So I liked surrounding myself with you. It made me feel somehow more of a man." He laughed. "You must have been somewhat aware of this, seen the incredible irony in it.

"Of course, I see all of this in a whole new light now, but when you told me... told me you have this gay side, I had to reconsider. I mean, *what* exactly does it mean to be a man? I couldn't find a way to label you as *sissy* or *effeminate* or *fairy;* those terms just aren't you, even if I now knew that you made it a habit to suck on other men's cocks. And when I saw you and Hank together that time I stopped over here, I saw two men together — two masculine men. And I knew the two of you were doing things with each other that were considered completely unmanly. But you were men, undoubtedly. It was right after that that I made progress in seeing you and Jeff together. It was like this major breakthrough; a huge brick wall had been miraculously smashed to pieces. Somehow, the realization that I didn't need to stop thinking of you as a man, allowed me to understand you and Jeff wanting to physically express what you felt for each other.

"So okay, all right," Derek waved his arms around expansively, "all was well now. I got it, comprehended homosexuality. I could go on with my life. But Christ... I was like this possessed creature. To make sure I'd truly gotten it, I put myself through a series of tests. Just like I would with any physics' theory. Could I imagine you two French kissing — yes, check; having oral sex — yes, check; anal sex — yes, check. You know, so it was like, all right, I'm not daunted by this anymore. Good job, Derek, pat on the back, all that. Phew, glad *that's* over. But *then*," Derek almost spoke in a whisper, "I would be, for example, riding my bike to school, and there Jeff and you would be in my mind's eye doing all sorts of lewd and lascivious things with each other. And I'd go, okay this is *enough*, and I'd force myself to think about antimatter, the beginning of the universe, semiconductors, what have you, and bam, I'd drive up to a red light and there you and Jeff would be again, fucking lustfully.

"At first, I brushed this off as a psychological process, dealing with so drastic a change in thinking, part of me was still trying to work it through. But slowly I began to doubt this. And then," Derek settled himself into the corner of the couch, and his voice became steady, calm, happy even, "Friday, two weeks ago, I was riding through Golden Gate Park, running a bit late on my way to Alice's, and one of those images came into my head. I was tired of fighting them, and the thought struck me, maybe it would be better *not* to fight them. Maybe I needed to let my mind do what it wants to resolve this. So, I let the scenario run itself like a movie through my head. But soon, utterly horrified, I realized I had an erection. I was so shaken by this, so disturbed, that I pulled my bike off the road. I sat on a grassy slope staring stupefied at the whizzing cars going by. And it dawned on me then, that in this scenario, I had put *myself* in Jeff's place. It was Jeff I saw in my mind, but it was *me* experiencing what it was like to be touching you. I knew then that the reason why these images kept coming to mind, was because I had an overwhelming desire to be able to do with you, what Jeff had done with you, what Hank was perhaps doing with you right at that moment.

"I sat there in the park thinking about this, not knowing *what* to think, not knowing how to feel, until finally I decided to just get to Alice's.

"When I got there, I felt desperate to be with her — a woman — in bed. But while we were having sex, I couldn't stop thinking about what that would be like with you. It was the best sex I'd ever had with her, but it hadn't even really been with *her*. I knew then that this wasn't something that was going to go away. And the more I thought about it over the next days, the more I didn't want it to go away. And the more I thought about it, the more I cared about little else. It was what I wanted."

Now Derek slowed his voice, his words becoming very precise distinct entities. "And the more I thought about what you said when you came out to me, about not being sexually attracted to me, the more I realized that that was bullshit. I know you might not realize that yet, but you will."

I sat motionless, seriously doubting my hold on reality. This simply could *not* be happening.

Finally, I said numbly, "This is some sort of bizarre nightmare."

Derek smiled. "You probably need to be alone. But I want to say one more thing before I go." Frowning with seriousness, he said, "I know what Hank and Rebecca mean to you. I see how good they are for you. I don't want to in any way interfere with what the three of you have. It's important that you understand that." Derek got up then.

On his way out, he paused and touched my shoulder. "I'll see you in class Monday morning."

I looked up at him; who the hell was this? And he left.

Chapter Thirty-one

I was unable to move for nearly an hour. I was, plainly and simply, in shock. Eventually though, an overwhelming urge to brush my teeth got me mobile again. I dug a bottle of antiseptic mouthwash out of the back of the cabinet and gargled with that too.

When I was able to make *any* sense of my thoughts, I tried to decide if I should be angry as hell with Derek, or if I should feel sorry for him because he'd gone crazy. And then, in a great sweep of self-pity, I thought, of course! Everything was going along all too well. I was out; Derek had accepted it; I had him for a buddy and a physics partner, and had Hank and Rebecca for lovers. Everything was just too good, too perfect. I was all too happy. Something had to give. Poor Derek. I had bewitched him. What had I done!

For a good while my thoughts went on like that. I hated him. No, felt sorry for him. No, felt sorry for me. He'd gone crazy. No, I was crazy — this never happened. No, actually the universe was coming to an end; all hell had broken loose — all the physicist's theories and predictions were dust in the wind.

Wait! Wait! I thought at one point, it's a joke! Derek's playing one hell of a joke on me. No... no... Derek's getting back at me! It's a joke, but a mean spirited one. It's revenge. But I knew immediately that this was only wishful thinking. Derek was serious. This was no joke. Derek had in fact, for whatever confused, crazed, reason, decided that he wanted me for a lover. And as this information finally, completely, sunk in, I found myself grabbing my keys and heading out the door. I was under the impression that I was going for a ride to clear my head, but I soon discovered that I was heading towards SOMA. When I parked across from HUNKS, I knew two things: I wanted to get drunk, and I wanted to get laid.

Love, Sex, and Understanding the Universe

As I fought my way through the crowd, a pretty boy with all the affects, limp wrists, lisp, etcetera, shouted loudly to his friends, but practically right in my face, "I'd go straight for Stevie Nicks!"

I put my hand up to my ear and dismissed this unsolicited information, brushing it away as if it were an insect.

When I finally got to Danny at the bar, he pointed at me. "Howdy stranger. Heiny?"

Thinking suddenly of Bill, I said, "Give me a Cruzan and soda."

"Cruzan and soda?" He looked at me suspiciously. "So, what's troubling you?" Like he's my father looking after me, not sure he's willing to give me hard liquor.

Needing to confess Derek's sins, I blurted out, "My best friend French kissed me."

Danny raised an eyebrow. "Male or female?"

"Male."

"And you're upset about *that*?"

"He's straight."

"Oh no he ain't!" Danny laughed uproariously. He made the drink and handed it to me, still laughing. I'd made his day.

The drink felt good; the music felt good; the hand on my ass felt good. I went back to his place — the guy who belonged to the hand on my ass — after another drink, and another drink and then a fourth bought for me by the guy with the hand, "for the road," which I downed at the door, giving the bouncer the empty glass with a wink.

He had nice hands, the guy with the hand on my ass, the way they explored my body, inside and out. I played passive the whole time, no energy for much else, no mind for much else, just take me away, remove me from this nightmare. We enjoyed this, the guy with the hands, and I.

266

In the morning, when I awoke in my own apartment, the drive back home a vague blur, I felt relaxed and refreshed, slight headache. But as I got up and started moving around, the headache came on stronger. Then anxiety and anger returned — slowly working their way through my body, as I recalled Derek's kiss, then his monologue.

"You arrogant son-of-a-bitch!" I shouted at the space on my couch where Derek usually sat.

****

"Do you have time to talk?" I fiddled with the phone cord.

"I have to meet Bob pretty soon, but until then... I'm just watching TV." Jeff's voice was welcoming. It was Sunday evening. I'd spent the day being depressed, angry, confused.

"Watching TV sounds wonderful."

"You hate TV."

"I know, but I need something mindless right now."

"Sounds drastic; what's the matter?"

"Derek kissed me."

"Hold on, let me turn off the tube." There was a pause. "Okay. Now, what did you say?"

"Derek kissed me."

"Derek?"

"Yeah." To make it perfectly clear, I said, "He put his tongue in my mouth."

There was a long silence. Finally Jeff said, "Well, how do you feel about it?"

"Like I want to vomit."

After another long pause, Jeff asked, "What did he say?"

I relayed the gist of Derek's speech. And again, it took Jeff a while to respond. Eventually he said quietly, almost not at all, "Maybe you should consider it."

"What?"

"Gotta admit, he's got a great body."

This time there was silence at my end.

"Don't tell me you never noticed!"

I'd always liked Derek's face. I liked what it said about his personality, that grin, and his eyes — dark, untelling, deep; I saw so much depth in those eyes. I liked his face and that's what I looked at. And yeah, he had nice hair too, jet black, thick... But his body? I knew he was slightly shorter than me, like Rick, and was probably a little stockier than me... or not? Wait, why were we talking about Derek's body?

"You had to have noticed his chest," Jeff insisted.

"This is San Francisco;" I protested, "people wear jackets all the time."

"Derek doesn't wear a jacket when he's studying at your place. He usually has on a T-shirt."

"Oh, I guess." That sounded about right.

"A tight one."

"Really?"

"You're kidding," Jeff said incredulously. "During that heat wave he wore shorts all week. Didn't you take a look at his legs?"

"No! Why would I?"

"It's just normal, Jim." Jeff's voice expressed impatience, like a teacher who can't get a concept through to a student. "His thighs are..."

"I don't want to hear about Derek's thighs!"

"There's something really strange about your inability to have noticed Derek's body in even the most casual of ways."

"He's my *friend*!" I was getting angry.

"He wants to be more."

Harrie Farrow

"He's confused."

"Sounds like *you're* confused."

"Why are you doing this to me, Jeff?" I was about ready to hang up.

There was an exceptionally long pause. Just as I was about to check if he was still there, he said quietly, sadly, "I always wanted to believe there was a good reason why you were so willing to sacrifice our relationship."

"*Not so* willing."

"But you sacrificed us non-the-less. And I never thought for a moment it was for Carol's sake. It was for Derek."

"For our *friendship*." This confession surprised me; I had never thought of it that way before, never thought Derek was what kept Jeff and me from staying together. But of course this was true — I would not come out, and that was because of Derek.

"Call it whatever you want," Jeff was saying, "but there's something very deep there. I know how much I meant to you — don't think it escaped me — yet Derek meant more. People don't go around giving up love for the sake of ordinary friendship. I believed you when you told me that you weren't interested in Derek sexually, but I could see what you two had, and it wasn't common. Love doesn't have to be sexual; that's how I saw it."

"Well, fine, whatever." What was Jeff saying? What was I agreeing with? "So, I want it to continue that way. What I love is the relationship that Derek and I had until last night. I love that friendship, and I don't want to lose it. What am I supposed to do, sleep with him just to keep him as a friend? I'm *not* attracted to him."

"Maybe you need to rethink that. You told me he turned you off just by virtue of the fact that he was hetero and homophobic. You said that he was too "he-male" for your tastes, that you didn't like men who were always on-guard, could never let go. All that fit Derek to a T, but think

269

about it, Jim, all that has changed by what he did the other night. Kissing you is hardly hetero, homophobic behavior, hardly on-guard. You came out to him, and he tapped into a part of himself he'd been keeping buried under some pretty heavy-duty camouflage. You might not have been attracted to who Derek was, but he's gone through some changes. Maybe your relationship with him needs to go through some changes as well.

Things have changed. Derek has changed. Who the hell was he now? I felt immensely unhappy. "All this is really fucking with my head," I told Jeff.

"You'll sort it out. You're smart, remember?" His tone was sarcastic.

"You're still angry with me."

"Of course I'm still angry with you. I try to forgive you, but it's not easy. After you called and told me you came out, I got angry all over again. Why couldn't you have done that for me? But still, I was glad you finally stopped being such a chicken-shit. In a way, it redeemed you in my eyes. But now this! Look, Derek's who you've always wanted. He's who you love, and I don't appreciate you crying to me about how he kissed you."

"*Hank* and *Rebecca* are who I want."

"Did Derek ask you to give them up?"

"Well, no. He said he doesn't want to cause problems for us. He made a point of saying that."

"Do Hank and Rebecca expect you to be faithful?"

"No."

"Do you spend less time with Derek now than you did when I was there?"

I thought about this. "Probably more. I'm at Hank and Rebecca's on the weekends and then with Rebecca on Tuesdays."

"That's about how much time you spent with me."

I thought back. Two, three, nights a week, some mornings, some afternoons. "Close to it."

"Then you spent time with Carol too."

"Yeah, some."

"Well, okay."

"Well okay, what?"

"You can have Hank and Rebecca *and* Derek. Have your cake *and* ice cream, and eat all of it too. You have plenty of time to spend with Derek, already do spend lots of time with him; the only difference would be that now he'd spend the night after studying instead of going home."

"Oh great; I'm glad you have it all figured out. Derek spend the night with me? You might as well suggest I have cat food for dinner."

"Thou dost protest too much! You're really pissing me off. Get over it and *enjoy* him."

Enjoy Derek?

Jeff came back with a mellower tone of voice. "I know I'm being hard on you, but you'll thank me; it's what you need. Anyway, you deserve it. Just try not to hate me too much."

"I could never hate you," I said.

"Well, I've tried to hate you and I can't, so we're even."

"That's nice to know."

"I really need to go now. I'll call you in a couple of weeks to see how you're doing."

We said our good-byes, and I was left to pick through the chaos in my head. The one thing that Jeff said, that I couldn't work around, was how all the reasons why I'd felt I wasn't attracted to Derek no longer existed. The facts now added up to a picture that I didn't want to face: Derek meant the world to me; he was good-looking — and if I took Jeff's word for it — had a great body; he wanted to sleep with me and had the guts to tell me so with a lusty kiss.

I kept running this around and around in my head, and still I could not imagine myself in bed with him, could not bring myself to think of this as desirable. It left me cold at best, disgusted at worst. But another fact, something I hadn't told Jeff, gnawed at me. When I first felt Derek's mouth on mine, I had responded by kissing him back. It wasn't until my conscious mind had a chance to process what was happening that I had pulled away. Even though I knew it was essential that I face the implications of this, I tried hard not to. Instead, I focused on the hopeful idea that Derek was just confused, that he'd snap out of this, and all would be normal between us again.

Lying down to sleep, I had no clue what I would do or say when I saw Derek the next morning. Restless in the dark, I began to feel angry with Derek again for what he had done to us. Everything had been going fine; why did he have to flip out? Shit, Derek! I fell asleep cursing him.

Chapter Thirty-two

During all my years at San Francisco State, I'd woken up by myself in plenty of time to get to class, but I always set my alarm to an hour before I needed to be at school, just in case. Monday morning I awoke to the alarm.

"Damn!" I pounced on it. Damn, because not only did I find the noise first thing in the morning irritating, but also because it meant that I would need to rush like a bandit.

"Damn," and then, "Whoa!" as I became aware of the dream I'd been ripped out of. What tipped me off was the tremendous hard-on I had — a good bit more urging than your typical morning erection. In the dream, Derek was giving me that kiss. Only this time I didn't pull away. This time I got into it. We were there in my kitchen, our mouths united, my hands groping his ass, Derek's hands feeling my cock through my jeans.

Though acutely aware of how late I was running, the dream's image had dug its talons into me. I started to jack-off, at first using the dream for fuel, but I soon found myself imagining Derek and I in much more graphic scenarios, and was shocked to discover how easy, how *very* easy this was to do. The fantasy was so pleasing that I held off as long as I could, and only gave in when it became unbearable, the resulting orgasm leaving my entire body shaking spasmodically.

On my bike, cool wind hitting my face and bringing me fully awake, I felt exhilarated. I recalled the morning, a long five years ago, when I rode home after spending the night with Farm Boy — my first bar pick-up — the joy I'd felt then, knowing I was at last free, free to be me, Jim, a bisexual man not afraid to face the world. The irony of what I'd felt that morning had hit me many times over the years, but now that sense of freedom was back, and this time it wasn't going to turn out to be an illusion. I'd thought that coming out to Derek would be the key that would unlocked the prison I had incarcerated myself in, but now I understood that the fortification around this prison had been much more complex than I'd ever imagined.

I jogged with the near-buoyancy of a moonwalk to the physics' department, but as I slowed down to round the corner and head down the hall, it struck me that I hadn't had time to think about what I'd say to Derek.

The professor was lecturing, moving hands dramatically to emphasize his point, the topic for the day scrawled on the board: "Weed Out the Irrelevant." Derek wasn't listening. He was staring at the floor, looking scared, looking like a wreck, the empty seat beside him beckoning to me. I stepped in; a few heads turned; I'm never late. Derek looked up and met my eyes, his expression an odd mixture of relief and fear.

I hesitated. A concept came to mind: cognitive dissonance. How to put the feelings I had together with the setting I was in. Everything seemed disorienting, dream-like. But this surreal sensation lasted only a second, and then, like a camera coming into focus, everything became very clear, and I became very present. I broke into an enormous smile, directed at my buddy Derek, and he responded with that sexy grin of his.

****

After class, as we left the physics' building together, I veered off the path, and stopped under a tree.

"How was your weekend?" I asked Derek promptly.

"I was doing great until you didn't show up for class on time." He said this in his usual expressionless way, only this time he stood much closer to me than he ever would have in the past.

"You were that sure of yourself?"

A faint smile stole across Derek's lips, but he said nothing.

"I had a lousy weekend," I told him. "I was really upset about what happened Saturday night." Reconsidering, I said, "Distraught is more the word."

"You looked pretty happy when you came into class; what happened?"

"I called Jeff."

"Jeff?" After processing this, Derek asked, "What did he say?"

"That you're who I always wanted. He got pissed, said it was absurd for me to be complaining to him about you kissing me, when I'd sacrificed my relationship with him for you."

Derek raised his eyebrows.

"I didn't like most of what Jeff said..." This wasn't the point, I realized, not the point at all. Not what I needed to say to Derek. My voice suddenly became deadly serious as, seizing his eyes with mine, I said, "Listen, Derek, I'm not going back in the closet for anything or *anyone*."

"Are you saying you'll have sex with me?" He could barely contain his excitement, like a kid: *are you saying you'll buy me ice cream?*

"What about Alice?"

"You *are* saying you'll sleep with me!" He smiled an altogether un-Derek-like smile.

"What about Alice?" I demanded sternly.

"She'll either deal with it or she won't." He shrugged, "Likely won't."

"You'll tell her?"

"Of course."

Of course. Well. "What about the rest of the world? Here — school?" I looked out towards the lawn, the student union.

Derek looked about vaguely, searching. "What do you mean?" But he knew what I meant because he then said, "I don't hold hands with Alice in public; I'm not like that."

Sure, I thought, some change Derek's gone through. No way was I going to let him off the hook... But I now became suddenly aware of Derek's specific personal smell. I wanted desperately to drown in it, and I realized I'd always felt this when I was with him. It was a drug, a potent tonic, a need within me. This knowledge passed through me, a shocking revelation, and then I said, feeling the urgency to get back to the business at hand, "When you give Alice a ride on your bike, what is she holding on to?"

"My hips," Derek responded impatiently. "But I use to ride on the bike of a girl I dated in high school, and my hands were always on my seat. That's just me."

Sure, sure, Mr. Macho. "Well," I countered, "when I've ridden on bikes belonging to guys I've picked up at bars, I'm holding on to *them*, not the bike.

"Fine," Derek responded, "when I give you a ride you can put your hands wherever you want."

"Really?" I asked suspiciously.

"Wanna go for a ride?"

A bit taken aback, I looked him over, thinking. Thinking that this was Derek I was talking to. *Derek!* "I might just take you up on that after school."

He stood unwavering.

Feeling that this had been resolved, I didn't know what the next step was. A bit flustered, I said meekly, "Can we go get coffee now?"

****

As we sat down with our Styrofoam cups, I leaned over and looked under the table at Derek's black jeans. Sitting up again I said, "Jeff said you have nice legs."

Derek laughed. "I never thought about it."

"You wouldn't."

He looked hurt until I added, "Oh, you're not the only one. Jeff thought there was something pretty strange about the fact that I'd never noticed."

"Is that what convinced you?"

"Maybe it was what he implied about your big strong chest." I watched Derek for any sign of discomfort at hearing me talk about him like that, but he was too busy grinning. I couldn't help but grin back. Derek. Derek and me? I blushed, overcome with lust.

"Is that really you?" I peered at him.

He was glowing. "It's really me."

"Good God."

"When?"

"What do you mean?"

"Tonight?"

"What? Oh! Tonight? Tonight?" I was horrified. Pleadingly, I said, "I need some time..." I wanted him then, right then and there.

"Tomorrow," he said resolutely.

"Okay," I said, burying my face in my hands, feeling like a bashful adolescent, "tomorrow."

Chapter Thirty-three

After our last class the next day, we sipped our coffee in silence, looking at one another in long glances, looking at one another within a whole new reality.

"I'm scared," I said finally, in a quiet voice approaching whisper.

Derek leaned forward. "Of what?"

"That you'll freak out."

"About having sex with you?"

"About engaging in homo behavior. I'm not sure you're facing the reality of what it is you say you want to do. All your life you quiver in disgust at the thought of two men together, and all of a sudden you want to suck my cock. What are you smiling about?"

"The thought of sucking your cock."

"Jesus Christ, Derek."

"You want me to run screaming in horror?"

"It'd be more in character."

"Jim," he leaned in real close, "I want to have sex with you. That's one thing I'm absolutely certain of."

The intensity in his voice, and the seriousness in his eyes, left my body and mind lost in a frenzy of excited panic, and I could not respond.

Derek stood; I followed. By the time we were in the parking lot, I got a grip on myself. I had to keep my head together, make sure I handled this right. We'd decided to have an early dinner first, but hadn't talked about where we'd go. I got on my bike and motioned for Derek to follow me out onto 19th Avenue. I led us up into a light fog on Twin Peaks, then down onto sunny Market Street, and settled the bike on a quiet road just off Castro.

"You testing me?" Derek asked, as he pulled off his helmet.

"Get use to these surroundings," I said a bit harshly. "Soon as you spend the night with me, you're queer. No

278

matter how attracted to women you are, or how many you fuck, or how passionately you fuck them — once we're lovers and open about it, you're going to be called a fag."

He looked at me intently. "Where's the restaurant?"

I stared at him as it sunk in that this was maybe going to actually happen.

We walked onto Castro, dance music blaring from a bar on the corner, which I knew in a few hours would be full of writhing and laughter, pathetic stares and sexy smiles. A whole world Derek knew nothing about. Most elements of the gay scene: drag queens, burly bears, S&M leather studs, etc. made their appearances here, but this bar mostly catered to Castro Clones, with their trim dreamy mustaches, well groomed but not-too-short hair, and firm, sculpted, torsos — health, vigor and desire oozing out of their pours.

As we rouned the corner, past the entrance, three men about our age stood outside, smoking, looking at us appraisingly. I felt Derek's hand slipping into mine. Did he do this to ward off these men, to let them know he was taken? Did he do it to reassure me that he was undaunted? Or did he just feel like holding my hand? I don't know. I do know how good it felt.

The Jungle Bistro's dining room was a patio setting with heat lamps strategically scattered about. Sophisticated lighting bounced off large plants with a soft green glow. The host — a handsome young thing who appeared to love his job, and batted his eyelashes flirtatiously at us — sat us under something with umbrella-like leaves.

A guy at a nearby table smiled at me, offering a cute little wave with raised eyebrows. I smiled back, nodding.

This transaction did not go unnoticed by Derek. "Who's that?"

"I almost picked him up at a bar once," I pushed an intrusive leaf back behind my chair, "but his boyfriend showed up and snatched him away."

Derek glanced at the guy, frowned disconcertingly.

"What?" I asked.

"I imagine you with someone more like Hank... or me."

I looked at Derek, a bit bewildered, amused. As much as I desired him, the idea of us together still seemed such a departure, not at all a normal thing to do. I turned to get another glimpse of my almost-lay; he *was* looking rather effeminate. But still it was easier to imagine myself going home with him than with Derek.

"He was wearing leather that night," I said. "And he's got the sexiest voice... anyway, look at those eyes, those lips, don't you find anything alluring there?"

Derek took another peek. "No."

"So who here *do* you find attractive?" I gestured about the dining room.

"You."

"Besides me."

Derek smiled patiently. "It's kinda difficult to think about anyone else right now."

"Oh, come on." I came across sounding calm and collected, but my knees were shaking. "If a totally hot chick walked in here half naked, you telling me you wouldn't take a good long look?"

In a thick deep voice Derek said, "I don't think you understand how desperate my desire for you is."

My mouth fell open. But I was rescued by a waiter with excessively tight blue jeans, who showed up for our order.

Shortly after our soup — a tasty corn chowder — arrived, I said, licking a flavor packed spec of basil off my lip, "Maybe it wasn't so nice of me to drag you down here tonight."

"No. I understand why you brought me here, and I can handle this. All of it." Derek leaned forward and added, "You could have taken me anywhere tonight. I've never gone dancing, but you could take me to the raunchiest gay bar, and I'd dance with you, if it meant I could feel your body move against mine."

A sharp gasp was the only way I could express the intense fear now giving way to an even more intense desire to get back to my place with Derek.

Chapter Thirty-four

A faint wind danced through our hair as we removed our helmets in front of my apartment, the light above my door just barely illuminating our faces. For a long moment we looked each other directly in the eye, and in this stern, silent, conversation, I told Derek that this was his last chance, that he'd better opt out now, or be damned sure of what he was doing. Once I got him in my apartment, I wasn't going to take a, *No, I'm sorry*, very well. He understood every word I wasn't speaking; I could see that, and he said clearly, silently, back, *I know what I'm doing.* We garaged the bikes, walked up my steps, and crossed the transom, into an other world.

After locking the door, I turned around and there was my buddy of five years, standing there — just waiting for me. I couldn't imagine how even someone dismantling a bomb could be more nervous than I was. Derek had made the first move, three nights ago with that kiss, so I could make the next. I reached out and peeled back the shoulders of his jacket, and lowered it down his arms, letting it drop onto the floor. Yeah, Jeff had remembered correctly — tight T-shirt, muscular chest. I exhaled the breath that had momentarily stopped short in my throat.

Wearing a completely alien expression, Derek removed my jacket in the same manner, only much more confidently — which set off a five alarm warning to every erogenous zone in my body, and stripped me of any sense of composure. With certainty and wonder, Derek explored my now bare arms with his fingertips, while I, with trembling hands, explored his. His bones, veins, and thick hair felt frighteningly exotic. As our hands arrived at each other's shoulders, I brought my mouth to Derek's. Suddenly, I was drowning in the vast ocean of the universe. Every moment over the years that Derek and I had unknowingly — or more recently knowingly — desired one another, all rolled into one now. I could not contain myself; I was outside myself, everywhere and nowhere, and then — as if a super nova collapsing — I pulled back into myself, became completely, wholly, me, completely wholly with Derek. When we separated from the kiss, we stood barely as separate people, yet somehow, I was Jim, and he was Derek, and we were in love.

Fueled with this knowledge, I regained a sense of myself as a man who knew how to love men, even this man, *especially* this man. With total confidence now, I brought my mouth to Derek's cheek, slowly grazed my hungry lips on the slight stubble there, tasted his saltiness, smelled a trace of shaving lotion mixed in with Derek's scent. Intoxicated, I moved on to his ear and then his neck. Derek was moaning, his hands — like lost souls home at last — searching the territory of my ass, his body falling, melting into me, writhing in agonizing pleasure. Oh yes, Derek wanted me. Oh yes. Oh yes.

In a haste of impatience — I suddenly had to see Derek's body, touch it naked — I pulled his T-shirt over his head. His broad shoulders, muscular hairless pecs, and taunt stomach, were absolutely shocking in their beauty. With a particularly luxuriant rush of desire, I placed my mouth on his erect nipple. But Derek tensed. Ah, I thought, something he had not included in the fantasies he'd had of me, something Derek wasn't use to. I silently cursed all the women whom he'd ever slept with, for denying him this pleasure. Ignoring his discomfort, I licked and sucked vigorously. Now he relaxed, gave in, breathing out with excessive syllables, "Oh, Christ."

I knelt to undo his belt and unzip him — his hard-on pushing against his jeans, crying for release — but before I could get his pants down, he lowered himself, bringing us face to face. Becoming the aggressive one now, Derek practically tore off my shirt. Then he kissed me with a thick probing tongue while guiding me down to the floor, pressing his body on mine. He placed a hand between us, feeling my erection through my pants, pushing and rubbing against it until I screamed, low and deep, and wrestled him onto his back.

Straddling him, I admonished, "Do you want me to come in my pants?"

"I want you to come in my mouth."

Though not what I'd normally consider a comical matter, I laughed anyway, after all, this was me and Derek. Then, while handing him the almond oil off my nightstand, I offered my conditions. "Not until after you fuck me."

There wasn't anything shy or uncertain about the way he complied with this request. As I lay on my back, while he moved inside of me — at first a slow, careful, thrusting — I watched his face, *Derek's* face. I took in every modicum of his pleasure, feasted off of it, until I was unable to distinguish it from my own. Then Derek began to drive into me with urgency and power, and my arousal spiraled off into near madness. When he came, Derek called out my name over and over, and then — as if in total surrender — he collapsed on top of me, the weight of his love now mine, a glorious burden to bare.

After taking time to catch his breath, Derek took me in his mouth, a bit too ravenously for my tastes, making me come way too soon, but oh how sweet to see him drink me in like a nomad at an oasis.

✳✳✳✳✳✳✳✳✳✳✳✳✳✳✳✳✳✳✳✳✳✳✳✳✳✳✳✳✳

Around about midnight, we sat at my table eating the strawberries I'd bought on Haight Street that morning specifically for this purpose. Candles I'd lit during an earlier hiatus in our lovemaking, flickered from around the room. Light from a street lamp streaked in through the space between my curtains and landed on the strawberries, highlighting their seductively red gleam.

"Why haven't you fucked me yet?" Derek threw this out casually, as if discussing football scores.

I smiled. "I've been waiting for an invitation."

"Okay, well, you are cordially invited to..." He cut himself off and I saw that serious intenseness that he'd been scaring me with lately. "I want to feel you inside me." It was Derek's voice, Derek's face, yet this was not Derek. Yet this *was* Derek!

I walked over to my nightstand and put a drop of oil on my fingertip. Crouching before him, I touched the oil to his lips, and we kissed — a delicious almond-strawberry kiss. I was in love with Derek, in a profound inexplicable, bigger than life sort of way. I felt that I should tell him, that I should never wait again to tell Derek anything I needed him to know. With my face only inches away from his, I spoke slowly, "I love you."

Now Derek, using the same low tone, watching my eyes, said what he needed to say, "I love you."

On the bed a little later, I focused on Derek's expression as I slowly, carefully entered him. There was a long sharp grimace but then, as I began to move, oh so gently, I saw something melt away from Derek, a harshness, an anger, which had always been a part of him, a part of who I understood Derek to be. Now it was gone, disappeared. Bliss took over his expression, and I knew he was going to a space where both of us had already been several times that night — a space where there was only the two of us, our lovemaking, the void enveloping us, bathing us. I stayed outside that space for a moment to watch him, and then with a steady thrusting, I joined him there.

When I felt I couldn't hold out much longer, I shifted my weight onto one arm and with my other, oily, hand stroked Derek's cock. As I climaxed, long, deep, *oohhhs* of ecstasy poured out of my mouth in a series of spasms. But Derek came screaming, like you'd imagine he might, had he been shot in the back by a machine gun.

Chapter Thirty-five

After class the next morning, we sat in the cafeteria with our cups of coffee. Normally we'd start chatting about something that came up in class, today instead, there were soft smiles and long deep stares. We sat this way for an amazingly long time.

Derek broke the silence, nearly laughing. "We don't have anything to say to each other anymore?"

"I think we said it all last night."

We went on smiling, taking in the joy plastered on each other's faces. Then Derek suddenly sat-up straight, composed himself, and after taking a sip from his cup, said with his deepest most masculine voice, "Damn good coffee, don't you think?"

Truth was, the coffee sucked. I knew Derek was aware of this because sometime during the first week we'd met he'd remarked on this fact. We'd been drinking this same horrendous coffee together all these years, and had never discussed it again.

"It's god-awful," I said. Then I confessed, "One of the booths in the Food Court has some real good Costa Rican roast. I go there when you're not around."

"Really?"

"Yeah."

"Why didn't you tell me?"

"It's called Croissant Corner."

Derek looked at me, clearly not comprehending.

"You know, Real Men Don't Eat Quiche... real men don't eat croissants..."

"Are you serious? That's why you didn't tell me?"

"Yep."

Derek broke-out in uproariously loud laugher that momentarily commanded the attention of others at tables around us.

286

Neither of us made a move, though, to walk the fifty feet or so to get some of that good Costa Rican roast. Instead, we sat there talking physics once again, and nursing our dishwater with milk. The best damned dishwater I ever had.

****

That night, as Derek and I lay resting between bouts of lovemaking, I suddenly thought of Alice. Had he told her? If he hadn't, would he? When? It wasn't that I didn't trust Derek, but that I knew how I'd myself handled such situations in the past, and that was enough to raise within me a respectable level of panic.

"I told Alice," Derek said suddenly. We were on our backs, knees bent, our arms, hips, and thighs touching.

"You did?"

"This afternoon; just before I came over here."

I reached for his hand, held it lightly in mine, resting them together on his still sweaty stomach.

"Her reaction?"

"She was horrified." The room was almost completely dark. Derek's low voice rumbled softly through it. "It was like her worst nightmare had been realized."

"What did you actually say to her?"

"She said, 'you seem different today.' And I said, 'I am different.' She got up from the table and walked towards the kitchen, like she didn't want to know, and I said anyway, 'I'm in love with Jim. We made love last night.'"

Derek's words spun over the bed, then fluttered upon us like soft rain.

"She demanded that I break things off with you. I told her that I could no longer help myself when it came to you, and that I very intensely did not *want* to be able to help myself when it came to you. That's when she told me to leave and not come back."

A feeling within me hinted vaguely of regret, but the over-ridding emotion was relief. I had never liked the idea of Derek and Alice together. "Was it bad for you?" I asked, concerned for him none-the-less.

"I was prepared for that. When I told her, weeks ago, that you were bi, I got a good idea of how she felt about these things."

"I didn't know you'd told her." I was rather surprised.

"Yeah, well, I probably wouldn't have, but I saw her that same night. She called a couple of hours after I left A Kiss of Heaven. I was really a mess." He grasped my hand. "A real mess."

I could feel within him a reliving of the experience.

"I didn't want to talk to her," Derek continued, "I said something probably pretty strange and hung up. Then I returned to pacing the room. I was going nuts. I had to practically restrain myself from pulling my hair out of my head. I was angry, and scared, and so damned *uncomfortable*. I couldn't make sense out of any of it — what you had told me, what I was feeling in reaction. Finally, in desperation, I called Alice and told her I was coming over." He paused for a moment remembering.

"I thought once I got there I'd calm down some. But of course I didn't. I was all over the place, couldn't sit still for a second. Alice didn't say much, just watched me. Though I hadn't intended to tell her, I found myself spilling out the story. My sentences were garbled, practically incoherent — it took a while for her to get the gist of what I was saying. But when she did, she was utterly appalled. Her face... you should have seen it. She didn't say anything at first, but when I finally ran out of words, she said, 'You'll transfer to another school.' The thought of this, the idea! Not that there's anything so amazing about State — I mean I'd thought seriously about applying to Stanford for my sophomore year — but I knew then, when she suggested this, that I wasn't going to let anything you told me interfere with what you and I are to each other. I didn't answer her. I just looked at her, kind of wondering who she thought I was. It was a strange feeling, because who she thought I was, was who I thought I was, and on some level I must have begun to have had an inkling that that wasn't me at all."

Derek considered for a moment, then added, "What an odd thing for her to have said. It's like she knew all along about you and me, knew she should separate us..." Apparently not wanting to dwell on that point, he continued, "Anyway, I slept with her that night, but I didn't like it, and things weren't ever really the same between us after that. It was on the ride home the next morning — I'd left early, about four — that I realized that I needed to understand you." Derek was quiet for a long while, then he added, "In the end, it was me that I finally began to understand."

"A fact I'll be eternally grateful for," I said.

Derek rolled over and on top of me. Hugging each other, his head on my chest — I not caring to remove the strand of his hair that fell across my lips — we soon fell asleep. Twenty-some minutes later we awoke with erections, and proceeded to, once again, show one another with our bodies the depths of our feelings.

Chapter Thirty-six

The man with the hands, I could have told Hank and Rebecca about this, or not, and felt comfortable either way. What happened with Derek, of course, was another matter altogether, and I was uncertain how they'd take it. I did not expect that even they would have been able to predict their reactions. Yes, we all understood that within our relationship, fidelity was not sought after, but how many pieces can you cut your heart into? How much love do any of us have to give? How much time and energy? I now knew that, personally, I had a great deal of love to give, and I knew that aside from physics, I could find no other way that I would want to spend huge chunks of my time than with people I love. I could be with Derek and physics simultaneously. I could be with Hank and Rebecca simultaneously. It sounded like a crazy life, but the more I looked at it, the more it didn't seem like a juggling act beyond my capabilities. Could I get Hank and Rebecca to see this?

We sat around their kitchen table. I had told them I wanted to discuss something, and just came right out with, "Something pretty bizarre happened while you were gone."

"Bizarre?" This was Hank. He was wearing one of those damn pair of thin cotton drawstring pants, a coffee color. I knew he had no underwear on, and he knew those pants made me mad with lust. I looked at Rebecca; her eyes were inquiring, excited. I couldn't wait to get into bed with her and Hank. But I found it extremely inconvenient to be thinking about sex at this moment, and vaguely wished they both didn't turn me on quite so much.

"Bizarre," I confirmed. "And..." I smiled to myself, "beautiful. And maybe a little scary." Looking into Hank's eyes, I felt a surge, a rush of emotion. "It's Derek," I said now. "He kissed me." I smiled at my choice of words.

Derek kissed me. *Derek kissed me*. I still had not quite gotten over that first kiss.

Hank and Rebecca checked each other's faces to make sure they heard me correctly.

"We slept together," I said.

"You and Derek?" Hank asked, disbelief setting his voice an octave higher.

"Me and Derek."

"The same Derek you're not attracted to?" Rebecca asked. "The straight one?"

"That's what makes it bizarre."

They were both studying my face, trying to read it.

"It's not... This isn't..." I shook my head trying to think of a way to say this that wouldn't come out awkward. Giving up, I finally said simply, "I've missed you two a lot."

There was some relief in their expressions, but I knew they were anxious to know what happened, and so I summed up it for them. "Derek kissed me — no warning. I freaked. Big time. He said he had wanted to understand my homosexuality and eventually — he explained the whole process — eventually he ended up understanding it a lot more than he ever bargained for, ended up obsessed with the idea of sleeping with me. He added that he didn't believe I wasn't attracted to him, even if I didn't realize it. He left me in a catatonic state that night. But before he left, he made it a point to say he didn't want to — in any way — interfere with what I have with you two." I looked at them to be sure they got this.

Rebecca looked skeptical. Hank looked impatient to hear the rest. So, I went on. "I was so disturbed by the kiss, that the next day I ended up calling Jeff — the guy who left me because I was closeted — and..." I smiled as a lost childhood phrase came to me — from TV no-less — "well Jeff really 'socked-it-to me.' *He'd* understood what was between Derek and I. I protested Jeff's claims, but he was relentless, came right out and said Derek was who I always wanted. I cut him off there, told him, 'Hank and Rebecca are who I always wanted.'" I said this now just as loud and clear and insistent as I had to Jeff, then I paused to emphasize the point.

But Hank, immediately, asked, "When you slept together, how was it, I mean did he... you... enjoy it?"

I looked down at the table. "It was wonderful... We'd denied ourselves for so long..."

"Was there just the one time?"

"No. No. Not at all."

Very calmly, but almost stiffly, Hank said, "It would be naive to assume that Derek would be okay for long about the fact that you are involved so significantly with two other people."

Rebecca squirmed in her chair. "I don't like the sound of this." Clearly she was trying hard to keep it together. Now my own level of discomfort escalated.

"Just because Derek said he doesn't want to interfere with your relationship with us..." Rebecca continued. "People say all kinds of things... to get what they want."

Hank looked at Rebecca. "That's right, you've never met Derek. I don't think he'd be that manipulative. But he might feel, eventually..."

"You barely know him," Rebecca said.

"Jim does."

They looked at me. I understood their concern. I'd *expected* it. I would have felt the same uneasiness if one of them told me about a new serious lover. But I was angry at the thought of having to defend Derek, my relationship with him. I got up and walked into the laundry room. I stared out the window, which boasted the only real view from their flat. The towers of the Golden Gate Bridge stood out boldly in the distance, but buildings blocked any sight of the bay beneath it. I felt frustrated by this. I wanted to see the water. I wanted to swim in that water. I wanted to dive into the vast depth. I hadn't been swimming for years, not since Jeff and I'd taken a drive down to Santa Cruz one weekend. We'd ridden on the roller coaster, and eaten corn-on-the-cob, after splashing around in the cold murky ocean.

I stood on my toes, still no sight of water. I could just picture myself submersed in the dark solitude of the bay, like... Like a closet. I wanted to escape! Fuck that! I high-tailed it back into the kitchen. Rebecca and Hank sat patiently, apparently expecting my return.

Standing before them, immediately filled again with an annoying desire to get into bed with them, I said firmly, "I love you both tremendously. I'm not going to let anything screw up what we have. Derek's been a huge part of my life for years, so — as Jeff pointed out — it's not as if all the sudden I'm going to be spending a bunch of time with someone new. Whenever I'm not with one or both of you, I'm pretty much with Derek; that's how it's been; that's how will continue to be."

They looked at me, focused intently.

I sat down, hands folded before me on the tabletop. "Derek *knows*," I said, "that you guys are..." was there a word, a way to explain? "the..." and then it came to me, "the essence of my happiness."

I realized how vulnerable I was making myself by saying this; the moment was awkward. I was more naked before them now than I ever was when we were having sex. But I wanted this, wanted to be complete with them, no holding back, no defenses. Looking at them, I could see that they felt the awkwardness, felt it within themselves, and felt my awkwardness. Then, as the moment settled itself, I saw how relaxed they became, saw how much they hungered too for the no holding back, no defenses. Saw how all of us in this world yearn for that, yearn to be able to be completely vulnerable, to have others trust their vulnerability with us, and we had it, the three of us. I knew too, that Derek and I had, in the last few days, also reached that space together.

Things began to occur to me now, and I haltingly spoke them as I thought them. "I've been in love with Derek for a long time..." Quietly I added, "That's why I fought so hard to stay closeted... I loved him and didn't want to lose him..." Now very certain, I said, "Me falling in love with Derek... or him with me... is nothing new. We were in love long before I met you two. So it's not as if I've suddenly fallen in love with someone new."

"Understanding that you're in love with each other is new," Hank stated.

"Yes."

I looked at them, these two whom I loved so deeply, and saw that they understood that these revelations about Derek had just now occurred to me, and they were quiet, giving me the space to process. I saw love in their eyes, and I knew that ultimately they would be okay about Derek.

"Hank's right," I said to Rebecca as a final reassurance, "Derek wouldn't just say things to... He's not manipulative." Glancing out the window, looking at the roof garden next door, I said, very softly, perhaps mainly to myself, "Derek so much wants for me to be happy." I thought of us making love, just that morning. It all still felt so unreal. How many times had it been in the last few days?

Chapter Thirty-seven

"Hey, Derek, is it true you're a fag?"

Derek told me he'd been walking down the hall at school when this was shouted out as he passed by what he thought was an empty classroom. He said he took a step back and looked in. It was a guy who he'd hung out with briefly in high school, and who'd also been in a couple of our undergraduate classes.

Derek gave him a good hard stare.

"Rumor has it, you and Jim are ahh... *boyfriends*."

"We're lovers. What of it?"

Derek said his candor shocked the guy. Leaving him there open mouthed, Derek started up the hall again.

Then he heard, "Does his girlfriend know?"

Derek turned around, saw the guy standing in the doorway, and thought, *girlfriend*? Confused and thrown off balance, he said, "You mean Carol? They split up a long time ago."

"I don't know what her name is, but he was having dinner with her last night — beautiful redhead."

"Oh, Rebecca." Derek thought it funny that this hadn't occurred to him. "Yeah, she knows." Then he added, "So does her husband. Jim's doing him too." The guy's mouth dropped opened again.

We flirted in the hallways before classes, rode onto campus hands-around-waist on one another's bikes, kissed good-bye in the parking lot. We'd known it was only a matter of time for something like this to happen. Derek's reaction to this guy was a bit extreme. But, I thought, extreme is good. He placed his hand in mine after he recounted this story, and I gave him an affirming squeeze. We were in bed yet again. We'd come to the conclusion days before that we needed to get sex out of the way first, before we tried to study — by the time we got back to my place, or his, after school, we were desperate for each other.

So we'd just had a wild foray into the realm of uninhibited passion — gone right to it the minute we walked in the door — and now there'd been time for conversation. Derek's story left me full of pride, still I must have had an odd look on my face, because Derek asked, "What's wrong?"

How to say it? Express the questioning? It was as if I could not be convinced that Derek and I together was not a hallucination my mind had tricked me with.

"Such a shock," I said finally, "to people who thought we were so hetero." I wondered about the foundations we were unsettling. Like an earthquake, the waves spreading out far beyond the epicenter. And then there are the aftershocks...

"I could have used a shakeup like that years ago," Derek said, adding a moment later, "When I was a kid — eleven, twelve, around then — I became fascinated with earthquakes."

Realizing that this was about the right age, I asked, "What are your earliest sexual memories?"

He thought for quite a while. "I used to," he said, "fantasize about very masculine men having sex with busty women." He got out of bed and put on his jeans, then slipped his T-shirt over his head. "Gives the illusion of heterosexuality, doesn't it?" He glanced over at me as he sat on the couch now pulling on his socks. Before I could answer, before I could think about what he was implying with this question, Derek added, "Let's get in a game of pool before we start working."

I rose and sat naked on the couch next to him, giving him a deep kiss before getting dressed myself.

Our game at Lucky Paul's was filled with ease and laughter. We played one-on-one, no Real Bikers around to entertain us. Then, grabbing slices of pizza on the way, we went back to my place, studying hard and long before we fell into bed, sleeping like babies in each other's arms.

The next day, Tuesday, we had only an early morning class. I would spend the rest of the day with Rebecca and the night with her and Hank. After class, Derek and I walked together across campus towards the parking lot where our bikes were locked.

"Why were you having dinner alone with Rebecca Sunday?" Derek asked as we passed the tree where we'd almost stepped on the toes of the two guys kissing years ago.

I pointed to the tree. "Remember that?"

"What?" He looked at the tree confused at first. "Oh." His face turned red as he realized what I was referring to.

"That was one of the worst days of my life," I told him. "Every time I've walked by here over the years, I've feel such a sickness."

Derek put an arm around me as if in consolation, and it worked. I felt very happy, felt a special kinship now with those two brave boys who had sat there kissing, expressing their love, oblivious to the world around them.

I put my arm around Derek too, and not wanting to leave his question unanswered, I said, "Rebecca and I were dining alone because Hank had to entertain an out-of-town client. It was nice," I added, "and Hank was home by mid-night, so I got to spend some time with him too."

"You had an early class the next morning," Derek responded.

"Well, we were asleep by two. Anyway, Derek, I never have been getting enough sleep. Half the nights when you and I studied till way late, I was out at a bar half an hour later looking for some hunk to go on a sexual excursion with."

He squeezed my shoulder. "Did you have fun?"

"Yeah, most of the time. But there was so much sadness beneath it all. You have no idea."

"Yes I do," Derek said.

I was surprised to find myself realizing that he probably did.

****

Rebecca and I sat on the couch. Apples I'd put in the oven gave rise to cinnamon and orchard aromas, aromas heavy with memories — memories that rumbled quietly inside me, finding at last a way to settle. We looked through photos dating back to Rebecca's and Hank's college days. After enjoying a picture of Rebecca looking beatific with a ring of pink roses in her hair, I got up and built a fire. Newspaper first, then kindling wood. I turned a pile of sticks in my hand. Here was an example of the original definition of the word "faggot." I thought of the homosexuals burned as a prelude to make fires hotter for hapless "witches." A practice that gave birth to a new definition of faggot. Humanity! From whence we come! Then dismissing all this, I placed a couple of small logs on top. Striking a match, holding it to a corner of newspaper, I saw now a headline, *Americans Return to Churches in Droves*. With satisfaction I watched it go up in flames.

I sat back down next to Rebecca, put my arm around her. How perfectly, inherently, good this felt. We were both in quiet peaceful moods. Rebecca was still in her bathrobe. She'd awoken only as I'd entered the apartment an hour earlier. I'd put in the apples while she showered. Then, before moving to the living room with the photos, we'd sat in the kitchen over steaming coffee as she recounted the intense day she'd had at work yesterday.

"But a dream I had last night helped," she'd said, "brought the pieces together, like a puzzle, fitting them into place." She'd pinched a strand of her still wet hair between her fingers. A droplet of water fell onto the wooden floor.

Now — the fire crackling (cackling) before us — I looked at photos of college kids in the mid-seventies fitting together their own personal jigsaw puzzles.

"This is Ted," Rebecca said, jabbing a snapshot in my direction.

I took the picture from her. "Wow!" The word came out of my mouth un-elicited. Now, more purposely, I added, "He's beautiful."

Rebecca laughed, "Good old Ted."

"How come you never fell for him?"

"Oh, he was too much. You should have seen it, the scene he created. Boys and girls falling all over themselves for him. It was pathetic."

"Is that how you thought of Hank at the time?"

"Yeah, at first. But then as I got to know him, I began to understand. Consider, of all the admirers Ted had in those days, Hank's the only one he's still involved with, so something's different there. I saw that fairly quickly. They have a true connection."

I felt grateful — for Hank — that he had found Rebecca. This conversation gave me an even more profound understanding of their relationship. A more profound understanding of my relationship with them too. It was all about allowing one another the freedom and space to grow. Loving each other enough to want to not possess. And yet as a result, it seemed to me, we emotionally possessed each other so much more than any monogamy-oriented couple. How could I not appreciate them all the more for giving me the space to explore my love for Derek? How would I not feel anything but resentment and anger towards someone who tried to stand between Derek and me? Yes, we are all imperfect, full of insecurities and fears — these emotions had risen up in Hank and Rebecca when I first told them about Derek — how could they not; they were afraid of losing me. But by fighting this fear, not allowing it any power, they had secured me to them with a bond stronger than that of any superglue, than that of any vow of fidelity.

Chapter Thirty-eight

It had been an overcast day, and now fog crept across campus like a seedy villain. Derek and I, done with our classes for the day, walked to the parking lot together as we talked about a problem we'd encountered in our joint thesis. This was on a Friday, about a month after Derek and I became lovers. As usual, I'd be spending the weekend with Hank and Rebecca and didn't expect to see Derek again until Monday morning.

However, when we got to our bikes, Derek squinted at me and asked, "Which day does Rebecca have off this weekend?"

"Saturday."

"Are you going home Sunday night?"

"Yeah, thought I'd get some studying done, and maybe some sleep."

He was silent, looking at me.

"What?"

"I'd like it..." He shifted his weight from one leg to the other uneasily. "Would you come over Sunday after you leave Hank?" He was still squinting at me.

Fog seeped up my pant legs and nipped at my calves. I'd been looking forward to having a little time alone, and I knew Derek realized this. But he'd asked me anyway... Climbing onto my bike, I told him I'd be there around five. Derek gave me a quick kiss, and I roared off to see my other lovers.

****

Sunday morning, Hank and I got up early with Rebecca and the three of us had breakfast together — cardamom-walnut cake that we'd baked the night before, after making love, and blackberries in cream. Hank ground up a cinnamon stick with the coffee beans, and that along with the cardamom led us into a conversation about India, where we imagined the air to be steamy with spice-laden scents. When Rebecca left, I turned to my books while Hank went through some papers for work.

In the afternoon, Hank and I lazed about on "Hippie Hill" in Golden Gate Park. The fog had receded, and the day was bright and clear — the heat a tonic for bodies too long denied the sun's rays. The wind picked up occasionally, rustling the eucalyptus leaves. I ran my fingers through the grass as we munched on delicately crunchy plantain chips and drank from tall bottles of tamarind soda — island treats introduced to me indirectly by one of Carol's City College friends. We said little, enjoying the day and each other. At the bottom of the hill, a man in a black sports jacket, T-shirt, and blue jeans, played Frisbee with his golden retriever. They hopped and pranced about joyously — a man who obviously loved his dog, loved life. As we watched, I laced my fingers into Hanks.

From out of a stand of trees, three drug fiends strode up the hill. As they sat down near us, there was a protesting low grumble, "Fucking Queers," from the white boy in a bleached-blond mohawk. But the nearly emaciated black woman who had her arm around him said loudly, "They just lovin' each other, ain't noth'n wrong with dat," and shot us a quick smile behind her guy's back.

Their companion, a horribly young, green-haired, punker, who danced about them with the nervous energy of a flea, seemed oblivious to the entire exchange. His pierced nose sported a beautiful heart-shaped jade stone that I couldn't help but admire. I thought of the house at Cole and Page, Zeek and the purple-haired one. Now a man with greasy, graying, hair, filthy clothes, and a not-so-subtle stench, made his way up the hill. I'd seen him before on Haight and in the park. Undoubtedly he'd eked out a home somewhere in the underbrush. He approached the young derelicts eagerly, seeming to know them, and sat down with much pomp and circumstance. Then, after a brief search, he pulled a tomato out of his ragged army surplus backpack, and triumphantly held up this gleaming red jewel.

"Trade you this for a hit of acid," he said, his voice brimming with generosity. "I've even got a salt shaker. Always travel with a salt shaker!"

The bouncing flea snatched the tomato out of his hand excitedly. "Yeah, yeah, we'll give you a dose." The homophobe looked over his shoulder at us communicatively to the others. They all rose at once and walked off into the bushes.

When they were gone, I rolled onto my stomach. Hank's warm hands worked my shoulders, loosening knots. I closed my eyes, wishing for sleep, but a siren wailed in the distance, and I got to worrying about Rebecca. Being a paramedic seemed to me almost as bad as being a cop — the unsavory situations Rebecca was led into regularly. She had her tales, and I didn't at all like to hear them — partially due to my concern for her, and partially due to my intense aversion to ugliness in life. She only talked about these things when she'd had an especially grueling shift, but I was always the one left shaken; I could never do her job.

She must have realized the effect her recounts had on me, because she'd stopped telling me about the strangulated wives, the teenaged overdoses, the blood-shrouded drunks, the slit wrists accompanying desperate last words scribbled on old shopping lists with eyeliner. I felt that I should be able to be there for Rebecca, that I failed her, and I was glad that Hank handled these things differently. I thought about all this then, in the park, and did not find sleep. All the relaxing the sun and Hank had done on my muscles was lost, and on top of the tiredness, I now felt tense, vaguely frightened, and uncomfortably incompetent. The fog started to roll in again, thick and uncompromising — great billows of damp, bone-seeking chill.

We headed back towards the apartment. Hank would go upstairs to get dinner ready for a beleaguered Rebecca who would be returning from work shortly. I would go to Derek.

At the apartment door, Hank and I stopped to say our good-byes. After we hugged, Hank stood before me, a fine, unshakable work of art. He smiled a patient smile. "Jim, darling, do please try and relax more."

He got a little laugh out of me with the "darling" like he knew he would. "I'll try," I responded, appreciating how well he understood me. And too, I appreciated the warm comfort of his mouth as he gave me a tantalizing parting kiss.

I drove off experiencing some relief at the knowledge that Rebecca would soon be home and safe and in Hank's arms. The fog, now an almost dense mass of white, sent its tentacles up under my leather jacket driving at me like an army of arctic snakes. Though I'd shaken off most of my anxiety by the time I got to Derek's, I was, on top of being extremely tired, amazingly cold; I wanted a soft pillow on a warm bed with thick blankets.

****

With a great deal of weariness, I unlocked Derek's door. As I entered, he jumped up from the couch and greeted me, "Where the hell have you been?"

Confusion buzzed my head. "I said I'd be here about five. It's quarter of," I added, glancing at the clock on his desk.

"Right, but where the hell have you *been*?"

Remaining calm despite Derek's apparent panic, I said, "I was where you knew I would be, with Hank and Rebecca all weekend." I really wanted to at least sit down.

"Yeah. Why weren't you here?"

I blinked a few times. "Derek, what is this?" I thought about the now-tomato-less park dweller and wondered if he was having as bad of a trip as I was. I doubted it.

Derek sat down. I sat down too — thankful at least for this — and put my now throbbing head in my hands.

He said nothing. I looked over at him at the other end of the couch. "What's going on?"

"Alice called." His voice was zombie-like.

"Alice," I repeated. The name of a ghost, I thought.

"She wants to get back together."

"What?" I looked up, becoming hyper-alert.

Talking to his coffee table, he went on, "She wants me to break things off with you and get back together with her."

He looked at me now, and saw the alarm in my face.

"You've gotta be kidding!" he said. "I wouldn't leave you for her; you don't actually think that do you?"

The relief was tremendous, but I responded, "I didn't actually think you'd become my lover. I mean what the hell do *I* know?" I wrapped my arms around my waist to keep my teeth from chattering.

"Why are you shivering? You look terrible."

"I'm cold, Derek. It's a cold night out there."

"Why didn't you say something?" Nervous concern quavered his voice.

I looked at him, incredulous. "I didn't exactly get the red carpet welcome when I walked in."

Derek jumped up. "Sorry, sorry. Here," he walked over to me, "take off your jacket; I'll get blankets. And coffee."

"Coffee. Yeah."

He brought blankets, wrapped them around me. In a minute, shouting from the kitchen on the other side of the

305

room, he said, "Sorry about the attack when you came in. That was pretty fucked up. I've been a mess all weekend." As he milled about getting the coffee, he continued, "She called Friday evening. That afternoon, when you drove off to go to Hank and Rebecca's, I was feeling really down, had the whole weekend to face."

He brought a cobalt blue ceramic mug filled with rich black elixir. "I figured you wouldn't want milk," he said.

I was disturbed by him knowing this — had no idea how he could have, he was right, I didn't want milk tonight, just the pure unadulterated rejuvenating stuff — and too weary to respond, so instead, I just took a careful sip while he watched.

Derek smiled with satisfaction, then sat down on a chair across from me.

"Anyway, when I got home from school, I got to thinking about Alice, really for the first time since we split up. I just felt that it'd be real nice to have her sitting at the kitchen table with me, talking about baseball, or the people she works with."

Baseball? I didn't know Derek was into baseball. Okay, well, we all have our closets... I laughed aloud at the absurdity of this thought.

"What?"

I shook my head in an apologetic gesture. "I just didn't know you were a baseball fan."

"Well Alice was... and yeah, I sort of got interested." Derek looked so sad.

I sat up, tried to force my eyes open. "Sorry, tell me."

"Just, I was sitting there missing her, you know, for the first time, and it hit me that she was gone and that I had actually lost something." Derek slowly combed loose bangs back with his fingers — strong masculine hand through jet-black silk. "Our relationship hadn't ever been all that great,

306

mediocre really, and then getting into such an intense relationship with you... I'd felt like losing her wasn't any big deal. But Alice and I were together for a while... She was, anyway, someone who I'd gotten used to having around." After pausing a moment, he added, "I know you never understood it — Alice and me."

He knew; I'd wondered.

"But it was just this very comfortable situation, peaceful and quiet. That felt nice a lot of times. So I was thinking about all this, and feeling lonely, and then she called, and I really wanted to see her, just sit and drink Bud and play cards."

That's what I'd always imagined them doing.

"Just not have to think for a time, just not be lonely."

Now I understood.

"But she says, 'I know all this with Jim being a...a...*gay*, I guess, has been confusing for you, but isn't it time you got over it? Just walk away, and I'll forgive you, never bring it up again. You can get your Ph.D. at Berkeley.' And though I was horrified by her words, and simultaneously felt so bad for her, I was like, 'Alice, please just come over; I'd really like to see you.' But she got all incensed, 'No! First tell me you'll give up Jim.' And I just kept pleading with her to come see me. Finally she hung up saying, 'When you're ready to stop messing up your life, let me know.'

"After I got off the phone, I felt disgusted by her attitude towards you — you and me. That's when I started to wonder where the hell you were. I spent most of the weekend wondering that."

"Why didn't you call me?"

"I wasn't gonna do that."

"Why not? That's why I gave you their phone number."

"I *don't* want to interfere with you and them."

"If you need me, you're not interfering. If you need me; I want to be here for you."

"It's crazy," Derek said, "I kept thinking, where the hell is he? And I needed you, that's right, but I didn't want you to not be with Hank and Rebecca." He looked at me. "That got me to wondering, why aren't I jealous of them? If I love you so much, shouldn't I be jealous? If you love me so much, shouldn't you want to be with only me? But the more I thought about it, the more I knew how desperately I didn't want to, in any way, cause problems between you and them. They're good for you. Really good for you. And I'm not jealous. I actually want you to be with them." He held his hands up as if in helpless surrender. "So I couldn't call, but I couldn't stop asking myself where the hell you were."

"Next time, call. I mean it."

He shrugged. "See, I spent a lot of my spare time with Alice — when I wasn't with you or at school — I'm not use to being alone for long stretches. I start to think too much." Derek rubbed his temples with his fingers. "You know what I mean."

Sure I knew, the intelligent person's curse — how to put the brain on hold.

"Alice was real good at keeping me focused on the here and now."

I was awake now, wide-awake. Carefully, sincerely, but reluctantly, I said, "Maybe you *should* go back to her."

Derek stared at me in disbelief. "You'd give me up that easily? Just: 'Go back to her'?"

"I'd do whatever I had to, to do right by you. I mean, take a look at me."

He looked at me. "What?"

"I'm a man."

"No shit."

"Why would you want to do this to yourself? Embrace a life that most people don't understand, don't *want* to understand, a life that some people despise with a passion?"

Derek stood up abruptly and paced the room angrily. "I'm in love with you!" He gave me a fleeting hate-filled glare. "And hey, you know what else? I like sucking cock. I like being fucked. Isn't it pretty obvious to you, that I like touching a man, like being touched by a man?"

I looked at him sideways, trying to get it clear in my head what he was telling me. "Are you saying," I asked, "that if I dropped dead tomorrow, you wouldn't go running back to the straight world?"

"I can't go back to the straight world." He said this calmly with his head turned away. "I'm not straight."

I stared at him. "What are you saying?"

Derek turned and looked directly at me. "I don't know." He plopped himself down on the couch next to me. "I guess I'm aroused by women. You know, I mean, yeah... I guess I am. But I've certainly never enjoyed sex with a woman the way I enjoy sex with you. I don't know if that's because I'm gay, or because I've just never been with a woman who liked sex as much as you do. Maybe it's because I've never loved a woman the way I love you. Maybe I'm not capable of loving a woman. Maybe I never opened myself up this much before. And why is that? I don't know."

I could tell him about myself. Tell him how I'd wondered about my own ability to love a woman, until I'd met Rebecca. I could also tell him that I'd had plenty of great sex with women before then. But what would any of this knowledge do for Derek? He had to discover who *he* was, and that I didn't know.

"Maybe we need to spend more time together," I said, feeling like he needed me there to help him go through all this.

Derek was silent.

"So much has happened so fast, and we haven't ever had a good solid chunk of time together. I think we need it."

He looked at me with searching eyes.

I thought a bit. "I want to spend next weekend with you. I'll just let Hank and Rebecca know that it's important."

"*No*," he was adamant.

"My mind's made up." I could be just as stubborn as he. "I'll wrestle with you about it in the morning. I'm tired." I put my head on his shoulder and closed my eyes.

Derek helped me get undressed and into bed. Then he lay down next to me.

****

In the morning, I opened my eyes, blinked, shook my head, then laughed, so surprised was I to realize where I was and who I was with. I'd had a dream that took place during the time when I was still in the closet and Derek and I were still just friends. It had been a pleasant dream, the two of us alone in a vast uninhabited desert, a swift wind blowing cloud shadows across scorching sand. We had joy-filled faces. But we stood apart — stolid, masculine stances. In the dream, I had been very specifically aware of how happy I was. It was telling then, to realize, when I awoke, that this dream's happiness felt almost akin to depression compared to what it felt like to be in Derek's bed, him naked beside me.

He lay sleeping on his side, facing me. His shoulder was uncovered, and I marveled at it there, so available to my touch, once such forbidden fruit, once so beyond my wildest dreams. So wild a dream that I never even dared dream it, never even allowed myself to know I wanted it.

A strand of hair had fallen into Derek's face near his eye. I brushed it gently back. He awoke then, smiled at me smiling at him.

"Derek," I said, in my horse, whispered, first-morning-voice.

"Yeah?"

"It's really you."

He grinned, brought a hand from under the blanket and reached up behind my head, guiding my mouth towards his. We fucked good and hard that morning — a passionate, loving, fuck.

****

Later, after classes, over coffee at a Kiss of Heaven, I said, "In reference to what you were saying last night — about your desires, or not, for men and women?"

Derek was staring contemplatively out the window. "Yeah?"

"My advice would be to stay away from thinking in terms of absolutes."

He nodded.

Chapter Thirty-nine

In the shower, water streaming down Derek's face, his eyes closed, steam rising up around and between us, I studied Derek's body. I'd ignored *this* all those years?

I reached out a soapy palm and touched his taunt stomach. Derek shuddered, retracted from my touch. Then he opened his eyes. There was a moment of uncertainty. I, uncertain if he really wanted to be my lover, wanted to be with a man, and Derek uncertain, I realized quickly, whether he had upset me by his unintentional reaction. The uncertainty swirled down the drain, like the shampoo running out of Derek's hair, and we chuckled, perhaps nervously, at it. Derek, clearly in a gesture of assurance, pulled my sudsy body towards his. Feeling his hands groping hungrily on my ass as he kissed me, I understood finally that I needed to let my fears go — Derek was right; he was not straight. I was, it turned out, an incredibly lucky guy.

I had refused to accept Derek's protests about our weekend together. It was now Sunday morning, and it was clear to both of us that we had needed this time together, needed a space within which to establish our new relationship as lovers. Unlike with Hank and Rebecca — with whom an undeniable mutual attraction had been firmly established almost instantly there at the pool table, as if preordained — my love-affair with Derek had been drenched in doubt from the start. But I learned this weekend, from moments like that in the shower, that the doubt had been mine alone.

I had doubted Derek's sudden transformation, even doubted occasionally my own attraction to him. Even after having spent many hours in bed with him, the two of us loving each other with no less than the passion of ancient Gods — as if caught up in the very whirlwind of their

312

other-worldly existence — I still, when not touching or being touched by him, sometimes wondered if I had just let Jeff, and Derek, and the last five years of my life, carry me to a place I had not really wanted to be. When making love with Derek, all doubts would melt away; at those times I knew, understood completely, what had always been between the two of us, what we had both denied and hid from for so long. But when we were physically apart, even if in the same room sometimes, the doubt, questioning would start to creep back in. I think this was largely due to the fact that I was so committed to what I had with Hank and Rebecca. I'd been so happy to be out to Derek and have this couple as lovers, that I'd been reluctant to let go of those dynamics — reluctant to allow anything to threaten my relationship with two people, for whom my feelings had been so intense that I'd been forced, finally, to rescue myself from the excruciating hell of closet-hood. But during that weekend with Derek, I learned to completely face the fact that I was in love with, loved by, not two, but three people. This was how my life was, and though it filled me with fear, I could not help but revel in the outrageous beauty of it all. San Francisco had at last, for me, lived up to its promises, and then some.

In the shower, after our kiss, I had knelt, put Derek's cock in my mouth. I watched with great pleasure as one of his hands — fingers splayed — pushed against the green tiles of the shower wall, and as the other hand, eventually, suddenly, grasped and tore frantically at the shower curtain, ripping it violently off its rungs. We wiped the water up off the floor together with an old towel.

"Sorry about how I reacted when you touched me while I had my eyes closed," Derek said, a little later as we sat at my table for an early lunch, "I probably shouldn't be thinking about atom-smashers when I'm showering with you."

I smiled. "Atom-smashers?"

"I do some of my best thinking in the shower."

"I probably shouldn't be so paranoid."

"Don't worry about it."

I tried to imagine how it would be possible to love anyone more than I loved Derek. We ate silently, for a moment, our bacon lettuce and tomato sandwiches.

"Let's go for a ride up to Muir Woods next week," I suggested.

"Sure, why Muir Woods?"

"We went up to Stinson beach a couple of weeks ago, hung out by the ocean."

"We?" Derek asked through a full mouth, "Hank and Rebecca?"

"Yeah. Beach was nice; we had a beautiful time, but on the drive up, I kept wishing I was doing that part of Highway 1 on the bike. It'd be a great ride. It's a wonder we've never done it."

"Too romantic."

I looked at Derek, doubt attempting to creep back in.

"I mean," he said smiling at my fragile sense of security, "it would have been too romantic back then. It never would have occurred to you to suggest it, and if you had, I never would have agreed."

It was still easier for me to think of Derek and me in a closet infested relationship, than Derek and me as lovers, and I knew in an instant that he was right; it wasn't any wonder that we never rode up those roads. About a week earlier, Derek had made some comments about all the time we'd squandered — all the time we'd been busy pretending, when we should have been enjoying each other fully, completely. I hadn't quite gotten his point. Hadn't we had many good times anyway? But today I felt remorseful, realizing why we never drove up into those hills together, and I began to understand Derek's mourning of our lost past.

"I know now what I wanted to say to you that night!" This suddenly came into my consciousness; I could picture perfectly the crystal-ball moon on the soothing monster-dark sea.

Derek stared at me, for only a moment lost, then he got it. "Ft. Funston. I was thinking about that the other day."

"What was going on in your head that night?"

"The same mass of confusion that was going on in your head," he said quietly.

We had come that close, years ago. We looked at each other with sad eyes, consumed by the magnitude of the horrible crime we had committed.

****

That night, street light snuck into the room through the gap in my curtains, a single white candle with a steady flame held its own on my nightstand, while Derek and I were on my bed making love, taking it slow. We had all night. We'd had coffee at Twice Over, a game of pool at Lucky Paul's, Thai food out of little white boxes at my table. While we ate, we'd talked in near whispers about the sensuous aspects of lemongrass tea, coconut milk, and red curry sauce — our unfaltering smiles a mixture of great amusement at ourselves in this scenario, and pure joy.

And now we were in bed and still the novelty of touching each other was fresh and vivid — desert dwellers exploring tropical flowers for the first time, tactile sensations acute with pleasure, visual images triggering in the mind opiate-like solace, luxurious scents bringing into bloom the wild jungle of our souls.

****

Monday morning, after Derek left, following our breakfast of coffee, toast, and scrambled eggs, I sat alone drinking my second cup, and thought about my three lovers. I tried to reconcile how it could be possible to be so in love with each of them, all of them. Trying to comprehend this brought on a feeling, a feeling somehow reminiscent, and I tried to put my finger on it, tried to recall when I'd felt this way before. Searching backwards, over my life thus far, it hit me finally, and I laughed. It had been back when I was a kid just beginning to get a glimpse of the nature of my sexuality — when I was struggling to understand how I could be attracted to both males and females, and what this meant. Now I knew fully what it meant, what it meant for my life.

But all that rummaging through my past got me thinking of my family — something I hadn't done in... I couldn't remember how long — and I felt sad in a pensive resigned sort of way. They are forever gone; I have lost them. Occasionally, on dull nights, over the years, I'd engaged in a loose fantasy. Elizabeth or Jesse, upon encroaching adulthood, rebels and forsakes the family religious neurosis. I'll get a late-night call, or there one of them will be, on my doorstep. Maybe Elizabeth will grow up to be a lesbian... But now I realized what a disastrous thing that would be — with the brainwashing she'd received since early childhood. It would screw her up good — the born again dogma would eat at her from the inside out. I once, when spying on that damned neighbor, Marissa, and my mom, heard Marissa explain, "You plant a seed. After a while it begins to germinate and grow. Put the thought in their head, introduce them to Jesus' love — the seed, a little water, some sun, it begins to grow."

Some people, I thought now, take a blade to it, chop it down, but it never really dies. Like with my mother, turning away from religion in her teen years, only to have it come back in another form, all the more insidious, in later life. Like a disease that the body can fight, but never kill.

I lay down now for a quick nap, and had a funny dream about a naked Amy feeding me Carob Haagen-Dazs while I sat in a warm bath. I got up an hour later, aroused by the dream, and rushed off to class, to Derek.

Derek and I had had all Friday, Saturday, and Sunday together, relearning each other. Hank and Rebecca had been all right with the plan; I suspected they needed a little time for just the two of them as well. I'd slept over at their place Thursday night; we'd enjoyed the break in our routine; I think it was a relief for all four of us to see that there was flexibility in our lives. I'd spend the rest of today with Derek, at school and after, and then tomorrow I'd be back with Rebecca.

****

That night, Derek and I were getting ready to sauté mushrooms and onions for our steaks when he asked, "Did Jeff ever call you back?"

"Hmm?" I asked, wiping onion tears out of my eyes.

"Didn't you tell me he said he'd call you back?"

"Oh yeah. Yeah, he did say that." There was a pop and a sizzle as I brushed the onions off the cutting board and into the hot butter. I stepped back from the splatter and steam.

"Maybe we should call him," Derek said, handing me the mushrooms he'd just finished breaking the stems off of.

"Not yet," I said.

"Huh?"

"The mushrooms, not now — the onions need to cook a little first." I began to chop the garlic. "Stir that some," I said, gesturing towards the stove.

Derek took up the wooden spoon, hesitated, then placed it carefully in the middle of the pan and awkwardly stirred.

I put the knife down. "Haven't you ever done any cooking?"

He looked at me, a remorseful confused look. "No." Then he added, clearly ashamed of himself, "Women cook."

"Women and fags."

"Yeah."

As we dined by candlelight, I said, "Really? Call Jeff?" Derek didn't know how to cook, but he sure knew how to eat; I could taste each of his bites by watching his expressions. He was working through a mouthful of string beans. String beans suddenly became a delicacy. He had no idea what he was doing to me.

His answer waited for the string bean experience to complete itself. Finally, when he was finished chewing, he said, "Yeah. I feel like I should thank him or something."

"That would be weird."

"You don't like weird?"

As he placed a forkful of baked potato in his mouth, I said, "Have you ever looked at yourself in the mirror when you were eating?"

"What?" he queried through the potato.

God, the sour cream in his mouth! I was so envious. "Here," I said, holding up my glass of wine, "To Jeff! And to being weird."

Earlier, after classes, we'd been shopping for this dinner in Stonestown, and it dawned on me that I'd not gone near wine since that last night with Rick. I remembered, early on with Carol, telling her, "I don't like wine," and I'd managed to simultaneously convince myself that this was true. I'd even said it to Hank and Rebecca, honestly believing it. But as I walked past the wine aisle with Derek, it all came to me, and I stopped and grabbed a bottle of well-priced cabernet off the shelf. "Wine with dinner?" I asked enthusiastically.

Derek had hesitated, but then gathered some enthusiasm, "Sure."

Now he toasted with me. "To Jeff."

"It was bad for him, wasn't it?" Derek asked, putting his glass back on the table without drinking from it.

"Yes. I was bad for him. I was bad." I put my glass down too.

"Because of me."

"No, I'm responsible for my actions."

"But you did it for me," Derek said, "for us."

"I could have told Jeff anything that first night. I could have said, 'I'm tempted, but no it's better if we remained friends.' "

"That would have been good for him?"

"Probably not."

After dinner, Derek handed me the phone.

"Me?"

"I don't know his number."

"I'll give it to you." I put the phone down.

He pushed the phone back into me. "Call him."

"Do I have to call him while *you're* here?"

"Why not? Don't you want me to hear what you have to say? You gonna tell him what a bad lay I am?"

"Don't be preposterous."

He grabbed the phone from me. "You're chicken-shit; what's his number?"

I grabbed the phone back. "Don't call me that. Jeff called me that. I'm not chicken-shit." After a second I added, "Not anymore." I pointed to my bookshelf. "My address book's next to the *Tao of Physics*."

When Jeff answered, I asked, without saying hello first, "Should I have turned you away that first night?"

"Jim," was all he said at first. Then, "No." Then, "You don't know how grateful Bob is for you."

"Bob? Grateful?"

"Sure. If I'd had no one in San Francisco, do you know how guilt-ridden Bob would be? And suppose I fell in love with someone truly available — would I have gone back to him?"

"Would you have?"

"I don't know. How can I say?"

Knowing it was an unfair question, I still couldn't help but ask more specifically, "If I'd come out, would you have gone back to Bob?"

"Jim." Jeff said this as a mild reprimand, but then he attempted to answer. "I think we both knew, when it came right down to it. I mean, there was a time when I thought I would stay, when I thought, if only I could persuade you, but I was desperate and confused. The idea of going back to Bob was scary; what if he backed out again? But you and I were never meant for each other; we fulfilled needs in each other's lives at a time when we were both pretty needy." Then he hastened to add, "Not that it didn't hurt, not that we didn't love each other, just that we weren't right for each other. But I still miss you sometimes." His voice became very faint. "If I concentrate, I can still smell you." Back to a normal tone, he said, "Tell me about Derek."

"He's right here." I was still trying to take in what Jeff said.

"And?" he asked.

"And, everything you said was right — last time I talked to you, and... what you said just now." I tried to remember Jeff's smell. It wasn't coming back to me.

"You're lovers."

"Yes."

"How is it?"

"Strange," I was honest with him, "very unreal, for me still. But also the most incredible experience of my life." I smiled, I'm sure a totally sickening smile, at Derek. "You want to talk to him?" I asked Jeff.

"No. Oh, okay."

I handed the phone to Derek who said eagerly, "Hello, Jeff," then listened for a while before responding, "Yeah, there was some of that in the beginning; it was disorienting, but that wore off quickly. The thing is, up until now my life had always been confusing, so since I've come out, suddenly I'm actually a lot less confused."

Come out, is that what Derek had done?

"I still don't completely understand myself, but now at least I know that; before I was just stumbling around in a daze and wasn't even aware of it. Of course, being involved with Jim can be confusing all by itself."

Derek played with the cord, listening, then said, "Oh yeah, I'm sure you can." Then a moment later, "Thanks, maybe I will. I'll get your number from Jim." Derek asked some questions now about how Jeff was doing.

Watching him, I remembered again the night at the hang gliding ramp. The moon, and how Derek and I could not speak our love for each other, could not even allow conscious awareness of it, and I remembered how I went to Jeff's place afterward and lay awake for hours beside him. Now Jeff's smell came back to me, and there was a longing. But it wasn't sad; it was a longing that didn't ever need to be satisfied.

Derek hung up.

I looked at him with a questioning expression.

"He said to call him if I ever need to talk — if you make me too crazy."

"Oh thanks a lot, Jeff."

"He meant well."

"It would be nice if I didn't have that kind of effect on people."

"I don't think so."

As we indulged in our dessert of baked apples, which I'd insisted on making (something was missing, what *had* my mother put in them?), I watched Derek eat again and realized I'd always done this, always watched the way he ate, always got pleasure from this voyeuristic act. Yet never once, until tonight, had I had any awareness that I was doing this.

I reached across the table and touched the back of my curved hand along Derek's clean-shaven cheek.

"You *are* so lovely," I told him.

Chapter Forty

Tuesday, after our one early morning class, and a fresh kiss from Derek in the parking lot, I rushed off to Rebecca. Jeans and a torn white T-shirt this time, she wanted to go for a ride on the bike, to the ocean. We walked along the beach hand in hand tasting the salt air, Rebecca fighting the wind's swirling of her hair. An older couple passing us, smiled. A certain sort of smile. I didn't like it and didn't know why at first; it seemed so genuinely good-natured. Then I knew. Of course. A typical young heterosexual couple, that's what we looked like. Handsome guy, pretty girl, dream of white picket fences... I stopped suddenly, spun around to face Rebecca and asked accusingly, "Would you love me if I was straight?"

"You wouldn't be you if you were straight," she shouted back against the wind.

"Who would I be?"

"Some guy who dreams of picket fences; someone," she went on, "*really* queer."

"If I was straight I'd be queer?"

"Definitely."

"I love you, Rebecca."

She hit my arm, a little hard, in mock irritation.

"Is there a lion in the zoo here?" I wondered aloud.

"There must be."

****

The lion was lethargic, sprawled out in the middle of his pen. But Rebecca and I stood in front of his cage and roared joyously at him. He wouldn't even look at us. Smart lion, I thought. Then, in need of coffee, I drove us to a cafe in the Outer Sunset called Pleasure Espress. We drank too many cups, playing endless games of aggressively competitive backgammon, until it was time to go home and attack Hank with a caffeine induced mania. We ran up the steps shouting, "We're home, Mom!" Hank greeted us at the top, amused and laughing. Such a beautiful sight; I always got off on seeing Hank in his work clothes. Suit, tie, and all that, but somehow he still always looked like one cool dude. We jumped him, and he ate it up with gusto.

****

On my day alone with Hank the following Saturday, he told me that the Sunday when I was with Derek, Ted had called. Since Rebecca had been at work, and Ted's wife was off taking a class in non-violent civil disobedience, Hank had invited Ted over.

We were sitting on Hank and Rebecca's bed when he told me this. I glanced around the room. "Here?" I asked.

"Yeah," he answered, with an *of course* tone.

Somehow this fact felt weird, but not too. I settled into it. "Okay," I said, thinking that this was necessary.

Hank laughed.

"So," I asked, "how's he doing?"

"Very well, thank you," he said with exaggerated politeness, clearly amused at my awkwardness. "I told him about you."

"And?"

"And I think he was uncomfortable with it."

"Jealous?" I frowned.

"Yeah, but not what you think." Hank stood up and played with some pencils on his desk. "You and I have found a way," he said, "to have a relationship with both a man and a woman, and *openly*. I think Ted looks at this pretty wistfully."

"Well, I have an idea what he's going through."

324

Hank gave me a sudden look. "Yes," he said, remembering what he'd obviously chosen to forget — that I'd been a long time closeted. "The thing is," he said, getting over the unpleasantness of recalling who I'd been, "Ted doesn't really want what we have. He's spent a lot of years being at odds with himself, because the things he wants don't work together." Hank sat down on the desk chair. "Ted was a real jerk in college, but he's matured since then; he understands who he is now. But for him personally, it doesn't make much difference. I use to think Ted identified himself as straight because he was homophobic, but it was because he thought he had to make a choice: straight or gay. He didn't see any acknowledgment of bisexuality as a legitimate option. So straight or gay. What it came down to was that he felt like there was no way that he could be gay with the way women turn him on." Hank caught my eye. "He's very into women, sexually — more than you and me."

I looked at Hank skeptically.

"Okay, well more than me."

I wasn't surprised by Hank's self-analysis. Hank was attracted to women, but not like he was to men — though to see him and Rebecca go at it sometimes, you'd hardly know it. It's as if when he was being sexual with a woman he was completely there, but when he wasn't having sex with a woman, the possibility wasn't something that was necessarily on his mind all that much. Which wasn't true for him and men. He could hardly keep his eyes off an attractive guy on the street, but women who turned my head went unnoticed by Hank.

"Ted," Hank was saying, "does now accept himself as bisexual. But it's a straight life he wants. The problem is, his interest in men isn't something he can ignore. So he looks at you and me and thinks: how nice they can make their bisexuality work with none of the guilt of lies and deception. Personally," Hank continued, "though I don't want it for myself, I understand Ted's attraction to the nuclear family."

I shuddered. "The word, 'nuclear,'" I said, "implies some fundamental building block, which gives the concept too much weight; the hetero, monogamous, dynamic is just an option."

"Sorry," Hank said, laughing again, "I forgot I was talking to a physicist."

"Who did you think you were talking to?"

"A sexy young stud."

"You like that I'm younger than you!" I said with outrage.

"Let's just say it doesn't bother me any."

I gave him a disapproving look.

"Anyway," Hank said, "my point is, look at all the stuff we're fed as kids — in books, TV, movies, and from our families — about what we're supposed to do, how it's supposed to be, about the *ideal*: man, woman, kids, right? Ted, like most people, bought into it totally. The loss of this fantasy is a traumatic deal for a lot of gay people when they're first coming out to themselves. But, at least for Ted, his desire for the opposite sex makes "family life" not only possible but palatable. So when he looks at you and me and our lives, it's not what he wants, and yet he's attracted to the openness of our fulfillment, meanwhile, his traditional family dream is co-opted by the fact that he's not complete or satisfied without a man in his life."

"So," I said, "he found himself a straight wife and has illicit homosexual affairs on the side."

"Perhaps," Hank said, looking at me as if from a whole new perspective, "you understand that better than I."

"I understand it a lot *less* than you!" I said forcefully. I stayed closeted only because of my love for Derek. I never went for that straight-life all-American dream."

I could see in Hank's eyes I'd redeemed myself some. But then he said, "Well, two kids, two car garage, a dog and a swing set, *I* do *understand* the attraction there and I find it difficult to find fault in Ted for pursuing it."

"And what happens when Ted's wife finds out about him?"

"She won't."

"Oh please."

"All right, well if she does, it might not be too bad. She's big on civil rights, including gay rights."

"But she doesn't have any gay friends," I added.

"How did you know?"

"Because Ted wouldn't have married her if she did."

"That's probably true. Listen," Hank said, not liking the look on my face. "Don't get me wrong. *I've* never been closeted, and I didn't marry Rebecca because I wanted tradition." He shook his head in dismay. "*That's* the worst part of it, the way people treat us as a married couple — all the husband/wife role playing they assume, and the assumption of heterosexuality, the assumption of monogamy. But I try to understand Ted, have some empathy."

"Why *did* you marry Rebecca?" I asked.

"I love her, can't imagine my life without her. That much I know you understand."

"Perfectly."

"So we thought it'd be fun, have a wedding, big party, all our friends..." Hank's voice fell low. "It was the stupidest idea. I regret it totally. We should have just had a Halloween party. Yeah, Rebecca and I love each other, want to be together, we're happy, but all the hoopla — it was totally unnecessary and has caused me untold grief. People automatically put Rebecca and me in this very square box that isn't us at all."

"But you still wear your ring."

"Yeah well, it's a nice ring." He looked at his hand.

"I like it too," I had to admit.

Their rings were identical; eight strands of smooth dark gold braided tightly.

"You have a nice ring too," Hank said pointing at my hand.

"Yeah," I laughed, remembering the places my pinkie ring had unwittingly taken me.

"Hey, maybe we should have another wedding! Have a third ring made for you." Hank's voice was full of ironic enthusiasm. "Sure, we should do it too! Just to blow people away."

"Derek and Ted could be the best men," I contributed.

We both burst into laughter.

"You could track down Sheila to be the bride's maid."

Rebecca told you about Sheila?"

"Yeah."

Hank laughed even harder, "Oh God, she was a trip!" and he fell on the bed. Together we rolled around, doubled over with giggles, which soon turned to kisses.

Chapter Forty-one

Derek and I were doing our coffee-and-studying routine in the cafeteria. We had our notebooks open, focusing intensely on a possible solution to our thesis problem, when someone approached our table talking. Breaking our concentration, we realized that his words were directed at us.

"Jimmy, darling," he said in a mocking girl voice, "after we do our schoolwork will you come over to my place and suck me off?"

It was Yamada, a tall angular Japanese man who was also in the physics graduate program. He was surrounded by his lackeys, smaller Japanese guys, who were all presently snickering.

"They're switch-hitters," he explained to his groupies. "Swishy, switch-hitters Ha, ha, ha."

Derek and I were pissed, mainly for the interruption in our work. We glared violently at him, and Yamada started to back off, with the final comment, "Ta ta," a little wave of the fingers, and, "Guess we better leave the lover-boys alone."

As they moved away laughing, Derek looked at me. "Switch-hitters?"

"Bi," I explained.

"Oh." He stood up. "Yamada!" he shouted over the heads of maybe twenty people. Yamada was a good thirty feet away. He, his boys, and just about everyone else turned around.

"You homophobic?" Derek shouted. I've been there myself. But I'm over it. And yeah Jim and I are lovers. It's great; never been happier."

I was thinking how embarrassing this should be, but I wasn't embarrassed at all. I was thrilled. Thrilled that it had come to this — Derek publicly defending us as a couple, homosexual love as a concept.

Yamada was the one who looked embarrassed — supremely.

Derek went on mercilessly while the rest of the room was silent. "If you absolutely must express your distaste for this, fine. But *goddamn* it," now his voice was deep, harsh, threatening, "*don't* do it when Jim and I are working!"

Yamada affected a look to his buddies that said, *this guy's a psychopath, let's make a quick, quiet, departure.* Which they did.

As Derek sat down, satisfied, a blond pony-tailed woman at a nearby table clapped loudly. We turned to see, and she smiled at us. We smiled back nodding.

When we focused on one another again, I said, "Hey, Mr. Macho."

"How can you call me that?"

I laughed. "There was a time when you *thanked* me for calling you that."

"There was a time when I thought homosexuals were degenerates."

"Well, aren't we?"

Derek laughed, I'm sure thinking, as I was, about what we'd done in bed the night before. (Finally, I'd gotten to live-out the dream I'd had when I first met Carol — mixing sex with physics.)

I smiled at Derek across the table from me, here at the cafeteria, and said, "That little scene you just made was the most macho thing I've ever witnessed. And," I added, "it totally turned me on."

****

Derek and I walked to the parking lot to say our good-byes. We'd ridden in together that morning from his place, and now I was about to go off to another weekend with Hank and Rebecca. We were pumped up on coffee, and in chipper moods, laughing at silly things. A man in a lab coat outside the student health center, frantically sucking on a cigarette, had brought on macabre comments about doctors' perverse Thanatos desires, and that led to lewd giggling fantasies about doctors and oral fixations.

We were just about to say our parting words when some jocks, who'd sprinkled vaguely harassing comments in our direction a couple of times around campus, pulled up behind us in a Jeep.

"Faggots!"

There were maybe six of them. They could have beaten the crap out of us if they wanted to, but we knew that they were terrified of us. To Derek and me they were like pesky little mosquitoes. I guess what scared them was that we *should* have been frightened of them and we weren't. I knew sooner or later Derek and I were going to find ourselves in a violent situation; we were too out in public. When and where it would happen, Derek and I would be ready. And if we ended up in the hospital or dead, so be it; there was no way we were going to hide our love. We were doing what we had to, and thus were fearless.

"Faggots!" they'd yelled, like dropping a bomb that failed to explode.

Only slightly annoyed, we turned and smiled bored smiles at them. The jeep screeched off as if we had pointed 45s at their heads. The bravest of them, a cute blond, yelled delightedly out the back, "Cock suckers!"

Derek and I looked at each other amused.

"Think he's gay?" I asked.

"Maybe. Maybe." Derek laughed.

"See you Monday, then." I was crouched down, unchaining my bike, and wondering if we'd find our tires slashed one day; I imagined Derek and I holding hands in the back of a MUNI bus.

There was no response from Derek, so I glanced up at him. He had an expression I hadn't seen in a long time.

That holding-back Hetero-Man look that I use to find plastered on his face so frequently.

I stood up. "Just tell me."

He adjusted the strap on his backpack, grinning to himself. I waited.

Still grinning, but at me now, he said, "I have a date Saturday night."

"A date?" It came off sounding so funny, but I was wondering if perhaps this was not funny at all.

"Halley," he said.

"Halley?" Same old Derek; you had to pull things out of him.

"Like the comet."

"Derek, just *tell* me."

He smiled at my irritation. He liked this! I wanted to slap him.

He liked unsettling me, but he wasn't going to push it; it wasn't within his desires to be outright mean to me.

"She's the one who clapped," he offered.

"She," I said.

"That time in the cafeteria when I told off Yamada. The blonde."

"Oh." I saw now. A date with a woman. He needed to know, to know about himself and women.

"She works at Croissant Corner. I stopped there last Friday to try the coffee."

"So, how'd you like the coffee?" I found myself asking stupidly.

"Good," he said. "She's bi."

"Umm," I nodded, unable to think what else to say.

"She goes out with this other woman, kind of a romantic deal, they send each other flowers. It's fun she says. They're not in love, but they have a good time." Derek seemed fascinated by all this.

"And you?" I asked.

"We're having dinner."

That sounded nice enough. Derek would be having dinner with a bi woman while I was with Hank and Rebecca. I smiled. "Have fun." Then I kissed him, wet and full on the lips, hoping the whole world was watching.

Chapter Forty-two

I took Hank to observe handball matches in Golden Gate Park Saturday morning. He wanted to learn the game. Next weekend I'd take him out onto the court — a prospect that excited me a great deal. We watched quietly for a bit, then pointing to the court now and again, I explained the basics of the game.

It was an exceptionally sunny day and, even though the air was cool, heat permeated through our shirts. Pearl drops of sweat gathered gradually and then ran down our stomachs and backs in slow tickling streams. In turn, the heat and sweat gathered in my mind into the tastes, smells, and textures of salty male bodies. An intense desire washed over me like a tidal wave. I wanted to feel Hank's sweaty body rubbing against mine, for us to be groping madly, licking each other; I wanted his throbbing cock in my mouth. I enjoyed this jolt of sudden passionate imagery, and then, just as quickly as it came, it was gone, and I was left well satisfied to bask in the luxury of its soothing wake.

Now we walked together out of the sunlight and into the cool dark of the tree-canopied path leading towards Haight Street. On the way, we came upon the quiet area where elderly people lawn bowl. The field was pristine green, the players decked out in blaring white. The scene would have been comical in its surrealism if it weren't so serenely beautiful.

Hank rested a hand between my shoulder blades and said, in that deep sexy voice of his, "We'll be out on that lawn together when we're in our 70's." He stated this as an unequivocal fact, a fact that I had no problem accepting.

But meanwhile, we went to The Bagel Shoppe on Haight, provisioning for Sunday's breakfast. Blueberry or not blueberry? Two or three onion? Pumpernickel for Rebecca. Lots of lox. Then to the health food store — slab of fresh cream cheese. On to the produce store — red onion and tomato. We forgot the capers. Forget the capers. Then up to Clayton, to the Zazen bakery, where we sat down for bitter coffee and fluffy poppy-seed muffins. On the way back, passing Cafe Some Place Else, I checked the schedule. A gay comedian was performing later in the month. I made a mental note to suggest his show for a night out to Derek.

Back home — as I now came to think of Hank and Rebecca's flat — I showered, put on a pair of cotton boxer shorts and, while Hank showered, sorted through the fridge for dinner ingredients. We were going to make stuffed eggplant. Hank soon joined me in the kitchen wearing a new pair of chocolate-colored drawstring pants. They were loosely tied and hung way low on his hips. Delicious.

In a matter of moments, Rebecca came home from work exhausted but in a cheery mood. She peeked in to say a quick Hi, then disappeared for a shower and a nap.

A bit later, eggplant baking in the oven, Hank finishing up in the kitchen, I sat in the living room in an armchair staring blankly at the dark lifeless fireplace. Soon I became vaguely aware of Hank coming in and propping his legs up in the easy-chair across from me.

After a while, he spoke. "You really love him, don't you?"

Pulled out of my thoughts, I asked, "How did you know I was thinking about him?"

"You have this look on your face... like a concerned father."

"That doesn't sound too healthy."

"No, I just meant you look like you're worried about someone you truly care about."

"Well, I was actually thinking about fathers. Mine, yours, Derek's. I wonder if Derek's ready for all that's coming his way. I know he's going to want to come out to his parents. I met them a couple of years ago; they come into the city every once in a while." I said this, trying again, unsuccessfully, to imagine how it would be for them to hear that their son and I are carnally acquainted. I was certain they'd never even discussed sex with their only child. I added to Hank, "We're talking small-minded people, but Derek's had a decent relationship with them."

"He'll be okay."

"I wonder."

"He'll be okay because what he has with you will seem like a bargain at any cost."

I smiled appreciatively. "Thanks, that's sweet."

"I wasn't trying to be sweet."

I thought this over. It hit me hard, enough to allow me to temporarily let go of my Derek anxiety.

Silence settled over us for a while. And then I asked, "Why are you sitting all the way over there?"

"I can see you better from here; you're nice to look at."

I smiled immodestly. The city was still at the moment. No rambling buses shaking the building, no blaring sirens to startle Rebecca out of her dreams. Hank studied me. And I, in turn, studied him. He was amazingly attractive — rock-solid physically and psychologically. His face was nearly always calm, relaxed — except during sex when his expressions were primal in their intensity. It struck me again how everything about his body was super masculine yet with a tender quality. His shoulders, for example, were broad and strong, yet the muscles were not sharply defined, rather more like gentle hills. And the thick curls that covered much of his chest were soft as baby's hair.

Derek's chest was so different, yet equally alluring in its angular brawniness, just a trickle of longish straight hair running down the center. I remembered how shocked I was when I saw him bare-chested the first time, the first time we made love. In five years of close friendship, I'd never seen him shirtless. I didn't feel, thinking about it now,

336

that it was normal for two men to be such close friends, for that long, and to have never have happened to see one-another bare-chested. There had been a reason for this, a reason for lots of things in our friendship that I had never questioned.

Hank was looking at my body now in a totally lascivious manner. Imagining what thoughts were going through his mind, I became heavily aroused. I moved my gaze to his feet, which I'd found myself noticing more and more lately. Not having a foot fetish, I found it amusing how turned on I was by them. What engaged me so was their perfection; Hank's feet were neither too small nor too large, neither too thick nor too thin. His toenails were strong and healthy and impeccably trimmed — the toes themselves plump and hairless.

"I'd like to suck on your toes," I threw out for consideration.

Hank laughed. "Rebecca went through a phase like that."

"I went through a phase like what?" She stood in the doorway, her silk Chinese bathrobe tided lazily at the waist. The setting sun blazed in from a hall window behind her, and her hair — frizzed around her head from sleep — glowed like a fiery halo. I realized then how anxious I had been for her to wake up and join us.

"Getting turned on by my feet," Hank answered.

"I was just telling Hank that I'd like to suck his toes," I said.

Rebecca grinned. "I'll take the right foot if you'll do the left."

Not being one to pass up an offer like that, I eagerly took my place on the floor to Hank's left. Rebecca fell into position opposite me. We licked, sucked, and nibbled vigorously. Hank responded with a series of low groans. Rebecca and I, smiling conspiratorially at each other, began to compete to see which one of us could be more sensuous, lustier in this activity.

Hank complained, "You're torturing me!"

"Let's hear your pain!" I demanded.

From somewhere deep within him came a loud, frantic, "Ahhhhgg!"

Equally frantic, I reached up and grabbed his waistband, yanked off his pants. Together Rebecca and I worked our mouths up the inside of his thighs while he continued to cry-out like a wounded beast.

When we'd made our way up to his cock, we took turns licking with fast long strokes. Eventually, I settled on sucking his balls while Rebecca worked on the tip of his shaft. The top of her bathrobe gaped open and I could see the shadowy outline of her breasts, her erect nipples.

Hank began to scream, "No!" desperately trying to hold on to the pleasure for which he knew, an end was eminent. And then, unable to hold out any longer, he came in Rebecca's mouth with a long loud groan.

After, he lay with eyes closed, and an expression direct from Flash's sketch of Zeek after he'd just shot up. But Rebecca and I were still primed. A drop glistened on her lip. I pleaded, with my eyes, for her to kiss me. She moved around Hank to greet me, wide-eyed with desire. I licked her lip first, then probed deeper. The taste of Hank in her mouth was unbearable. I took her hand, and we went over to the futon couch, then I undid the sash on her robe. She lay down — the robe's oriental blue splayed out behind her — and parted her legs. Droplets of moisture accented her pubic hair. I paused for a moment; Rebecca and I looked into each other's eyes, smiled, and then unceremoniously, I removed my shorts and hastily entered her.

Wetting fingertips in my mouth, I placed them where I could give her the most pleasure while I thrust my hips, her hands on my ass, fingernails digging into my sweaty skin, my tongue luxuriating in the warm saltiness of her mouth. And soon, with deep moans, we both came.

Hank joined us on the futon then, tangling himself in with us. For a long while we lay there, all of us now like spent junkies, blissfully basking in our combined sticky body heat, until someone remembered the eggplant.

****

"Don't get too excited; it's just something fun," Rebecca said as she piled us into the car Sunday morning. She'd told us, after the lox and bagels, that she had a surprise for Hank and me.

We drove down to the Marina Green at the edge of the bay, where there's a spectacular view of the Golden Gate Bridge. Rebecca opened the trunk and pulled out... a kite — a pale blue kite decorated with an explosion of triangles — pink, green, and orange.

The eastern sun shone down at an angle. While high fog, coming in from the Pacific, rendered the top of the bridge's towers obscured in clouds, the rest of the bridge glowed royally. A steady breeze, coming off the bay, made the morning perfect for the task at hand. Despite Rebecca's warning, the kite and the setting excited Hank and I immensely, and the three of us ran like giddy children out into the field. After several humorous failed attempts, we got the triangles airborne. Taking turns holding the line, we ran in unison, laughing, as the kite sailed above us triumphantly.

Rebecca had just handed Hank the line, she and I dancing along beside him, when I heard the roar — a Harley — and then the beep. We looked to the road. It was Derek, with a passenger — hands on Derek's hips, blond ponytail wagging from beneath the helmet. Derek waved enthusiastically, the passenger looking at us as well. Rebecca, Hank, and I waved excitedly back while still running. Even when we all stopped waving, Derek continued to watch us run across the wide flat field. Though I saw no specific sign of danger before him, I began to get frightened. *The road! Look at the road! Goddamn it; look at the road!* I would have screamed it if I thought there was any hope of him hearing me. *Finally,* he turned and faced the long straight black tar that led towards the bridge. My eyes followed him.

And then, "Jimmy!" Rebecca's shout of warning, as she grabbed my arm. Hank tackled me, seconds before I would have likely broken my ankle in a deep animal-made crater in front of me. We crashed to the ground, Rebecca tumbling beside us. There was a second of giggling and gayety at the three of us jumbled together, there on the great green openness. But then, remembering the kite, we looked up and watched solemnly as it, newly liberated flew high up into the boundless sky, the triangles quickly disappearing into the vast whiteness.

I could still hear a faint Harley cry, and I looked far up the road to see Derek looking back at us, the pony-tailed head facing forward, scared to death like me, I was sure, that they'd crash.

And I wondered, where was he taking her?

Chapter Forty-three

Hank and I watched one-another admiringly, as we each ran a bar of soap across our own chest, thighs, crotch, etc., in the shower the next morning. Normally, we'd lather each other up which would invariably lead to sex, but there was no time for that today; Hank had to get to work. When we got out of the shower, I watched Hank's reflection in the mirror as he shaved. He looked a bit too much like Rick, a fact that had only recently occurred to me; I hadn't yet quite gotten over the shock of this, had only gotten up enough nerve to tell Hank the weekend before, and had not yet gotten around to mentioning it to Derek. Watching Hank shave now reminded me of watching Rick shave, and I had to let the pain, longing, loss, wash over me and finally bring myself back to the joy I had in Hank. He was watching me in the mirror too, reading my mind as he does — must have read the whole story, from start to finish. He didn't say anything, just seemed pleased when I was back in happiness.

In the kitchen, we drank our coffees, leaning against opposite counters, again watching each other. I was aware of not feeling freaked out over seeing Derek with Halley yesterday, felt Hank's awareness of, and perhaps perplexity over, this. But I had only put it aside, held it back for later. I'd been getting better at keeping my worries about Derek away from my time with Hank and Rebecca. Our only Monday class had been canceled, so Derek and I would have the whole day to deal with whatever we needed to.

Rebecca lay beautifully lost in dreamland as Hank and I took turns kissing her on the forehead then headed to the garage together. I rolled my bike out onto the sidewalk, steadied it with the kickstand, and stood with Hank in the light breeze spinning down Fulton Street.

"I'm totally infatuated with you," he said matter-of-factly. I responded with a kiss that expressed how infatuated I was with him.

****

I could smell bacon cooking when I let myself into Derek's place. His big adventure into the world of food preparation was bacon and ketchup sandwiches on toast.

He handed me a cup of coffee. "Hungry?"

"Yeah."

"Bacon'll be ready in a few minutes."

We took seats at his kitchen table and I waited for him to tell me about his weekend. I wasn't going to ask any questions — fully accepting that this might mean I'd find out very little.

But after taking a sip from his cup, Derek started right in.

"It turns out," — he smiled like he had some wonderful news that he knew I might not take too well — "that I don't have even the slightest heterosexual inclinations."

I was relieved that he wasn't telling me that he'd fallen for Halley, and upset at myself for being relieved by this, but what came out of me was exasperation over his assertion.

"Derek, just because you weren't attracted to this one particular woman..."

"No, Jim! I find Halley attractive; I'm just not interested."

"Just because a woman is attractive, that doesn't mean all even totally hetero guys, are going to desire her."

"You don't know that, Jim, do you? You don't know how hetero guys feel, because you're not hetero."

I frowned, "What's that got to do with anything? I like women, and for me to be attracted to a woman there has to be some kind of chemistry."

"But you slept with girls in high school that you weren't really into; didn't you tell me that?"

"Sure, but that was just some basic primal urge that I let myself get carried away with."

"Okay, so that's exactly it, I don't have any of that basic primal urge when it comes to women."

"She just wasn't right for you."

"We got along great! She's got this wonderfully lurid way of looking at the world. And she wanted me, and I just had to tell her, 'no, I'm sorry,' then I slept on her horrible couch."

"Bacon's beginning to burn."

Derek dashed over to the oven, and soon brought the sandwiches and refilled our coffees.

After taking a couple of hardy bites, I said, "You've slept with women before, Derek."

His sandwich was poised for a bite, but instead, he put it down — which frankly, shocked me — and said, "So, when I was having sex with Alice, imagining you on top of her, imagining your arousal, your hard cock — you're saying that's proof of my ability to have heterosexual response?"

I wiped ketchup from my face. "That's actually really embarrassing: me and Alice?"

"It has nothing to do with Alice! It never had anything to do with her at all."

"I was thinking we should go to the beach today."

"Why are you avoiding what I'm trying to tell you, Jim? I'm gay. Is that so impossible for you to grasp?"

Derek's gay, oh yeah, sure thing, easy to get. I balled up my napkin and dropped it on my plate. "Look, Derek, even putting aside our history together, the truth is, I don't understand how anyone — male, female — could not be attracted to women, not any woman, not ever, how anyone could not be attracted to men, never. It's mind-boggling. And all I'm saying is, you don't have to make a choice, you don't have to decide."

Derek stared at me for several seconds. Finally he said quite pointedly, "There is no choice for me, Jim, no decision to be made."

I watched him, uncomprehending, as he got up and returned our plates to the kitchen.

Then Derek said, making it sound like an obscene proposition, "Take me to the beach, Jim."

****

We lay on our backs, propped up on our elbows, looking at the sea. We were on the same stretch of beach I'd sat on arguing with myself, the day I'd scurried back into the closet for Derek.

Now, I found myself saying things I hadn't known I was going to say, hadn't even thought about before.

"If something happened to you, Derek, I'd be destroyed. It would be like someone had reached in, and torn out every single one of my organs. Like..."

"Do you really think you have to explain to me what that would be like?"

I looked away from the ocean and to Derek. "Of course not." I sighed, exasperated with myself. "How stupid of me."

"That's what always gets me," he said, "how stupid we've been."

"So much for being geniuses."

"So much for being geniuses."

We lay down on our sides, facing each other. I ran my hand down the length of Derek's arm and kissed him, losing myself in his mouth. He held me tight, welcoming me with his tongue. Then fearing that I might disappear

344

completely, I gave up the kiss and just clutched his body to mine.

With eyes closed, and Derek and I entwined, the sounds of the surf became huge. I felt the ocean rise, felt a wave wash over us, and then another. A gentle swell carried us in, bathed us with foam. Over and over again we were washed in soft popping bubbles. Another surge pulled us farther out, out into the deep, out and out until we were surrounded in dark vastness and then carried away into the universe. Our bodies spiraled off together, swimming in the soothing void of empty space, then eventually, we were returned, pulled back into the earth's atmosphere, back into the dark ocean, slowly drawn back towards shore, sliding through the foam, back onto the sand. Then the sun was warming our wet barnacle and seaweed covered bodies, as waves crashed softly near our feet.

A seagull cried overhead, its piercing call bringing me back. I open my eyes and loosened my embrace just enough to get a look at Derek. What all had occurred in his past that had brought him here into my arms, to be this man who would travel through the universe with me?

I brushed his bangs off his forehead and whispered, "What were you like as a caterpillar?"

THE END

Acknowledgements

Much thanks to the various coffee houses where this book was written. I appreciate your warmth, coffee, space, light, and kindness.

Thank you to the members of my former writing group for your encouragement, feedback, friendship, and support.

Thank you to the members of the community that is Eureka Springs for unquestionably accepting, acknowledging, and respecting, me as a writer even before you ever read a single word I wrote.

Thank you to Oak for being the first person ever to read Jim's story, and for providing invaluable proofreading and positive feedback.

Thank you to Kenny for giving me - in the most unobtrusive way imaginable - the love and support that made it possible for me to learn to see, feel, and think, again. Thank you for bringing me to a wholeness that allowed me to understand that finally publishing this book was what I needed to do.

Thank you to Peter for an extraordinary friendship.

Thank you to all of those who were there for me in my darkest hours - most notably Eva, and my mother, Jackie.

Thank you to my son for sailing off into the world as a strong and wise adult, allowing me to feel free to proceed by my own design.

About the Author

Harrie Farrow is a Life Coach for Bisexuals at Navigating the Biways. She had an idyllic childhood growing up on St. Thomas in the U.S. Virgin Islands. Her 20s were filled with adventure, travel, and education. She graduated summa cum laude from San Francisco State with a BA in Psychology and a minor in Human Sexual Studies. A brief carrier in freelance writing back in the Virgin Islands was followed by a move to the Ozarks, where she opened and operated a fine dining restaurant, raised a son, designed a beautiful house, wrote this novel, nearly finished another novel, and did more traveling. After the breakup of a 35 year long relationship, losing her restaurant and home, gaining a grandson, and a new romance, she returned to freelance writing, this time doing investigative reporting. Four slashed tires on her car convinced her to quit that line of work and instead focus on finally publishing "Love Sex and Understanding the Universe." Harrie, as Bisexual Batman on Twitter, Tumblr, and Pinterest, has been active in fighting bi-phobia and bi-erasure. She writes a blog about bisexuality, and is currently also working on finishing her novel, "The Man with the Camera: Bonita Verses Ivan Rastaman and the Monkey-Go-Round."

For more information, check Harrie's website: harriefarrow.wordpress.com